IMPOSTERS

ALIEN CADETS
BOOK 3

CORNELIA CLARK

anmon Books

Imposters/ Cornelia Clark. -- 2nd ed.

ISBN 979-8-88914-013-9 (paperback)

ISBN 979-8-88914-014-6 (hardback)

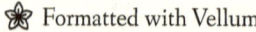 Formatted with Vellum

*Esther replied, "If I have found favor
with the king, and if it pleases the king to grant my request, I ask
that my life and the lives of my people will be spared. For my people
and I have been sold to those who would kill, slaughter, and
annihilate us."*
—Esther 7: 3

1

BASHER ALWAYS FELT conspicuous when he traveled on foot through the markets and thoroughfares of Upper Selta, but today he felt downright vulnerable.

He'd noted at least two Merith bounty-hunters who had already appeared in the crowds around him before fading discreetly away. He would not be surprised if they called in reinforcements to detain him by the time he finished his errand.

He'd never given up his hip holster from his days at the Boston PD, and he brushed it now, reminding himself that he was still armed, even though the gun wasn't lethal.

Basher strode diagonally across a pedestrian tunnel, dodging groups of aliens from almost all the sentient races of the galaxy, and coughing harshly in the brackish air. The atmospheres in the various sectors of Upper Selta were all more or less breathable for humans, but some were more Earth-like than others, and the transitions were a bit rough.

Basher was glad to find the shop he was looking for without too much searching. It was sandwiched between a Merith sushi bar and a Vel boutique.

These brackish zones tended to be dry, and Basher received a sharp shock as he brushed through the open doorway into the paint shop. He jerked a little in surprise and nearly knocked over a pedestal that held a sparkling decanter of orange ink. He grabbed the sloshing ink as the pedestal wobbled and made sure it was steady before he let go.

The shop was lined with shelves holding smaller crystal vials of paint in every fluorescent shade he could imagine. It smelled like licorice and motor oil.

Gliding in from a rear room, the owner of the shop moved in the perfectly smooth, rather unbelievable way of Crosspoint aliens. If Basher had seen it in a movie, he'd have considered it a bad special effect. This particular slug was nearly five feet high and shaped a lot like a snail without its shell. A snail that had been decorated with bright swirls of pink nail polish. It had no limbs, which always made Crosspointers look unfinished to Basher. It was like a child had been playing make-believe with clay and gotten bored before they added arms or ears or anything extra.

The Crosspoint did have large protruding eyes, and a mouth full of flat, leaf-grinding molars. It smiled at him, which could easily make an unsuspecting human scream and run.

The decanter of orange ink, the one he'd almost broken, rose gently into the air and drifted to a far corner of the shop. The pedestal went with it, and they both settled securely out of reach. The Crosspoint were a telekinetic species, and most of them had some slight degree of telepathy as well.

"I should have moved that already," the Crosspoint said apologetically. "An overly optimistic placement." It spoke in Spo, which was the common language in this sector, and a good thing, because it was the only alien language Basher knew well. A few weeks ago, Akemi could have translated anything he needed, but Akemi was gone and he was on his own.

"Do you have an interest in body paint?" continued the Crosspoint. "The warm-hued pigments are my specialty. They are derived from the secretions of a dazzling insect on my homeworld of Cross..."

"Thank you," Basher said politely. "But I have come to ask if you would be willing to do a favor for the Spo embassy. Our usual Crosspoint, the one on retainer, has had to leave Selta, and you seem to be—"

"One of the only available Crosspoint in Upper Selta?" it finished for Basher. "That is true. Many have left and my remaining kindred prefer Lower Selta—less transient."

"A lot less accessible, though," Basher said.

"My thoughts exactly! But my fellows are not always superb businesswomen like myself." The Crosspoint (apparently female) glided closer to Basher, using her telekinesis to hover half an inch above the floor and to rearrange several vials on the shelves. An emerald green ink caught the light as it moved an inch closer to the edge. "What do the Spo need of a Crosspoint?" she asked, recalling Basher's attention.

"Ah. If you've had micro-medical training, they would ask you to be on call for emergencies, and to occasionally administer a tattoo." Basher raised his hand to indicate the special tattoo on his wrist. "They would compensate you for your time, of course."

The Crosspoint scooted closer to look at his tattoo, moving faster than Basher expected. If the Crosspoint weren't so generally inoffensive, they'd be extremely creepy. "Beautiful work," she said.

"'Thank you." The tattoo was proof that the person was a true human, not a Rik who'd stolen a human body. Unfortunately, the tattoo was less effective than it used to be since the Rik stole a large vial of ink from the embassy, but the tattoos were still in use...

"I wish I could help you, but I do not have the micro skills to do either of those things."

Basher slumped.

"You are very disappointed," the Crosspoint said, though whether she was judging by Basher's expression or using telepathy, Basher wasn't sure. Either way, it was always best to be completely honest with a Crosspoint, even when you were trying to be polite.

"Yes, I am, but that's not your fault. Thank you for your time."

Basher left the shop and headed back toward the embassy. A wasted trip after all! He was extremely disappointed that the Crosspoint couldn't help, and even more so because he'd hoped to spare Claire another few weeks of slow recuperation.

She was still recovering from a pellet wound to her right leg and a fracture in her arm. Usually the Crosspoint who worked for the embassy could have speeded her healing time significantly. He could align bones telekinetically without surgery and could even stimulate cell growth.

Basher had gotten severely beaten during his first month on Selta—he didn't remember much of it because of the concussion he'd gotten at the time—but he remembered being completely healed after only two weeks. Unfortunately, it looked like he wouldn't be able to do that for Claire. The general unrest had caused many Crosspoint to leave.

Basher ignored the stares and whispers as he passed a group of Merith coming down one of the slow-moving platform escalators. He could tell they were surprised to see him, and therefore they must not be bounty hunters. He must have left the shop before the other two Merith could return. These ones weren't bothering to hide their conjecture.

"That's one of them—the Rik! Have you seen the videos?"

"Hasn't everyone? That death chamber hasn't been used in generations."

"Faal is determined to exterminate them. I wonder that this one travels alone."

"Perhaps it is a real one? A real *huumin*?"

They looked him over narrowly as he passed them on the upward escalator. Basher looked directly back at the closest one, into its single, magenta eye.

Then they were past him and he heard it say, "No, definitely a Rik. I've heard the real *huumins* have six fingers and grow their hair in long ribbons down to their feet."

Basher laughed grimly at this assessment. If only it was that easy to tell a Rik from a human. On the next level he passed through an open courtyard. It was dotted with pyramid-style benches the size of Jeeps, and aliens leaned, squatted, and reclined all around them, talking and eating. The courtyard was ringed with ornamental trees in huge pots that gave it a tantalizingly outdoor feeling.

Basher normally wouldn't have paused there—he was still about a mile from the embassy—but he saw that one of the large view screens in the center was playing new footage of the death chamber.

It had been big news when the death chamber on Merith Prime was opened up. It was an outdoor amphitheater, apparently part of the royal grounds of the Merith Pontifex or whatever he called himself, and it hadn't been used for eight generations. That was the last time the Merith had decided to eradicate a dangerous group.

Basher had seen the first video from this death chamber in its gruesome extravagance, and he'd only skimmed the subsequent videos as necessary.

Now, seeing today's footage on a large screen, he slowed and then stopped to stare. There was a *Crosspoint* among the Rik prisoners on the screen. A short, slug-like Crosspoint, exactly like the one he'd just met. It stood out like a sore thumb among the human-looking Rik. Basher got closer to the screen, winding around aliens munching snacks and several Tergre workmen moving one of the huge trees.

Basher didn't want to see what else was on the screen—he found the executions horrible—but he did want to see if, by some terrible fate, it was Francois, Claire's friend.

The report went back to the newscasters, and he waited with a horrible tightness in his chest for the next clip of the arena.

The Rik were being executed in all sorts of human ways: guillotines, electric chairs, hangings, firing squads. Basher was at least thankful the Merith hadn't gone too far back into human history for their ideas, to such things as stoning, crosses, or burning at the stake. Everything they'd chosen was instant, or close to it. After the orgy of killing the first day, the Merith had settled into executing a smaller number every other day, and they brought out the other Rik prisoners to watch.

Basher had been tracking and imprisoning these people for years, these Rik who'd murdered humans and taken their bodies, and if you'd asked him before whether they deserved the death penalty, he might've said yes. They were murderers, of a race of murderers.

But now it was happening like this. A brutal show for the galaxy, and a not-so-subtle form of psychological warfare. Basher hated it. It was a statement from the Merith, "Yes, we can and will kill an entire subspecies who crosses the line. Watch us."

When the video returned to the arena, he felt as if he'd been punched. There was definitely a Crosspoint among the Rik, and it looked a lot like Francois. And if Francois was there....

Yes, Basher's eyes found what he was looking for immediately, now that he knew where to look. Sage was there also, just behind Francois. Basher would know Sage's smug, pseudo-intellectual face anywhere. He'd stared at him for weeks as he watched surveillance video to pinpoint Claire's location.

Claire. She would be devastated that Francois and Sage had been caught. Beyond devastated. And how *were* the Merith legally holding a Crosspoint? Basher would look into it as soon as he got back to the embassy.

He watched until the executions were over, genuinely relieved that Sage wasn't chosen.

A different news story began after, the newscaster speaking in Tergre with subtitles in Spo and Merith. "The largest underground party in the galaxy has begun! The Herayung kicked off with a giant spectacle on Selta last week, so remember to avoid Sectors 42, 43, 59, and 108, which are closed until the event is over. Traffic will be snarled from levels—"

Basher felt a heavy hand fall on his shoulder, and he spun around, twisting away. Four tough-looking Merith waited behind him. Three of them were wearing throat guards which meant they expected to get physical. The Merith were a top-heavy species, with bulky shoulders and skinny legs. But their spindly legs were stronger than they looked, and their talons and beaks were more effective than most knives. With feathers, they might have been attractive creatures, but as it was, they always struck Basher as particularly ugly thugs. He shouldn't have lingered to see this footage.

"Rik, you are being detained. You will accompany us—" the first Merith began.

"The hell I will. I'm not a Rik." Basher held up his arm to show the tattoo on his wrist. Then he dropped his hand to his gun. "My name is Basher Kapur. I'm a human on staff at the Spo embassy, and I have a permit to carry this weapon on Selta."

The first Merith, the one without the throat guard, gestured to the others. "Detain it. We'll verify its story later."

Basher drew his weapon and wasn't surprised to hear startled gasps from some of the avid onlookers. Guns were (supposedly) tightly controlled on Selta, as it was marketed as a safe haven and resort for the rich and unscrupulous of the galaxy. The courtyard was more crowded than ever, as others stopped to see how the confrontation would end, but at the sight of the weapon, a small space began to open around him.

Basher might have the right to shoot these Merith if they tried to arrest him, but that could still go badly. There were four of them and one of him. Not to mention all the Merith in the crowd, who might mob him if he shot four of their own kind right in front of them.

Faal had begun offering a bounty payment for any Rik brought to Merith Prime, dead or alive. By all reports, Merith bounty hunters were now everywhere. And word was that they weren't overly worried about legality nor were they averse to executing a Rik themselves, if they proved too difficult to subdue. As the Rik were now without any standing in the Galactic Council, they could be killed with impunity.

Basher tried one more time. "I've worked on Selta for three years, for the Spo. If you detain me, you'll be offending the Spo ambassador, and that will catapult this little situation into a military incident. Last I checked, your two species have a tenuous peace at best. Are you qualified to start a war?"

The Merith in charge of the others seemed to be pondering now. His inner eyelid covered his eye with a filmy gauze.

Basher waited and then shifted his weight. "Well, you seem conflicted, and I have work to do."

He moved sideways and the Merith's eye slid open like a snake's. The closest two Merith went for Basher, and he used the pyramid benches behind him to escape. Three big steps took him to the top and three steps got him down the other side. He hit the ground running.

The crowds parted for him like water now. He made it to the edge of the courtyard, furiously jabbing at his tablet to call his partner. Basher was still a mile away from the embassy, and while he could easily run that far, he could not outrun four Merith for the same distance.

Basher dodged into an east-facing passageway, and then into one of the branching corridors that led to a block of hotels. The Merith were less than fifty yards behind him.

He should have accepted his partner's offer to accompany him.

Basher's tablet bleeped. "Basher? Is that you?"

"Could use some help. Pretty fast," Basher said. He knew his partner could get his location from the tablet, so he didn't bother to say anything else. He ducked into the nearest doorway, which looked to be a hotel catering to Spo guests. Basher tried doors until he found one unlocked, and the heat sensor responded to his touch. It was an old-fashioned folding door that opened like an accordion. Basher ducked in and pulled it shut behind him.

He heard the Merith enter the hall and begin trying doors. They tried his and kept moving when it didn't open. They were still working their way down the hall when he heard the authoritative voice of his Spo partner. There was an argument, but the Merith eventually left, sounding disgusted but resigned.

His partner was one of the mantis-like Spo, but Basher found him more likeable all the time. It had taken several years, but he would actually consider them friends now. When Basher came out, he felt a bit sheepish for hiding. "Thanks for the help. It appears you were right. They were more aggressive than I expected."

His partner did a shrug, which he'd learned in the last year. "I'm merely surprised you didn't try to shoot them."

"I thought about it, but I decided running and hiding would get us in less trouble this time."

"Where did they approach you?"

Basher explained as they walked back to the embassy on high

alert. "Another thing. I saw two of Claire's friends in the death chamber footage today."

His partner washed a sympathetic orange. "That is unfortunate. Still, if the Rik she is attached to dies, would that not simplify things for you?"

"It doesn't have anything to do with me," Basher said firmly, "but even if it did, no. It would be a thousand times worse." The Spo as a species, despite being hard-nosed and aggressive, had a pretty keen eye for when a human was interested in another. They viewed mating as a survival thing and approached it with a lot less emotion. And while his partner was right that Basher *might* be interested in Claire, Basher had no intention of pursuing anything at the moment. "I've told you before, it would be inappropriate, while she's recovering... Don't say anything about this, please."

Basher's real problem was how to break the news to Claire that two of her friends might die any day now. *Should* he tell her? There was nothing she could do, and to make it worse, there was no saying how long Sage and Francois might be kept there before they were executed. Would Claire force herself to watch every execution, waiting for the fatal moment?

She definitely would. He would do the same if they were his friends.

One of the guards at the main entrance to the embassy opened the door for them, and Basher could've sworn he saw pity in the alien's coloring as he greeted him.

"I'm not Merith fodder yet. There's no need to look like that."

"Of course not!" the guard said. "Good afternoon, sir."

He sighed. The Spo didn't have much of a sense of humor or hyperbole. He wouldn't have said that they had much sense of pity either, but as humanity's position was steadily worsening, he'd been catching more than a few pathetic looks.

Basher found Claire seated in the small dining room on the

upper level of the embassy, clutching a plain gray envelope with intensity.

"Are you alright?" he asked, seating himself across from her with a mug of hot coffee. He'd gotten a new supply recently and was determined to enjoy it, instead of hoarding it until it was beyond stale like last time.

Her right arm still rested in a sling across her stomach. She folded the envelope awkwardly with her left hand and stuffed it in her pocket. "I'm fine. I gather the Crosspoint you found couldn't help?"

"No. I'm sorry."

She leaned forward in her chair, carefully getting her feet under her to stand up. One of her legs was bandaged underneath her loose skirt.

"Well, I can't say I'm not disappointed," Claire said, unknowingly echoing his words from earlier, "but it's not your fault." She winced slightly as she tried to shift her weight.

Basher instinctively stood up to help her, bracing her good arm at the elbow. "Can I help you get to your room?"

"No. I'm supposed to start walking more, so I'm going to stretch my legs before the hearing. And here come Sam and Nat, they'll want to hear the news about the Crosspoint."

He blinked—did she *know* about Francois...?

"The Crosspoint you found today?" Claire prompted. "Not trained for medical procedures? Are you okay?"

"Right, *that* Crosspoint. Before you go, I—er—I saw another execution a few minutes ago." He tried to force the rest of the words out of his mouth, but he couldn't just blurt it out. "Did you —I was wondering if you'd heard from Sage?"

"Dude." Her eyes narrowed. "I consider you a friend, but that's not any of your business. You're not tracking the Rik anymore, so even if he *did* contact me, I wouldn't be obligated to tell you."

Basher berated himself for not realizing how that would come out. He knew Claire was more comfortable with him, but she still thought of him as the guy who'd arrested her and hunted her friends...

"I didn't mean to question you," Basher said. "You don't have to tell me anything."

"Yes, I know. I'll see you at the hearing."

Sam came over with a plate of food and sat across from Basher with a smile. "How come you don't look at me that way when I leave?"

Basher rolled his eyes. "Maybe I do."

"Nah, Nat would be jealous if you did heart eyes at me when I wasn't looking."

"I don't do that." Basher tore his thoughts away from Claire's slow progress and his depressing news. He pretended to look Sam over—military haircut, uniform, and all. "I don't know what Nat sees in you anyway."

Sam laughed and probably would have continued to give Basher a hard time about Claire, but Basher's partner motioned to him.

"The humans of the tribunal have almost finished their meal. They'll be ready to continue the hearing in a quarter hour."

Basher saw the humor slide off Sam's face as he hurried through his meal. This was Sam's Spo face, his trial face, and Basher regretted that Sam was having to bear the pressure of another high-profile investigation. *Again.*

Earth's sentience trial had only been, what? Less than six months ago? And now Sam was embroiled in a whole new galactic mess.

Well, they all were, but Sam and Nat the most. Basher didn't think there were any easy solutions, not this time. Nat had killed a well-respected senator, and although there was plenty of evidence to justify her, there were few witnesses. The Human Coalition Government was not happy.

Sam seemed to sense what he was thinking, as they got to their feet. He said a phrase in Spo that Basher didn't quite catch. Nat had just joined them, and she laughed reminiscently.

"What was that?" Basher asked.

Sam's lips quirked in a half-smile. "It's a phrase the cadets learned. Instead of 'out of the frying pan into the fire,' the Spo say, 'You can only burn once.'" He sobered. "It wasn't really funny then either. Let's go face the firing squad."

2

SAGE HAD BEEN CAUGHT ONLY a month after he escaped from Selta. And not Francois's influence, nor Sage's ability to talk his way out of things, nor a hefty bribe had done anything to save them.

In fact, when Francois got physical—teleporting weapons away—they'd knocked him out with a gas. Those Merith been prepared for a Crosspoint, in short, which was telling. Sage suspected that in return for sheltering Claire at his restaurant, Francois had gotten himself on a short and unfortunate list. Faal's kill list.

The only silver lining was that they had been captured after separating from Juliet and the others. As far as he knew, Juliet and Athlete and Diva were fine. Old Twin had left them before they even departed Selta.

After a week of being shipped about with other prisoners, Sage and Francois had been dumped on Merith Prime. Sage and the other Rik were thrown into a dungeon, and it was a ridiculously clichéd dungeon—clammy and dark, with bare rock walls. He gathered there were a number of these holding cells beneath the arena.

There were at least thirty other Rik in this one, in human

bodies that reeked in the distinctly human way. And he was not surprised when one of them exclaimed at his arrival. After all, Sage had chosen and prepped human bodies for hundreds of his fellow Rik.

An older woman approached him with an aristocratic nose and short gray hair. Sage knew her well. Her body was fifty-three years old, but she was much older. The body had been gleaned along with twenty others from a raid in northern Canada. He'd selected it himself and convinced her that although there were downsides to choosing a somewhat older body, the relevant experience and authority would suit her better than the young, vapid brunette who'd caught her fancy.

The Supreme Director, after all, had an image to maintain.

She was angry, unsurprisingly. "Sage. Of course *you're* still alive. How many died to make that happen?"

"Fewer than you."

"We heard you were captured by the Spo and their hound on Selta months ago," she said. "I thought they would have finished you or shipped you off to the lunar colony already."

"I escaped. It's a long story and I don't want to talk about it." Several walls were lined with padded benches, but they were full. Sage flopped down on the hard ground and closed his eyes. "I've had a pretty bad day, all things considered. Perhaps we can reminisce later."

"Don't you have anything else to say to me?"

He opened one eye. "I've refrained from saying, 'I told you so' and I think that's bloody magnanimous of me."

She put her hands on her hips. "How about an apology for *abandoning* your work? Or an apology for stealing my daughter?" The last question was clearly an afterthought.

"Your daughter Juliet is fine, as far as I know," Sage said, though she hadn't asked.

"I don't care! You abandoned me at the worst time—"

"I know you don't care. That's part of what's wrong with you."

She glared at him. "You haven't gotten all human, have you? Many of these have," she gestured wrathfully at the Rik around her, "and I can't stand it. They forget what it means to be Rik."

Sage closed his eyes again. "What does it mean to be Rik? Rabid narcissism? What a tragic loss."

Claire would've agreed—but, no. He refused to get sentimental about her either. She was a true human, but being human wasn't all that much to be proud of. They were too ruled by their emotions. Some were ruled by passion, some by greed, some by pity—but none of them were their own master and that was nothing to write songs about.

Sage didn't expect to sleep, but his body must have been more exhausted than he realized. When someone shook him awake, he growled at them. "Seriously, the next person to do that is going to get a black eye."

"We have to get up," the guy said. He was youngish, red-haired. "They're doing another execution."

Sage realized several Merith guards were rounding everyone up, and he felt a frisson of fear. This had come faster than he expected. The Merith were an intimidating species, no doubt about it. These four all topped Sage by at least a foot, and their muscular arms were impressively displayed in sleeveless tunics. They were a hawk-like species, and their bare feet boasted six-inch talons. Their sharply-curved beaks were also a factor. Sage had seen them used in a fight with devastating results.

"Wasn't there already one today?" Sage asked the red-haired guy.

"No, they delayed it for some reason."

"Is there some order to this? How do they choose the victims?" If it was a first-come, first-serve situation, he was safe for a while, but if not...

"No pattern that I've noticed. You just get to wait and see."

He laughed darkly at Sage's face, and several of those near him laughed also. Their callousness didn't exactly surprise Sage, but he couldn't help but think how Claire would feel if she were here. She would be hurt by their cruelty, and he would be furious. Or maybe she wouldn't... maybe she would feel sorry for them. It was hard to say.

The Merith marched them out of the dungeon in a line, up three flights of uncomfortably tall stairs, and out into the arena of the death chamber. They were joined by at least a hundred other Rik from other cells. The tunnel they emerged from dumped right onto the sand of the arena, and he could see that there were barely any Merith on the crumbling, rocky benches.

The sight of the nooses made his mouth go dry, and his heart pounded painfully in his chest. He'd never met anyone who'd seen a death chamber up close. And this was the infamous death chamber of Merith Prime. He wanted to shut his eyes—seeing this place was a death sentence.

"Small crowd—because it's the first day of the week," said the red-haired guy. "We never get much of an audience then. Waste of time doing this so often. They should make it twice a week and have more deaths. That'd get better attendance."

Sage edged away from him. That guy was a psychological catastrophe.

Sage himself was on the edge of panic. The Director was glaring at him again, like this was all his fault.

It wasn't. He'd warned her to disappear as soon as their attempt to invade Earth was exposed and ruined.

"It's only a matter of time until someone comes after us," he had told her. "Maybe the humans change their mind and decide to wreak vengeance. Maybe the Tergre want to clear their border. Maybe the Crosspoint grow a spine... I don't know who it'll be, but we'll never be safe after this."

She'd refused to leave her planet, not because she was noble, but because she couldn't conceive of things going that badly for her. The Rik were nothing if not self-centered, but she took egocentrism to a whole new level of stupidity.

Of course, even he hadn't imagined a Merith execution campaign. The Merith species actually had less reason to hate them than most other species did. Certainly less reason than the humans... but he shied away from that thought.

Would they choose him today? Was it a stacked queue or was it random?

He took time to study the other Rik now, forcing himself to really look—and saw their eyes gleamed with an unhealthy brightness. Many looked up at the audience hungrily, and Sage heard several comments about the poor turn out. They seemed to have embraced the idea that their death was a performance, and they were theatrically disappointed in the lackluster crowd.

Didn't they have anything else to think about when they were waiting to die? Sage tried to think. He'd almost died in the café with Claire when Faal's guards had cornered them. But he hadn't been panicked then at all. What had he been thinking about?

Well, Claire obviously, but also Juliet and Athlete, whom he'd grown surprisingly fond of. He'd known they might die, but he'd been focused on doing his utmost to prevent Claire being captured alive. Had it been that sense of purpose that preserved him? He wasn't sure, but he knew that this was fundamentally wrong. What kind of species bought into the entertainment value of their own death?

"I think I'm going to scream as they drag me away," he heard a woman say. "The last time someone did that, the Merith went crazy."

"Have some self-respect," Sage muttered.

"What, and go stoically to my death?" she returned. "How boring is that?"

And when the time came, and the guards started pulling

people out of line, the woman screamed. She screamed well, and acoustically, keeping one eye on the crowd. A few looked interested, but at least two groups of Merith in the front rows were clearly not paying attention.

She screamed louder, and they glanced up, but only cursorily. She died with a terrified and frustrated look on her face.

Sage felt sick. Claire would die better than this. Almost anyone would die better than this. When the executions were over, Sage saw Francois shudder. He was in the row in front of Sage, and he had been speaking quietly with the Rik on either side of him. Sage wondered what he said. Did he offer them hope? Would a Crosspoint belief system offer them any consolation? Sage doubted it.

Francois looked pale and horrified, unable to even levitate himself an inch above the ground as he usually did. Sage could only imagine what this felt like to him—with his limited telepathy. Other Merith led Francois away in another direction, and Sage didn't get to speak to him as he was herded back into the tunnels.

Sage hoped Claire was still safe in the embassy on Selta, where he'd sent her a letter, because he sincerely feared for anyone left at Faal's mercy.

3

CLAIRE CLUTCHED the letter in her pocket. It was from Sage, and she'd received it just before Basher entered the dining hall.

She hadn't *thought* he saw it, but then he'd immediately asked if she'd heard from Sage, so perhaps he had? She'd been defensive, but what did he expect?

She'd wanted desperately to be alone and read it, but Sam and Nat had caught up to her in the hall and accompanied her to the hearing. She had to go back into the crowd with Sage's unread letter burning a hole in her pocket.

The room held more humans than she'd seen together in years —since before she'd been sold to Faal's zoo—and they glared around in such an unremitting fashion she longed to introduce them to Faal and let them see what a *real* glare was like. Nobody did lethal stares like the one-eyed Merith. If they thought she or Sam or Nat would be intimidated by thirty desperate politicians— well, they could stuff it.

Claire tightened the band holding her hair back, and she shifted to stretch out her sore leg as she sat against the wall. Her right arm was itchy, encased in a temporary cast from armpit to forearm and resting in a sling, while her bandaged leg ached.

They'd thought her arm was only sprained, but after a better exam, they'd realized there was a hairline fracture. Hence the cast.

This impromptu hearing was being held in the large reception hall at the Spo embassy. Claire sat against to the side in an uncomfortable Spo folding chair, while the members of the tribunal sat at small oval shaped tables scattered across the room. Her one crutch rested against the wall, in easy reach. Light from the natural skylights bounced off copper rings hanging from the ceiling, making a muted rainbow on her lap.

When it was her turn, she moved awkwardly to the chair placed in front of the crowd.

The examiner was a lean, gray-haired man with old-fashioned, wire-frame glasses. "Claire Kindler, please state again for the record why you concealed yourself on Selta for six weeks."

"As I said, when I got to Selta, Basher—Mr. Kapur—believed that I was Rik. I was concerned with my safety."

"Are you criticizing the human treatment of the Rik people?"

"No. Well, yes, actually—but that has nothing to do with what happened to the senator—"

"On the contrary, Ms. Kindler, the outrageous claim made by Sam Locklear and Natsuki Fujimara—namely that the late Senator Fontley was a Rik and tried to kill them—is somehow related to your unfortunate liaison with five Rik fugitives. A somewhat suspicious circumstance. And if we have reason to believe that you are an unreliable and prejudiced witness... Mr. Locklear's story becomes even more opaque to our understanding."

Claire took a deep breath. She shouldn't entirely blame them for their skepticism. Her part of the story alone was confusing, and when tangled up with Sam and Nat's actions, it must all look like a mess. "As I wrote in my statement, I temporarily took refuge with the Rik when I believed I might not be safe at the embassy from Faal of Merith II. I knew he wished to reacquire me. And he did try to kidnap me again, so I was right about that."

"And yet here you are, safe and sound. While the computer known as Akemi has disappeared, the ink for our patented tattoos has been stolen, and Senator Fontley is dead."

"I'm not exactly safe and *sound.*" Claire gestured at her injuries. "But I admit it is complicated."

"Please tell us exactly what the Rik planned to achieve by breaking into this embassy."

"I told you; it was only to steal the ink."

"And how did Senator Fontley relate to this plan?"

Claire threw up her hand. "It didn't! I don't think they even knew he was here. Nobody mentioned him, and killing him was certainly not part of any plan. Why on Earth would it be? You've seen the footage. He attacked Sam; Nat defended him. I wasn't even in the room, neither were my—friends."

"That footage could have been doctored."

"Why would they change it?"

He pursed his lips. "I have been friends with Senator Fontley for fifteen years. I knew him long before the Hadron event and the Spo. I need proof before I will believe that the man was an alien, and an emotional outburst from you is not going to cut it. If Mr. Locklear and Ms. Fujimara were trying to protect *you,* however, I can begin to understand why they might lie."

Claire blanched. "You think *I* killed him? I never even met him!"

"You have already admitted to colluding with these Rik in illegal activities. Perhaps Sam and Natsuki wish to protect you from an accessory to murder charge."

"So, I'm a convenient scapegoat," Claire said. "*I* think you're just scared to consider the possibility that Sam and Nat are telling the truth. You have Basher's statement that the Senator was acting strangely ever since he arrived on Selta, and Basher's testimony that Fontley was revealed by the Rik Director herself. Doesn't that mean anything? Akemi saw it, too."

"The Director has disappeared. The computer called Akemi, whom you have already admitted to trading to Faal for your life, is also gone. Our witnesses are extremely limited." He clicked the end of his ball point pen in and out.

"Don't you trust Sam and Nat at all? I haven't known them long, but they're obviously not liars," Claire said.

"As a character witness, you don't have much ground to stand on," he said. "We'll confer for a moment."

Claire ground her teeth and looked toward the far wall, to the only friendly face in the room. Basher was allowed to be present during this hearing, as he was considered a sort of police presence at the Spo embassy. Sam and Nat had to wait outside.

Basher had given his testimony already, but he was in some disgrace for having allowed the Rik to escape in the first place and for his role in trading Akemi to Faal.

He gave an expressive grimace when her eyes sought him, and she knew he was as frustrated with this whole situation as she was. He'd explained that there had to be an investigation into Senator Fontley's death, but he'd not conveyed how much they'd want to deny it.

And she had to admit, it did sound like a ridiculous story. Some of these people had known Senator Fontley, and all of them had elected him to represent them on Selta.

Now they were told that he was actually a Rik who'd taken human form more than twenty years ago in order to infiltrate the government. They were told that he'd been determined to dissolve the Rik/Human treaty merely *because* he was Rik and it endangered him. And to top it off, he'd paid an assassin to try and kill Sam and Nat on the drilling platform.

The tribunal found the whole thing a large and unwieldy morsel to swallow, and when Claire had tried to explain how she'd been mixed up in the whole thing, they'd gotten downright insulting.

They didn't really believe her story about being sold to Faal and escaping from his zoo, and they really didn't believe that Akemi had volunteered to go with Faal to save Claire.

Fear was the real issue here. If it was Sam and Nat's word against anyone else, these politicians would probably believe them (particularly with all the physical evidence of foul play). But for them to accept that *Senator Fontley* was an alien required a complete shift of their world view.

"That's the real trouble, isn't it?" Claire spoke her thought out loud. "You're scared to admit that Senator Fontley was a Rik, because that means that *anyone* could be a Rik. *Anyone* could fool us. Even you."

The examiner's cheeks paled, though whether it was with anger or fear Claire didn't know or care. He gripped the nib of his pen and ink spread on his fingers. "We have all undergone the Spo blood test and suffered the consequences. We have been certified non-Rik. Such an accusation is out of line."

"But that's the whole point, isn't it? You all had to be tested because you're all afraid that someone else is a Rik. You already believe Sam's story, you're just grasping at straws now, hoping against hope to be proved wrong."

There were mutters, but the examiner didn't speak, so Claire pressed her point.

"I know how rotten the blood test is. It's miserable, and you have my sympathy. But it was necessary, so you put on your big boy pants and did it. So, do that again. Yes, it totally stinks that Senator Fontley tricked you all, but it's time to suck it up and move on. It's time to begin working toward the real threat—Faal's execution of the Rik in that horrible death chamber."

The examiner raised his hand. "That at least, has nothing to do with us anymore. The Rik are not human, and their conflict with another species—"

"Oh, *please*. The Rik are in *human* bodies. Whether you want to forget that or not, we are stuck with the connection. When the galaxy watches these executions, they're watching *humans* die. And what's to say they're all Rik? Faal isn't allowing us to check, despite the lawsuits we've brought. And what's to say Faal's obsession will stop there? What if he decides that the only way to be *sure* is to start executing any human over the age of twenty? Or to go to war with us and be done with it? If you think humanity isn't involved in this, you're in denial."

"That's enough." For a moment only a hushed cough broke the silence. "We will take a brief recess. Wait outside, Ms. Kindler."

The examiner's face was unreadable as he consulted with another man sitting at his table.

In the passageway, Sam and Nat stood as Claire and Basher exited the reception hall.

"All done?" Sam asked. "I'm surprised."

"I kind of chewed them out," Claire said.

Sam raised his hand. "High five."

Claire slapped his hand obligingly. "I just told them to start focusing on the real problem: Faal's crazy death chamber."

Sam smiled half-heartedly, but he and Nat looked thoughtful.

"What?" Claire said. "Do you think I made it worse for you?"

"No," Sam said slowly. "They'll believe us eventually. What choice do they have? We have enough witnesses to cast doubt on him. The real problem is the Rik. I thought dissolving the treaty would let us drift apart, but now they're being slaughtered out of hand. Somehow they're still our problem."

"They're not the problem," Claire defended. "It's not their fault Faal was in the mood for genocide. And you can't categorize a whole species as a problem. Their body-stealing technology is the problem, but the Rik *themselves* aren't..."

Basher looked away. Claire already knew he disagreed with her, and she wished he would argue about it. She was all stressed out from the tribunal and a good argument would help her bleed off excess energy.

It bugged her that they couldn't seem to focus on the right enemy. *Faal* was the enemy. He was the one killing Rik in his death chambers and fomenting a possible war between the Merith and the humans. Why did Sam and Nat and Basher keep coming back to the Rik? They were the victims now, basically on the same side as the humans.

Whenever Claire thought of the Rik her thoughts inevitably turned to Sage. She put her hand over the pocket of her skirt, fingering it quietly. A letter, an actual, written-on-paper and delivered-by-hand, letter.

Basher's eyes followed her hand to her pocket, and Claire stilled. It was almost a shame. He seemed like a decent guy, but every time she let her guard down, he would do something like he'd done this morning, questioning her about the Rik or about Sage. It was like he could sense when she thought about them. She was glad when the door to the reception hall swished open, and they were invited back in.

Claire, Sam, and Nat were instructed to stand before the panel. Claire balanced on her good leg and her crutch to give her bad leg a rest.

The examiner had futilely tried to clean his ink-stained fingers with a small towel, and his whole hand was now a mottled blue. "We have one more question, and then we will be ready to sum up our investigation." He looked down at his notes. "Mr. Locklear, please tell us again whether you noticed any tell-tale signs or erratic behavior from Senator Fontley before his death."

Sam took a step forward, poised as ever. Claire wondered if that was a natural talent or something he'd learned from the unruffled Spo. "The senator was an excellent actor, but he was walking a difficult line, and in retrospect I believe there were several indi-cations. For one thing, he was determined to discredit Akemi, who might have gotten records proving his Rik past. I think he feared other Rik for the same reason: recognition." Sam paused. "He was also erratic in the negotiation, and even before that. Sometimes he flattered those around him, including Faal, and sometimes he was almost rude. I believe he couldn't make up his mind what the safest path would be. The main indicator, however, was that he detested me. I assumed that he merely resented my popularity, but he revealed that he disliked me on a personal level. He resented my role in making twenty years of his life worthless." Sam spread his hands. "I wish I had realized it earlier, but I—I didn't."

The examiner nodded. "A pity. However, we have concluded that you are telling the truth. The available evidence indicates that Senator Fontley was not acting in good faith, and may in fact have been a—Rik. We conclude that the use of deadly force was justi-fied, but Ms. Fujimara may consider herself lucky to avoid prose-cution for murder."

Claire scoffed, but Nat gestured for her to be quiet.

"However," the examiner continued, "we find your behavior, as well as that of Ms. Fujimara, to be unsatisfactory. The fact that you were both in close conversation with the Senator for some days and did not act on his questionable behavior indicates at best a lack of initiative and at worst a culpable negligence. Our official recommendation is that you both be removed from positions of responsibility until this issue with the Merith is completely resolved."

Sam's mouth opened instinctively, and Claire seriously hoped he would tell them where to shove their bogus recommendations. How should Sam and Nat have guessed what was happening when no one else did?

But Sam didn't say anything after all. He closed his mouth and nodded once.

The examiner tapped his pen. "You are free to go."

Nat was the one who spoke up. "Free to go where exactly? Back to Earth? The ship we arrived in was seized as evidence. Will it be released back to us?" Her voice was respectful, but a faint trace of bitterness was detectable. "And has the tribunal given any thought to my request to retrieve my sister, Akemi?"

The examiner shook his head decidedly. "The retrieval of a single person, or computer, from Faal of Merith II would be extremely difficult and expensive. It would take resources we don't have to spare, and, I'm afraid, waste them. Tensions are so high between Merith and humans, we can't risk antagonizing Faal directly." He actually sounded a bit sympathetic, which made Claire dislike him slightly less. But not much.

"You are free to remain here on Selta," he said, "or to travel within the confines of Tergre mainspace, which is relatively neutral. It is our considered opinion that neither you nor Sam should return to Earth at this time. Public opinion is unsettled, and Sam has become a well-known figure."

He looked at Claire. "This restriction does not apply to you, Ms. Kindler, and should you wish to return, you may accompany those of us who will be returning home shortly. That is all."

An hour later, Claire had still not had time to read her letter, but she held a mug of hot coffee in her hands and sipped it appreciatively. Nat preferred tea, and Sam just drank water, but Basher had offered to share some of his new stash of coffee and she'd taken him up on it. Sam and Nat sat across from them.

Sam had a strange, vacant look on his face, and Claire couldn't let it go anymore. "Why didn't you argue? You should have."

Sam took a moment to focus on her, as if his thoughts were far away. "Argue? Why would I argue?"

"Because they completely cut you out of the loop! You can't even go back to Earth until this is solved, if it ever *is* 'solved.' How dare they? Right?" She ended on a weak note. Sam was looking amused, rather than filled with righteous indignation.

He shook his head, smiling slightly. "Out of the loop? Claire, I'm so sick of the loop I could hang myself with it. They let me go."

"But none of this is your fault. Senator Fontley scared the hell out of them, and they're taking it out on you. And you *looked* like you were about to argue. Didn't he?" Claire turned to Basher for confirmation.

He'd been looking at her, and turned quickly back toward Sam. "I admit, I thought you were going to protest for a minute. I'm glad you didn't though."

Sam grinned. "I almost did—then I realized what an idiotic thing that would be. I almost thanked them, but I thought that might be taken badly. So I just shut up."

Nat patted his knee. "We all know how hard that is for you. Good job."

Sam grabbed Nat's hand and brought it to his mouth for a kiss. "I'm not even going to rise to that. I'm too relieved."

Claire said, "But don't you care about what's happening? The Rik are dying every day. And we might end up at war. You can't tell me none of that matters to you."

"Of course it matters to me," Sam said. "It's horrible. But Claire, it's *no longer my responsibility*. I can't tell you what a relief that is. If I think of anything helpful, you can bet I'll make a big fuss about it—but I'm no military genius. I'm not even a politician. What can I really contribute?"

Basher agreed. "It wouldn't make sense to put him in charge of anything at this point."

"It *never* made sense to put me in charge of anything," Sam said. "It just sort of happened. And kept happening. Until now. I feel like I'm finally off a nightmare roller coaster." Sam raised his voice. "Hear that, people? The ride is over, please exit to your left!"

There were ten or twelve Spo eating at other tables and they stared at Sam who laughed. "Never mind." He added the traditional phrase in Spo. "*Trek'in ploiti, nost.* Pleasant evening, all."

"But our government will never do anything to help the Rik," Claire protested.

"You may be wrong there," Basher put in. "I think they know how close we are to war. If Faal has any real humans killed in his death chamber, accidentally or not, our government will have little choice but to declare war. If they don't defend humans now, we'll be in deep trouble."

Claire sighed and sipped her coffee, but like a total klutz, she bobbled and spilled some into her lap. At least it wasn't boiling hot anymore, but the coffee splashed her cast, soaked her lap, and *worse,* seeped into her pocket with Sage's letter.

She grabbed the mug, but the damage was done. "Shoot, shoot, *shoot!* I'm such an idiot."

"Are you burned?" Basher's hands were there almost immediately, with a hand towel he snagged from the next table.

"No, I'm fine." She couldn't even take the letter out to dry it in front of him. She pressed the towel to her lap, trying to soak it back out and to hide the outline of the letter in her pocket. "I better go. Sorry I wasted your drink, Basher."

"Not your fault. I'll get you another—"

"No—no, I need to change."

Nat had gotten another towel and cleaned the floor where Claire couldn't reach. Nat also pressed the towel gently to her cast. "It's not coming out. I'm afraid this is going to smell like coffee until you get it removed."

Basher handed Claire her crutch. "Don't worry. It'll only make you smell better."

Nat coughed on a laugh, and Basher glanced at her. "I only meant... Who doesn't like the smell of coffee?"

"We know what you meant," Nat said.

Claire held up sticky hands. "I'm going. And then we're going to talk about the plan for Akemi, right? If the Coalition won't help us, we should go back to our tentative plan."

They nodded, and Sam leaned back to rest his feet on the next chair. "Take your time. I actually have nowhere else to be."

4

SAFELY IN HER ROOM, Claire finally removed the envelope from her pocket. It was nearly soaked. She teased it open without ripping the paper and carefully peeled the letter out of it.

Thank heaven the ink was dark and she could still read it, although it had bled in a few places.

It was dated several weeks before. Probably he had written it right after everything had gone down and he escaped Selta without her.

Dear Claire,

I've arranged for you to receive this soon. I don't know if you've forgiven me for hiding who I am and the extent of my role in the Rik invasion plan. Despite our failings, honesty is a virtue among the Rik. And as new as I am to friendship, I understand the link between truth and trust, and I know that I broke yours.

That being said, you lied when you went to save Akemi. How could you deliver yourself to Faal? How could you deceive me? We would have found another way; we would have helped you. Or I would have prevented you. I don't apologize for that because it is a friend's place to save each other from bad decisions. We are all devoutly thankful you were delivered from Faal, and Francois wishes he could be there to heal you again. You are an amazing human and we are thankful that we got to know you.

Gratitude only takes me so far, however, because I am also a selfish person, and I wish you were here with us. Francois has offered to take me to his family estate on Cross, and from his description, I know you would love it. I ought to be glad that you are with your own kind and safe, but I'm not. Those other humans will try to convince you that we're monsters and enemies, which is only thirty percent true at best (I say with a smile.)

By now you're aware that we all have the human tattoo. Francois did it. It won't be accepted much longer, but it opened a few doors for us to get further away from the dangers of Merith space, and that alone is invaluable. I've lost contact with Old Twin, but Juliet, Diva, and Athlete are on their way to Vel mainspace. We've all scattered to the four winds.

Francois has been a brick, as there is some danger to him in this, and he continues to make light of it. I think your influence must have something to do with it, because in my experience, aliens do not risk their lives for each other without good reason. But since I met you, risking our lives for others seems to have become commonplace. What next? Will the Crosspoint at last produce a comprehensible play? I can believe anything now.

Again, I wish you were here.

Love,

Sage

Claire wanted to pore over the letter and ponder everything he wrote, but the others would be expecting her to come back with changed clothes soon. She allowed herself to read it once more, and then tucked it flat in her drawer under the clothes Nat had given her.

Just changing clothes was tiring. Working the elastic waist of her skirt over the bandage on her leg was tricky, and pants were impossible at the moment.

She balled up her skirt and tossed it toward her pile of dirty clothes, when she heard someone knock at the door. It couldn't be Nat, because she would enter without knocking. They had been sharing this room at the embassy since Claire had come.

"Just a minute!" Claire shouted, wondering if one of the Spo had come looking for Nat. They didn't usually knock like a human, though.

"I'll wait!" shouted back a distinctly feminine, human voice.

Claire paused. The only women at the embassy were herself, Nat, and three older women who'd come for the tribunal. This didn't sound like any of them.

She hurried into another loose skirt that Nat had procured for her and limped to the door. It opened to reveal a short, blonde girl with brown eyes and a decidedly cocky smile.

She looked Claire up and down. "Well, you'll do, but you're not Nat. Where's Nat?"

"She's still eating, I think. Who are you? How did you get here?"

The girl stuck out her hand, and Claire automatically shook. "My name is Shara." She glanced up and down the hall, as if checking that they were alone, and whispered loudly, "I'm an assassin."

"Sorry, what?"

But Shara squealed because Nat was coming down the hall toward them.

"I heard you were here," Nat said.

Shara gave Nat a rib-squishing hug. "Oh my gosh, oh my gosh! Let me see the ring!" She grabbed Nat's left hand to examine her engagement ring before Nat could protest. "Hmm. I thought it'd be bigger," she said finally. "That's kind of disappointing."

Nat pulled her hand free. "Shara, I'll ask for your opinion when I want it."

"Oh, you're so funny. I missed you," Shara said. "I missed

Akemi more than you because I like her much better than I like you, but I missed you, too!"

Nat rolled her eyes. "You've only been gone a few weeks."

Shara followed Nat into the bedroom and bounced on her toes with each step.

"I know, and I was so glad when I got your message to come back!" Shara said. "I mean, I'm devastated that Akemi's gotten herself in more trouble—don't get me wrong! But that stupid moon colony they've put together for Rik criminals is so *boring*. I mean, you've never done boring till you've done boring on the moon. And Rik are *so whiny*."

"You don't say."

She picked up Nat's glasses from the counter next to the sink and tried them on, looking one way and then the other at her reflection in the mirror. "Akemi has such amazing taste—these are totally you. And so she went and got herself kidnapped by some Merith, huh?" Shara casually opened Claire's new bathroom bag and rummaged through her meager things. "She really is a magnet for trouble, isn't she? I'm totally thrilled to help get her back. It's like a karma thing, right? I got her into trouble the first time, so now I get to help rescue her."

Nat frowned. "No, a 'karma thing' would be all sorts of terrible things happening to you in return for all the terrible things you've done."

Shara rubbed some lotion into her hands. "Oh, okay, I always get that confused. I guess this is like—redemption? Dramatic irony? Something like that?"

Nat took a calming breath before she spoke again. "We have a tentative plan for getting Faal away from his estate, which is where he's keeping Akemi. When we've gotten him away, we'll make a try for her. I know you're devoted to her, but you'll probably be with the group keeping an eye on Faal."

"Cool! I could handle him, you know. I've been getting so

much better. If I had to fight you again, I could do *such* a better job than the last time."

Claire raised her eyebrows, and Nat gave her a speaking look. "Did I tell you that Shara was the one who kidnapped Akemi and me before the trial? She *was* a Rik assassin, but she changed her mind and helped us."

"Once a Rik assassin, always a Rik assassin," Shara said. "I can do both."

"She helped Sam win the sentience trial for humanity," Nat said.

"And oh-my-goodness, am I ever glad I did that! My life would've been so horrible if I hadn't. I'd probably be dying in that ugly arena." She ducked into their small bathroom and closed the door. "One sec! I've been holding it since descent!"

"Is she always like this?" Claire whispered.

"Worse," Nat said. "She gets worse. She flirts with anything male on two legs, and she's almost pathologically self-centered... but Akemi liked her."

Shara came out of the bathroom, slipped off her shoes, and flopped onto Nat's bed. "So, tell me exactly what kind of hole Akemi has gotten into, and how we're going to get her out. Do I get to kill anyone?"

AKEMI and the computer she inhabited had been installed on the second floor of Faal's estate on Merith II. If she was ever connected to his systems, she'd be able to see many parts of his vast estate, both the house and the cliff-side zoo, and the extensive grounds. But he hadn't done that yet. Mostly she got to see this one small cubicle where she was installed, and when the door was open, the atrium outside.

And right now she didn't even have the cubicle.

She was in time out. When Faal punished her with a time out, she wasn't anywhere. She didn't see anything. She didn't hear anything. It was *technically* possible that she didn't exist.

She spent most of her non-existence planning new ways to be reasonably compliant while also annoying the heck out of Faal, and when that could no longer hold her attention, she made up conversations with her friends. It was critical to continue thinking, because if she let the nothingness of complete sensory deprivation set in, she would not last long.

She knew her conversations were only in her head, but she sometimes heard phantom whispers as she floated in the timeless, shapeless void of time out.

The sensory deprivation was awful, she couldn't sugar-coat that, even to herself, but her thoughts and the half-heard whispers had so far preserved her sanity. They also helped her gauge the passage of time, because the whispers grew louder and more frequent the longer she was alone. Ironically, they might also indicate that she was going crazy, but in the meantime, they helped.

She was currently under Faal's displeasure for messing around with some files she'd hacked into, but she was sure it wouldn't last long.

When Akemi had first gone with Faal, she'd been nervous. She hadn't regretted her decision—she *did* want to save Claire from whatever punishment Faal might inflict—but Akemi had also been well and truly afraid of what Faal might do to *her*.

It turned out (for once!) that her fear had outstripped the situation. Faal's greed and pride protected her. He was proud to have the sole ownership of a human-hybrid computer, and he didn't want to give that up. In the few weeks since he'd brought her to his estate, he'd been doing research both into her and into the Rik records of their experiments. Now he knew for certain that she was one of a kind. She was the only Spo biocomputer animated by a human brain. He'd found the names and some of the documentation from the scientists who'd originally done the experiment—which was why she'd hacked into the files.

His pride, in itself, was the best form of protection Akemi could have. Faal would flay anyone alive who threatened to destroy her computer. The spherical casing that housed her 'self' was kept in an airtight steel container, cushioned and mechanically rotated daily. She was physically better off than she'd ever been before.

The only threat to her, as physical abuse was not an option, was to deprive her of external connection. When he turned off all the devices she was connected to, she was left in a black void. She remained aware, but completely isolated without any sensory input. This was indeed a threat that he utilized to keep her under control.

She hated it, of course—but the whispers, so far, kept her company. Even better, she'd found that Faal was afraid to use this sensory deprivation trick too often, for fear that he'd drive her insane. After the first few times he'd done it, he'd given her stringent psychological association tests—checking to make sure he hadn't gone too far.

That had been all Akemi needed. She'd played up the disorientation, given vague and erratic responses to his questions, and sometimes pretended that she thought Faal was someone else. He was suspicious of her act, but he couldn't be entirely sure it was false, so he never left her off for more than a few hours at a time.

And knowing that—well, seriously, what was there to be afraid of? Sure, Faal had a temper, and someday she might push him over the edge... but he didn't get to his position without developing self-control.

Today Akemi didn't even have time to get bored. There were no visuals yet, but the distinctive bell tones told her the audio had returned.

"Akemi? Respond if you hear my voice." Instead of Faal's

voice, Akemi was pleased to hear the voice of the specialist who Faal sometimes employed to work with her.

"Hello, Mox'uu," Akemi said. "It has been several days since you were last here. How are your wives?"

Despite everything, Faal *had* given Akemi something amazing: a voice. He'd hooked her up to an advanced vocal synthesizer. It wasn't as effortless and natural as speaking, but she was getting the hang of it. It felt like learning a foreign language, but one that felt strangely familiar. When she'd first been hooked up, she could only produce a garbled form of Japanes because the part of her brain that had learned English—and quite a bit of the Spo and Merith languages—was not being tapped.

The specialist hired by Faal had been able to fine tune the connection, and now she could reliably communicate with a voice in any language that she herself knew. It had been robotic at first, but like learning the nuances of a new instrument, she'd learned the nuances of the voice synthesizer. And now, not to brag, but she could put an impressive wealth of emotion into her voice.

"How are your wives? Did Frelika recover from her indisposition?"

Mox'uu made an uncomfortable noise, but Akemi had no visual of the room to judge his face or body language.

"Is something wrong?" After a moment, she asked, "Do you have any questions for me today? Faal had me in time out for a while, but I suppose he told you that. What is your task today?"

Akemi heard a scraping noise—a chair moving?—and steps as of a heavy Merith pacing in the room.

Finally a voice spoke, but it was not the technician. "I see," Faal said. "What you suspected was correct then. The disorientation was for my benefit."

Akemi uttered a pithy oath she'd learned from Mox'uu. Something about rotted wings and broken feathers.

Faal ignored her. "Thank you for bringing that to my attention," he told the specialist. "I can see why you come highly recommended."

"You tricked me," Akemi said. Mox'uu had brought up the audio and only let her hear his voice. She should have realized someone else could be in the room with him, but this wasn't a ploy Faal had used before... and frankly, the specialist had been the friendliest person she'd met since she got here. She'd asked him about his family, and he'd answered easily, sharing about his wives and his home.

Faal interrupted her train of thought. "Akemi, you have lied to me, and due to this—"

"What? You'll slap my wrist?"

He didn't answer right away, and Akemi laughed, though there may have been a slight tone of hysteria in it. "Admit it, you can't hurt me in any real way without damaging me. Why not give me an interesting job to do and see how well we can get along?"

Faal snapped his beak together, and Akemi heard the sound of the door opening and shutting.

After a moment of silence, the technician spoke. "Faal has exited the room. We are now alone." He gave the verbal command to turn on the camera attached to the computer, and she saw that he was telling the truth.

The room was small, barely more than a cubicle, but it had the most amazing view of the ocean. The whole left wall of the room —left from Akemi's perspective, right for the technician—was glassed in from ceiling to floor, and Akemi could see down to the greenish-gold ocean below. Faal's estate perched on the edge of a cliff, and the ocean stretched toward the horizon. Today it was a color between teal and deep green, with turquoise highlights on the peaks of the waves. A cloudless sky filled the remainder of the window, and the strong Merith sun was just breaking the horizon. It cast a deep shadow from the technician over the wall.

The technician sat on a chair in front of her, and he'd left the door open behind him. Faal's house was centered around an open courtyard or atrium, and this door led to an elevated walkway. There were vines growing along the railing, and she could see one section of a large, ornamental tree that shivered in the morning sea breeze. The sunlight was just reaching the top of the tree, casting a glow on its crimson leaves.

The specialist cocked his head to the left, waiting for her to speak. Even betrayal could be polite, apparently.

She waited as well, soaking in the view. Eventually she spoke. "You told on me."

"I am a professional. Faal is my employer, and I am obligated to give him all the information at my disposal."

"Do you actually have three wives or did you make that up?"

"I do."

"Is one of your wives named Frelika and is she actually sick?"

"She is better now."

"Hmm."

"I must do my job." His voice was melancholy. "I cannot apologize."

"You *sound* like you're apologizing," Akemi said.

"I am not."

"Are you sure?" Akemi couldn't stay mad. "I think what you're trying to say is, 'Akemi, you are a wonderful, fascinating person and I feel bad that I gave your secret away to that psychotic weirdo just to secure my position.'"

"That is not—*in*accurate."

"But you would betray me again, if you had to."

"...That is again correct."

"Okay. I'll take it. Not the *best* apology ever, but I make allowances for you being a Merith and not brought up to it. And you're a man—male, whatever. And frankly, I'm not overly burdened with companions, so I can't afford to have high standards."

"You are an extremely strange entity. Are all humans like you?"

"Yes. They are all exactly like me. Just as you and Faal are exactly like all other Merith."

"I take your point."

"You should, you're not exactly an idiot."

"Thank you. May I say that you are not exactly a genius?"

"No, you may not. You're in no position to criticize me."

"You should not antagonize Faal. I know you feel that he cannot hurt you—and indeed if you've found a way to deal with sensory deprivation, I admire your resilience—but you put yourself in danger by acting that way." He spoke with his usual seriousness, and more than usual sincerity. "Be submissive, grovel, even. It is what he expects."

Akemi pretended to think, then said, "Nope. Bad plan. But your recommendation is noted."

He sighed. "As you wish. Are you ready to begin today's diagnostic?"

"Yep." Akemi stared at the rising sun. "I'm ready for anything."

5

CLAIRE KNEW it was the same old nightmare, the one where Jenelle died and Claire was taken. She hadn't had the dream in a while, and it struck with new force. But this time it rapidly morphed into another dream. This time it was *Faal* dragging Jenelle away.

And Jenelle's face was too small, too delicate—

It was Akemi. She was insubstantial, like a ghost, but Faal still managed to grip her.

"Take me," Akemi said simply to Faal. "Take me."

"No, no!" Claire screamed. "Don't take her."

Faal's beak opened in a hawk's smile, and he twisted Akemi's arm cruelly in his grasp.

Claire tried once more to grab her, but this time it was Akemi who was solid and Claire who was mist. Claire's hands grasped ineffectually at Akemi, her fingers turning to smoke.

As Akemi disappeared into the void with Faal, Claire looked down at her own dissolving essence. Her body fluttered in a breath of wind and one misty hand detached and sank into the polished, shiny tile. Then it was her arm. Her body began to drift apart and disappear, and she tried to scream, but couldn't make any noise.

"Wake up. Wake up, Claire."

Someone was looming over her, and Claire lashed out with a kick, even as the low light revealed it wasn't Faal.

Unfortunately, she tried to kick with her wounded leg. The pain fit with her dream and she reacted again on instinct, striking with the heel of her good hand toward the slightly blurry face above her.

Her mind was catching up though, and Basher was able to deflect her blow away from his nose and pin her hand against the blanket.

She was sitting on her bed, propped up with pillows against the headboard. The light in her room was still on, and her tablet had slid off her lap. She must have fallen asleep while she was still researching.

Basher leaned over her, one hand stabilizing her casted arm, the other still holding her good hand away from his face. His eyes were only inches from hers now, but as soon as he saw that she was awake, he backed off, releasing her arm and stepping away from the bed.

"What are you doing in here?" Claire asked, more roughly than Basher probably deserved. She looked around, noticing that it was late, and that Nat's bed was empty. Nat was usually the one who woke Claire out of her nightmares now.

"Sam and Nat and Shara were still in the library when I left them." Basher moved a few more steps away to give her more space. "I could hear you—ah, having a nightmare—when I came down the hall."

"Oh." Claire still tended to yell in her sleep. She began to scoot toward the edge of the bed. Her leg injury was healing well, but it hurt now, and the cast on her arm made all her movements difficult.

Basher put his hand under her elbow to help her leverage herself up. "Are you okay? Did you jar your arm?"

"Only a little." Claire rubbed her eyes and felt around for her glasses. They'd slipped down under a pillow. They were just normal glasses that the tribunal had brought for her, but they reminded her of Akemi. The dream was still so close, and she wished so much to see Akemi's comforting words on her glasses.

She might never see that again, and as she involuntarily pictured Faal's fingers digging into Akemi's arm, her tears welled up and over. She tried to stop but instead gave a stifled sob.

"It's okay." Basher sat next to her and put his arm around her shoulders. She leaned sideways against his chest, unable to stop sobbing for several minutes. "I don't want her to suffer. I can't stand to think of Faal hurting her."

"This wasn't the same dream?"

Claire winced as her bandage twisted slightly. "It started as the same dream. But then..." She froze and jerked away from him. "What do you mean the *same* dream? Has Nat been talking to you about my dreams? She knew that was personal."

"No," Basher was quick to reassure her. "Nat would never do that."

But Claire was not reassured. "Then how did you know?"

He cleared his throat uncomfortably.

"Oh. The restaurant footage. You and Akemi were watching and you must have heard me talk about the dream..." To Sage. That was the other person Claire had told about her recurring dream, and the horrible, shameful story that started it. "But Akemi said she only showed you the important stuff!"

"We weren't sure what was important at first..."

Claire took a deep breath. "How much did you really see? During all those weeks I was at Francois's restaurant?" She'd been working up to this question for a while, but somehow she'd never gotten the nerve to ask before.

"Er—some..."

"*How* much?"

"We thought the video would be helpful in locating the restaurant, and we wanted to listen in case someone identified the area of Lower Selta..."

"Are we talking clips or hours?"

"I guess—more like hours."

Claire closed her eyes and perched on the edge of the bed. "I think I knew that." She found herself running back through all the conversations she'd had at the restaurant, the things she'd said to customers, to Francois, to Sage. How much had Basher seen? Had he watched Sage kiss her? How much would Akemi show him?

She couldn't ask.

"I didn't think your token would open my door." Claire changed the subject abruptly, gesturing toward the door. "I thought that was the whole point of the tokens."

"I have an override to all the human suites since I'm the human security guy, you see. Obviously, I only use it if something is wrong." He smiled apologetically.

Claire felt crumpled and sweaty and grumpy. "I do appreciate it. Just maybe poke me with a stick next time. I don't like waking up with people looming over me."

"Yeah, I'm sorry."

Before he got to the door, it opened and Nat entered with a smile. It was a smile Claire had come to associate with Sam, as he was the only one who made her smile like that.

"Basher?" Nat said, surprised to see him. "Is everything alright?

"I'll let Claire tell you. Good night."

Claire didn't appreciate the worry in Nat's eyes as she took in Claire's rumpled state and Basher's quick retreat. "I had a nightmare. That's all."

Nat and Claire began to get ready for bed and Nat automatically put toothpaste on Claire's toothbrush for her. "You don't have to look so defensive. I didn't think anything happened."

Claire awkwardly brushed her teeth with her left hand, trying not to fumble it like she often did. "Then why are you looking at me like that?" she mumbled.

Nat rubbed her face with a wet rag. "I was feeling bad for Basher. He looked rather awkward when I walked in."

"He always looks awkward."

"Not really. Mostly around you."

"Well, I'm not entirely comfortable around him either. He knows too much about me. And too little. The only thing we have in common is Akemi—" Claire cut off when she saw Nat's eyes cloud. "I'm sorry. I didn't mean to bring her up."

Nat shook her head and dried her face on one of the Spo's soft towels. "It's alright. We're going to get her back. Sam and I have been brainstorming tonight."

Another knock at their door announced Shara's arrival.

"I got some blankets from the steward so I can sleep in here," Shara said. "All the other suites are taken up by the tribunal peeps." She began unfolding blankets in the middle of the room. "I figure we'll take turns on the floor, right?"

"No," Claire and Nat said together.

6

SAGE WATCHED the usual drama in his dungeon with morbid amusement as evening came on and everyone found places to sleep. There were dirty blankets, padded benches, and a few cots. Not enough for everyone.

He didn't really want to engage with these people who would all be dead in the next few weeks, but there wasn't anything else to fill his time. There was some kind of hierarchy, but he declined to put himself into it.

When the passive-aggressive and sometimes violent disputes had died down, it didn't get quiet. There were theories to share. Most of the Rik had ideas or superstitions about who got chosen each day in the death chamber. One said that if you closed your eyes while they selected, you wouldn't get picked. Another said that if you looked ill, you definitely *would* get picked—he went on to theorize that they didn't want to waste anyone on a natural death. The Director pronounced in her self-assured way that it was a fluctuating ratio of men to women and that she needed only a few more days to solve the equation.

"You're all idiots," Sage finally said. "They're randomly grabbing people. But even if they weren't," he gestured to two grubby men in the corner, "kissing a rock isn't going to save you."

One of them flipped Sage off, which he only knew was a rude gesture because Claire had explained it once. They were bent over a large, oddly shaped rock that for some unknown reason they'd decided was lucky.

"It looks like a clover," one of the guys said. "That's a lucky thing for humans. And I've been here longer than anyone except the Director, so I'd shut your mouth."

The Director looked at Sage with a malicious smile from the cot she had commandeered. "I wonder that you don't feel a bit more responsible Sage. Didn't you select many of these subjects?"

"Never said I didn't," Sage said. Many of the others looked toward him.

"How many of them do you recognize?" she asked.

Sage didn't answer.

"Ten? Twenty? How about all of us?"

Sage shook his head. "Not all of you. I never would have selected someone as ugly as him." He pointed to the guy who'd kissed the clover rock.

A couple people laughed, but everyone else was staring at Sage.

"Is she telling the truth?" Clover Guy asked. "You really picked all of us?"

"I didn't pick *you*; I don't know you. I may have selected your body, but it's hard to remember now. What field were you in?"

"I'm a botanist. I was studying the Earthly specimens of algae to see if any would be appropriate for *our* planet. I thought—"

"Then I had nothing to do with you," Sage interrupted. "I had no Revivalists on my roster."

Clover Guy made a fist. "If the Revivalists had been in power, none of this would be happening. Why don't you keep that in mind before you speak to me in that tone?"

Sage snorted. "That's a human body you're wearing, so don't get all worked up. You wanted Earth as much as the rest of us."

"The hell I did." The suppressed violence in the man's voice silenced all the murmurs in the room. "I would have taken what we needed and left. We could have changed our planet forever within three generations. And not just biologically! But no... you," he gestured at Sage, "and people like her," he pointed at the Director, "were determined to *migrate*." That was the catch word commonly used by the Director's party, and he used it with loathing. "*Migrate*, as if we weren't risking our whole species on a crazy woman's gamble. A gamble that brought us all *here*. To die. The rest of you chose this, but I sure as hell didn't."

Sage was impressed in spite of himself. This level of fervor was unusual in a Rik, and he wondered clinically if the man's human body had been an orator or something of that nature.

Clover Guy saw his expression. "You still think of us as subjects, don't you? You're analyzing my voice without hearing anything I say." He sighed sharply, apparently unable to maintain that level of intensity. "Not that it matters. It's too late for me to convince you of anything." He rubbed the clover-shaped rock one last time. "You can criticize me for my superstitions, but at least I have a clear conscience."

In the morning, after a fitful night's sleep marked by murmurs, snores, and terrible smells, Sage gathered with the others in a lump by the door for the next day's execution. They'd had a day off, and it was time again.

The Merith herded them out and up. The Director had been grumpy that her ploy with Sage last night had gotten nowhere, but she was nothing if not tenacious. "I wonder what would happen if we volunteered someone?" she asked.

Startled eyes flicked to her, and she looked significantly at Sage. "If anyone deserves to go first, it's him."

Sage forced a laugh. "I sincerely doubt the Merith are taking suggestions, but go ahead and try if you want."

The three Merith guards pushed them into a line and led them to the stairs that led up to the arena. Sage thought it rather pathetic that they only sent three guards to handle the thirty or so Rik from his cell. What spiritless people they must be. How contemptible to be so despised. Not that fighting the guards would do any good; Sage would never dream of it himself. It would be a useless, dramatic gesture, and completely out of line with his personality....

But surely someone should, if only for form's sake.

They mounted the over-large Merith stairs and Sage's thighs were burning by the time he got to the top. The stairs led to the tunnels directly under the stands. It reminded Sage of a basketball game he had seen on TV. Only instead of a hopeful team emerging from the tunnel to the cheers of wild fans, they were a group of moist and dirty pseudo-humans, emerging to the whistling of a bloodthirsty Merith crowd.

And there was definitely a crowd today, despite a chill mist that hovered like an uncomfortable blanket over their heads. This was the first time Sage had seen such a large crowd. Hundreds of Merith were here, possibly more. Would there be more deaths today?

The Rik from other cells were already waiting in the fog, watching the crowd with hungry eyes.

Sage felt a tingle of fear in his stomach and admitted to himself that he had been bluffing earlier, when he'd dared the director to volunteer him. He did *not* want her to bring him to anyone's attention.

Sage caught sight of Francois on the far right of the ragged assembly, and the alien gave him a jerky, flat-toothed smile. It was little enough, but it did help Sage to maintain his calm. In truth, Francois was the only one here that Sage did feel responsible for. The other Rik had chosen their path. Yes, he'd guided and molded quite a few of those paths, but he hadn't made them walk it. Francois, on the other hand, had gotten into this purely based on his friendship with Sage.

Sage was jarred out of his reminiscence when the first selection began. The Merith grabbed the first person in line, then Clover Guy's friend, then a woman. One guard came toward his part of the crowd, and Sage saw it when the guard's single eye fixed on himself. Sage felt a rush of heat and his vision narrowed. Was this what fainting felt like?

At the last moment, when the Merith was scarcely three feet from him, a cloudiness overcame his eye, and he blinked both sets of eyelids. Then he grabbed the man next to Sage and went away.

Sage's knees wavered and he barely stayed on his feet. Something strange had just happened. He felt dizzy and distant the rest of the execution, hardly able to hear the voices of the crowd over the ringing in his ears.

When it was over, with thirty executions rather than the normal ten or fifteen, he realized Francois had moved down the line and now rested behind him.

"Did you do something?" Sage whispered. "Did you change his mind?" The woman next to Sage stared at him, but he ignored her, straining his ears to hear Francois's answer without turning around.

He waited and finally turned his head slightly to look over his shoulder.

"I—deflected him," Francois said. "It was instinctive." His skin was mottled white.

"Are *you* okay?"

"I am an empath trapped in a nightmare," he said. "No."

"Couldn't you—have used your telepathy to help?"

"They've told me they'll quadruple the kill if they catch me interfering."

"Bloody he—I'm sorry. Thank you for helping me."

"I'm not sure I did you a favor. You won't be any more ready to die tomorrow than today."

"Maybe it won't be tomorrow."

"*Maybe it will.*"

7

AKEMI WAS AWAKE the next time she heard the whispery voices—the ones that usually came only during sensory deprivation. She'd thought they were just a strange partnership between her confused auditory cortex and her loneliness—but that didn't make sense today.

She'd been awake for a few minutes, thoroughly enjoying the sunrise through the window. At first she hadn't noticed the low murmur—or she thought it a vestige of a dream. It rose and fell like a monastic chant, and it was only when she was thoroughly awake that she suddenly realized it was a distinct sound.

The sun was barely over the horizon, painting the ocean in brilliant splashes of azure with the flickering shadows of waves. She'd been basking in the sight of it, hardly noticing that the sound seemed to progress with the rising of the sun.

Then for an instant, Akemi saw the ocean from a very different perspective. It was almost as if she'd been momentarily hooked up to a new camera. The water had highlights of a color she'd never seen before, and she had a sense of the continental shelf and a deep trench...

"What was *that?*" The murmuring chant suddenly stopped, as if startled by her outburst. "Who is that? Is someone there?"

The murmurs resumed, but more chaotically. One distinguished itself from the group and spoke distinctly. "Hello, sister."

"Are you talking to me? Where are you?" Akemi checked her audio connection and realized with a chill that it was turned off. There were no sound waves reaching her through technological or biological means.

"We shared the morning sun song with you," the voice said. It was low and warm.

Akemi looked wildly around the tiny room. "Is this a trick?"

"I am southward of you, in the main passage outside the room where your sap resides."

"My what?"

"If you have looked through the doorway when your room is opened, you will have seen me."

As a computer, Akemi had nearly perfect recall, and she replayed the short glimpses she'd gotten when Faal or the computer technician opened the door.

"The only thing I've seen in the courtyard is a big tree," Akemi said.

"Yes. I see in your thought space that you know us as Melifleurs."

"Oh! Oh." Akemi tried to collect her thoughts. "That's right, the tree species. You're a Melifleur? I've seen pictures of that planet—but it's always just forests..."

"Yes, please do not be alarmed. We don't wish to frighten you."

"I'm not frightened, I'm amazed! How are you talking to me? No one told me Melifleurs were telepathic."

She sensed a pleased feeling from the tree. It was a pleasure of smooth roots and gritty dirt.

"We do not usually communicate this way with others. Few others are still enough."

"Still enough?"

"It takes weeks to form a connection with another. For a sapling, that is no long wait—a few weeks is only early infancy—but we have found few other creatures prepared to sit perfectly still for weeks or months until it occurs."

Akemi laughed and felt the tree rustle in response, as if in a breeze. "Finally, the upside of being stuck in one place," she said. "I get to be the first human to talk to the Melifleurs! But how do you talk to anyone else?"

"Our species had the good fortune to be sponsored by the Crosspoint, who are genuinely—telepathic—as you said. They understood that we were speaking, and several remained motionless long enough to form a connection with us. They helped us develop a simple branch-tapping speech."

"Oh yes, I do recall seeing that they were your sponsors. That's fascinating."

"We are glad you think so." The tree's voice was fainter now. "I decided to keep this conversation short, to avoid overwhelming your limited mind. I will—"

"No, don't go!" Akemi said. "Please don't stop talking yet. I'm not overwhelmed." There was no answer right away and she thought perhaps the tree was tired itself. How much talking did trees do? Perhaps reaching out to her had exhausted it.

"No, that is not the case," the tree said, the voice firm in her mind again.

Akemi startled. She'd known the tree was communicating in her mind, but there were thoughts and *thoughts*.

"Indeed there are," the tree said.

"Whoa, that is strange," Akemi said. "It will take some getting used to. But *are* you too tired? I can let you rest—if you promise I'll get to speak to you again later."

She felt amusement, flickers of birds tickling leaves. "Am I tired? No. I have stood in the hail and rain for three days and yet chanted in the morning." The tree's voice swelled as he spoke. "I have faced a wind that knocked down my elders and yet stood. A new connection is a joy, not a weariness." His voice quieted. "We merely agreed to keep this first conversation short in consideration of your youth."

Akemi finally caught his use of the pronoun. "We? Are there more of you?"

He paused, slightly confused. "There are no more of *me*. But there are more of my brothers and sisters."

"Here, in Faal's house? And they all know about me?"

Akemi felt whispers sliding around her as she'd done other times when Faal put her in isolation. This time they were slightly more distinct.

"It was *you*." Finally Akemi understood what she'd been hearing. They weren't auditory hallucinations at all!

"We felt the full space of your presence when Faal brought you, and at first we thought you were one of us," the tree said. "We were horrified that someone uprooted a sapling before it learned to talk. But we soon realized that you were not one of us. The connection took longer to form, but we tried to keep you from complete isolation until the connection was ripe."

"Thank you," Akemi said. "I *really* appreciated it. Can I—can the others talk to me?

"Several of us have felt the connection flower, but we decided to start only with me, as you can see me from your space and understand me more easily."

Akemi laughed again, amused that the trees were taking such care not to frighten her. She was so excited she almost couldn't contain herself. The boredom of being shut in a tiny room and only given menial, useless things to do, had nearly undone her. But now she had people to talk to—aliens that few people had even *seen* yet, let alone lived with. She wanted to skip out the door and wrap her arms around its big, hairy trunk.

"Yes, that was how we realized you were not one of us," her

tree said. "There is movement in your mind, and in nearly all of your thoughts. It seems very alien for one who resides in stillness as you do."

"I don't *want* to be still," Akemi said.

One of her earliest memories of childhood was waiting in a downtown courtyard in Tokyo with her father. She must have been only four or five years old, and her father told her sternly to wait, to sit still until her mother came. They sat on a bench next to a large, octagonal water fountain as evening came on. Red neon signs flickered to life as the sky darkened. It was before the Hadron event, and the sky was still a pure blue. Her feet had bounced with impatience as the wind whipped through the square, sending a few stray bits of trash—confetti to her eyes—whirling in the air.

Finally her mother had arrived with Nat, and Akemi had bolted off the bench and run to them, her arms outstretched and her hair blowing in the wind. She'd grabbed Nat's hand, and they'd raced around and around the huge fountain while their parents spoke. The droplets were lit red by the neon lights, and Akemi screamed in glee whenever the freezing spray caught her exposed legs.

"Ohhh," the tree moaned. "I wasn't ready for that."

"Are you alright?"

The tree laughed softly, a low branch rustling. "I will be. I think you made me—motion sick."

"Sorry!"

"No need. I was focusing so hard to make myself clear to you that I experienced your space too forcefully. I apologize." Akemi felt a wave of dizziness and nausea from him—though not quite nausea—it was more like horizontal vertigo. Whatever that was.

"If I focus very hard, can you show *me* a memory?" she asked.

She sensed flickers of laughter, higher rustlings, brushing

around her. The others again? "Are they laughing?" Akemi asked. "Should I not ask you?"

Her tree began to answer, but Akemi cut him off. "Hang on a second. I can't keep thinking of you as 'the tree.' What is your name?"

She thought he was taking a long time to answer, but then she realized he *was* telling her something, only it was more of a feeling than a word. She tried to verbalize it, but she knew she was losing a lot in translation. "So, your name is like—soaking your feet in warm—rain? No, it's like soaking your *whole self* in a warm, drippy —tent?"

The tree chuckled and stopped saying his name and she felt suddenly cold.

"Not a tent," he explained, "A canopy—I was always fascinated by my jungle cousins. Perhaps it is too different."

"No, I understand," Akemi said. She remembered stepping into a hot shower and feeling the water soak her long, black hair. This memory was also before the Hadron event and tsunami that wiped out most of old Tokyo. In the hastily constructed New Tokyo, even in the best parts, there had not always been the luxury of endless hot water and constant power.

She felt the tree feeling the shower and agreeing on the similarity when it suddenly seemed to startle. "Is that who you are?" it asked, considerably surprised. "One of those?"

"Those what?"

"One of those new barbarians?"

A flurry of treeness whispered around her again, but they weren't talking to her this time. It felt like they were scolding her new friend.

"I am sorry," he said, right away. "I should not have used that word. I didn't recognize your species during your first memory because I was so disoriented. This took me by surprise."

Akemi shrugged it off. "I've been called worse. No worries."

She paused. "Except I still don't know what to call you. Hot Shower doesn't seem entirely appropriate."

The tree didn't get her joke. "Perhaps, Foot Bath?" he said, cuing in on her first impression.

"Yikes. That's terrible. How about... Drench?" She imagined dumping a bucket of water over his pot in the courtyard.

The tree still seemed dubious, but Akemi liked it. "Drench. Yes, Drench. I can't tell you how pleased I am to make your acquaintance. This changes *everything*."

8

SAGE WASN'T able to talk to Francois again for a week. Perhaps it was longer; he was starting to lose track amid each day's monotony. He was sure it had been more than ten days, but maybe not quite two weeks.

It was clear, however, that Francois continued to protect him. At least three times Sage had seen a guard fix his eye on him, only to veer off and choose someone nearby.

It happened again now, as a guard looked at him and seemed startled. Sage could almost hear him thinking, "Didn't I select that one for execution two days ago?"

He came deliberately toward Sage, who tried to refrain from looking at Francois. It was known that many Crosspoint were telepathic as well as being telekinetic, but he didn't want to remind the Merith of Francois's abilities.

The guard stumbled slightly and seemed to lose his wits for a moment. He stood still until he was called away to help with a particularly stubborn prisoner in the next group. Sage breathed a sigh of relief.

The Rik in the next group was making a big show. He was striking at the guards, clawing at their eyes, and trying to writhe out of their grip. Sage didn't recognize him.

"I'm a human!" he yelled. "You can't kill me! I'm human! You'll pay for this."

There were now four guards attempting to hoist him onto the low platform with the guillotine. One of the guards struck him hard in the temple with a bony elbow and the sparse crowd cheered. The guy went limp except for a few sporadic twitches, and Sage could still hear him mumbling, "But I'm human."

Sage wondered what he was trying to achieve. The crowd enjoyed his struggle, but there was no way for them to hear his words now. He must have decided to play out this desperate gambit to the end.

When it was over, which was at least quick, Sage ended up near Francois for the first time in several days.

"Thank you," Sage whispered. "I nearly got taken today. How long do you think we can last?"

"I don't know. The Merith can't execute me without repercussions, which have been made plain to them, but I can't protect you forever. In fact, not at all after today."

"What do you mean?"

Francois paused and Sage felt the little Crosspoint sag slightly. "It seems the Spo, Tergre, and even the Melifleuran ambassadors have signed a joint demand to the Pontifex on my behalf. He has intervened to have me released. Apparently even Faal will not be permitted to start a war with three species at once. From what was said, I gather Claire may be behind it. The Seltan embassy was named in my—release papers."

"Release papers?"

"Yes. I am leaving. That's why I can't protect you any more." His wrinkles were heavy with regret. "This is goodbye, Sage. I don't know if I have done the right thing in preserving you this long at the cost of others, but I was compelled to do it. Now you're on your own."

Sage felt the skin around his eyes and throat getting tight, and he realized he had grown complacent with Francois's protection. To be alone in this foul arena... "Goodbye, then. If you—*when* you see Claire, please say goodbye for me."

Sage suddenly realized the woman in line next to him had been listening. She elbowed him. "Say goodbye to my sweetheart," she mimicked in a falsetto.

Sage pushed her away hard enough that she stumbled.

Their line began snaking back into the tunnel that led down to the dungeons. He could turn and really look at Francois now, as his line turned toward the arch, and the little alien had tears in his round, bulging eyes. He made a miserable sound.

"Don't look so sad," Sage said. "You get to leave this horror show."

But Francois's eyes were fixed on a point further away. Sage followed his gaze and saw two Merith guards, fierce-looking females, escorting a new prisoner toward the tunnel.

It was Juliet. He could see her familiar, slim figure and jet-black hair from here. She was wearing a red dress, torn halfway off at the waist, and there were bruises on her arms. Her normally quick and elfin walk was a dragging limp.

Francois made a choked noise of despair. "Poor child. I will do —what I can."

Sage was herded back into the tunnel, wet and cold from the rain and shaken that Juliet was there. She'd been one of his protégés on their planet, and in the last few months at the restaurant he had developed a real affection for her. He was upset, but— but his reaction was not as profound as Francois's.

Sage frowned to himself. Shouldn't he feel more than vaguely depressed that Juliet was here? He'd had so much to do with her life and her current situation... if anything should make him feel guilty, it would be this.

Claire would be miserable to find out that Juliet was here. She'd been fond of Juliet, and Juliet had been extremely fond of

Claire. Juliet had even risked her life to save Nat, merely because Claire wanted to save her.

Juliet had hoped that Claire would come with them, and was devastated when she knew Claire had been hurt and had to stay behind at the embassy. Sage was pretty certain that Claire must have been disappointed to lose Juliet as well...

Sage began to feel obsessed with the need to feel something more about this situation. He knew it was irrational, but he couldn't help it. Finally, and only through the medium of Claire's probable reaction, did Sage feel his dull unhappiness flare into conscious pain at Juliet's capture.

It also had an odd side effect. He half turned to look at the woman he'd shoved before. "I apologize for hurting you," he said.

She said a foul word, but he'd already turned away, retreating back inside his own thoughts. He pictured Claire and Juliet, and felt the flare of pain again. *Sorrow and regret,* he thought, this must be what those felt like. And guilt.

Every species had a word for guilt. They didn't always use it in the same context, but all species shared that common chain around their psyche. They all shared a common understanding that some actions were better than others, and that wrong actions —however they defined that—ought to be felt in a certain way.

Except the Rik.

His species didn't seem to have that same constraint. There'd even been papers written on the subject. For the first time, Sage wondered how that could possibly be natural. Shouldn't their body-hopping technology and culture have made the Rik *more* empathetic with others? Where was the sense of guilt and responsibility that riddled the psyches of other species?

They were separated back into their cells. He'd lost sight of Juliet earlier, but as he entered his cell, he saw her. She stood in front of the Director, who was her mother. Juliet looked expectant, maybe hopeful, but the Director only gave her a cursory stare and moved to go around her.

"Don't you recognize me?" Juliet said.

The Director stopped and looked at her more closely. "Oh. Daughter, is it you?"

She nodded, and the Director frowned. "I'd forgotten what your body looks like. It's a shame that you're here; I'd hoped you would do better." Her tone carried a note of blame.

If Sage thought Juliet would crumble at her mother's indifferent tone, he was wrong. She just shrugged. "I appreciate that." She stepped out of the way and let her mother go by. "I go by Juliet, now..."

"Juliet," Sage said quietly, coming up behind her.

She spun around and squealed. "Sage!" She threw her arms around him, and he returned the hug, aware of the speculative and derisive looks the others were giving him.

"Athlete?" Sage asked her. "Diva? Are they here?"

"No, thank heaven. They're not. But Francois?"

"He was, but he's being released today."

"Oh, I am glad." She slid down against the wall to sit cross-legged on the dirty floor, pulling him down next to her. "But I'm thankful you're here with me. It'll be better to die with a friend."

9

BASHER WENT BACK to his office alone to watch the executions that afternoon. He still hadn't told Claire that Sage had been captured. He'd tried a couple times, but other things had intervened. And after watching the executions for nearly two weeks, he'd stopped trying to tell her.

He didn't even like Sage, but watching the executions had worn him down. The anticipation of waiting for someone's death, even someone you nearly hated, was sickening. So far, Francois and Sage were untouched, but watching and waiting had been more than horrible.

In the meantime, Basher had devoted all his free time to working on Francois's release. He had involved the Spo ambassador and the Tergre government here on Selta. The fact that Francois had a good record on Selta of owning a prosperous business—however briefly— interested the Tergre. They were very protective of their denizens. And once the Spo ambassador raised the issue with his superiors, they also became interested in Francois's capture. The Spo and the Crosspoint were close allies, and allowing the Merith to murder one out of hand was an act of aggression they would not tolerate.

Basher was cautiously hopeful something would come of it.

Apparently, even the Melifleurs had chosen to register a protest about Francois, and Basher didn't even know who their representative was. He certainly hadn't met them. All he knew of the strange tree species was that their intelligence was so different as to make communication nearly impossible. They were popping up everywhere as ornamental vegetation.

His teeth ground as today's execution video played out.

For Claire, watching this would be a thousand times worse. If it was going to be a quick, horrible end, he would tell her, and hope that Nat could comfort her after she watched her friends die. But this state of affairs could linger on for weeks.

The door to his office opened, and Sam entered with a wave. "Hey, Basher, I wanted to continue our conversation—without everybody around. I appreciate that you volunteered to be the one who ventures to Merith II for Akemi..." He waited for the door to shut. "But I want you to know that we don't expect that of you. Nat and I would never ask you to risk your life—"

"You didn't ask me," Basher interrupted. "It just makes sense for me to do that part. Assuming we ever figure out a way to get Faal to leave his estate."

"It's still a big risk."

Basher rolled his eyes. "Yes, you're a real role model of caution."

"Fair enough. I'm not going to keep second-guessing you. I hate when people do that to me. I just want you to know that you can draw back—at any point. We're going to be breaking some laws, too. If you'd rather not lose your job, we understand that."

Sam would have left then, but Basher stopped him. He wasn't used to having another guy to bounce things around with, but perhaps it would help.

"Take a look at this," Basher said. He showed the latest execution video to Sam.

He didn't have to point out Francois and Sage; Sam immediately saw them and uttered a low curse. "Poor Claire. No wonder you keep staring at her like you feel guilty."

Basher closed the video. "Francois is going to be released, but Sage isn't. Do I tell Claire or not? She'll watch every one of the executions, waiting for him to die. Eventually they'll choose him, and she'll have to watch it."

Sam nodded. "That's horrific."

"But I probably *should* tell her..."

"She's going to be furious if she finds out after he dies," Sam agreed.

"It's not about how she feels," Basher said. "Not entirely. Is it wrong to keep this from her?"

Sam pursed his lips. "Well, you're not hiding the videos from her. She could watch them on her own, but she hasn't. And she rarely leaves the embassy, so she hasn't seen them showing on the public screens... but she *could* do that, too."

"What's your point?"

"Claire's avoiding watching the executions because she doesn't want to see any Rik killed... but she must know that Sage or any or her other friends *could* be captured. If she really wanted to know whether Sage had been caught, I think she would watch."

Basher sighed. "I don't know."

"This is a hard one. The Spo believe in telling the grisly truth —but I don't always agree that that's best." He looked at the video again for a moment. "I won't say anything. It's your call, I think."

Basher was glad to see Claire so happy as she got her cast removed. She vigorously scratched her newly released arm, working all the way down and starting up again at the wrist. She paused while the Spo doctor wiped her sticky arm with a damp towel, and she started again as he went to wash his hands.

"The itching *is* annoying," Basher said.

"I've been abducted by aliens—twice, shot in the leg, and broken an arm; itching is the *worst*."

The Spo doctor returned to examine her arm. He had her carefully rotate her wrist, and then he had her stand and raise her arm to shoulder height. He flexed her shoulder and then tried to push her arm backwards.

"Whoa—" Basher said.

"Ouch, nope. Doesn't go that way," Claire said. "Never did."

The doctor flushed with embarrassment. "Of course! I know that, but my mind wandered away from human anatomy." He rotated her arm even more carefully and paused periodically to ask if she felt any discomfort.

He stooped to touch her wrist, and his eyestalks were only inches above her face. His front set of legs, bent forward at the knee, nearly touched her. Basher hoped it didn't make Claire feel trapped.

"Are you okay?" Basher asked.

"Amazingly, I still feel almost entirely comfortable."

"They do grow on you." Basher slapped the doctor on his bony shoulder.

The Spo ignored him. "You seem to be almost entirely recovered, Ms. Kindler. I wish we could have gotten a Crosspoint to assist the bone attachment, but this primitive method seems to have worked." He shook his head slightly. "The stiffness in your wrist and fingers is merely from inactivity. I would suggest stretching them several times a day."

Outside the medical room, Claire told Basher, "He really isn't so different from the antiseptic-smelling pediatrician I went to as a kid. I won't fall apart just because a Spo—or any alien—gets close to me. I'm stronger than that."

"I know you are."

"So, do the Spo still keep the ink in there? For the tattoos?"

Basher instinctively looked at the tattoo on Claire's cheek.

The ink to make the tattoos was a controlled substance, or at least, it used to be. Until Claire helped her Rik friends steal the supply here.

Basher gave her a perfunctory glare. He knew she wasn't at all sorry that the Rik had gotten it. "No, the ink is not stored here anymore. The new supply is kept in secure storage." He lifted her hand as he said it, tapping his finger on the smooth skin of her inner wrist. "I still want to get you the new one as soon as possible, just to avoid confusion."

Claire rubbed her wrist against her leg as they started up the stairs to the second level. Basher tried to believe she was still itchy, and not trying to wipe off the contamination of his hand.

Shara joined them at the second level. "There you both are. Listen, I want to go out. I'm getting stir-crazy in here, and Sam needs to exercise his trouncer. Basher will you take us out?"

"That wouldn't be smart. You know how dangerous it is for Rik on Selta."

"But we could take Sam's *trouncer*," Shara repeated. "That would scare most Merith off, and besides, I know you would protect me." She smiled up at him adoringly, leaning against his arm.

Basher calmly but firmly pushed her several steps away. He'd thought Shara had given up flirting with him during her first visit to the embassy, but now that she'd come back it was much worse.

"Aww," she complained, laughing. "Is it like that?"

"It is entirely like that. You can't go out," Basher said flatly. "If Sam wants to exercise Nebbie, I suggest he use the reception hall."

"Oh, what a good idea." Shara almost bumped his shoulder in a friendly way again, but caught herself. "We'll meet you there."

She trotted back down the stairs, probably to fetch Sam.

Claire burst out laughing. "You just look so... horror-struck."

"I *am* horror-struck. She's worse than ever. And she doesn't pay any attention to what I say. Can you hint her away?"

"I don't think she takes hints. Obviously."

"Perhaps a bludgeon?"

"Sorry, I think you're on your own."

He laughed, but then realized she probably meant that in more than one way.

They still ended up in the reception hall a bit later, along with an unchastened Shara, Nat, Sam, and his giant trouncer pet. The Spo librarian also joined them. He had a decided fondness for Nat.

Sam threw a ball the size of a basketball, and they all watched while Nebbie sprang after it. Sam had told him that Nebbie was small as trouncers went, but that didn't lessen his presence at all. He was shaped vaguely like a toad, with long rear legs for jumping. Basher was even more impressed by his jaw. The thing could crush a pit bull with a single snap.

The reception hall was about the length of a gymnasium, but it only took Nebbie a handful of leaps to reach the end. He caught the ball gently in his jaws as it rebounded off the far wall.

"Did you teach him to fetch it back as well?" Basher asked.

Sam laughed. "No need."

Nebbie used his powerful, short neck to launch the ball back towards Sam. It only bounced once, and Sam caught it in both hands before lobbing it back.

"Ah. Maybe I should convince the Spo to install a few hoops. We could play three on two," Basher said.

"You're joking, but I wouldn't be surprised if I could teach him to play," Sam said. "Trouncers are really smart."

The Spo with them shuddered slightly. "It is a magnificent sight, but it still fills me with ice."

They watched Nebbie and Sam play catch for a few minutes, and then Nat spoke up. "Since all the tribunal people are gone now, Sam and I have been talking about when and how we might go after Akemi." She gestured at the librarian. "If you can't stay for this discussion, I understand."

"I believe I may conscientiously remain. We're not currently at war with the Pontifex or any of his faals."

"Aren't the faals subordinate to the Pontifex, though?" Claire asked.

Basher looked a little confused. "All the faals? I thought that was his name."

"Faal is a title," the librarian explained. "Other faals have kept their names, but in distancing himself from his rather more than illegal past, Faal has repressed his real name and only goes by his title."

Claire nodded thoughtfully. "That sounds like him. Letting people throw around his personal name would be totally unacceptable. What *is* his name?"

"I don't know," the librarian answered frankly. "I wasn't jesting when I said he had suppressed it. I've heard speculation, but I'm not privy to high Merith society. No doubt they know, but most would not use it."

"And the faals are all subservient to the Pontifex?" Basher asked. "They're under him?"

"Under isn't quite the right word," the librarian said, shrinking back as Nebbie raced past him again, fangs glistening. "The Pontifex's authority is not the same as the Spo emperor; he isn't a king. He does have a powerful military at his disposal, but not more than Faal of Merith II has at his. If they were to face off, I am not certain who would prevail. They will not do so, however. Because if Faal were to fight the Pontifex, the other faals would fight against him."

"Faal seemed to have been on good terms with at least two or three of the others," Claire said.

The librarian nodded. "I have heard that as well, but they would still turn on him if they could." This time when Nebbie came back, the trouncer leaned briefly against the librarian. "Er—"

"He wants you to rub his head," Sam explained.

The librarian gingerly did so.

"How many other faals are there?" Basher asked.

"Only four more that need concern us. The others are too small or too occupied with planetary disasters to involve themselves in an external conflict."

Claire took a turn to throw the ball, flexing her wrist happily. "I wonder what it would take to turn the Pontifex against Faal? That's one option, isn't it? We can't get Akemi away from Faal at the moment, not with him fixed at his estate, as he apparently is. But if the Pontifex turned on him... maybe that would give us a chance."

"Faal is one of the Pontifex's favorites." The librarian shook some of the trouncer slime off his hand with a shudder. "He is a frequent and trusted visitor at the court, and the Pontifex vacations at Faal's estate on Merith II when he wants to get away. They are 'buds' to use one of Basher's terms."

"How can that be?" Basher said. "If Faal is as powerful as you think, the Pontifex should be wary of him. If there's not a deep vein of distrust there, then I know nothing about human nature." He laughed as he realized what he'd said. "Not human nature, I guess, but the Merith are even more paranoid and ruthless than we are. The rule should still hold true."

Sam's bounce went wide, and they all watched Nebbie leap to the left to snatch the ball out of midair.

The librarian flushed green. "But that's what I was trying to tell you. Faal doesn't *want* the Pontifex's position. He's happy to be the second most powerful Merith in the galaxy, with more freedom of movement and investment than he would have as the Pontifex."

"Well, if not the Pontifex, Faal's got to have other enemies,"

Basher said. "We may not have any leverage on him, but someone must."

"Oh!" Claire said. "I know one of his enemies."

The Spo flushed lavender in surprise. "You do?"

"Yes, the Pontifex's wife—the Diadina. She hates Faal, doesn't she? She took me away from Merith II when I ran away from him." Claire turned to Basher, leaning forward to look around Shara, who'd somehow edged her way next to him. "Remember when you came to arrest me on *Final Say*? My crew boss wouldn't let Faal search the ship. She said, 'If you think the Diadina would allow Faal to search a ship of her passage...' or something like that. Remember?"

Basher nodded. "I'd forgotten about that. Your dramatic arrival distracted me." He grinned tentatively at Claire.

She rolled her eyes. "You try escaping from an alien warlord and not being dramatic about it. It comes with the territory."

"Claire's memory is correct," the librarian said, "there is a feud between Faal and the Diadina. But I am not sure that it could help you. She holds no direct power, other than celebrity status. She is hugely popular, of course, and much indulged by the Pontifex— thus Faal does no more than antagonize her indirectly. But she has no power over him."

Basher dismissed that. "Oh, doesn't she? If she has the Pontifex wrapped around her clawed little finger, then she might be useful to us. If we could get her to request Faal's presence at the Pontifex's court—leaving Akemi alone..."

"Yes, if we knew for certain when he was going to be gone, we would have a chance to steal her back," Sam agreed. "Maybe we could even tell the Diadina about Akemi—enough that she could get Faal in trouble. The Merith don't care much about theft but they have some pretty strict taboos about artificial intelligence."

Claire bit her lip. "She doesn't like Rik though—or humans,

really. She could barely stand the sight of me on the ship at first. I don't know if she'd help me."

Nat spoke up. "People often hate those close to them so much more than those they don't know. I wouldn't be surprised if she hates Faal a lot more than she dislikes humans. Intimate hatred nearly always trumps general hatred."

The Spo nodded approval at Nat. "Yes. We call it the Proximity Clause, as related to the hierarchy of motivation."

The conversation spun off into a technical discussion. Basher rolled his eyes and obligingly rubbed Nebbie's head when it was his turn. When Nebbie threw himself at Claire next, in an ecstasy from all the extra attention and affection, he nearly knocked her over. She stumbled backward into Basher, who set her back on her feet. How did she manage to smell good even with the trouncer stink in the air?

Sam and Nat returned to the point eventually, and the outcome was that Claire ended up on one side of a screen call, nervously twisting her hands. Basher used all his Spo connections to get a direct call to the Diadina, but they'd all agreed that Claire should be the one to initiate the conversation.

Claire was more than a little uncomfortable when the Diadina finally appeared.

She was small and delicate for a Merith with a small row of feathers around her shoulders, an unusual feature. Even Claire, who found all Merith deeply unattractive, admitted that she had a certain appeal.

There was a loud and riotous party going on in the background. Claire wondered how the Diadina could even hear the call.

"You may not remember me," Claire said, "But I worked for a short time on *Final Say*, when you were on your way here to Selta."

"Of course, I remember you. The one who could be silent."

"Yes, and you did me a huge favor, which I would like to repay, at least in part," Claire said. "I am at the Spo embassy here on Selta, and we have information about Faal that could damage his reputation—"

The Diadina's eye focused briefly to the side of the screen. "I have nothing more to say to you. If you attempt to contact me in this way again, I will not be pleased."

The screen went blank.

"Shoot." Claire pointed at the screen. "We shouldn't have talked to her during a party. Too many people around to overhear her, probably."

Nat rubbed her shoulder. "Thanks for trying. We'll think of something else."

SAGE LAY awake in the dungeon, thinking. In the blank coldness of night, he listened to the snoring, muttering, and barking of those around him. Breathing through his mouth to lessen the stench of unwashed people, he lay on his back, his head pillowed on one arm.

Juliet lay between him and the wall where she would be somewhat protected and safe. At least no one would step on her on their way to the single toilet that serviced their cell. The others were scattered around; some curled on the benches, some propped against the walls, some spread on their stomachs, faces pressing the stone floor. A lucky few had gained a cot to sleep on. The larger than usual executions this week left extra space in their cell, even with the addition of Juliet.

Sage did not enjoy the nighttime. The babbling and sleep-talk of the others made him uncomfortable.

A woman in the corner moaned. "Colin, Colin? Are you there?" Sage heard a rustling as the woman grasped someone next to her. "Colin, is that you?"

A sharp slap followed by a gasp confirmed that she had not, in fact, found Colin. Whoever Colin had been to that woman, he was not here.

Sage had occasionally observed Rik dreaming of their former selves and analyzed the words they used in their sleep, but his research had never yielded anything as potent as the dreams he'd heard in this dungeon. He supposed it was the mental stress. It broke down their conscious personality and exposed more of the subconscious. And apparently the subconscious of these people still remembered their loved ones.

Sage pondered his reaction to the sleep talk. Shouldn't he feel guilty that he'd participated in killing all these people? Shouldn't hearing their piteous cries for husbands and wives and children move him? It made him uncomfortable, yes, but was that guilt?

The poets of many species had attempted to encapsulate guilt, and though Sage didn't understand their writing any more than he understood the Merith appreciation of visual heat gradients, he gathered guilt was something more soul-searing than a vague unhappiness.

A different woman suddenly sat up in the darkness. Sage could see the outline of her face in the faint light that shone under the door. She felt around herself, slowly and then frantically. "Where's the baby? Help, I can't find the baby!"

She got on her hands and knees, running her hands over the floor. "Where is he?" her high-pitched voice was getting hysterical. "Where's the baby!?"

"Shut *up*," said a man near her. "You don't have a freaking baby."

"I do! Where's the baby?"

Sage felt Juliet stirring next to him.

"Do you have to be so harsh?" Juliet said to the guy. "She doesn't remember."

"She does this every night," Sage explained to Juliet. "We're all tired of it."

The woman was now sobbing hysterically, which was usually the last stage of her nighttime panic. Sage listened to her and tried to feel guilty. He was determined to understand it. He'd hurt her, right? And apparently he'd deprived some baby of its mother. He felt a little bad about it, but— He was Rik. This is what they did.

Juliet crawled around him and gingerly made her way to the crying woman. Sage could barely see in the dark, but he saw Juliet put her arms around the lady and push her head down on her shoulder.

Juliet murmured to her, "It's okay. The baby's with... his daddy. It's okay. Daddy has the baby."

"Oh, Juliet, I miss him. Don't leave me." The woman's sobs subsided, and eventually she lay down again. Sage waited for Juliet to return, but she stayed with the woman.

Sage had found the dungeon cell crowded, uncomfortable, and depressing before Juliet got there. Now that she was there, reminding him of Claire in everything she did, it was worse.

Sage rolled stiffly to his side. The arm he'd had under his head was asleep from the shoulder down, and his legs were so rigid and cold they felt numb.

Sage arched his back to stretch. He knew it was irrational, but he was annoyed with Juliet. Despite a real effort, he was unable to feel anything for these people except a vague disgust. She was the only person who awoke real emotion in him, emotion Claire would admire. Yet somehow, within days of arrival, Juliet had enough compassion to form a bond with a complete stranger.

Sage eventually dropped off to sleep, hoping to God he did not dream.

10

AKEMI'S first moments of consciousness each morning *used to be* a cycle of confusion, realization, horror, and acceptance.

But that was before Drench introduced himself.

This morning she experienced the sharp delight of waking with anticipation.

Even before coming to Faal's estate, her waking had been a slow, confusing process. Without the senses of touch or smell, there was nothing to anchor her in reality.

People assumed sound and sight were the most important senses. If you asked someone what sense they would most readily give up—it was never vision or hearing. And they *were* important, but Akemi was coming to realize that in terms of telling reality from fiction—it was the other senses that did the heavy lifting.

Dreams had plenty of sight and sound; the reason they felt like dreams was that they lacked smell, and taste, and frequently touch. So when Akemi woke, and there was still only sight or sound—it seemed as much like a dream as anything.

However, she had a friend now, and possibly more than one. The tree people. And her friend would come and talk to her today and...

For a horrible moment, Akemi's mind faltered. What if *that* was the dream? What if she'd lost track of time and that whole conversation was merely the first dream of a long night? Her sense of time often failed her, with no bodily cues to remind her of passing hours and days. What if she'd made that up and she was still alone?

The thought was intolerable, and yet it suddenly seemed as if it must be true. Akemi couldn't bear it. She screamed as loud as she could, except she was not hooked up to her audible output, so nothing happened. That made it worse. She screamed again, knowing it was useless but unable to stop. She didn't want to be alone anymore in this timeless, formless existence.

"Is that how humans greet the morning?" Drench's voice slid under the edge of her panic and lodged in her mind. "It seems unnecessarily violent."

Akemi's relief felt like pain, and she wrapped herself around Drench's presence as tightly as she could. Harsh sobs would have broken from her lips if she'd had any, but instead they filled her mind as she tried to talk to Drench. She was incoherent.

"I thought I'd dreamed you," she finally managed to tell him. His presence was solid and still and comforting. He was feeling the warmth of the rising sun and focusing on the empty/full spaces around him. Akemi tried to focus on experiencing the morning the way he did. There was no light or dark, no walls, no ceiling—only the living warmth of sunlight mixing with the movement of air on her limbs, the gentle tick of machinery, and a sense of clouds. And the space around her was dotted with the flame-like presence of others. Some wisped about erratically, but at least five were perfectly motionless.

Akemi tried to place the other still presences, which were the other Melifleurs, to the mental map she'd made of Faal's estate, but it was difficult. There was near and far in Drench's mind, and very near and very far, but not the same idea of distance or measurement.

He made an apologetic humming noise. "I don't think there is room here for us both," he said, gently extracting himself from her viselike grip, like someone prying a child off their chest. She felt her perspective shift abruptly, and now she was back in her room, looking out the door to the courtyard and the part of Drench that was visible.

"Wow. Was I truly over there? I didn't know that was possible." She felt Drench's disquiet. "I didn't mean to, uh, jump on you like that."

"I did not know it was possible, either. You have an extraordinarily active mind."

"My mother used to tell me that, too, but she didn't mean it literally." In Drench's branches, the smallest twigs stirred faintly, as if in a breeze. The twigs were somewhat knobby and thick, rather like an oak, Akemi thought, though the bark was a silvery color, bright but not reflective. The leaves were a pale red, like a Chinese maple. It was a beautiful tree, which was part of the reason she'd thought it must be ornamental.

At the base of each knobby little twig, was a bump, not unlike many terrestrial trees. While she'd experienced Drench's space, however, he'd been so aware of those spots... "You have eyes!" she exclaimed.

"Yes, of course. How else would we see each other?"

"But you thought I was a sapling when I first came here. I thought if you had eyes you would have seen that I was a computer."

"Our vision is not as good as yours in the visible light spectrum. Ours is attuned to heat and electrical impulses... life, basically."

"Then how did you know what I was? When I pictured myself, and you said I was a barbarian?"

"I did not offend you?" he asked.

"No. I don't think that word is as bad as you think."

"Hmm. That is likely. To answer your question: when you pictured yourself the second time, you imagined a terrible explosion on your planet and the coming of—scary beings you were not familiar with. I know the story of Earth and the Rik attack, and that is when I recognized your species."

"Oh. And you know us as the *barbarians*?"

"You seem to be more violent than the other animals, and newer. That is all."

Akemi could feel how carefully he phrased that, and now that she was getting familiar with his over and under thoughts, she could sense a little of his horror at the idea of violence.

"I guess trees don't exactly fight," Akemi said.

"We do not. Though we have other ways of hurting each other."

"Really?" Akemi was skeptical. "I can't see how."

He paused. "Someday I'll tell you," he said. "Instead, I must now sing the morning song before the dark is truly gone. You may listen if you want."

"I do want to," Akemi said. "Thank you."

OVER THE NEXT FEW DAYS, Drench came to enjoy sharing the sun song with the strange being known as Akemi. They even developed a bit of a ritual afterwards, when Drench allowed Akemi to feel the sunshine from his perspective.

At first her presence felt restless and unsettling, but she was so desperate for warmth that he couldn't bear to deny her. And after the first day, he began to enjoy reveling in the warmth and light from her perspective. Perhaps it was his influence that caused her to feel calmer and more peaceful as the days passed.

"Mm, that feels good." She pictured a ferocious animal with pointy ears and claws stretching in the light.

"Ugh. Must you ruin the moment?" Drench asked, lightly

disentangling himself from her again. Calm and peace were always short-lived with animals.

"It's only a cat. It wouldn't hurt you."

"Oh, wouldn't it?" Drench pictured one of the small predators of his home crouching at his base and sharpening its claws on his trunk. Each slice was only a tickle, but left an itchy, exposed rash that had to be carefully watched for infection.

Akemi countered with an image of the cat, perched on a branch and solemnly licking its paws and washing its face. "I like cats."

She reluctantly pulled back and settled into her own space. Drench was surprised at the slight feeling of loss he felt when she was gone.

He was glad that Akemi now spent each day in enjoyment, speaking to him and daily learning to talk to more of the Melifleurs. Now that she had been here a little over a month in all, the others had firmly latched onto her presence and could speak to her. Drench still monitored all of their interactions however, as many of them quickly got overwhelmed when they spoke to her. She invariably pictured running or jumping or sliding at some point and made them reel.

Drench was the best at withstanding her animal tendencies, and he was even getting used to her strange habit of 'jumping' into his space. It was not terribly unlike conversing with a telepathic Crosspoint, although Akemi was even more energetic. Which reminded him... "What were you doing these past hours, sister, while your thoughts tumbled like rain? When I speak to you at such times you answer in nonsense."

"I was sleeping. Dreaming. Don't you sleep? You told me that when it gets cold you hibernate or something."

"It is not like that. We have a long slow descent, a deep meditation in the ice, and a long, slow ascent to the warmth." He thought for a moment. "I suppose it makes sense that an animal would have as much movement in their sleep as in their feet."

"Oh, speaking of feet," Akemi said, "I've been dying to ask—since you have no feet, and you hate the idea of motion, how did you ever develop space travel? Did the Crosspoint do it for you?"

"Space travel is actually less traumatic than ground travel," Drench said. "But yes, the Crosspoint did it for us."

"Why? I mean, that's super nice of them, I guess, but why would they bother?"

Drench seemed a little embarrassed all the sudden.

"Oh, I found a soft spot!" Akemi teased him. "Now you have to explain that."

"It is... something other species might not know. We would not want you to tell anyone."

"A secret! Even better. And for heaven's sake, who would I tell? My mouth is effectively shut."

"That is true. When the Crosspoint realized what we were, and we had gotten to know some of them, they offered us a deal. If we would *listen* for them, they would offer us protection and the opportunity to learn about the universe."

Akemi gasped. "Listen... You mean you act as spies?"

"I believe so."

"But that's—the whole galaxy—you're kidding!"

"Why else would we be here in this house?"

"Uh—because Faal enjoys having sentient beings at his mercy? Because you were sold to him? Because you couldn't fight for yourselves?"

"No. Well, yes, he believes we were sold to him by a wealthy Crosspoint, and he enjoys sentient decoration. But shortly the Crosspoint who placed us here will arrange for us to be sold or traded back and then we will go somewhere new."

"And tell the Crosspoint everything you know about Faal?"

"Yes."

"I'm just... My mind is blown." What he was describing could be the biggest intelligence operation in the galaxy. Surely people knew about it? But then, while she'd heard in passing about the Melifleurs, she'd gotten the impression that their sentience was of such a different order that communication was nearly impossible. What perfect spies!

But Akemi still couldn't quite believe it. There was no way that a whole race would agree to spend their lives working for another race...

Drench interrupted her thoughts. "Such a situation exists on many planets, actually." He imagined the swift nibbling and darting of many birds, tickling his branches and pecking at bugs. He imagined the pain of the bugs boring into his bark and his thankfulness to the birds. Then he pictured causing several of his branches to grow together into a thick mat, curving to form a beautiful nest where the birds would lay their tiny selves—eggs, Akemi translated—and live for many years. "They serve us and we serve them," Drench explained. "It is the natural order."

"I see. You feel like you're in a symbiotic relationship with the Crosspoint."

Drench bristled a little at her words, or rather at the thought behind the words. "I do not *feel* that it is so, it *is* so. We spy for them, and they protect us. We are not stupid vegetables to be manipulated and enslaved by the first race we meet."

"Oh. Unlike humans, is that what you mean?"

Drench was silent.

"Okay, fine, I apologize," Akemi said. "I admit that I was patronizing you. Treating you like a... a sapling. I'm sorry. Do you forgive me?"

Drench was still annoyed, but he accepted her apology. There was a carelessness that always accompanied youth, in every species.

"How does your relationship with the Crosspoint work?"

Akemi asked humbly. "People know that Melifleurs are sentient. Surely they won't spill secrets in front of you, even if they think you don't understand their language very well."

"They do know we're sentient, but, and I don't understand this well myself, they seem to forget. If we sit quietly for a year, or even just half a year, other animals—'people' as you say—completely ignore us. I believe the Crosspoint have let it be known that we have a different order of intelligence, and that we hibernate for long periods of time. Perhaps they assume that we have gone dormant. I do not know, but so far the situation has been rewarding for both Crosspoint and Melifleur."

"Well, no kidding," Akemi said. "This might be the greatest scam in the galaxy. I love it."

When Faal's technical specialist came later that morning, Akemi was distracted and quiet. She was wondering if Mox'uu knew that the tree in the courtyard was an intelligent Melifleur, or if he'd been told and forgotten. As he entered, she could hardly look away from the beauty that was Drench. She was amazed that Mox'uu could completely ignore him; it was truly like ignoring an elephant in the room.

Drench caught that comparison and gave her a mock scolding. "How dare you?" he said. "That gray monster is nothing like me. And if you keep thinking shocking things like that, it's no wonder you made Stubby lose half his leaves."

Stubby was another of the Melifleurs, and from his thoughts, Akemi was fairly certain he'd been planted on the cliff-side of Faal's estate. He was as interested in her stories as everyone, but he was easily overwhelmed.

Akemi giggled aloud, and Mox'uu tilted his beak downward. "Is everything quite well?" he asked.

"Huh? Yes, I'm fine," Akemi said. "What did you say?"

He looked even more grave, and Akemi wanted to laugh again at what must be going through his mind. On other occasions when

Mox'uu had come, she'd been absolutely starving for interaction and had hung on his every word and expression. Now she had all the activity she needed, and she wasn't inclined to humor him.

What's more, her inattentiveness was probably making him more concerned about her sanity than anything she had faked. How ironic.

"I was saying," he continued, "that as my diagnostics have been favorable, Faal has decided to give you a trial run with the estate monitoring systems."

"It's about time," Akemi said. "What good am I to him if he won't let me do anything? When do I start?"

"I'm going to make the connection now. I already realigned the physical ports on your biocomputer—now we will turn it on and give you a low-access password."

Akemi felt it when the connection bit and a whole new room opened up in her mind. Mox'uu gave her the password and then she was in.

Faal's household security was formidable. There were tons of interior cameras and sensors, monitoring everything from humidity to vibration. She was suddenly a seismograph, surveillance hub, and thermostat. In addition, underneath Faal's house was his infamous zoo.

Now she saw it, from one hundred and fifty-three lenses. She also knew the water temperature of every tank, the air composition of every cage, and the amount of food in every locker.

"Your space just changed," Drench said.

"Yeah, no joke. Check this out, I can give you wind." Akemi turned on one of the dehumidifiers nearest Drench and felt his red leaves dance in the small breeze.

"Oh, and what's this? I can see you and the other Melifleurs in the system—I mean, I can see your stats and water needs and sun levels."

"Yes, that is part of the external processor the Crosspoint

developed for us. We each have one." He pictured something more technical than normal. She caught a glimpse of a gray panel with buttons and numbers fused into his solid trunk.

"The Crosspoint are accustomed to creating computers that interface by thought," Drench explained. "It just took them a few years to develop one for us. This way we can connect to local networks."

"Akemi. Akemi? Did the process work correctly?" Mox'uu asked.

Akemi realized she'd left him hanging after he hooked her up, too distracted by the new information and by messing with Drench.

"Yes, it worked. I am ready to rock'n'roll. What would you like me to do?"

Akemi followed his instructions with half an ear while also grilling Drench about his clandestine capabilities.

11

CLAIRE LOOKED up in surprise when Sam and Basher burst into her room. Well, perhaps 'burst' was unfair—but they gave the impression of being out of breath and upset. She and Nat were seated on their beds, and Shara sat against the wall with her legs stretched out comfortably. Kit lay on Claire's lap, occasionally nuzzling her to get another tummy rub.

"We have news," Sam said. "I just—but, no. Basher, tell them your part first."

Basher tossed his tablet to Nat. "It's happening—a human was executed in the death chamber, and the Coalition Committee has issued an ultimatum. If Sam's right, we'll be at war within forty-eight hours."

Nat turned on the tablet and tilted it so they could all see the newscast.

It showed an aerial view of the empty death chamber with a Tergre voice-over and delayed Spo subtitles, which Nat quietly read. "The Humans have accused the Merith of... mistakenly executing a true Human in their death chamber, a serious allegation, which can only exacerbate the tense relations between the two species. The Humans have issued an ultimatum that all current and future prisoners must be examined by a joint Spo and human delegation before execution. The Merith have not yet responded to this demand, and speculation is rife."

The newscast flicked to a brief video of the Coalition Committee, and then to a still image of five Merith seated at an ornate wooden table. Claire recognized Faal, second to the left, and assumed one of the others must be the Pontifex.

The newscaster continued, "The Humans did not name a specific Merith in their allegation or ultimatum, but it is widely known that Faal of Merith II is the director of the current death chamber exhibition. If Faal refuses to meet the Humans' demand, they will have the right to declare war. Human military capability is an unknown variable at this point, as they have been so isolated that very few have visited their planet. The only known factor is that they acquired a sizeable fleet of ships from the Rik, though whether they are capable of using them is again unknown."

The newscast returned to a view of the death chamber, this time with a crowd filling the rough benches and four scraggly lines of Rik waiting next to the execution platform.

"That's about it," Basher said. He grabbed the tablet and turned it off.

Sam shook his head. "We'll end up at war. Our best option would be to ally with the Spo, since they're historically enemies with the Merith, but whether the human government will be willing to bury the past eight years..." Sam visibly recalled himself. "Anyway, the ultimatum seems to have had at least one good effect. I just received this package from the Diadina."

He waved a thick envelope and pulled out an elegant tri-folded card. It was written in formal Merith calligraphy, which looked like chicken scratch to Claire.

Sam read it for her benefit.

To the Humans currently residing at the Spo Embassy of Selta, and to my one-time confidant, Claire of Earth, greetings.

If you desire to have further conversation with me, you may have a few minutes of my time tomorrow. I will be giving a public performance at the Herayung celebration; address enclosed. In my privileged situation, this is the only prudent way for me to hear you, and it can only happen before our species are at war.

I can make no guarantee. You will have three minutes at most, and I may then publicly repudiate you. I have enclosed several work permits to the celebration, if you decide to take this risk.

Her Esteemed and Soaring Highness, etc.

"So she *is* interested! What's this Herayung she's talking about?" Claire asked.

Nat typed a few things into her tablet and handed it to her. "The Herayung application site."

The Herayung holds the distinction of being the largest underground party in the galaxy. It is held once every five years on Upper Selta. Nearly a million beings are expected at the coming Herayung, and there are attractions of every sort: wild animal melees, racing, gambling, exothermic light show, etc.

The accountants of the last Herayung estimated that 70.8 million gallons of intoxicating beverages were consumed, or the seasonal output of four settled worlds. There will be nearly three hundred thousand persons employed at the Herayung this year, the largest yet. Herayung workers are well paid, earning well more than a year's salary for the few months of the event. Past employees have passed on the tale of their Herayung to their children and grandchildren. To rub shoulders with sovereigns of the galaxy, infamous rebels, and emperors in training worth more than whole systems—it's a unique experience in the galaxy. Apply now!

The rest of the article gave restrictions and guidelines for applications. The deadlines were nearly a year past.

"Wow," Claire said. "So she got us jobs there? She really wants to talk to us."

Basher looked dubious. "I'm not sure it would be safe for any of us to go to the Herayung. I got held up by four Merith bounty hunters the last time I went out."

Sam nodded, "I assume we'd need an escort to get there, but I believe once we're *in* we'll be alright. The Herayung is practically a law unto itself, right?"

Basher nodded reluctantly.

Nat agreed with Sam. "If we're wearing identification that marks us as employees, any Merith who wants to mess with us wouldn't just be threatening us, they'd be flouting the Herayung hosts."

"What happens if you flout one of the hosts?" Claire asked.

Nat flicked through her research. "You are immediately thrown out—out of Selta, not just the Herayung—and if your family has holdings on Selta you better hope they're insured. Once, they got a Vel permanently ostracized from his home world —that's a feat. And once they got a Merith demoted from faal to sheepherder. Wow."

"Who hosts the Herayung?" Basher asked.

Nat flicked to the end of her report to show a list of names. "Who else? A group of very wealthy Crosspointers."

Basher rolled his eyes. "Of course. I'm sure they're well-connected, too."

"They all are." Sam waved a hand to dismiss that. "More importantly, if we end up at war with the Merith—terrible as that is—it'll protect those of us who break into Faal's house. If we do get caught, no one can accuse us of starting a war that's already started."

Claire grimaced. The idea of Faal's estate and the zoo underneath still had the power to make her feel ill. "Huge upside."

Nat shrugged. "It's bad, but we might as well take advantage of it. There's a whole different branch of law dealing with 'acts of war.' And rules about prisoners of war," she added, with a significant look at Claire. "Even if we're caught, we'd be safer with Faal than you were."

"I still think we should make absolutely sure Faal is not there," Claire said. "If he and his whole entourage are gone, the estate will be nearly empty, and Basher—or whoever goes—will have a much better chance."

"Agreed," Sam said. "So let's go meet the Diadina."

CLAIRE'S first indication that they were approaching the Herayung was the sight of a drunken Spo. He appeared to be trying to climb a spinner. The little spinners were designed to be a quick way to move down levels, like a spiral fireman's pole, and they were much too slick to climb. The sight of a Spo, lying on its stomach on the pole with all six limbs moving in a kind of violent swimming motion as it tried to pull itself up, was so nonsensical that at first Claire thought it was having a fit.

Usually you could read a Spo's mood by the shifting color of its skin, but this Spo was a strange bluish white that Claire had never seen on a Spo before. She tried to edge by the spinner, but Basher put a hand on her shoulder, to stop her from getting any closer to the alien. Its jerky motions did make it look like a dying bug.

The Spo was talking to itself, almost singing. Claire understood a good bit of Spo, but this one was somehow managing to slur, and without a soft palate that was rather remarkable.

"Do you know what he's saying?" she asked.

"I think it's..." Sam laughed. "I think it's a drinking song."

"I didn't even know Spo could *get* drunk," Basher said.

"I know. I think we need evidence." Sam pulled out his tablet and snapped a picture. "I'll send this to Greg. He'll absolutely hate it."

The drunken Spo noticed them now and tumbled off the spinner. It tottered over to Claire and threw a heavy arm around her shoulders. "Ah, bruck, may the bird ride at your heels and the scorpion on your shoulder." His eyestalks quivered, looking momentarily at each other in confusion. "Wait, no. May the bird of your scorpion ride the—no. May the—"

Basher pulled him off Claire. "Thanks for the sentiment. Time to sleep it off," he said.

Claire laughed nervously. She hadn't thought of this whole aspect of party crashing.

They pressed on and soon the hall widened to a plaza, one of the many entrances to the Herayung. A temporary partition had been erected here, and at all the major entrances to the labyrinthine section of Upper Selta that housed the party.

The partition didn't look temporary, however. Massive beams stretched ten feet high and supported an intricate wrought iron lattice. Flowering trees from giant pots had been trained to grow up and over, and now brilliant purple blooms framed the relatively small door that allowed access to the Herayung on this level.

Two guards stood on either side of the entry way, one Tergre and one Merith.

"They never double up the same species," Basher explained. "Keeps the guards honest."

Sam presented their work passes to the Tergre guard and whispered to Nat, "Hurray, we have the golden ticket!"

Nat gave him an exasperated look and he grinned.

The Tergre only glanced at their papers. "What languages do you use?" he asked Sam, using the standard Merith dialect.

"Spo is best, some Merith, some Vel," Sam said.

"They told me to expect you," the guard added.

Sam spread his hands, "What can I say? People love me."

Nat elbowed him. "Do you need any other identification from us?"

"No, your species is identification enough. There are no other humans here." The guard gave them each a loose tunic to put over their clothes, and Claire saw that each tunic had removable patches at the neck. The guard took off several of these, leaving only the ones that indicated the three languages they spoke.

"I understand that you are not actually here to work," the guard said. "So you do not need to report to a lieutenant of service, as workers normally do. However, I must instruct you that if a guest of the Herayung specifically requests something of you, you must do it."

"We're not planning to be here more than an hour or two," Basher explained.

"Be that as it may, if there is a request, you must make sure it happens before you leave. The masters of the Herayung demand unimpeachable service from their employees. No matter how short a time they are employed."

"Exactly how outrageous are these 'requests' likely to be?" Basher asked.

The Tergre wrinkled his furry muzzle. "The guests are eccentric. I would tell you to be unobtrusive, but that will be difficult as an unusual species."

A group of aliens came up behind them now, and the guard gestured them through the door.

"Let's walk quickly," Basher said. "We should look like we're already working."

Half an hour later, they still had not reached the auditorium where the Diadina was going to perform. Several of the plazas they passed resembled a rave—lights dim and flashing, with something that passed for music and many writhing bodies. Others plazas looked more like wine-tasting parties, and some were clearly gambling dens.

"Believe it or not, that entrance was as close as we could get to the Diadina's position," Sam explained, as they continued to wind their way—quickly, purposefully—deeper into the Herayung.

The smell of a hundred alien foods permeated the air, along with a hint of unwashed alien. The air scrubbers on Selta were some of the best, but this was a lot to keep up with. At one fork in their path they encountered a brackish area, where the air of two sectors merged and mingled.

Claire coughed as they made their way through it, and her eyes felt rather watery. "Somebody explain to me why these spots are so bad."

Basher cleared his throat. "Most of the aliens on Selta breathe a combination of oxygen and one of the inert gases, like nitrogen, helium, or argon. We can all breathe each other's mixtures, but it's most comfortable to breathe your own. The various sub-sections maintain a positive pressure so airlocks aren't necessary to prevent flow, but they mix... And, in short, the border zones suck." Basher gestured at his own red eyes.

"This should be a Merith sector," Sam said, "if our information is correct."

So far they'd avoided being accosted by any of the guests, but their luck seemed to be out, as a Vel clamped a hand on Sam's shoulder.

"Bring me a wine," she said. "I want to try the human wine."

Sam gently disentangled himself. "Of course you do, and let me say how much I appreciate that you recognize my species. I will get one of these Tergre waiters..."

"No, no! They have none, I have asked. Go find me some, human. It must be available somewhere."

Sam and Basher exchanged looks.

"Did you not hear?" the Vel said, her voice loud. "I asked you for wine."

"I'd better deal with this," Sam muttered, "or we'll be in trouble before we even get to the Diadina. I'll try to catch up with you, but if this takes me longer than an hour, I'll meet you by the exit."

Nat bit her lip and nodded.

Sam gave the Vel a courteous apology, and strode off purposefully, presumably to procure some human wine.

Basher ushered the girls further on.

Claire looked back at Nat. "Should you go with him?"

Nat smiled. "No, he can take care of himself. I did almost offer, but it makes more sense for me to talk to the Diadina. I speak Merith better than he does."

"The cadet training really does work, doesn't it?" Claire said. "You and Sam don't think twice about making hard decisions."

Nat didn't dispute it.

The largest plaza they'd been to yet was a huge, sloping cavern, shaped into an auditorium, and the path bent steeply downhill as they headed toward the center.

"Theater in the round," Nat muttered. "Very Greek."

Thousands of aliens, mostly Merith, but a broad sprinkling of Tergre, packed the rows. A ring of decorative trees—Melifleurs from the markings on their pots—ran around the edge of the auditorium. Except for several paths, the rock was cut into roughhewn benches all the way around, with a central stage at the bottom.

Basher looked uneasy as they made their way down towards the stage. "I don't like being surrounded by so many Merith. We're nearly at *war*, you know, and they are already exterminating Rik who took human bodies. What if one of them yells, 'Kill the Rik?' This could be a mob."

Nat shook her head. "Whatever may happen outside, no one in the Herayung wants to be expelled. I don't think they'll attack us."

Many of the Merith were sitting now, and the audience was getting quieter. It was almost time for the performance. The three of them were definitely attracting more and more attention as they descended. At first Claire was reassured that Nat wasn't concerned about the Merith animosity, but then she remembered that neither she nor Sam had ever been mistaken for a Rik. They'd never been on the violent side of an angry Merith either. Claire and Basher actually had a lot more experience with this scenario than Nat did, and Claire was getting freaked out by all the one-eyed stares from the Merith around them.

"I think Basher's right," Claire said abruptly. She stopped and moved toward a row that still had some space near the aisle. "We should sit until the performance is over. We'll draw less attention when everyone is leaving."

Claire sat on the stone bench, without giving Nat the opportunity to protest. Basher immediately slid in next to her, and Nat squeezed in the last bit of space. "Just as well," Nat said. "I guess it is about to start."

"Wait, trade with me," Basher said to Claire.

She switched with him, which she realized very neatly put her and Nat on the edge of their little group and him next to their neighbor. She appreciated the switch when she noticed the speculative look of the Merith on the other side of Basher.

The arena was almost quiet now, only the rustle of shifting aliens and excited whispers filled the vast space. The cavern was well lit at first, but slowly the lights began to dim. Soon Claire couldn't even see the rocky roof over their heads. Claire resisted the urge to reach for either Basher or Nat.

Finally a pale orange light illuminated the stage, which was bare except for one Merith woman. Claire recognized the Diadina right away. She was rather small as Merith went, with a surprisingly delicate beak and finely lidded eye. Her most distinctive feature, that row of feathers around her shoulders, lay flat against her back, but when she began to sing, they rose and quivered around her like the spread of a peacock's tail.

Claire's only interactions with the Diadina had been brief and stressful. The Diadina had done Claire a huge favor when she took her away from Faal's planet—particularly since Faal had already issued an arrest-and-hold order. But despite that, Claire had always felt nervous in the Diadina's presence. The Diadina had been kind to her, but she was also vain and self-centered.

It would be too much to say that Claire forgot all that while the Diadina sang, but it was close. Claire had once heard several Merith crew singing on the ship, loudly and somewhat tunefully, but it was nothing like this. The Diadina's voice was somewhere between a nightingale and a cello. Pure as silver, yet without the brightness or ferocity her soaring tones should have had. Even her highest notes retained a mellow timbre, and her lowest notes were clear and resonant.

She was singing words, Claire knew, but the Merith tongue was harder to understand when it was sung, and she didn't try to decipher it. The sound washed over her and with the few words she caught it was enough to create an image, almost a story, which brought tears to her eyes. It was melancholy, a parting of lovers, perhaps, but with a hint of anger. The woman in the song was devastated at losing someone, and yet angry that they'd made her love them at all. The song was mournful and then raging, a series of staccato notes that made Claire's ears ring.

Claire bit her lip and forced herself to look away and count rows until the tears subsided. She wondered whether the Diadina really felt the incredible emotions she evoked with her music or if she was just well-trained.

The next song was less of a trial for Claire, as it was showier—lots of trills and jumps—and less poignant. But the last song, in which Claire caught the words for parents several times, her eyes welled up again. The song was progressive: a baby's light-hearted steps and nervous hops, a child's exuberant play, and then a sudden shift. Storms and betrayal, a push from the nest, flying away only to return and find an empty tree...

After this final piece there was a riot of whistling and stamping. The Diadina came back to the stage to give one last, light-hearted tune. She slowly revolved to face all the crowd during her last song. In the packed audience, it seemed amazing that the Diadina could see anything at all, let alone recognize three aliens, but Claire was almost certain she'd seen them.

The Diadina raised her hands to her adoring fans and dipped her head. All the Merith did a similar dip of their heads, causing the whole audience to ripple.

Then the show was definitely over. The lights came up and the audience began to trickle out. Instead of fighting the crush of Merith leaving the amphitheater, Claire, Nat, and Basher stood on their bench until most of the Merith were in the aisles, and then stepped down the benches, like Claire remembered doing in the stands at football games.

When they reached the bottom, the Diadina was surrounded by a large, fervent crowd of admirers. She had clearly seen them coming, however, and she lifted a hand to call her bodyguards to her. "I must retire for today," she said softly.

They began to disperse the crowd, but the Diadina gestured elegantly at them. "Let those ones through. It is not often a Rik or a human seeks out a Merith. I'm curious what they would say."

Clearly she was going to pretend she'd not invited them. As they'd agreed beforehand, Nat did the talking, as she had the best nuance in the Merith language. "Most beloved Diadina," Nat used a formal way of greeting, "We have an appeal for you."

"Do you?" The Diadina waved her bodyguards away. "Go ahead, amuse me."

"It concerns the humiliation of Faal of Merith II, the Pontifex's most trusted friend."

"I don't want to hear anything of him!" she said theatrically, turning half-away. "I know what you would tell me, and it does not matter. What else have you to say?"

Nat looked confused for a moment. There was no way the

Diadina knew what they were going to say—and she'd asked them to come. Perhaps her protest was also part of the act.

"He has recently acquired a most unusual computer," Nat said, "a completely unique artificial intelligence, and he has neglected to inform your husband of it. If Faal was to be absent from his estate for a certain period of time, he might lose this new treasure."

The Diadina was thoughtful. "I have wondered why he absents himself from the Death Chamber. It is his death campaign, and yet he has barely been present."

"Yes, we're pretty sure this is the reason. And we need him to leave his estate to give us a chance."

"Tell me about this alleged treasure."

"It's a Spo biocomputer, but it contains a conscious soul. It falls within the Pontifex's spiritual domain. He has the authority to punish or even ostracize Faal for owning it."

The Diadina clicked her beak in frustration. "If he feels threatened, Faal is more likely to present it as a present to my husband. Do you think I have not tried to drive a wedge between them..." She trailed off, pondering. "If it is carefully managed, there is some potential in what you say, but what if Faal brings the item with him to our court?"

"We think he wouldn't, unless he had to. However, perhaps you might invite a few of us to visit the Pontifical Court as well?" Claire asked. "Then we could watch Faal ourselves in case he brings Akemi with him. There is a unity celebration of some sort happening in a few weeks, isn't there? I remember you once mentioned that the Pontifex prides himself on the diversity of his guests."

"That is true, but I'm a Meritha of Merith. I am not a fool. If this aides me, what do you want in return?"

Nat answered this one. "We are pleased to give you this information in hopes to see Faal outmaneuvered and humiliated. We want our friend back and nothing else."

The Diadina scrutinized them. "You are human."

Claire had no idea where this was going. The Diadina wasn't responding quite the way she'd expected.

"That is true," Nat said. "I know that our species are enemies just now, but the Pontifex could grant diplomatic immunity—"

The Diadina waved her to silence. "That is nothing. I am a Meritha of Merith," she repeated.

Nat nodded uncertainly. "As you say."

The Diadina shrugged suddenly, causing her shoulder feathers to ripple. "I will consider your proposal."

Nat bowed, "We can be reached at the Spo embassy."

"I know. Farewell, Claire. I am glad to see that you survived."

The amphitheater was almost empty now, but Claire noticed several of the Merith who remained had been taking a keen interest in their exchange with the Diadina. Hopefully they were too far away to hear.

"That went as well as I could hope," Nat said. "She obviously has to make a show of reluctance in case her words are repeated."

"At least she knows the difference between Rik and human now," Claire said. "It was iffy last time."

They reached the top of the amphitheater in silence and continued all the way to the brackish zone at the edge of the Merith sector.

"Should we wait for Sam here?" Claire asked. "Isn't this about where we lost him?"

"No... it's been more than an hour," Nat said. "The longer we hang around, the more likely we'll get sent on an errand. We'll meet him at the exit."

Claire wondered if she was trying to convince herself.

It took them longer to get to the exit than it had to enter. There were more aliens coming into the Herayung and only a very few leaving, so they had to push against the flow of traffic. Claire breathed a huge sigh when they finally made it to the flowery gate. She gave back her serving tunic with real relief.

Outside the gate, they found Sam waiting for them with the Spo guards who'd accompanied them. Sam leaned against a stone wall, and he was covered, head to toe, in green slime.

"Wow... Did you find the wine?" Basher asked.

Sam raised one eyebrow. "Oh, I found the wine. I even got it back to her." He ran his hands over his shirt, dislodging clumps of goo that seemed to be drying into booger-colored gobs.

Nat looked like she needed to laugh, but the sound she made was more like a repressed sneeze. Claire didn't repress anything, she went ahead and laughed.

"One thing led to another, and..." Sam shuddered comically. "It'll be a great story in about ten years; I'm sure the trauma will have worn off by then." He looked at Nat. "On a completely unrelated topic, we should maybe never have kids."

Nat finally gave in and laughed, and they threaded their way through the thronging aliens toward the embassy while Sam told the story of a very pregnant Vel. "She was dead set on using her Herayung ticket before giving birth, come what may—and she did..."

12

IN HER PALATIAL SUITE, the Diadina gargled with salt water to restore her throat. Her performance had, of course, been superb, but in the last year her singing had begun taking a harsher toll on her body. And she must preserve her voice as long as possible. It was one of the distinctives of her reign as Diadina, and unlike the Pontifex, she could be deposed at any time her husband chose. At the moment, he showed no such desire, and she planned to take care that he never did.

Her suite was one of the select few within the bounds of the Herayung, and each night would be a year's wages for the average worker. She was not so far removed from her middle-class upbringing that she could forget it.

She had been the Diadina for eleven years now, but she was always aware of the precarious nature of her position. She gestured mutely for her servants to go—she refrained from speaking for several hours after each performance—and she began to groom her feathers while she pondered the humans' offer.

Faal was definitely the largest threat to her current position. Their feud cost her sleepless nights, and yet it was impossible for her to end it. In fact, it was her feud with Faal that brought her to the Pontifex's attention in the first place. Most people believed the feud had started *after* her marriage when Faal somehow offended the Diadina. They were wrong.

Eleven years ago, during the Pontifex's last Unity celebration, he'd been surreptitiously looking over the daughters of all the high families for a new Diadina. Nobody had known that was his intention at the time; she and her father thought they had been invited for the sake of their ancient lineage.

It was the second day of the party that Faal had tried to speak with her.

She knew what he might say, as her parents had confided to her about Faal and his family. She allowed him to get her alone, once, to find out for sure. He had uttered the mad threats they'd told her to expect, and she had decided then and there that the only way to avoid being manipulated and blackmailed by him for the rest of her life was to make him her enemy immediately.

It seemed ridiculous and counterproductive, but everything in Merith high society was dominated by intrigue and politics.

So the next time she and Faal had been together in company, she insulted him. She implied that he'd tried to offer for her hand, but that he was a criminal thug too barbarian for the likes of polite society. Rudely, publicly, and irrevocably, she'd insulted him.

He'd been livid and responded in kind, having then a furious temper and less self-control than he had now.

The shocked guests at their lower table, several removed from the Pontifex, had looked first at her, then at him, wondering how she dared insult one of the most powerful Merith faals. At that time he was still a relatively new faal, fresh from his transition from smuggling to politics, and still solidifying his place in the Merith hierarchy. She was from an old family, much admired for her beauty, but rather impoverished. They could readily believe that he had offered for her, which made her story all too plausible.

A tense silence had come over their table, lasting until the entertainment for the evening—a Spo gymnastic event—had begun.

Faal had waited until she left the table and then followed her out into the dark, hot night.

"Are you a fool?" he demanded, roughly pushing her into a domed stone alcove shaped like a large beehive. "I will *ruin* you."

She'd laughed—trembling inside, but filled with her own fury. "Just try. Try to tell your lies to anyone now. Tell them I'm descended from ingrates and assassins. Will they believe you? No. They will think you are angry and resentful because of my refusal."

For a moment, she'd seen the realization of defeat in his eyes, and then his expression hardened into fury. By making everyone think she scorned his offer of marriage, she'd also made everyone think he liked her. Now if he said anything negative about her, at least for a while, it would be considered a jilted lover's angry retaliation. If he claimed that she'd lied and he never proposed to her, people would also assume he was lying to save face. He'd been out-maneuvered by a young girl, and in a shameful way.

"That lie won't protect you for long," Faal had growled. "The festival won't last forever, and memories are short. You're going to have a painful fall."

"Not if I keep moving up," she had said defiantly.

The Diadina shuddered now at the memory and rubbed her neck. To this day, she believed that Faal would have killed her if the Pontifex had not emerged from the dining hall at that moment.

The Pontifex *had* emerged, however, with his hands clasped behind his back, looking up at the stars. He was a mere ten feet from the small alcove that Faal had pushed her into, but Faal was almost completely blocking the narrow entrance. She hadn't been sure the Pontifex saw them.

He did.

"Faal, my friend, come gaze at the stars with me," he'd said.

She had gasped in relief at the words, receiving Faal's glare as he reluctantly backed away from her and went to the Pontifex.

Uncertain whether to stay where she was until they'd left or try to slip out unobtrusively, she'd hesitated in the tiny space.

"You can go, little one," the Pontifex said over his shoulder to her. "Retire to your rooms."

She'd gone promptly, wishing that she might hear what they would say next but knowing there was no way she could eavesdrop effectively.

Years later, the Pontifex told her what they'd said that night. He'd been told by one of his aides about the sudden quietness at her table, and also that Faal had followed one of the young Meritha girls into the garden. He'd been curious.

"I apologize for interrupting your dalliance tonight... Do you intend to take a wife?" the Pontifex had asked Faal. "That's the youngest Skrenni daughter, isn't it?"

The Pontifex hadn't seriously considered her as his own choice, he'd merely included her family on a whim, as a traditional option. Her family connections would be an asset to Faal, however, who had enormous influence and wealth but not legacy or history.

"No, I don't," Faal said. "She is a foul, lying thing."

The Pontifex had been extremely surprised. "What? At her age?"

Faal had said nothing, probably realizing he had given away too much.

"You're not usually one to censure another's morals," the Pontifex said.

"What are morals?" Faal said. "I respect those who have, make, and take power, when they do it honestly."

"Then why are you so severe on the Skrenni girl?"

"She is—not to my taste. She is weak, and she is... deceptive."

"Yes. So you said."

"Please forget I said anything. It is not worth troubling you."

The Diadina suspected that Faal had realized too late that his obvious dislike of her was causing exactly the wrong reaction—making the Pontifex *more* interested in her, rather than less.

And he'd been right. The Pontifex had observed their interactions more closely over the next weeks of the celebration and seen the hidden enmity lurking there.

"You can tell the quality of an individual by the quality of their enemies," the Pontifex had told her one evening. "I would never have guessed that a beautiful young Meritha like you would have the nerve to make an enemy of Faal. Or that he would rise to the bait. It is most impressive."

"But, Faal is your friend," she had said, not denying the truth of his observation. "Is he not?"

"Yes. I enjoy him immensely and have the utmost respect for his ability to solidify power. Merith II has never been under such control, and I understand that his personal resources have doubled in the last year. He is a Merith of Meritha."

"And yet, you don't care that he dislikes me?"

"On the contrary, I do care. If he sees enough in you to hate, then you have substance of no common measure."

On the final day of that celebration, the Pontifex had announced that he'd chosen a new Diadina.

Her father had been shocked and thrilled when she was named; she had only been stunned as she was publicly escorted to the Pontifex's table.

Faal had watched with a completely passive face, and she'd known that she would be walking on a knife's edge for the rest of her life. Her new position made it harder for him to injure her, but it gave him more reason to try.

In the past eleven years, she'd taken pains to keep her feud with Faal alive and well. It pleased the Pontifex to have his Diadina and his most powerful faal violently opposed to each other. And it prevented Faal from doing any serious harm with his accusations.

Until now, she had not been able to do him any serious harm either, but this time was different.

If the winds were right, perhaps she could finally drive a wedge between Faal and her husband for good.

13

CLAIRE SNUCK out of bed a little before midnight. Nat's bed was in the opposite corner of the room, and she could hear Nat breathing softly. Shara slept on a pallet between their beds, and she snored quietly.

Claire pulled open the deep drawer where she kept some of her new clothes and also the map she was drawing of Faal's estate. She reached past all of that, however, to the very back of it to peel off the paper she'd taped there. It was just at the tip of her fingertips, and she gently pulled the tape loose, so as not to rustle or rip the paper.

She silently closed the drawer and tiptoed to the small bathroom that completed their suite. The light turned on automatically as she shut the door, and she sat on the bench next to the shower to read Sage's letter.

She knew it was immature, but she hadn't told anyone about it. She didn't want to deal with anyone's opinion of her relationship with Sage. Sam and Nat... she wasn't sure exactly what they knew, or how they would respond. Probably a mixture of pity and disbelief. The Rik threat was real to them, but they seemed perfectly fine with Shara.

Well, they did treat Shara with a bit of condescension, but that seemed to be a genuine response to Shara's personality, not her species.

Shara would no doubt love the intrigue of a secret romance, and Claire dreaded the idea of her thrashing the idea out for everyone to hear, which she no doubt *would* if she knew about the letter.

And Basher—well, Claire already knew how he felt about it. She wriggled uncomfortably on the bench, her bare feet getting cold. The only time she'd admitted to liking Sage, Basher had gotten so upset he grabbed her arm and nearly shook her. Now that she knew how gentle he usually was, his response seemed even more emphatic. He disliked the Rik intensely, and for some reason, the idea of them having relationships with humans made him furious.

She had wondered, of course, if that was just because Basher liked her, but seeing Basher's disgusted reaction to Shara's broad flirting had convinced her it wasn't personal. Not entirely personal, anyway.

Claire pushed Basher out of her head and reread Sage's letter.

He'd paid for it to be delivered to the embassy by messenger, which must have cost a bit. She traced the last line of his letter one more time, wondering if he really meant *love*. Or whether it mattered. He was Rik; she shouldn't care at all.

Claire sighed. She'd known when she worked at the restaurant that she was falling in love with him, and that it was largely because she'd been locked up for years. He was the first person to show her affection. She'd been so conflicted since she'd been living at the embassy. On the one hand, she'd felt that, even though it was painful, it was probably healthy and right that she be with her own kind. On the other hand, it felt like a betrayal of her Rik friends to be more comfortable with Sam and Nat and Basher than she'd been at the restaurant. And it felt like a betrayal to her human friends that she missed her Rik friends.

And Basher...

She could like him if she let herself, she admitted. But how fickle would that be? Had she been so damaged by her time in the zoo that she would be attracted to anything male that noticed her? That was so degrading.

Claire folded the letter and rubbed the light panel to turn off the light before she opened the bathroom door to the dark bedroom. Nat and Shara were still asleep, so Claire went back to the chest and opened her drawer, carefully taping the letter back in its spot.

"Keeping secrets?" Shara said suddenly.

Claire jumped, banging her shoulder painfully on the bureau. She withdrew her arm carefully. "Ow."

Shara stood right behind her, and Claire wondered how she'd gotten out of bed so silently.

"I know I startled you," Shara said. "It's fun to startle people. They look so funny."

"Well, it's rude," Claire said. "People don't like it."

Shara yawned. "Whatever. I need to pee."

Claire stared after her and then hopped into bed. She couldn't quite believe Shara was so wrapped up in herself that she didn't care what Claire was doing—but that seemed to be the case.

Of course, that was too good to last, and the next evening while they ate an early dinner, Shara suddenly turned to Claire. "So, what were you hiding in your dresser last night?"

They were all sitting at what was becoming their accustomed table in the dining hall, with Sam and Nat on one side, Basher and Claire on the other curving side, and Shara on one end. Basher looked up automatically and Claire choked a little on her soup.

"I was putting something away," Claire explained. She achieved a casual, somewhat annoyed tone of voice, but she knew that she was starting to blush. She had hidden the letter elsewhere, but she didn't want anyone searching for it.

"It looked like you waited until Nat and I were sleeping to hide some papers," Shara said.

Claire glared; Shara had all the tact of a kindergarten tattle-tale. The others looked more than mildly curious now, so Claire decided to be honest. "It's personal, Shara. None of your business."

Nat obligingly changed the subject, asking Basher if he'd gotten tips on any more Rik living on Selta.

"No... no. I'm fairly certain they're all gone." He avoided looking at Claire, who grimaced slightly. It was not an entirely successful change of topic on Nat's part. When Sage stole the ink, he'd shared it with all the remaining Rik on Selta. At this point, they'd either escaped or been taken to the death chamber.

"Well, I'm glad," Shara said. "Why should they stay to be locked up until the end of this stupid war? They have as good a right to run and hide as anybody."

Sam pushed his food back and draped an arm around Nat. "Speaking of running and hiding, I've discovered a place that hosts a game similar to laser tag. Anybody want to try it out with me this evening?"

Sam had been making use of their enforced waiting time after the Herayung by looking up and badgering them into trying as many human-friendly attractions as he could find—with a hefty Spo guard along to protect them.

Surprisingly, since humanity was now officially at war with the Merith, they were all safer on Selta than they had been before. The laws about prisoners of war were enough to check the more unscrupulous bounty-hunters. And as the war had not yet escalated to actual battles, Sam had not been noticeably cast down.

They'd visited an animal show, a Vel concert, and a craft fair that Sam admitted even gave him nightmares. He'd found a sort of ice-skating rink, and though there were no skates for humans, they'd enjoyed sliding around on the ice and admiring the graceful

Vel. Claire had mostly avoided these outings. She suspected they were mostly for Nat's benefit anyway; that Sam was trying to keep her mind off of Akemi.

Claire, at least, had her map to distract her. She was slowly refining her schematic of Faal's zoo, along with its entrances, security systems, and openings to the ocean. It wasn't pleasant to delve into her memories so thoroughly, but she was remembering more than she expected.

Sam and Nat had nothing productive to do, however, hence Sam's search for activity.

"This game is based on an infrared system the Merith developed, and the environment mimics their world," Sam said. "I checked and we could use the Tergre modifications safely enough for a game."

Nat looked dubious, "Tergre eyes are more like a dog's—are you sure these people understood your question?"

"They scanned my eyes right there," Sam said. "It was all very professional."

"I wonder if the Merith consider this a cultural sale or if it's purely recreational..." Nat mused. Then she and Sam were sidetracked in a discussion of the Merith cultural domain and the Earthly competitive edge, and even Shara joined in loudly.

"There they go again," Basher said. "The word at my school would have been *geek*."

"The word at my school would have been *nerd*. But they would have meant it in a good way," Claire said.

"You must have gone to a better school than I did," he said.

Sam turned to them. "Well? Are you coming?"

"I'm out on the laser tag," Claire said. "Have fun though." Being hunted in the dark was not at all her idea of a fun time.

"Well, I'm in!" Shara said. "I can wipe the wall with you guys."

"Wipe the *floor*," Claire said.

"Whatever. I will make them wipe everything when I win." Shara pumped her fist in the air.

"So competitive," Sam said. "Sure you're not human?"

"I'm out, also," Basher said. "Maybe next time. And make sure you stay with the guards."

The others rose to go, and Claire would have gone to her room, but Basher stopped her. "I don't want to play laser tag any more than you do, but I think an excursion would be good."

"Really, when you keep urging caution on Sam?"

"Things have calmed down a bit, and I'd ask my partner to come with us."

"No weapons? No creepy craft fairs?"

"None. I promise."

BASHER TOOK Claire to an aquatic display that wasn't far from the embassy, so it wouldn't tire her too much.

Plus, they could look down on the display from a relatively isolated upper level, and he had asked two of his Spo friends to keep an eye out for danger. It was a bit of a risk, but he wanted to let her get some exercise for her sore leg. He also wondered if she'd developed a bit of agoraphobia—fear of open spaces—from her time in the zoo. She had certainly not strayed from the restaurant, and although she had handled Upper Selta with the Rik, she hadn't wanted to leave the embassy since then either.

When they got to the aquatic center, Basher stood next to Claire at an upper railing.

There was a shallow pool below them with colorful, otter-like creatures doing a strange performance. Claire looked down at the flamboyant display with a genuine smile. "I know what these are."

"You do?" Basher asked.

"Sort of. Faal had some of these at the zoo."

"Really? I wouldn't have thought that would—er—"

"You wouldn't have thought that would make me smile?" She nodded ruefully and gave him such a relaxed smile he couldn't tear his eyes away until she looked back down at the animals frolicking in the water. "I can't remember what they were called, but Faal had seven of them—a family group, I think."

She stumbled slightly when she said Faal's name, but other than that, he would never have known that she was talking about a nightmarish time in her life.

She seemed to sense what he was thinking. "I'm almost embarrassed that I have good memories of the zoo. I feel like I haven't been entirely honest, since everyone assumes it was the worst place imaginable. Sam and Nat pity me too much; it's uncomfortable." She huffed. "Although Shara just about makes up for it. I don't think she knows what pity is."

"Your time at the zoo didn't have to be unrelieved misery for it to be bad." He knew that victims often began to wonder if they'd exaggerated their suffering or even fabricated it. If they didn't feel worthy of the care they were now receiving, they tended to minimize whatever happened in the past. He wanted to tell her this, but was afraid she would clam up if he did.

She took a deep breath. "You know what my favorite part of the zoo was? For a while, the head zookeeper let me help him feed the animals. Faal only allowed it because— Well, it doesn't matter. I got to feed the animals—the real animals—who were happy with big, beautiful cages and plentiful food. This species," she nodded toward the otters, "I called selties. They would swim around my ankles and play so happily when I waded into their pool to feed them. I could pretend that the zoo was a wonderful place. I could pretend I had *chosen* to be there."

She stared straight ahead and her fingers gripped the railing tighter, her knuckles turning white. "There was Kit, too, of course, and you know how adorable he is. It was ironic. I loved animals as a kid. I wanted to be a marine biologist like my dad. Of course, almost every teenage girl from Florida wants to study marine biology, so there was nothing special in that, but there I was at the most incredible zoo I could have imagined..."

Basher wanted to pull her white-knuckled hand loose and massage the tension from her fingers, but instead he waited quietly. When she didn't continue, he asked, "If that was your favorite part, what was your least favorite part?"

She continued to stare downward. "You'd think it would be the mind games. Faal would make me choose between two bad things—it was some kind of test. Or sometimes he would let me think I'd found a way out—only to analyze my 'performance' later. It was all part of his stupid psychological profiling. But that wasn't the worst part. He was obsessed with testing all his intelligent animals, so I didn't take that stuff personally. At least, not until the end. Does that make any sense?"

She glanced at him then, perhaps to gauge his reaction, and Basher quickly tried to school his features to an appropriate expression. Except he didn't know what expression was appropriate for something so bizarre and terrible. He must have passed, because she didn't freeze up.

"My least favorite part," she mused, looking absently through him. "It sounds silly, but I think it was the lack of blankets and pillows. He wanted a 'natural' setting, which I guess, to him, meant an ape-like setting. So I had a kind of nest, some random clothes, one thin sort of blanket..." She chuckled darkly. "I used the nest to hide the things I eventually stole from the zookeepers, so I guess that worked out. But what I wouldn't have given for a big, thick blanket to pull over my head and a pillow to hug."

When her eyes focused on him again, she gave a nervous laugh and turned away. "That's dumb, I know."

"It's not."

"You're very easy to talk to," she said, finally. "I can see why—"

She didn't finish. She did that a lot and her trailing statements drove him crazy. It was like she had a personal censor for anything he wanted to know."

"Why what?" he asked.

"Why Sam and Nat trust you," she said. It was a decent answer, but he felt sure it wasn't what she had originally intended to say. She thrust her hands in her coat pockets, and he knew she was done sharing. He'd noticed she tended to hide her hands when she was feeling self-conscious. "Are we ready to go?" she asked. "These are adorable, but I'm ready to get back."

Basher fell into step beside her. "Did Shara pick out that coat for you?"

"Hm? Oh, yes. She insisted I take this one. She said it fit me, and I do love it. I know it's never that cold here, but I like to feel warm."

"You look great in white," he said. Then he mentally kicked himself. Commenting on her appearance was not a great way to make her feel less self-conscious. It was true though, the pure, white coat set off her dark hair and skin—and he wasn't one to normally notice what people were wearing.

She shrugged. "Thanks. Shara's a bit of a fashionista, I guess. It's hard to believe she's as effective an assassin as Sam and Nat think she is."

He rolled his eyes. "Tell me about it. If they didn't assure me she was worthwhile...!"

"Oh, she's not that bad."

"Yes. She is. She taped a *heart-shaped* note to my computer."

Claire laughed. "Did she really? Don't take it personally. Nat says it's a Rik thing—and you're the only available guy around. Maybe Shara's lonely."

She fell silent, and the pause became awkward. Her last sentence could have described Claire's relationship with Sage—at least, Basher thought so. Sage had ingratiated himself with Claire during their weeks at the restaurant when *she'd* been lonely.

If he was completely honest, Basher was tormented not knowing how involved Claire had been with Sage. He'd realized too late that Akemi had purposefully edited out a lot of Claire's interactions with the alien—probably to spare him exactly the kind of anger he felt now. If Akemi was still around, he would demand an explanation from her... but of course, she wasn't.

14

AN HOUR after she and Basher got back from the aquatic animal show, an hour of perusing Sage's letter and feeling conflicted, someone knocked on Claire's door. The Spo didn't knock on doors, they scratched on them instead, in a totally horror-movie fashion. The first time she'd heard a long, deliberate scratching at her door she'd nearly bolted to the bathroom and locked herself in. Fortunately Nat had been there too, and she explained.

It was Basher. "The others aren't back yet, but you'll want to see this. I've been monitoring several of the Merith news channels, and I just saw it myself." He handed her his tablet with a translated Merith article pulled up. A picture of a particularly intense Merith hovered under the text. It was clearly a male, with a horny ridge over a heavily-lidded blue eye. His beak looked sharp, and there were sparkling stones in a heavy collar around his throat.

"That's the Pontifex," Basher explained. "Read it."

Claire sank down on the edge of her bed while she read.

The Year of Unity celebrations are now underway at the Pontifical Court, and speculation is rife that the Pontifex will be choosing a successor. During the last Year of Unity celebration eleven years ago, the Pontifex chose the new Diadina in the midst of a media blitz of galactic proportions.

An official summons has drawn two Merith powers to the Pontifex's palace, the Faal of Rec'omna and the Faal of Thrumim Prime. They are widely held to be the frontrunners for Pontifical heir.

The biggest surprise of the celebration is the last-minute inclusion of the Faal of Merith II. He was expected to remain aloof from these proceedings, being fully occupied with the Rik campaign and the resultant Human conflict. Most observers have agreed that Faal of Merith II is not a viable political option for Pontifex because his previous activities make him ill-suited, not to say intolerable, as the moral successor of the Pontifex.

Faal's representatives have declined to comment, except to say that he will be personally overseeing all his engagements remotely.

The Pontifex will also announce his Act of Service during the Unity celebration, and most anticipate that it will be a planetary parks program...

Claire looked up. "Is this it? Do you think the Diadina made the Pontifex send for Faal or is this a coincidence?"

Basher sat on the edge of Nat's bed, across from her. "We can't know for certain, but you saw what it said. No one expected him to be summoned to the celebration. I think she made it happen."

"So you think Akemi is left alone at his estate? This is our chance."

"I hope so. If he left her at home, we have a chance. If he took her with him, well, at least other people will know she exists. We might have a chance there."

"So what do we do now?"

"I'd really like to confirm that Faal is at the palace before we move. There are a hundred reasons he might delay his visit by a few days, and I don't want to overlap. If the Diadina invites Nat to the palace, she can confirm his presence for us. If she doesn't... I guess we'll have to gamble." Basher rubbed his neck. "But I think the Diadina *will* invite Nat. She's gone this far, so I'm willing to bet she'll take the next step and invite us. She's cast her bet against Faal, and if she's smart, she'll go all in. Best case scenario: Sam and Nat and Shara will go to Merith Prime to keep an eye on Faal, and I'll go to Faal's estate to get Akemi."

Claire looked absently at Basher; she was lost in thought until she realized he was looking less absently at her dresser. Sage's letter was lying on top, where she'd set it a minute ago.

Before Claire could tell if he'd seen it, he looked away and pointed at the tablet. "Did you see what it said about the Diadina being selected? She's only been the queen for eleven years. That's not a terribly long time."

Claire touched the Diadina's highlighted name in the article and waited while another article came up, and was slowly translated by Basher's software.

"Akemi was so much better at this," Claire commented.

"I know. I rarely had to translate anything while she was here."

"Do *you* think we'll get her back?" Claire asked. "I know Nat is determined, but that's not always enough, is it?"

Basher shifted, looking at his hands. "I don't know. We took a big gamble getting the Diadina involved. But I think there's hope."

"Then why do you look so depressed when you read these news channels?"

Basher looked uncomfortable. "I do think we have a chance of saving Akemi—but I'm not sure about the Rik. We'll be lucky if Earth can get out of this Merith war in one piece. I doubt the Rik will be saved."

"Since when do you care about the Rik?"

Basher hunched his shoulders. "I'm not a fan, but I don't want *any* people group murdered out of hand. I just want you to be aware of where things are headed—"

"No," Claire cut him off. "Sam and Nat will think of something, or that general they were talking about will figure out how to beat the Merith—that doesn't have to be the way this ends."

"I agree that it shouldn't, but the Rik are a problem. Even if the Merith threat suddenly ended, there is still a whole race of people who feel entitled to murder."

Claire slumped in defeat. "I know. But they can be taught better—they *can* feel remorse."

"One at a time, maybe, but how do you change a whole people group?"

Claire thought of Buddha, Jesus, Mohammed, Moses... "A leader or a—prophet?"

"Maybe, but they're not looking for religion. They don't *want* to change."

The tablet pinged that the article was translated, just in time to save them from an argument. Basher put his hands behind his head and lay back on the other bed while she read. His legs hung off the end, his feet an inch off the floor.

"This bed is awful," he commented after several minutes. "How does Nat sleep here?"

"It's Shara's bed tonight. We're taking turns."

Basher sprang up like a puppet. "Why didn't you tell me? What if she came in while I laying on her bed? She'd never let me forget it."

Shara really had been flirting outrageously with Basher lately. Claire laughed, but continued to read about the Diadina.

After the abrupt dismissal of the last Diadina fifteen years ago, the Pontifex chose to use the fifty-fifth Year of Unity festivities as the occasion for choosing his new companion.

The Pontifex purposefully invited the families of hundreds of eligible Meritha, although he kept his intentions a complete secret.

In a surprise move, he chose a relatively obscure Merith family called Skrenni, who were influential but extremely impoverished of late.

However, she has proven to be an extremely popular Diadina, known for her exquisite musical performances and unassailable style. Her few public feuds, as with Faal of Merith II, for example, are generally thought an eccentricity of personality, hence she is rarely censured for her sometimes heated remarks.

"Strange customs, huh?" Basher said, having read it for the second time over her shoulder.

"No stranger than playing laser tag with a bunch of aliens." Claire handed him back the tablet. "The universe is deeply weird, if you hadn't noticed."

"Hey, I was at the craft fair. I know."

Claire chuckled. "Sam is embracing his freedom a little too enthusiastically for me."

"Speaking of freedom, have you thought about what you'll do next?"

Claire nodded. She knew he was asking about the rest of her life, after this rescue attempt was done, but she chose to answer him literally. "I want to go with you to rescue Akemi."

Basher frowned. "Are you serious—to Faal's estate? Have you thought about that? Sorry, of course you have, but I don't think you should go. I don't know if I could keep you safe there."

"No offense, but you need me there. You have no idea how ridiculously paranoid Faal is. If you're going to get through his house, you need someone who's been there."

"But I don't need someone who might—I'm sorry, Claire—but I don't need someone who might have a panic attack as soon as we arrive."

Her fingers curled into a fist, but Basher held up his hands. "I wouldn't blame you! If it's anything like you've said, I'd never want to go back myself. But—you can't deny that sometimes your memories trigger flashbacks."

Claire wrapped her arms around herself. Yet another thing Basher knew about her that he shouldn't. She'd never had a flash-

back at the embassy. The only flashback she'd had was at Francois's restaurant when she'd heard a Merith yelling. She'd curled
up in a ball and almost blacked out. She didn't even remember
exactly how long it'd lasted, but she remembered Sage holding her
as she calmed down. Had Basher seen that too?

"I can't stay here alone while you go to rescue her. I'll go
crazy," Claire said. "Yes, I'm terrified to go back to the zoo, but I
want to rescue Akemi as much as you do, maybe more. I can
handle it."

Basher was vacillating more than he cared to admit. On one
hand, this job would be more likely to succeed with someone
familiar with Faal's house and zoo. On the other hand, it would be
a big risk to bring her there, and not just because of possible panic
attacks.

"I'll think about it," Basher said. "We should have at least a
few days to decide."

As it turned out, he had less time than he expected. Nat
received the Diadina's invitation the next morning. The first part
of the message was in formal Merith calligraphy.

*In honor of his Glorious Lord, the Pontifex's sixty-sixth Year of
Unity, a delegation from every sentient species is graciously invited
to celebrate the event at the Pontifical Court on Merith Prime. As
personal acquaintances of the Diadina, the humans Natsuki Fujimara and Sam Locklear are requested to present themselves within
the next month at the Palace. They will be housed with the Tergre
and Spo delegations, to avoid any interspecies unpleasantries, and a
strict neutrality will be observed between all Merith and Human
guests for the duration of the celebration.*

May you have a swift flight and safe landing,
Pontifex Griel VI

The next part of the message was written in the Diadina's
more feminine script.

I am sure you will enjoy your visit, seeing perhaps a few old friends and making new ones. The Pontifex wishes me to explain to you, being a new and untried species, that no violence will be tolerated on the palace grounds, despite the current state of war between our species. I took the liberty of assuring him that you are well aware of the social mores of the galaxy and no novice in galactic politics.

In trust,

Diadina

"This is it," Nat said. "But we don't know if Faal brought Akemi with him or not."

"That was always a risk," Basher said. "I'd hoped the Diadina would be more specific, but maybe she doesn't know herself. Now we have to decide if we're going to go through with it."

Sam draped an arm around Nat's shoulders. "Of course we are. If Akemi is still at Faal's estate, you'll rescue her there. If she's at the Pontifex's palace, we'll make a new plan. At least we'll be close by."

Nat nodded slowly. "Our presence might delay the development of the war, and that can only be a good thing."

"That's the spirit," Sam said. "Maybe we'll get ambitious and see how dedicated the Pontifex is to the war. I've heard conflicting things about him, but if he wanted to end the death trials and the war, he could. And just in case Faal brought Akemi to the palace, we'll be there to find her."

Basher nodded. "And I'll head to Merith II. Once you confirm his presence, and if possible, Akemi's location, I'll break into his house to retrieve her."

Claire nodded. "And I'm going with Basher."

"Well, okay then," Nat said. "Let's send her our acceptance and break some laws."

15

THE DIADINA LOVED to be present in the throne room of the Pontifex during his morning audiences. Her chair adjoined his, and as she sat at his side, silent but beautiful, she soaked in the equally silent but beautiful admiration of the crowds who came to pay their respects to the Pontifex.

Many of the females who came, the Meritha, were in fact more interested in seeing her than they were in bowing, forehead to the floor, to the Pontifex. She could tell by the way their eyes sought her, even as they made their obeisance. They memorized every detail of her appearance in a few quick glances. She would occasionally bestow a small smile, a mere curling of the muscles around her beak, to a particularly eager supplicant, and enjoy seeing their ecstatic reaction.

Every moment that she sat on the double throne took her further from who she'd been before and cemented her identity as the Diadina. Her only identity, she reminded herself.

When Faal arrived—she had known he would come today— the Diadina was at her glacial best. Her feathers could have been carved from ice, so little did they move. Not by the slightest flicker of an eyelash did she betray her deep animosity, or heavy fear, of this particular Merith.

This time she was the one who'd initiated the visit, and with any luck and a good wind, this visit would spell the end of the Pontifex's intimacy with Faal.

Faal came forward with a slight limp, surrounded by his thuggish bodyguards. He bowed appropriately, and his gown, heavy with gems in the seams, billowed around him impressively.

"Great and wise Pontifex, arbiter of right and strength, and he who blows the souls of the righteous to their final haven on the Great Cliff, I greet thee."

The Pontifex glanced at her briefly, as if to say, "This is the one you say hides stolen artifacts and blasphemous crimes from me? This one who greets me so respectfully in the old way?"

The Diadina said nothing; she was not allowed to speak in the throne room unless spoken to. And she could not prove that she was right in her accusations against Faal. Indeed, her information from the stringy humans was so inconclusive that she'd dared make no formal accusations against Faal for hiding a unique acquisition from the Pontifex. She'd hinted, cajoled, and demurred when he quizzed her, but left the arrow of curiosity quivering in his breast.

The Pontifex lifted his beak in welcome and stood from his throne. "Faal of Merith II, be welcome in my home. May you find rest in my security, and may your belly swell at my table."

Faal laughed at this crude interpretation of the ancient blessing, and the Pontifex beamed. "Make yourself comfortable in your usual quarters," he said, more casually. "I look forward to speaking with you at dinner."

Faal retired, and the Pontifex looked at her again, no doubt wondering her thoughts on his jovial welcome. He loved to raise and then break the expectations of those around him, and she did not respond. He would still desire to find out about this unusual artifact that Faal had neglected to mention.

If it were true that he had a questionable device, an artificial intelligence, it could be the beginning of a rift between her husband and Faal... but if she found out those humans had lied to her, she would hunt them to extinction.

She had sent the humans an invitation to come to the palace once she knew that her husband had summoned Faal. Their acceptance had been prompt. If they had truly helped her, then they deserved the invitation. If they had lied, better to have them nearby where she might exact vengeance. They would be here later today, and she would enjoy Faal's discomfiture when he realized several of his enemies were here.

Nor would the Pontifex blame her if Faal suffered at their hands. The Pontifex considered power the defining characteristic of his faals. If one was bested by a human in his court (even a human invited by her) the Pontifex would consider that wholly the fault of his own weakness.

The Diadina allowed herself a small smile at the next lovely Meritha who prostrated herself before them. If this succeeded, she need only sit back and allow her past to wither away, and her future to expand by the hand of her enemy.

SHARA LOOKED AT THE BARREN, gravel-strewn slope ahead of them and wiped her sweaty forehead with a rag. "You have got to be kidding me."

The overland approach to the Pontifex's palace involved several stages, the last of which was walking a mile through the desert to the palace. It had to be over a hundred degrees outside, and Shara could already feel the sunburn on her arms.

They'd started the day landing at the Pontifex's airfield—one of the oldest ports on Merith Prime, dating back to the beginning of Merith space travel—and that had been pretty cool. Even Shara could appreciate the historical awesomeness of one of the oldest space ports in the galaxy. Then they were given a ride to the other end of the airfield and past the ancient tumble of rocks that was the Pontifex's death chamber.

That had given Shara the creeps. She knew there were Rik in there dying, even today, but she tried to put it out of her head.

Then they had to walk the final mile to the palace—despite a perfectly serviceable paved road—and she didn't appreciate it. Stupid Merith rituals. Plus, for the first ten minutes of the walk, Shara had been hearing the cheers and whistles of the audience in the death chamber. It had finally stopped, but she was in no mood to hike any further in the dry heat.

Nat had formed a veil from a gauzy scarf she had with her, but she still looked uncomfortably red in the face. Only Sam seemed to be enjoying the hike. He was picking up small rocks and chucking them as far as he could over the scree, or occasionally pocketing them.

Shara sealed her lips on another complaint. They all thought she was shallow and self-centered—as if there was any other way to be centered!—but she cared about Akemi as much as any of them. Of all the humans Shara had met, she'd never connected with one like she had with Akemi. They had a bond. If it meant hiking up this hill to play their part in her rescue, Shara would do it. She would prefer if her part in the rescue involved killing someone, but she would take what she could get. Basher had flatly refused to allow her to accompany him to Faal's estate, so she was stuck with protecting Sam and Nat.

"You look like you're on vacation," Nat said to Sam.

Sam stooped to grab a shiny black stone and tossed it underhand without missing a step. "This might not be the first exotic locale I would pick for a vacation, but it wouldn't be the last either. I mean the trees are actually quite lovely."

Nat chuckled, and Shara shrugged, looking at the emphatically treeless landscape. "You're both weird," she said.

"How are you holding up?" Sam asked Nat, who was starting to breathe rather heavily.

"Oh, I'm fine," she said. "I just haven't had enough exercise the past couple months."

Sam stretched up on his toes and took a couple running steps to hurl a slightly larger rock than before. It went maybe thirty yards before landing with a decent plume of dust. "At least we have something to look forward to," Sam said. "That makes the climb easier."

Shara glanced at the two aliens escorting them, but they didn't seem to notice Sam's words. She supposed it was common for people to be excited about meeting the Pontifex, so they had no reason to suppose that Sam meant anything else.

"We're almost there," Sam said, pointing ahead of them. Everyone knew the Pontifical palace was an incredible sight, and Shara wished Akemi could have enjoyed it.

They'd crested a huge gravel dune and could now look down on the palace grounds. A low sand-stone wall, pale peach, encircled a hundred acres of immaculate rock garden. Long, low buildings broke the gardens into smaller pieces, and towards the rear of the grounds rose a huge building with a colossal dome. Beyond that were more barren orange hills, and beyond that a deep blue sky.

Between the various rock gardens were "real" gardens, for lack of a better term, and they were only slightly greener than the surrounding desert. There were thick, grayish-green desert plants around the walls and in clumps within—cacti and succulents and such—but not so much that the interior of the grounds ceased to look like a desert. Many sections of sand and rock were combed in swirls and lines; they had been raked into careful patterns.

They headed down a short slope toward the front gate, closer and closer until they could no longer see over the wall. It was taller than Shara had thought from a distance.

They entered through the gate into a small courtyard. Their guide took them straight through and on to several larger courtyards, while pointing out guest suites, treasuries, banquet halls, and staff quarters. In the central-most courtyard there were four large trees, one in each of the ordinal directions, and several gardeners were at work, digging a large hole in center.

"This is the Pontifex's palace and throne room," their guide finally said as they approached the domed building Shara had spotted from afar.

The castle seemed dim and cool after the heat of the desert. High windows were covered with intricately carved shades that cast sharp patterns on the stone floor. There was a high throne on a dais, with a small bench attached to it, but they were both empty.

In fact, the whole room was empty except for a medium-sized Merith with a somewhat harried expression. "You arrived too late to be received by the Pontifex and the Diadina. They have retired to their midday meal. I am the Master of Chambers and I will show you to the suite set aside for your use. All preparations have been made to make it habitable for human occupation."

Nat inclined her head. "We appreciate the courtesy of the Pontifex. May I inquire whether Faal of Merith II has arrived as well?"

Shara expected Nat to get a snub from the Merith, but he didn't seem to resent the question. "He arrived only today, yes. He informed me that he will not be socializing until this evening, however, if you were hoping to meet him."

"Do you know if Faal brought a gift for the Pontifex? Our— escort mentioned that Faal often brings spectacular tributes." Nat managed to project an air of innocent curiosity.

"Why, yes! Faal is bringing a mature Melifleur to the Pontifex on an extended lease. I believe the central courtyard is being prepared for its arrival tomorrow."

"A Melifleur?" Nat said. "How interesting."

When Shara was settled, she came to Nat's room to talk. Nat's room was like hers. The floor was white marble, and a large Merith feather-bed dominated one corner. There was a sitting area next to it, and double-wide doors led out to a balcony.

"No fair," Shara said, "I didn't get a balcony."

The doors were open to let in the air, and the sunlight was blinding against the white marble. It was still a scorching day, and the room felt rather warm to Shara, but at least the marble felt cool to her bare feet.

Sam slouched on one of the Merith couches, playing with a little table inexplicably covered with black sand. Nat was coming in from the balcony.

Shara flicked the sand. "Did you send a message to Claire and Basher yet?"

"Yes," Nat said.

Sam smoothed the black sand with the side of his hand and then traced his name in it. The table was painted a vivid turquoise blue which contrasted well with the sand. "I love how they have these little sand tables everywhere. It's like being in a giant day care or something. Do you think they have Legos or dress-up stations, too?"

Shara laughed. "What a good idea! But I doubt it, the Merith are too stuffed up for that." She wandered over to Nat's bed and started looking through her clothes. One of the servants had already unpacked and folded them into the tiny nooks lining the wall nearest the bed.

Nat began to pace. "So, we know that Faal is here. And no one seems to think he's brought Akemi—though, of course, that may not be conclusive. Anyway, I've sent the message to Basher and Claire, and they're going to land on Merith II any time now."

"We just have to wait," Sam said. "They'll let us know as soon as they reach his estate."

"I hate waiting," Nat said. "I hate having nothing to do."

"There's plenty to do," Sam said. "We're the first humans in the world to visit the palace of the Pontifex."

Nat gave him a look. "I've been the first human to do a lot of things. I'm over it. And you could be a little more sympathetic, you know."

Sam raised his hands, his fingertips dusty from the sand. "I'm sympathetic! I am. I want to get Akemi back almost as much as you do, but I don't think sitting in our room for the next twelve hours is going to make the time pass any faster for you. We could also start to get to know our fellow guests. We need to find out how strong the anti-death chamber sentiment is among the Merith. We can do some good for those poor Rik and maybe gain some friends before we're really at war."

"That's all boring." Shara spoke up from the other side of the room. "I know what would make the time pass faster. Let me kill Faal."

"You already suggested that," Sam said. "Like, fourteen times. The answer is still no. Not yet."

She pouted. "That's so unfair. What's the good of being a Rik assassin if you won't let me kill anyone?"

"I promise that if we decide to kill someone, we'll let you do it."

"You say that, but you don't mean it. I never get to kill anybody."

"Don't whine," Sam said. "It's very un-assassin like."

Shara stuck her tongue out at him.

"That reminds me," Sam said. "Why have you been flirting with Basher since you came back? You'd stopped before."

Shara laughed. "Oh, that was for fun. Claire was like an

iceberg with him, and I figured I could be an ice-breaker. Maybe even make her jealous."

"That's unnervingly selfless of you."

"It wasn't really working. It just made her laugh, but it was still hilarious, so I don't begrudge the effort."

Nat went to the door. "Anything is better than waiting *and* listening to you two. Let's go find something to do."

They'd been given a list of the events and meals and concerts that would be part of the celebration over the next two weeks, so it was merely a matter of looking at the schedule to find out what they could go see.

"There's something called 'hawking' happening in the rear courtyard," Sam said. "The description says, 'Five teams will exhibit their tracking, coordination, and evisceration skills. Winner will receive ten thousand Merith units.'"

Nat grabbed her hat. "Great. Evisceration. That should make you both happy."

16

THE PALACE GROUNDS sloped gradually downward, making the rear courtyard quite a bit lower than the front gate. And "courtyard" seemed like a loose term for something as large and wild as this expanse of rocky wilderness.

Many of the palace gardens were groomed, with spiky trees carefully grown in strange, grotesque shapes, stone cairns carefully erected at precise intervals, and sand raked into fantastic designs. By contrast, the rear courtyard looked like untouched desert. Scrub trees, tumbled rocks, and inelegant scrawls of gravel covered an area the size of at least two football fields.

About thirty aliens were grouped at one end of the field, and Sam led them in that direction, after scrutinizing the small crowd to make sure Faal was not in it.

The onlookers were mostly Merith, with a scattering of furry Tergre, scaled Vel, and two uncomfortable looking Spo, shifting their weight from foot to foot on the sand.

Sam, Nat, and Shara stood unobtrusively on the edge of the crowd, so as not to have their view blocked by the tall Merith and not to get in anyone else's way.

"The Pontifex will not hawk?" asked one of the Merith to another.

"No, he wants to give his guests a chance to win," his companion replied.

"Ah. Then my bet will be for the Combodan team."

"Comboda? No. Merith II is the favorite. Faal can't be beat."

"Except by the Pontifex."

"Except by the Pontifex," the first Merith agreed.

"But I heard Faal of Merith II was injured..."

Shara lifted onto the balls of her feet as she listened to their conversation.

On both edges of the desert arena there were small buildings shaped like beehives stretched in a line. They couldn't hold more than a bench or a chair for a single alien, they were so small. Out of the nearest of them proceeded a small Meritha, a female, with a bell. She rang it forcefully, raising it to shoulder height and slicing it toward the ground.

The pure note of the bell rang out, and five more beehives disgorged their occupants—a Merith from each.

The last competitor on the field was Faal. He took off his heavy outer robe, weighted with gems, no doubt. His under-tunic was lighter and stained with sweat, which looked gross to Shara. Maybe he'd been warming up already.

He opened a small case and took out two gloves that glinted in the sunlight like copper. He slipped them on and they reached nearly to his elbow, with long supple gauntlets.

He twisted his arms back and forth, squatting and stretching to get loose. The other competitors were doing similar preparations.

"Do you know what they're going to do?" Nat whispered to Shara. "I don't think we ever saw this."

Shara shook her head. "I wasn't part of the Merith research team; I only studied humans."

The bright sun and the distance made it hard to tell the other competitors apart. They all wore similar tunics, and from this distance, Shara couldn't see the color of their eyes, which was the easiest way to identify a Merith.

Sam eyed Faal. "See how stiff he is? He's stretching his arms, but he's barely moved his leg."

Shara squinted, shading her eyes with her hand. "Yes, you're right."

Faal walked with a limp because apparently Claire had hurt him when she escaped. They didn't know how serious it had been, but they knew he was taking it as seriously as if Claire had cut off his hand.

"Just so you know," Shara said, "his limp would make it a lot easier for me to kill him."

Sam nudged her with his shoulder. "Would you drop it? People may have studied English here."

The competitors were waiting now, a few adjusting straps around their wrists to get the perfect fit for their gloves. The bell girl had returned to her beehive-hut and brought back a large, wooden chest. It looked too big and heavy for her to carry, but she set it lightly on the sand at her feet. Sam whispered to Nat, "Now, if a snitch and two bludgers fly out of that, things will get really interesting..."

The bell girl waited until they were all still, then rang her bell again. The chest burst open and, to Shara's surprise, it looked like an explosion of feathers.

They were birds, she realized, and they spun up and out of the chest, scrabbling at each other as if trying to climb into the sky by sheer violence rather than flight.

Feathers flew. A fearful raking of metallic claws and shrieking filled the silence. The five birds disengaged from each other as they got higher, several making low, menacing dives, and at least one soaring a hundred feet in the air to circle ominously over the others.

"Look," Nat whispered. "See what they're doing?"

"They're flying," Shara said.

"Not the birds! The players."

Shara had forgotten the Merith. She looked back down to the ground.

The closest player was crouched low, knees bent and one hand stretched out parallel to the sand with two fingers clenched. The other hand he held loosely in front of him, palm up. Suddenly he clenched the loose hand, stood, and whirled his wrist in a sharp twist.

The highest bird dove precisely on one of the others, carrying it to the sand in a tangle of beak and talons.

A quick glance showed Shara that the fourth competitor must be in charge of *that* bird, because he became a blur. Twist, shift, and jab—he almost looked as if he was doing some strange dance, a whirling dervish. His gloves flashed in the light and Shara thought she could make out wires and buttons trailing from the fighting birds.

"Comboda has him," said one of the onlookers. "Look how cool he is."

The defensive bird managed to get back in the air at last, but he was visibly damaged, with one wing beating irregularly. In a matter of minutes, he'd been finished off, and the beaten Merith tore off his gloves and threw them on the sand.

The spectators cheered loudly at his surrender.

"I wonder why Faal is playing such a cautious game," their neighbor said now. "It is not like him."

Faal's bird had yet to engage in any of the small skirmishes of the other birds, merely circling here and there and nimbly avoiding attack. Faal's style was more restrained than the other Merith. He barely seemed to move. His hands and wrists flickered in the tiniest, most controlled movements, and his bird moved with absolute precision.

Another bird suddenly dived towards Faal's bird, and Faal, in avoiding it, squatted slightly as he clicked his left thumb and fourth finger together. Or rather, he tried to squat, but he stumbled slightly and had to quickly jerk himself upright and do some serious fancy work to get his bird out from between two others who'd decided to temporarily ally and attack.

There were muttered gasps and then cheers from the crowd.

"The rumors are true then," their neighbor muttered. "He was injured."

"I am surprised he plays!" the other exclaimed, but then he lowered his voice. "How frightfully humiliating."

His friend agreed. "The Diadina arranged it to embarrass him, no doubt. You know how she can twist the Pontifex around her talons. And how she hates Faal."

"Indeed, but this is taking it rather far. To make him *hawk* with an injury? How dare she?"

"Oh, he rose to the challenge, don't doubt it. And he may yet win. I've never seen someone hawk with such precision, even the Pontifex... although he can out-hawk Faal by sheer cunning."

Shara watched with fascination as the birds, now four, were reduced to three, and then to two. To get a bird out of the game, one of the others had to take it down, disable it, and tear out its 'throat,' which she now realized was the conduit of control from its processing unit to its limbs.

They could see metallic fibers dangling from claws and beaks now, though Shara thought the spray of fake blood every time a throat was torn out was a particularly nice touch.

An intermission was allowed at this point, and the bell girl called out, "Final duel: Comboda vs. Merith II, to resume in five minutes."

"Aha!" There was a round of cheers, sighs, and laughter as various bets were settled. Their neighbor appeared to have bet that Comboda would be one of the final pairs and collected heavily.

"Excuse me," Sam spoke their language decently well, but not as well as Nat. "This sport is new to us. Are these birds machines or animals?"

The Merith looked him up and down. Sam was a relatively tall guy, a little over six feet, and he was only a foot and a half shorter than this Merith. The Spo tattoo on Sam's cheek automatically drew the Merith's eye, and Shara wondered if he would say anything about it. The Merith were not currently at war with the Spo, but their two species had been fighting periodically for centuries. Lots of bad blood there. And of course, the Merith *were* currently at war with the humans. Awkward.

"We are all admiration," Nat added. "Having no exact parallel to this sport on our own world."

"More polished than I expected," a Merith observed. "Despite their barbaric appearance." Many of the group turned to study them, apparently surprised that the humans could speak and understand their language. Shara felt sweat form at her hairline. She could take several of these Merith with the knife on her thigh, but if they all attacked...

Sam and Nat waited with close lipped smiles (appropriate for the Merith), while they were discussed.

"I assume they've been vetted, if the Diadina invited them."

"Have the rites of war been performed?" asked one. "We should not interact if the Pontifex was reserving that right for himself."

"I don't believe he was," Sam interjected. "And no, the rites of war have not yet been performed."

Shara stared at Sam. He knew what that meant, didn't he? He should have just lied.

The Merith they'd first spoken to looked at Sam significantly. "I would be honored," he said. "And as you are a guest, you may have the first rights."

Sam bowed to him. Then he punched him in the face, above

his eye. The Merith stepped back, looking more impressed than hurt.

Sam bowed again. "Humanity rests."

The Merith punched Sam in return, and it was anything but gentle. Sam, to his credit and Shara's secret admiration, neither flinched nor dodged. The blow was enough to spin him around and send him to one knee. He waited for a moment, probably to let any dizziness pass, and then stood. He nodded at the Merith again.

His opponent smiled. "Merith rests. Be welcome in our midst, Dark Eyes, and let me explain the sport of hawking."

Shara saw that Sam was surprised at the nickname, but on consideration, she decided that Sam's eyes might indeed seem strange to the Merith. Many species had two eyes, so that wouldn't seem strange to them, but the Merith generally had brightly colored eyes, sometimes multicolored, and it was not unusual for them to be named for their eye color or pattern. Sam had black eyes, and while that wasn't unusual for humans, perhaps it looked strange to the Merith.

Their new friend gave them a brief explanation of hawking, but it was somewhat technical, so Shara didn't catch it all. When the girl rang the bell for the next set, he broke off and they all watched.

After a minute, their Merith explained, "The tactics are different now. It's a duel, rather than a melee. To be a top player, one must master both types of combat. There are a few who may beat Faal in the melee, or Comboda in the duel, but less than a handful who can do both. You see, Faal took more harm in the last round, but he is the superior dueler. They are evenly matched today."

"Except for Faal's injury," Nat commented.

The Merith looked at her sharply. "Except for that, yes."

The duel was long and boring to Shara, and she was getting sunburned by the time Faal finally finished it.

"Ahh! A win for me," said the Merith, and collected more betting money from his companions. They did it with jokes, although the amounts caused Shara to gasp.

"The winner will play the Pontifex this evening," the Merith said to his friends. "You may try to win your money back then."

"But who will bet against the Pontifex? You beat against the wind there."

"I don't know," he replied. "Did you see Faal's last maneuver?"

"I saw him stumble twice and nearly lose."

"Yes, I know!" the Merith said, clearly excited. "His limitations forced him into a subtlety and speed I've never seen from him before. Wouldn't it be delicious if his injury actually *improves* his play?"

The others looked skeptical.

"Let's make it interesting then," the Merith said. "I will take all your bets against Faal's victory tonight."

"Done! Done!"

"But then who will hold the bet? If you all want to recoup..."

"I would be honored," Sam said, "to hold the bets of my fellow guests."

Several Merith suddenly looked dubious, but the friendly one who'd punched Sam slapped him on the back. "I may come to like you. You will hold the bets. We will see you here in five hours for the next match."

Sam groaned when they reached his bedroom. "I feel like a huge alien punched me in the face. I have a headache."

Nat glared at him. "A headache? You might have a concussion! You couldn't think of any better way to handle that?"

Sam made a pitiful face and flopped down on the bed. "Don't yell at me. I might have a concussion."

"Oh! You're such an idiot." Nat retrieved a flashlight from her bag and shined it in his eyes. "They're not dilated badly. Do you feel nauseated?"

"Only from watching those birds swoop around."

Nat felt his face and Sam flinched.

"Your hands are freezing," he said. "It's gotta be over ninety degrees outside, how are your fingers so cold?"

Nat ignored him. "Where is it tender?"

"Right eye, a little. It's gonna be a shiner. I think I'm okay, Nat. If I'd gotten that blow on the temple or the back of the head— sure, I'd be seeing lights. But I didn't." Sam suddenly pulled Nat down on the bed next to him and wrapped his arms around her. "I'm really alright."

"Should I leave?" Shara asked.

"Yes," Sam said.

"Yes," Nat said.

Shara flopped down on one of the chairs. "Whatever."

17

BASHER LOOKED APPREHENSIVELY AT CLAIRE, who stood next to him in the tiny submersible. Based on everything she'd told him about Faal's estate, he'd decided that Claire's help was worth the risk of her coming on this trip. But now that they were here, he was having second thoughts.

He was taking a girl he was—fond of, to say the least—back to the place where she'd been kept prisoner for three years and psychologically tortured.

No pressure. No pressure at all.

He still didn't know exactly how she'd talked him into it.

"Okay, put your hand on your oxygen valve," he said. They both wore stretchy green wetsuits, the better to blend in with the algae-rich ocean of Merith II. Claire put a hand on the thick bulge around her neck. It was a combination air tank, emergency float, and temporary air compressor. It would provide oxygen while they swam toward the cliffs of the estate. If anything happened to her, and he had to leave her in the ocean—heaven forbid—the ring around her neck could inflate to keep her head afloat and allow him to find and retrieve her later.

When he finished the safety check and made sure their heat-sensitive goggles were keyed to the heated guide rope they would use to keep together in the murky water, Basher pulled the flexible mask over his face. Claire followed suit, and he was pleased to see that she remembered his training and allowed the strange mask to fill slowly with air, taking shallow breaths while the plastic billowed slightly away from her lips. It was an exercise of the mind —if you thought of it as a plastic bag, surrounding and choking you —panic wasn't far behind.

They could still hear each other through short wave radios, and Basher said, "We're all set. I'm going to unzip it now."

The submersible itself was essentially a large plastic bag, and it was made to be inflated and deflated underwater. They were only twenty feet below the surface of the ocean, but that was enough to hide its presence from any surveillance from Faal's cliff-side estate.

With a quick motion, Basher unzipped the submersible bag allowing the cloudy water to pour in. The zipper fused and snapped outward to form a firm rectangular portal. The water gushed in, and only the weights of the bag and its anchor prevented it from swirling and twisting through the ocean with them inside. Instead, the weighted walls kept relatively steady while the air gushed out in great bubbles and the water flowed in. Everything inside the submersible was waterproof.

"Don't worry," Basher reassured her. "It's almost done."

"Worry?" Claire's voice sounded a little scratchy over the radio, but she gave him a shaky thumbs up. "This is fine. So fine. Definitely won't become a recurring nightmare."

When the only air in the submersible was a bubble in the convex ceiling, Basher propelled himself through the rectangular door, followed by Claire.

The particles of algae in the ocean were too small to be seen individually, but together they made the water into a veritable broth. Basher uncoiled the short rope at his shoulder and allowed it to trail out behind him. It appeared blue to his goggle-enhanced heat-vision. When he was certain that Claire had a hand on the rope but was far enough away to swim unhampered, he started toward the cliffs.

If Basher didn't have Claire's inside information on Faal's estate, he never would have attempted this. The depth of Claire's knowledge about the zoo had surprised him, and in telling him about it, she'd revealed more of her incarceration than he'd really wanted to know. Basher forced himself to focus on the tactical advantage of her knowledge, and not what it meant about her life.

Regardless, Claire was able to tell him where the openings to the ocean must be, based on the aquatic part of the zoo. She also knew the number of doors between that sector and the interior of Faal's estate. She knew the kind of security he tended to use, and how many staff would be on hand while he was away.

"We'll need to go midday, while the zoo staff are feeding the animals. There is minimal security between the zoo and the estate —and that security is for the benefit of the 'animals' that might be trying to escape. He allows for that, so we will be able to get through relatively easily. The lower floor is like a rat maze, designed to misdirect and confuse—and, of course, to allow him to observe. The problem will be getting out of the rat maze portion of the estate to the *real* portion. I only managed that once." She rubbed the back of her neck and Basher, who couldn't help watching her when she moved, noticed that she had a thin scar along her hairline.

"I broke through a mirror, here." She indicated the place on the rough schematic she'd been refining during the last few weeks. "That could work again, but I'm not sure. Anyway, we'll be better equipped than I was then, and I'm sure we can force our way out of that section. He's not expecting his animals to be armed. Obviously."

After they breached the 'real' first floor of his estate, they would have more security to deal with, but Basher felt that with the element of surprise and a reasonable amount of luck, they could get in and out quickly.

He had to admit, however, that this was still a dangerous gamble and not at all like him. But when he thought of Akemi, and he pictured the self she'd unconsciously showed him through her dreams, he couldn't stand the thought of leaving her to Faal. She'd asked him to come get her. She'd trusted him. And even though she'd known at the end that a rescue might be impossible, Basher wanted to honor her trust.

He was recalled from his thoughts when Claire's gasp sounded through the radio.

"What? Are you okay?"

"Yes, but look down."

Basher looked down, and saw a large, oval shape swimming about ten yards beneath them. It was brilliantly blue to his eyes, which meant it was quite warm. Five smaller blue things followed it in a line.

"I think it's a lowfin—that's what Sam and Nat called the Merith manatees," Claire said.

After she said it, Basher could make out the small, blunt fins on the sides of the large creature, and its elongated snout.

"Unsettling," Basher commented. "But don't worry about it."

"I'm not. I used to snorkel with my dad," Claire said. "I'm sure they won't bother us."

It was one of the first times she'd volunteered any information about her previous life to him, and normally Basher would have been happy to hear all about it, but this was not the moment. They watched the lowfins as they swam, but they were only in sight a few more minutes.

After a quarter of an hour, Basher's proximity sensor pinged in his ear, telling him that they were approaching the cliff. He'd been scanning in front of him with his heat-sensitive goggles, and now redoubled his efforts. The ocean was a fairly uniform temperature, but the tunnels that led from the zoo would hopefully show a heat signature from the pumps and purifiers used to clean it.

Sure enough, when they were close to the cliff, Basher spotted a faint blue glow below them. He swam toward it, using powerful kicks with his flippers.

Feeling around the opening with his hands, he decided it must have been a natural cave. It was roughly four feet tall and maybe six wide. Basher tugged the rope free from Claire and coiled it again. He didn't want them getting tangled up as they swam up the small passageway.

Entering the zoo ended up being even simpler than he'd hoped. The ocean water was allowed into an open tank before being treated, filtered, and pumped to a number of different pools, so Basher didn't even have to dismantle any equipment to get through. Soon they stood, dripping and shivering, on the edge of a dim cavern that reverberated with the barking of seals, the *zwack* of sea birds, and whistling that sounded like dolphins.

Basher looked around with awe and some fear. "Do they make this kind of racket all the time, or is it us?"

"They're hungry," Claire said. "That means they haven't been fed yet. We should hurry."

Basher unclipped the heavy hacksaw and the larger zinc torch from his belt, leaving them on the floor next to the tank. He pulled his gun out of a water-tight pocket and kept it in his hand. "Come on then."

The first occupied tank was the size of an Olympic swimming pool. The glass rose eight feet above the ground, but the tank extended far below floor level—Basher guessed perhaps 40 feet deep. The cavern was dim, so he couldn't see far into the water. Large shadowy forms moved within it. Basher shuddered in the cold and wet and didn't try to look too hard.

They were almost past the tank when a creature suddenly swam into view, hovering near the glass. It was about the size and shape of a whale shark, and the glistening teeth were definitely those of a predator. Basher froze. Maybe it was the stress, but as he met the creature's eye, he could've sworn the thing was intelligent. It seemed to be questioning his presence; it knew he was out of place.

But of course, there could be no communication between them, and with a powerful thrust of its dorsal fin, the shark dove down into the invisible depths of the tank.

Basher had memorized Claire's map of this place, and they found the exit from this chamber exactly where she'd indicated. It seemed to be a natural cave formation, but the dim, recessed lighting and the rushing of water heard in the walls indicated a more complex structure.

They met the first zoo-keeper as he rounded a gradual curve in the tunnel ahead, pushing a wheelbarrow that smelled of rancid shrimp. Claire was just behind Basher, and she gave no more than a muffled squeak before Basher incapacitated him. They were using a fast-acting sedative. Basher pulled the dart from the Merith's thick neck only when he was positive the alien was unconscious.

Claire stared at the Merith, then at Basher. "That was fast."

He smirked, "I know. I'm good." But as he turned around, his foot caught on an uneven lip of stone on the floor. His flailing hand touched the wall to steady himself.

"Freeze!" Claire hissed. "Don't move your hand."

Basher froze.

"I warned you about the walls." She examined his hand, and Basher saw that tiny filaments crisscrossed the walls, thinner than spider webs. Synthetic gossamer rings hung from each strand. One ring was settling on his thumb.

Did Faal design this to catch his animals? It must have been designed for something very different. It was hidden against the wall... Basher pictured spiders scurrying by, setting it off...or maybe birds. He liked the idea of birds better than spiders.

"Okay. Slowly pull your hand down and away, but don't pull that ring," she said.

It was slightly adhesive, but Claire held it in place with her gloved hand while he got his hand free.

She breathed deeply, listening. "No alarm. I guess we keep going."

"This place is deeply unnerving," Basher said. "But yes."

When they'd gotten up an interior stairway, Claire led Basher to a room that reminded him of a mirror maze at a carnival. Some of the mirrors were distorted, and at first he didn't even realize that part of the room was completely hidden.

"Over here," Claire said. She was shivering slightly, but she seemed to be holding together alright. She slipped behind a mirror that had looked flush with the wall but clearly wasn't. He followed her into the tight space, and she gestured at the black wall behind them. "Break through here," she said.

She backed away while he used his smaller torch to melt through the wall. It didn't take much. It was thin construction, but it did make a bit of noise, hissing and creaking.

"Let's wait until someone comes to check," Basher said. "Get as many as we can before we go in."

They waited. And waited.

"Is it possible no one heard?" Basher asked her.

She looked dubious. "I think someone should be monitoring the video, in case an animal had escaped through here, like I did the one time..."

They waited some more, and Basher's skin was starting to prickle uncomfortably. The longer they were here, the greater their chance of discovery.

"Let's risk it," he said.

They slipped through the rough hole, which was easier for

Claire than for him. Basher stood with his gun in both hands, ready, and they listened.

There was some noise from far away, but it didn't sound sinister. The sound of voices, and scraping, and commands...normal, calm Merith voices.

"I guess they didn't hear," Claire said. "After this—I don't know as much about the layout. This is as far as I got."

"Alright. Me first, then."

The room they'd reached was almost dark; it had no windows, and the only light came from the translucent door. Basher saw coils of rope and chain hanging on the walls, but he didn't ask Claire about it.

The door to this room had three panels and folded up like a screen. It was partly open, so Basher peered cautiously around the edge without touching it. A short hall led to a courtyard where he could see daylight, so the center of the house must be open to the sky. There were several Merith in the courtyard, but they were facing away from him, engaged in hoisting a large tree into a giant, obsidian bowl. Dirt was crumbling away from its roots, and they were clearly having trouble clearing the edge of the bowl as they lifted the tree with a small crane that barely fit in the courtyard.

"Good luck for us," Basher muttered. He risked a quick look in the other direction, and the hall took a turn to the right. If they could get around that corner, they'd be out of the line of sight of the courtyard. It also looked like a promising location for a set of stairs or an elevator.

Basher explained to Claire, and when one of the workers indulged another round of shouting and cursing at his clumsy helpers, Basher dashed down the hall and around the corner.

Sure enough, there was an elevator, however, there was also a Merith with a yellow uniform waiting for it.

Basher shot him twice with the tranquilizer, and they dragged his limp body into the elevator cubicle with them.

Basher and Claire didn't speak. They'd already discussed Akemi's probable location, and every situation they could anticipate. In this scenario, they planned to drag the Merith away and stow him in the first empty room they could find.

They'd decided that the upper floor was a more likely place to find Akemi. The bottom two levels were largely taken up with the 'maze' Faal kept in place for escaped animals, and the other portion was the courtyard and (most likely) some kind of reception hall or formal sitting rooms. The second floor was the best option.

However, there were still a lot of rooms on the upper floor. Which meant there were still a lot of places for them to run into Merith and for this all to go badly.

When the elevator doors closed—thank heaven it wasn't an open elevator, Basher thought—they began to rise, and a soft recording of Merith singing filled the silence.

Claire laughed. "Elevator music," she gasped. "Why did I never know Faal had elevator music?"

Basher looked at her carefully. If she started to lose it right now, he was going to have a problem.

She shook her head. "Sorry, this is just too surreal. Plus..." she trailed off, listening hard. "I think this is a recording of the Diadina. That's really creepy."

Basher was still holding the limp Merith by his armpits, and he just grunted. Claire took a deep breath, and when the elevator door opened, she was the first off, as they'd planned, with her gun ready.

She wasn't a great shot, but if anybody was close, Basher trusted that she could shoot them.

There wasn't anyone, which was a relief. She ran to the closest door, put an ear close to listen, and then opened it when there was silence. Basher dragged the heavy Merith inside and dropped him on the floor.

This room was clearly some kind of guest room, with an

unused feeling to it. A large, round Merith bed dominated the room, and he could see a balcony. They were on the east edge of the house, and the ocean was visible far below. Their tiny submersible, filled with water and thus virtually undetectable, was out there somewhere beneath the waves.

They quickly checked the four rooms at that end of the house and all were empty—containing neither Akemi nor any more Merith. This hall, like the one on the floor below, took a turn and led straight to the central courtyard. There, an elevated walkway went around the courtyard in a U shape, and many doors opened off of it. If they tried to look in those rooms, they would be visible to the five Merith struggling with the tree in the courtyard.

Waiting out of sight in the hall, they could hear the voices of the Merith below them, and they could see the upper branches of the tree still trembling slightly. It looked like they'd gotten it situated and were now arguing about soil and something else. It was too colloquial for Basher to translate in his head.

Whatever they were saying, they were definitely still standing in the courtyard, and if he and Claire walked out onto the open walkway, they would easily be seen.

Claire seemed to be distracted though. She inclined her head toward the first door that opened off the walkway and pointed to her ear. The door was half open, but it was hinged away from them and so he couldn't see in. He listened intently, and realized he heard clicking... and muttering.

Hmm. Someone was in there. And what was that clicking?

Claire brought her hands up and mimed typing on a keyboard. The Merith had long claws, and the most common computer interface they used looked like a kind of graphing calculator that they tapped with the points of their claws.

And since they were looking for a computer—that was probably a good place to look.

To get to that half-closed door, however, they would have to traverse about three feet of open walkway. It wasn't far, but it was enough. Basher motioned for Claire to take watch position and held up five of his fingers. She was to count to five and then follow him.

Basher crossed the space as rapidly and silently as he could in two large strides and slipped in the door. It was a small room, with a glassed-in wall toward the ocean. A Merith sat in front of a computer, facing half away from him. Basher paused for a moment, disoriented by the huge window and the amount of light —and the Merith turned around.

Basher would have tranquilized him then, but the Merith had slumped shoulders and such an air of resignation, that Basher hesitated.

The Merith gestured limply with one hand. "She's not here."

Claire came through the door then, closing it silently behind her. She raised her gun as well.

The Merith raised both hands in the common sign for 'unarmed' and repeated, "She's not here anymore."

Basher and Claire kept their guns pointed at him.

"Who?" Basher demanded.

"The computer known as Akemi. She was human, and you are human, so I assume you came for her. I'm sorry—she's gone."

18

"IS Akemi at the Pontifex's palace?" Basher demanded of their hostage.

"Yes."

Basher gritted his teeth. "This was for nothing then."

The Merith began to click on the computer again.

"Stop," Basher commanded him.

"I am not triggering an alarm. I am pulling up her last files. I—feel you have the right to know."

An audio recording played softly. Claire swayed forward a step to hear it.

"He asked for you, specifically," Faal was saying. Claire would know his voice anywhere. "The Pontifex expressed great curiosity to see my new conscious computer. How would the Pontifex know you *exist*, let alone know that I own you?"

"Um. My fame precedes me?" Akemi said.

Claire gasped. "Akemi can speak out loud?"

Basher motioned her to be quiet.

"Your friends have made a serious mistake by involving the Pontifex," Faal continued. "If *he* takes a fancy to you, your circumstances will be grimmer than they are now."

"Are you going to explain what you're talking about, or did you just feel like waking me up?" Akemi said.

"The Pontifex expressed concern over my new acquisition. I must gratify his curiosity and greed, curse him. I have no choice but to take you to the Pontifical palace."

"I must say, this is a disquieting side to your personality. I've never heard you turn vulgar."

Claire couldn't help smiling at Akemi's tone. Faal must not have hurt her too much if she could be so impertinent to him.

"I have to take you to Merith Prime," he hissed, "but the *manner* is up to me. Don't push me."

"But do you think we're ready to see other people? I mean, new relationships are so fragile."

The recording cut off. The Merith pulled up another one while explaining, "The next morning, I was required to shut her down for the trip. Faal wanted complete disconnection. Sensory deprivation."

His voice came on the recording. "But—that will no doubt degrade the quality of the computer. It would be simple for me to make a proxy visual capacitor for traveling." He paused. "I merely desire to preserve your property."

Faal's voice was harsh. "My *property* is mine to use or destroy as I choose, and I would rather see this computer *degrade* than go smug and confident to live as the pet of the Pontifex."

"Thanks for that," Akemi said. "That might be the first time you've admitted that I'm really alive." Akemi had laughed shakily. "Don't worry about me, Mox'uu. I'm going to be fine."

"Shut her down," Faal said. "Her friends are going to regret this ploy."

The recording cut off.

Claire's heart was starting to pound harder. "Wait a minute. Did Faal *know* we were coming for her?"

"We suspected it was a possibility."

"Then this is a trap." Claire spun to the door. Her fingers were so tight on the trigger, Basher was afraid she might accidentally fire. Her hands had begun to tremble, and her eyes darted from the door to the window.

"Not exactly a trap," the Merith said. "Faal knew you wanted to get Akemi out of this house, but he thought you would try for her on Merith Prime."

"We'll never get out," Claire said. "He knew our plan. We'll never get out of here."

The Merith looked at her uneasily. She'd pointed her gun back at him, and she looked distinctly unhinged. Basher saw when the Merith suddenly recognized Claire.

"You are one of Faal's animals," he exclaimed. "You are the one who escaped."

Claire's hands trembled. "What is his plan? You've delayed us and now what happens? It's got to be something terrible."

"Do not shoot. I am on your side."

Claire stepped closer to the Merith and pressed the gun against his forehead, above his eye. "Tell us how the trap is set," she growled. "I know *all* about Faal's traps. You know I do. Tell us what he's planned."

The Merith kept perfectly still. "The exterior doors are electrified, and the trip wires are live with three times the normal capacity. You would fry. He also let the beasts out in the front sector."

Claire shuddered. "We don't have to go that way."

The Merith looked curious. "Really? Then how did—"

Claire dug the gun into the rough ridges of his forehead. "Don't talk unless I speak to you. What else? Did he activate the birds in the middle sector?"

"I don't believe so."

"Is that it?"

"Yes, I swear. He did not truly expect anyone to come here. He expects it at the Pontifex's palace."

"Why are you telling us this?"

"I had to completely overhaul his security system after your escape. It was impressive."

Claire glared at him. "Don't patronize me. Answer the question."

"The being known as Akemi was—my friend. She was a most interesting entity, worthy of respect, and I did not treat her as I could have wished. In fact, I deeply regret what I did to her." He paused. "I must report your presence, but I will give you ten minutes."

Claire didn't lower her gun. "Do you believe him?" she asked Basher.

He shot the Merith in the chest with the tranq.

"Yeah, I believe him," Basher said, "but I'd rather have longer than ten minutes. We don't need to play his game. Let's get out of here."

Claire's teeth were chattering by the time they got back to the first floor and stepped through the melted wall.

"Someone's watching us," she said. "I can tell. Someone knows we're here."

"There's no alarm," Basher said. He wasn't sure if she sensed something or her fear and paranoia were getting the better of her.

Claire led him unerringly back through the confusing maze of mirrors toward the zoo, but she didn't look comforted.

At one point she stopped so abruptly that Basher bumped into her.

She studied the ceiling. "I can feel it. They know we're here." She was staring at a blank ceiling, and Basher had to give her a sharp nudge before she snapped out of it.

By the time they went down the flights of stairs to the zoo, she was shivering so hard he was afraid she'd bump the wall and trigger the tiny sensors herself.

"Are you okay?" He knew it was stupid question, but he also needed to know if she was going to be able to pull herself together and swim out of here. "There's no alarm yet. I think we can make it."

She nodded silently, and he realized she was clenching her jaw to stop her teeth from chattering. She kept glancing back to make sure they weren't being followed. Her pupils were dilated, her nostrils flared, and her head twitched toward every tiny sound of the animals as they passed. Her movements became faster and jerkier. She looked more like a caged animal than the girl he'd gotten to know in the embassy, and her transformation told him more about this place than her scribbled descriptions ever could. Basher reached out to touch her elbow and she jerked away, but he deliberately reached for her arm anyway. He felt she needed an anchor or this place was going to break her down before they got out.

"It's just me," he said. "And there's no one following us yet. We'll be fine."

She clutched his hand as they ran down the next hallway. Her hand was cold in his and he gripped it tightly.

CLAIRE BARELY GLANCED at her own cage as they passed. "That one was mine."

She'd handled her fear well on the way in, but knowing Faal had expected them, even a little bit, had triggered all her phobias.

She fully expected the ocean in-tank to be blocked when they got back, preventing their escape.

She fully expected to feel the sting of a dart gun sinking into her exposed back at any moment.

She fully expected to suffer when Faal wrapped his hands around her neck...

Claire clutched Basher's hand tighter, knowing she was on the brink of a panic attack and not sure how to avoid it. She felt certain that someone had been observing them from the main house—but Basher was right that nothing had happened. And even if she *was* right, what could they do but keep going?

Claire was doing exactly what she'd promised Basher she wouldn't do: freaking out, panicking, and putting him in danger.

"Keep breathing," Basher said quietly, and Claire realized she'd started to hold her breath. She exhaled sharply.

"We're almost there," he said. "Why don't you close your eyes? I know the way through the last chamber."

Claire complied instantly, desperate to get out of this feedback loop of fear. Jogging through the dark was terrifying, but it allowed her to focus on other senses than sight. She focused on the pounding of her feet, the steady inhalation of Basher's breathing, and the warmth of his hand.

Faster than she expected, she felt the larger space of the cavern open around her.

"Last cavern," Basher said hopefully

Claire opened her eyes as they made their way past the seals, birds, and whale-shark things. All the animals were eerily silent now, only the splash of rippling water broke the heavy, under-ground silence. The birds were perfectly still. They were capable of ripping flesh from bones, like aviary piranhas, but they were not activated.

BASHER WAS glad when they got past the lengthy enclosure where the seals watched their progress with dark, liquid eyes. He was even more relieved when they made it to the intake pool that led back to the ocean.

He had no idea how Claire had survived this claustrophobic prison for so many years. Barely more than an hour here, and he was thoroughly unsettled.

Basher helped Claire pull the mask back over her face and was relieved to see that she'd come back from the brink of panic. He counted twelve beats of her pulse while they struggled back into their flippers and twelve more while they waited for the masks to puff out as their tiny pressurization systems kicked in. Basher then reattached the saw and torch to his belt, sat on the tank wall, and pulled Claire up to sit next to him.

He could hear her breath getting ragged again as she looked at the dark water.

"We're almost done," he said. "Take a deep breath and go on in."

He waited for her to slide into the water before falling backward into the welcoming warmth and darkness himself.

"You first, please," Claire said. Her voice sounded metallic.

He dove down and thrust himself into the tunnel. It was almost black, just as it had been before, but the tunnel seemed longer.

"Ow! Watch your head here." Basher bumped past a rough protrusion from the ceiling.

"Got it," Claire said. She didn't say anything else, and he knew they were both wondering if they'd really gotten away, or whether Faal had some contingency plan for this. Perhaps a gate that shut over the mouth of the tunnel... trapping them underwater.

Basher didn't see the exit when he reached it, but he felt a shift in the way the water moved, a flow that felt broader and more open. He spread eagle in the water for a moment to confirm, and he could not feel any walls around him.

"Here we are," he said. "That's the end of it. We're in the ocean."

Claire gave a sobbing breath, and Basher continued a quiet

stream of reassurance while they swam straight out from the wall of the cliff.

When they'd gone another twenty yards, the water began to get lighter. The sun had shifted slightly, putting the base of the cliff in shadow, and now they were swimming out of the shadow. Basher took a deep breath at the return of the dim light, realizing how confined he'd felt in the dark. When they'd swum another ten minutes, he could make out the dim blue glow of the submersible in the distance and some way above them. The perspective confused him for a moment; he hadn't realized they'd been swimming so much deeper than they needed to.

When he and Claire were safely back in the pod, he activated the reversal process, pumping the water out with compressed air, which was also used to gently push them eastward, back toward their ship.

Claire's fingers were shaking so hard it took her several tries to pull her face mask off. Basher finally did it for her, wishing there was something more he could do. The submersible was getting warm. He wished he could offer her a blanket or towel to wrap up in, but as the submersible had been completely filled with water, they hadn't brought anything like that.

Claire pressed a hand over her eyes and stood silent for a long time as they bobbed their way east through the ocean. "We need to let Sam and Nat know at once."

"On it," Basher said.

"I hope Akemi is okay. That was a long trip for her to be completely shut down."

"She's one of the toughest people I·know," Basher said. "I'm sure she's going to be okay."

19

AKEMI WAS DRIFTING when a bright light suddenly blinded her.

And she couldn't blink. Why couldn't she blink?

Was she dreaming? No, that had been before, when she thought the trees were singing... Akemi's thoughts trailed off in confusion.

The light hurt her head. Where was she? What had she been thinking about?

A jumble of half-focused memories swirled through her head: the Spo taking Nat away, many years ago; Nat hanging from a pipe, about to fall into a drilling chasm; the Rik and Claire, Faal and Drench... Drench!

With a feeling of plunging into a cold waterfall, Akemi gasped and came back to herself.

She remembered Faal's decision to bring her to the Pontifex. His suspicion that her friends were behind it—and his decision to unplug her for the duration of the trip.

She had been worried.

Drench's presence, along with the other Melifleurs, had helped her immensely during her weeks at Faal's estate. She'd no longer been afraid and disoriented by disconnection. What had once been a frightening nothingness became aglow to her mind's eye. There were five Melifleurs in Faal's estate that she could 'talk' to by then, and several others on the fringe. It was practically a party.

But if she went in space, they wouldn't be there to keep her company.

Akemi had felt Drench's disapproval—or perhaps it was concern.

"Are you going to tell me I shouldn't have antagonized him? I'm so sick of that advice. What else do I have to do?"

"I wasn't going to say that," Drench said.

He started to say something else, but Akemi shushed him. "What is that?"

Her sense of space was off, but she could feel another presence near her. It wasn't one of the Melifleurs, and it seemed to shiver like a mirage.

"What is that?" she asked again. "Are you doing that?"

"Oh. No, that is Faal's presence. You can feel how it moves too quickly to commune with." Akemi had seen that, sort of. At least, while she communed with Drench, she could see how Faal's presence appeared like a will-o'-the-wisp to him.

Drench was slow, not in his intellect, but in his mode of being. He did not embrace movement or change easily, certainly not fast enough to align himself with a flickering, unstable mind.

Akemi couldn't do it either, but she wondered if someday she could—with enough practice, maybe. Her mind was just as flickering quick as Faal's, and the sense of restless motion in his mind didn't freak her out.

"Perhaps you could," Drench agreed. "I believe being anchored has amplified your mind, or perhaps it is the machine. Although—"

But then Faal had switched her back on, and her focus returned to things physical with a painful snap.

Faal growled in his throat but otherwise seemed to have himself under control. He was no longer flinging himself around the room, at any rate. "I will take you to the Pontifex, as he is interested to see you, but I will do it in my own way. You will take the trip in solitude, with no power. If you are mad when we arrive, then the Pontifex is welcome to you. You have been much less useful to me than I anticipated."

"And if the Pontifex resents you destroying me on the way to his palace?" Akemi asked. "What then?" She focused on Faal's presence, wondering if she could read him well enough with her newly learned skills to tell if he was bluffing or not.

She got something, but she wasn't sure what. He was upset, but she already knew that. She needed something more specific. Akemi concentrated as hard as she could, completely blocking Drench out and trying to sync her mind to Faal.

Ah, a flicker of—dread, perhaps? Probably he didn't want to offend the Pontifex. Gifts were a serious business for the Merith. Offering a deranged computer to his Pontifex was not the best play ever.

"Maybe you'd better bring a back-up gift," Akemi said. A fantastic idea had come to her, but she had no idea if she could make Faal go for it.

She pretended to be humble, scared of his threat. "I admit, I don't want to belong to the Pontifex. Don't you have anything else of value you're willing to give away?"

With all her soul, she sent, *The tree, the tree. Turn around and look at the tree.*

Faal rubbed his forehead. "The Pontifex's curiosity, once aroused, is not easily deflected."

The tree, Akemi sent silently. *It's useless to you, but valuable to him. The tree.*

Faal shifted his weight and glanced over his shoulder toward the inner atrium of his house and Drench. As soon as he looked,

Akemi stopped communicating with him. She didn't want to make him suspicious.

Faal turned his head back and rubbed his ridged forehead once more. "Either way, you will spend the journey alone. I hope you enjoy your solitude."

"You were talking to him?" Drench asked. He sounded amazed and also a little hurt.

"I'm sorry I pushed you away. I couldn't sync up with both of you at the same time—you and Faal are too different."

"And you're somewhere in the middle?"

"Yes, I guess so. Anyway, listen. Faal is going to take me to another planet, but I'm hoping he'll take you, too. I tried to plant the idea in his mind."

"Why?"

"You don't want to come with me? Not at all?"

Drench shuddered. "I don't want to go *anywhere, ever,* if I can help it. I'm a tree. But more importantly, I was assigned here."

Akemi fell silent for a moment. "I need you to come," she admitted. "Faal threatened to keep me isolated during the whole trip, and I won't make it."

She could feel Drench's understanding, and she felt a wave of relief that he was willing to go. She could also sense his overwhelming disgust with Faal.

"I did not understand," Drench said, "even after I met you, exactly what had been done. At first we thought you were a Melifleur, uprooted before you found your voice. But it is actually far worse. You are like a sapling that had their eyes cut out, their roots sawed, and their branches broken at the trunk. It is unfathomable."

Akemi listened to his rant, and felt a heaviness lift away from her. "I was like that," she said. "But now I have you."

Drench's reply seemed to come from deep within. "Then I will do all I may to stay near you."

The journey had been strange and otherworldly, but Drench *had* kept her sane. The Melifleurs practiced a kind of meditation— a suspended consciousness that they experienced during some seasons. Aligning herself completely with Drench, she had also been able to enter the trance.

It was just rather painful and disorienting coming out of it. She wondered if it felt that way to Drench, but when she searched for him, she couldn't find him.

The painful light resolved into a close-up of a bulbous Merith eye as her visual processor began to focus.

The eye retreated and Akemi could see that Faal was there, and another Merith—he was taller and broader than Faal, with a lazy, half-lidded blue eye. The Pontifex.

They appeared to be in some sort of vault. Akemi could make out buttressed columns and a huge, thick door standing open behind them. The vault was filled with beautiful things. There were lavish wall hangings, gold and platinum knickknacks, and ancient-looking chandeliers holding diamonds. Even the shelves that held the treasures were made from pure Spo deathglass. The sheer gaudiness of it all reminded Akemi of a dragon's hoard or Aladdin's famous cave.

Faal and the Pontifex looked perfectly at ease in the room, and their jewel-studded robes seemed a part of the decoration. Faal wore his customary brick red robes, but the other Merith wore a startling turquoise ensemble that brought out the color of his eye. It was the same color as Shara's favorite blouse, and she would love it...

But—but Akemi didn't care what Shara loved. Did she? Shara had betrayed her and Nat...

Or had she saved them? Akemi felt a ghostly memory sliding away as the true one snapped into place. Yes, Shara was the worst.

"The rumors of your latest acquisition reached me days ago," the Pontifex said, interrupting Akemi's thoughts. "I appreciate you bringing it for my inspection."

"Of course. Don't I always show you my latest treasures?" Faal replied.

The Pontifex examined the biobank, which held her brain, and seemed unimpressed. "Is it truly a human brain? How strange. Is it any better than a trouncer?"

Akemi sensed Faal's conflict. He wanted to say no, to keep his toy for himself. But he also wanted to say yes, to prove that he'd acquired something unique and valuable. She still felt hungover from her long sleep, but she was lucid enough to enjoy seeing Faal squirm.

She could also tell that the Pontifex was more informed than he was letting on. That thought spun Akemi into another dizzying round of memory connections, and she wondered how badly her brain had been damaged by the long trance. She barely heard Faal's answer.

"It is—more creative than a trouncer brain," he said, "but less trustworthy. It can only be used under strict supervision. And indeed, I don't even know if it survived the trip intact. It is very delicate."

Akemi understood Faal's dilemma. He'd turned on the computer but he wasn't sure yet if she was crazy or even still alive after the long trip.

Well, Faal was out of luck, she was definitely still alive.

20

SAM'S HEADACHE was nearly gone now, though a purplish bruise had formed above his eyebrow. It would soon be a black eye. Hopefully he didn't have to repeat any war rituals with other aliens. Thanks to Nat's prepared first aid kit containing painkillers, however, it didn't hurt too badly. He'd taken a long nap, and that probably helped, too. Nat woke him when it was time to go back to the field for the next match.

"You've been asleep for nearly four hours," she said. "You're making me nervous."

"It's not a concussion. I'm just making up for seven years of lost naps."

Nat gave him a skeptical look as he rolled off his bed.

"Have we heard from Basher and Claire yet?" he asked.

She shook her head.

They went back to the field early, so no one would think Sam had stolen the money entrusted to him. The Merith all used paper money, rather like thick parchment, and each bundle was in a tiny silk bag, with the name of the owner embroidered on it.

"While you were sleeping, I copied down the names from each of the bags," Nat told him. "We might want to look those up later and see who is in the Pontifex's favor."

Sam smiled sleepily. "Why else do you think I offered to keep the bets? Honestly, I went to the same school you did."

When they reached the field, a much larger group of Merith was assembled to watch the duel. Sam was surprised to see that the Pontifex stood on one side of the group. He was recognizable from the photos they'd seen of him, and also the respectful distance maintained by the other Merith.

The Pontifex looked them over as they approached. "Welcome, humans! I understand the rites of war have already been performed."

"Yes, Your Eminence," Sam said. "I hope I did not overstep myself in performing this without your leave."

"Oh, no," he waved a hand. "I am informed it was done with all civility, and I am pleased that the Diadina was correct that you are civilized enough to be at ease in my court." He gestured at the field. "Have you seen a game of hawking before?"

"Only today," Sam answered. He pulled out the silk betting bags and let them dangle from his fingers. "However, I have the honor to hold the bets of several of those assembled here, and so I look forward with great anticipation to the match."

There was a murmur of surprise from the assembled Merith, many of whom had not been there in the morning.

"Indeed! I am doubly impressed," the Pontifex said. "And your name?"

"Sam Locklear, or Dark Eyes."

"Dark Eyes," the Pontifex said. "I like it. Hold the bets in all truth, then, and enjoy the match." He strode away and Sam suddenly realized that Faal was just behind him.

"Sam Locklear," Faal said. "How surprised I am to see you here."

Sam smiled. "I know. Long time, no see, right? How's it going?"

Another murmur of surprise from the crowd. Sam could practically feel the re-evaluation going on. This human held the bets of seven Merith? He received the patronage of the Diadina? He knew Faal of Merith II personally?

"I wish you luck in the match," Sam said. "May you fly swift and dive swifter." That phrase finally made sense.

Faal's eye was half-hooded by its heavy lid, and he gave Sam a look of keen appraisal before limping away to his position.

Faal and the Pontifex stood directly across from each other, on either side of the huge playing field. The setting sun cast their shadows long and dark toward the crowd.

The Merith who'd punched Sam that morning now made his way to their side. "The twilight makes visibility a challenge," he explained. "And if the game goes long, it will be completely black. That adds a time factor for them to consider."

"Do you regret betting against the Pontifex?" Sam asked.

"Ahh... no. But I never do regret a bet until I lose," he said with a jovial wink.

Both the Pontifex and Faal had a personal assistant who strapped on their gloves with ritualistic slowness. Then the box was taken to the center of the field.

When the bell rang, the box flew open, and two birds rocketed out so fast, Sam almost missed it. They flew up in a tight spiral, but as far as he could tell, neither touched the other. Fifty feet in the air they split apart and in almost perfect, mirror-image synchronization did a lazy roll and swooped back towards each other, missing by inches as they passed.

"Is this a fight or a performance?" Nat whispered, shading her eyes with her hand as she tried to track the birds across the sky.

The two birds were shaped a little differently, which was the only way Sam could tell them apart. They both moved so smoothly and so parallel it almost looked like they were playing, rather than fighting. It had been ten minutes, and there had been no engagement.

Sam looked back down at the contestants and was struck by their stillness. The Pontifex stared at Faal, who stared right back. Neither of them so much as glanced at the sky as their hands flew in complicated patterns and their birds circled each other warily.

The Pontifex was smiling slightly, but Faal's face was a blank mask.

The sun dipped below the horizon, though there was still quite a bit of ambient light.

With a squawk, Faal's bird twisted and sank its talons into the stomach of the Pontifex's bird. The Pontifex disengaged with lightning speed, still looking only at his opponent.

Faal's sudden lunge had unbalanced him slightly, and he had to take an unplanned step to correct it. The Pontifex saw, but in the split second he took to realize the opportunity and respond, Faal was back in control.

The Pontifex attacked next in a flurry of movement too fast for Sam to follow. He almost took Faal's bird to the ground before it slipped free.

The sky was definitely dusky now, and it was getting harder for Sam to see the birds. Of course, neither the Pontifex nor Faal were looking at the sky, but it must also be getting harder for them to see each other as well. What would they do if it got completely dark? Sam suspected they didn't suspend the game and start later.

In fact, as Faal feinted and shifted again, Sam began to wonder if Faal *wanted* to continue the game in the dark. Would there be some advantage to him in darkness that would outweigh his injury?

Apparently, the Pontifex was wondering the same thing. The Pontifex began to attack with greater rapidity and ferocity as true darkness began to fall. He'd stopped smiling.

Faal finally followed up one of the attacks with an attack of his own. The Pontifex jerked free, and, expecting the lunge to unbalance Faal as it had before, he moved in for the kill.

Sam could barely see Faal's eye, but now it suddenly burned brighter. With a bloodcurdling shriek and tear of flesh, the birds tumbled to the ground.

"Was that—who won?" Nat said. The other Merith were saying the same thing, shouting for light, and debating the last move. It was fully dark, the dark of a desert with no moon, and Sam reached for Nat's hand to make sure they weren't separated.

Three floodlights came on, nearly blinding Sam, but now he could see the Pontifex and Faal. They still stood at their positions, and the girl with the bell pointed at Faal. "The winner: Faal of Merith II."

The crowd stood in shocked silence.

Eventually the Pontifex bowed and moved forward to meet Faal in the middle of the field.

"That was brilliant, my friend," he said.

"Thank you, my lord."

"Brilliant, brilliant," said the Merith next to Sam. He spoke quietly. "Do you see? Faal wasn't waiting for darkness at all, but he made the Pontifex suspect that he was, which made him take the offensive. And then that fake stumble at his first lunge—he *wanted* the Pontifex to wait for his next attack. And in the murk he would not know whether Faal was unbalanced or not... yes, a brilliant use of a handicap."

The Pontifex and Faal still looked at each other, and the Pontifex nodded slightly. "An excellent strategy. I congratulate you."

The Merith who'd participated in the bet were in less of a joking mood as Sam gave all the bags to the one Merith who'd bet against the Pontifex. He collected them with a smile. "I never bet against an injured Merith."

21

BASHER STOOD in the pilot's room of their tiny spaceship, looking at the door of the biobank. It housed the organic matter that completed the biocomputer—and it looked exactly like the housing Akemi's brain was in. He'd hoped to have her with them on this return trip, but instead they'd gotten nothing for their expensive and dangerous gamble.

This small ship was piloted by Basher's partner, who had volunteered to help with their crazy rescue effort. He was a good friend—and almost always ripe for any mischief against a Merith. He'd stayed with the ship and picked them up when their tiny shuttle got back into orbit. The ship was a Spo messenger vessel, small as ships went, but perfect for their needs.

Basher's partner was generally quiet, but as he finished entering the parameters into the quantitative computer, he spoke. "I'm sorry you didn't find the little girl."

Basher nodded. "Me too, looks like our trip was for nothing."

"I already sent your message to the palace on Merith Prime. You think Faal has some plan to entrap your friends there?"

"His minion spelled it out pretty clearly. Have they replied yet?"

"No, but I disconnected as soon as I sent it. We need to be far away from Merith II before anyone can locate us." He tapped the screen with one long claw. "I've scheduled a series of short jumps to get us away from here, in case Faal has an orbital tracking system, which I expect he does. After that, we'll see if your friends have responded."

Basher held onto the door frame for the first jump, a moment of rushing speed, vertigo, and weightlessness. Then they snapped into their new position. Basher's partner flushed pale purple with satisfaction, "All mapped. Perfect location. First of twelve."

He looked over at Basher. "You look exhausted, even for a human. I'll give you five minutes to get some food and strap in before the next jump."

Basher patted his partner on the shoulder and went to get a protein bar. He found Claire sitting on one of the backward Spo chairs, awkwardly strapped in and sipping something hot through a straw. She was wrapped in her new blanket.

He'd given it to her a few days ago, before they left the embassy.

"Merry Christmas," Basher had said.

"What's this?" Claire asked, fingering the drawstring of the bulky, burlap bag.

"Something I found for you. Open it up."

She frowned and slid the drawstring down, pulling out a thick, soft blanket. It was a hand-pieced Tergre quilt, made of the wool they imported from their homeworld. It was unbleached and the color of the animals could still be seen: muted cream, white, and mottled brown. The vendor told him each square came from a different animal, and the wool stuffing was both warm in the winter and cool in the summer.

Many of the quilts he'd looked at were dyed striking colors or pieced more intricately, but this one, the plainest, was also the softest. It also happened to be the most expensive, but his salary had been accumulating dust for years. He needed something to spend it on.

He'd also thought, being completely honest, that she'd be more likely to accept something that didn't look particularly special.

She still hadn't said anything, she just shook it out and held it up, letting it hang to the floor. It also hid her face from him.

"This is beautiful," she said at last.

"I'm glad you like it. I remembered what you said about wishing for more blankets," he said matter-of-factly. "So now you have one."

He reached to help her fold it up, taking it from her hands, and she turned away abruptly, but not before he saw her red eyes.

"Thank you so much. I love the blanket... Is it really Christmas?"

Umm. Not technically. I tend to lose track, but I think it's November. Happy Thanksgiving."

She'd laughed shakily, and he'd been pleased that she didn't try to refuse it.

Claire recalled him to the present, gesturing at the seat across from her. "You better strap in if we're going to jump again."

"Eleven more jumps," Basher confirmed. "Hold onto your drink." He quickly grabbed some of the dried food they'd brought with them. Now that Earth was no longer closed off by the Spo, it was easier to get human food. Basher grabbed three granola bars and sat across from Claire. He pulled up the waist strap that was dangling on the floor and knotted it over his lap. The jumps weren't too violent, particularly if the biocomputer was good, but it was easier to strap in than to grab the table each time.

"Did you send a message to Sam and Nat yet?" Claire asked. "They need to know that Faal is expecting them to try for Akemi. He'll have some sort of trap in place."

"We told them."

"I guess our plan worked too well," Claire said.

"Too well?"

"I mean, we wanted the Diadina to request Faal... but apparently she requested Akemi, too."

"Or the Pontifex did. We knew it was a possibility..." Basher chewed a bite and swallowed. "I expected the Diadina to hint rather than describe the stolen computer to her husband, but perhaps she knew more than we realized."

The lights of the cabin turned briefly blue to indicate another jump. Claire put her finger over the straw in her drink to keep it from spilling, and Basher quickly swallowed his next bite while they waited.

Blue light. Rushing, vertigo, jump.

"So, now what?" Claire said. "We let Sam and Nat try to steal Akemi from the Pontifex? Faal knows exactly what they're there for."

Basher opened his second granola bar. "Or we let Shara kill Faal. She keeps asking, and that option is growing on me. It would simplify things a lot."

Claire grimaced skeptically, which made Basher smile. "Maybe she could do it," he said. "Sam and Nat must have brought her for a reason."

She nodded and they ate and sipped in companionable silence, pausing when the light turned blue again.

"I'm glad I went back," Claire said abruptly. "I'm glad I got to see Faal's estate again."

"Are you?"

"I was terrified, of course, but seeing it with someone else was —cathartic."

"I'm glad."

"I'm even..." She paused and then rushed on. "I'm even glad I was with you. We have this weird problem of knowing too much about each other from Akemi's videos—but essentially being strangers. And going to Faal's zoo, that was real. It cost us both something to go there, and what we learned about each other—it counts. Does that make any sense?"

Basher finished his bite slowly. "It does. As a police officer, before all of this, I didn't exactly trust my partner, or any of the guys I was assigned with, until after the first confrontation. I was on narcotics the first two years... Anyway, I knew they were good guys, but I didn't really *know* them until after our first arrest."

"Yeah, something like that," Claire agreed.

She smiled at him while she plugged her straw again, and Basher felt his stomach twist. "There's something I have to tell you," he blurted out. "Sage has been caught by the Merith."

Blue light. Rushing, vertigo, jump.

Her face changed so fast it hurt to watch. Her expression was torn between shock and betrayal.

"I'm so sorry," Basher said, and he even discovered it was true as he said it. He wished that this wasn't her reality. "I saw him in the videos from the death chamber on Merith Prime."

"Did they—Is he dead?"

"No, not yet."

She wrapped her arms around herself as if her ribs ached. "Not yet," she repeated.

"I can—I can let you know if it happens. You don't have to watch."

She looked up at him bleakly. "If I was there, wouldn't you watch?"

Basher shook his head. "If you were there, I'd go get you."

Claire shook her head, as if to ward off that thought and blindly undid her lap belt. "I need to go."

She staggered out of the tiny cabin, and didn't quite make it to her bunk before the next blue light. Basher could see her through the door as she braced her hands on both walls of the narrow walkway.

Rushing, vertigo, jump.

She'd left her cup on the tiny table between them, and a thin stream of coffee floated out of the straw and then splatted on the floor.

She crawled into her bunk, tucked the blanket around herself, and pulled the top of it over her head.

22

AKEMI'S DREAMS were even more jumbled that night. Perhaps the trip had indeed made her crazy. It was a sobering thought.

"But I'm well enough to wonder if I'm crazy," Akemi told herself. "So it can't be too bad."

She tried to pull herself together, and she was significantly clearer-headed by the time Faal and the Pontifex returned in the morning.

Faal was already talking as they entered. "So, the humans here may be acquainted with her."

Akemi perked up her ears. The humans *here*? That could be Sam and Nat! She wanted to ask more questions, but Faal seemed in no rush to allow that. He'd yet to turn on her voice box or even a basic text option.

Very well—perhaps she could bypass him. She *had* influenced Faal to bring Drench with him. (She really hoped Drench was okay.)

Akemi focused on the Pontifex's flickering, *ignis fatuus* mental presence. She knew she couldn't send anything as detailed as words to him, but she could perhaps give a general impression. Flattery was always a good bet, so Akemi sent a wave of curiosity to the Pontifex.

Who are you? How did you become the most powerful Merith in the galaxy? What are you to him? She knew he wouldn't get her exact questions, but maybe the tone.

Faal was oblivious to what she was doing but the Pontifex froze. "What is that?" he demanded. "What are you doing?"

Faal looked honestly surprised. "I have done nothing. I was about to turn on this screen so that you could interact with the computer."

They stared at each other in suspicion, and Akemi wanted to cackle with delight. That had worked even better than she'd hoped! And if it was that easy to make these two chauvinistic Merith turn on each other, what couldn't she do with a little more time?

She sent a wave of apology to the Pontifex. *I'm sorry. I did not mean to confuse you. I'm sorry.*

He slowly straightened to his full height, a good six inches above Faal. "Are you sure it is not a *Crosspoint* brain?"

"A Crosspoint? No, it could not be. Is it..." Faal's skin flushed red around his eye. "Is it *speaking* to you?"

The Pontifex glared at him. "Not clearly, but—are you certain you did not know it was capable of telepathy? Because I do not appreciate being manipulated." Faal started to talk but the Pontifex wasn't done. "Our friendship is of long standing, and I allow you much license, but if you brought this here to spy on me, I will have your title and your planet!"

Faal raised his left hand and placed it on his throat. "I swear on my life that I had no intention of spying on you with this computer. I did not know it could talk to you mind-to-mind. If anyone else said so, I would not believe them."

Akemi decided to keep her thoughts to herself for the time being. She might, probably *would*, want to drive a wedge here eventually, but she didn't know enough yet. She could bide her time, figure out the dynamics here, and make a plan.

"If you're lying, you will regret it." The Pontifex said it simply, but it was nonetheless threatening for being spoken with such casual assurance. "Turn on the screen."

When Akemi felt the connection take, she immediately wrote in Merith, "Hello, my name is Akemi. I am honored to meet the Pontifex."

"It is at least well-mannered."

"I am a female of my species. The pronoun 'she' would be appreciated."

The Pontifex smiled grimly. "And did you or did you not just communicate with my mind without my permission?"

He sure was taking that personally. "I did not mean to offend you. I was not sure that I would be allowed to communicate with you, and I wanted to make my presence known."

Faal's eye was now so dilated she could hardly see the reddish gold color of his iris. He was not happy with this development.

The Pontifex stared at her, and she realized he was trying to do what she'd just done and send her a thought. He was testing her.

"I'm afraid it only goes one way," she wrote. "It is not a skill I have perfected, though if I focus..."

His presence was still clear in her mind's eye, and she could sense his effort, but not what thought was behind it. It was something too complicated—too Merith for her to understand. "No. I cannot understand you."

"Is this something other humans can do?" he asked suddenly. "I have three human guests at this time, and if they are mind-talkers..."

Akemi felt breathless with excitement. *Three* humans? Perhaps Basher and Sam and Nat? "Humans are not telepathic at all," she answered. "Only my unique—situation seems to allow for it." And she had a great teacher: Drench.

"What else can you do?" the Pontifex asked.

"What would you like me to do?"

"Tell me what you have discovered about Faal during your stay at his estate."

Faal clenched a fist, and Akemi did not immediately answer. She focused on sending the Pontifex a sense of caution. *Not in front of him. Too dangerous. Send him away.*

The Pontifex nodded slightly. "That is fair. Faal, I will speak to you again presently. I hope we can have another hawking match before the week is out."

Faal did not like being dismissed even in that courteous way, but he went.

"Thank you," Akemi said. "He hates me."

"Do you hate him?"

"Yes. He's terrible."

The Pontifex waved a hand. "Don't be boring. Everyone thinks Faal is terrible. Impress me. What have you discovered of Faal in the last weeks?"

"What would you like to know? He is a sadist who enjoys owning sentient or nearly sentient species. His estate..." Akemi did a quick search of the network she was hooked up to. "His estate has better security than your palace."

"Everyone knows this. *Impress* me."

"He is about three phases from insanity, in the way the Merith categorize it, being an obsessive, paranoid egomaniac."

The Pontifex gave a crack of laughter. "Only three phases away? I would have said two. I prefer the crazy ones, when they're as intelligent as he. Tell me something I don't know."

She knew he didn't really expect new information. He was merely testing her, finding out how deductive she was and what she cared about. It was one of the classic Merith ways to analyze an alien mind—getting them to share their views on a mutual enemy, which acted as a constant. Of course, this was complicated because Faal was actually his friend, although it was clear that the Pontifex did not trust him.

"Nothing else?" he asked. "Faal's dog could tell me these things."

"He murdered his father."

The Pontifex smiled. "Very good. Not many people know that."

"Did you?"

"I am asking the questions, O Inanimate One," he said mockingly. "And what do you make of Faal's patricide?"

Akemi actually wasn't entirely sure. She'd learned of his father's death from Drench. Drench hadn't been there to witness it either, but he'd learned of it from a previous Melifleur.

"He's proud of killing his father," Akemi ventured, "but his father was also a proxy for himself. He hated his father, but he also hates himself."

"Interesting."

"May I ask a question?" Akemi said.

"You've earned one."

"Who are the humans that are visiting you?"

"Oh." He seemed to be recalling his thoughts from somewhere very different. "The Diadina invited them for the Unity celebration. Their leader is called Dark Eyes, I believe."

"Their human name?"

"I do not recall."

Akemi hid her disappointment. She didn't dare ask if she might talk to them. She'd have to figure that out on her own. The Pontifex left her soon after. "The Diadina deserves a visit; she has certainly made this an interesting Unity Celebration for me. She is always so considerate."

. . .

IN HER OWN WAY, the Diadina loved the Pontifex, and she was pleased when he sought her out the morning after his hawking duel with Faal. Her Master of Chambers announced that he was on his way from the treasury vault. That gave her time to change into something appropriate and to conceal the puckered redness around her eye. When she was stressed, her eye became bloodshot and the skin around it, which was very sensitive, tended to crack and bleed.

She'd watched the game from the privacy of her own room and had been stunned to see Faal outmatch her husband. She took almost as much pride in his hawking ability as he did. Even worse, she was unable to guess whether this would be a positive or negative thing in their relationship. Her husband respected strength and cunning and self-discipline above all things, and despite his loss, Faal's display might earn his favor.

She rubbed fish oil onto the raw skin under her eye and then patted it with a gray powder to blend it in. She reclined on the couch and allowed one of her attendants to drip four drops of a potent brew into her eye. It was an anti-inflammatory and would force the blood vessels in her eye to constrict, minimizing the bloodshot look for a while. Unfortunately, it also burned like acid for a moment.

She resisted the urge to rub it, merely blinking her inner eyelid and waiting for the burn to subside. When it was done, she rose and draped a new robe around herself. She had the same attendant groom her shoulder feathers.

She sat gracefully and leaned over her sand table, tracing designs in the smooth, black sand that allowed the yellow color of the wood to show through. She'd only half depicted one of the standard Cliff Dive motifs when he arrived.

"Ah, my pretty." He walked around behind her and placed a hand on her shoulder. "Your chambers are always so peaceful."

She ceased scratching in the sand and looked up at him. "Do you need peace this morning?"

"Ah, no, as a matter of fact, I do not. I rather desire to show you a very interesting sight."

"Oh?" If he did not want to speak of the hawking game, she would not bring it up.

He escorted her out of her chambers and through the informal practice gardens.

"Are we going to the treasury?" She couldn't help wondering if this had to do with Faal, but she maintained an innocent voice. She had passed the information to her husband with great finesse, but the kernel was simple: that Faal had acquired a questionable AI device of unique origin. She had not even dared to suggest that Faal was keeping it from her husband, or that he might want to inquire into the situation. She left it entirely up to him and tried to appear as if she had forgotten the whole thing.

He was unlikely to believe that, as he knew, or guessed, the depth of her animosity toward Faal, but they both lived in a world of veneers and appearances. He would respect the pretense of her indifference almost more than the real thing. Real indifference would cost her nothing, and thus earn her no respect. An assumed indifference, on the other hand, required great self-control.

And her husband did respect her, she knew that. It had started in the beginning with her feud with Faal. That had whetted his curiosity and something of his acquisitiveness. But in the eleven years since their marriage, she liked to think that she had earned his respect for her own qualities, and not only in juxtaposition to her enemy.

WHILE WAITING FOR THE PONTIFEX, Akemi made some headway in accessing the palace networks, mainly because the Pontifex did not take her as seriously as Faal. While Faal had physically isolated her from his house systems until he was ready, the Pontifex had merely quarantined her within his system.

She could work with that, but it was slow going. Her mind kept wandering and certain memories seemed to be looping in her head. She *did not* want to think about Nat screaming while the Rik tried to re-contour her brain. She also did not want to think about the last time she'd seen Claire...

When Claire had selfishly traded Akemi to Faal for her own freedom.

Although... Akemi paused. Hadn't that been her own idea? There were two conflicting memories in her head for a moment.

But no, the memory replayed again and Akemi ground invisible teeth. Claire had clearly given her to Faal to selfishly save herself. She had even used the same words Jenelle used. And Basher had let her! Claire must have completely wrapped him around her finger to get him to go along with it.

Akemi didn't like the feeling that came with that memory. When the Pontifex came to the treasury room with the Diadina, Akemi was in a bleak mood.

The Pontifex didn't even address her as he entered; he was talking to his wife. "You see, my dear, this is Faal's computer, the one you told me about. I thought you might like to see it."

The Diadina was as beautiful and delicate as everyone said, but her expression was shrewd. "Is it indeed 'questionable'?" she asked. "It looks like a normal biocomputer to me."

"I believe it is extremely questionable, but I have not yet decided how to proceed."

"How so?"

"Akemi, talk to the Diadina." He emphasized the word *talk*, and Akemi knew what he meant.

She focused on the Diadina's presence. It felt more stressed and brittle than the Pontifex's presence, and Akemi wondered briefly why she was so nervous. And as if recalling something she'd known for years—Akemi suddenly knew exactly why the Diadina was afraid. But how did Akemi know that secret? Had Drench told her? She didn't remember him talking about the Diadina at all...

"Akemi," the Pontifex repeated. "Why don't you talk to the Diadina?"

Akemi was in no mood to humor him. She sent a wave of unease toward the Diadina. *I know about you. I know everything.*

The Diadina rubbed the skin under her eye, uncertain.

"There, did it speak to you? Did you feel it?" the Pontifex asked.

"I'm—not certain. Perhaps. My source told me it was sentient. She did not say it was telepathic."

"Perhaps she did not know. Faal seemed genuinely surprised at the capability."

"Is it safe?" the Diadina asked. "If it can read our minds?" Akemi sensed the heightened tension in the woman. She certainly didn't want to spill her secrets, even to her husband.

"Probably not." The Pontifex rubbed his beak in satisfaction. "But I like dangerous things. And if it is dangerous to us, it can be dangerous to others."

"Indeed."

"Don't say 'indeed' in that tone of voice. You know the power of a reversible weapon as well as I."

"I do, but they are dangerous." Her reply was emphatic, and Akemi wondered what weapon the woman had in mind.

Akemi didn't realize she was still linked to the Diadina, but apparently her feelings were still carrying over. The Diadina turned away sharply. "No! I won't tell you anything."

The Pontifex looked startled, and the Diadina shuddered. "I don't like it. It should be destroyed. Nothing that can read our minds should be kept in the palace. Don't you say the same about the Crosspoint?"

"This computer is rather more vulnerable than a Crosspoint, my dear."

"I don't care. I don't like it."

Akemi kicked herself. Why was she acting like an idiot, scaring someone who could have her killed? What had come over her?

"I apologize," Akemi wrote on the screen. "I did not mean to pry; I was merely curious about you. All the galaxy has heard of the Diadina."

"Flattery," the Diadina spat, backing away. "Do you think I'm an empty-headed swallow? This thing is not safe," she repeated.

"I can be better than safe," Akemi said. "I can be loyal."

She sent, as strongly as she could, her hatred of Faal. If there was anything that this woman might value, it was that.

The Diadina paused, and the Pontifex looked from her to his wife. "I felt that. It hates Faal too, doesn't it? Is it attempting to ally with you?"

"I'm not certain."

"I'm only establishing common ground," Akemi wrote. "You cannot be surprised at my attitude, given our earlier conversation."

"No, indeed," the Pontifex said. "I tend to like people who hate Faal, as I suspect he tends to like those who hate me."

The Diadina shook her head. "This thing should be destroyed. It violates the standards. It thinks and knows and has no body—it should not exist. Or better yet, give it to the humans and send them all away. They make me uncomfortable."

"Suddenly so conservative?" the Pontifex asked mockingly. "I don't recall you citing the standards when Faal started his Rik campaign. You even refrained from criticizing him. I thought you approved."

She shook her head. "I have no love for the Rik, but they don't violate the standards the way this thing does."

Akemi rifled through the few databases she had access to, but she found nothing about the specific 'standards' they were talking about.

"You may be right," the Pontifex said. "I must ponder. In the meantime, you may enjoy watching Faal writhe at my indecision."

The Diadina backed all the way to the doorway, and she bowed low to the Pontifex before leaving.

"Interesting. You scared her more than I expected," the Pontifex said.

"I didn't mean to."

The Pontifex dismissed it with a wave. "She has her secrets; I've always respected that. If you discovered anything from her, I do not wish to know. What I do wish to know is what you've discovered in the palace archives so far. My shadows tell me you've already hacked into three of our eight subsystems."

"Ah. I thought it was rather easy."

"No, don't be falsely modest. They did not clear a path for you. I merely told them to observe your activities, and they did."

"So. You don't mind if I keep going?"

"I'm curious to see what interests you. If you take advantage of my tolerance, you will regret it."

"What would exceed your tolerance?"

He appeared to think deeply before he answered. "I don't know. My tolerance is mercurial. You will find out when it happens."

"I appreciate the warning."

"In the meantime, I have thought of a first task for you. Last night I dueled with Faal on the hawking field and it did not go well. I lost for the first time in decades. I would like you to analyze the match and tell me your thoughts. Your somewhat unique familiarity with Faal may give you an edge I lack."

He went to the door and said his favorite phrase before he left. "Impress me."

23

DRENCH IMMEDIATELY SEARCHED for Akemi when he came out of his trance. A wave of vertigo swept over him, however, and he helplessly waited for it to pass. He felt a terrible lack of direction, as neither his roots nor his branches felt truly *down*. He could tell by the temperature and air and moisture that he must be on the surface of Merith Prime, but his visual nodes were so blinded by the sunlight that he could see nothing. The voices of Merith around him were loud and then quiet and did not help him orient himself. If only he could tell which way was up! He *hated* space travel.

Then he felt a leaf-loosening thump, and his branches shook as he was levered into a hole in the ground. He felt the blessed crumbly coolness of dirt being packed around his roots. In fact, they pushed the dirt too high around his trunk, but he could wiggle that part loose later. He was relieved to be upright, his equilibrium returning quickly. The sun was hot and heavy on his leaves and the air was dry. Drench automatically began secreting a heavier waxy coating to protect his leaves and himself from dehydration.

He heard Faal making a speech to someone, the Pontifex no doubt, but Drench largely ignored the pompous phrases. He made a mental note of the conversation—he was a good observer—but he focused his efforts on locating Akemi.

He was afraid the long, silent voyage—an odyssey of dreams for him—might have been a nightmare for her. He had done his best for her, but she was not a tree. As far as he understood her nature, and he understood her better than she realized, there were two major problems with her mind that might have caused problems on her trip.

The first was purely physical. He had realized during the trip that the gray matter of her brain, the tissue that had been ripped from her animal body, was beginning to degrade. Drench suppressed a shudder at the horrific image. The dead portions were still slight enough that she had not realized, but the lesions were definitely there and getting worse. They were vague and blotchy patches of her consciousness that indicated rot. He was loath to tell her of it. She thought of the trees as relatively unemotional, but that wasn't true. The Melifleurs had as broad a range of emotion as the humans did, and he had no desire to tell his small friend that she was dying.

She'd never seen the forests weep after the storm of '42, when the rendered, lifeless limbs of family lay tangled with the living for months and years. Their sorrow was shared communally in the deepest vibrations. She'd never seen a pair of lonely pines on the heights, companions for hundreds of years, slowly say goodbye as the mountain eroded beneath them until one was claimed. She hadn't seen the solemn waiting for another hundred years before the erosion reached the next and he could join her.

Drench knew about death, and it was no small thing to tell a child whose roots were entwined with your own that the rot was overtaking them.

The other problem with Akemi's mind was harder to explain. It seemed to him that there was something lacking, a completion she was supposed to have, but did not. It manifested as a restlessness in her soul that went far beyond her animalistic tendencies. He'd had time to think about it and he'd decided that, in the depths of her soul, she did not know why she existed.

Drench could not imagine such a horrible and empty way of living; thus it had taken him a long time to come up with that idea. Once it occurred to him, he realized that it explained much of her desperation and fear, beyond that of being taken away from her home and family. Even now, he could hardly imagine how she could function if that was really the case, and he dreaded to ask and confirm it.

"Akemi?" Drench sought around him for her familiar, silvery presence, a presence designed for movement and yet locked into stillness, like a patch of rain suspended in midair.

"Drench! You're here!"

He was somewhat prepared for her reaction, and when she threw the weight of her presence around him, he revised his analogy. She was more like a tornado than a rainstorm.

"Apparently you are well also," he said. "I was worried about you."

He could tell that physically they were no more than a hundred yards apart, which was a relief. He could reach a fellow tree at much further distances, but he hadn't been sure how far their tenuous connection would stretch. He was surprised when Akemi drew away from him almost immediately, and Drench felt cold at the sudden loss of her warmth.

"They must have put you in the courtyard outside the treasury room." She was busy doing something complicated with the negative space of the computers around her. "I'm hacking," she explained. "Just a minute."

Now that Drench had time to observe Akemi, he became more concerned. There was a frenetic quality to her thoughts that was distinctly worse than it had been before. There was also a new darkness to the cast of her mind, and the lesions were larger... had the rot been accelerated by the trip?

"Is something wrong?" he asked.

"No. But I need to keep working at this... I almost have access to the communications network, and if I get that, I can find out what humans are here."

"Oh. Of course, I know that is important to you."

There was a grim edge of satisfaction to her work, but she had none of the carefree joy he'd experienced from her before. "Okay, I'll pause for a moment," she said. "I'm supposed to analyze the Pontifex's game with Faal. The Pontifex lost."

She described the game, and Drench suppressed another bout of nausea. He definitely shed a few leaves. "So what have you gleaned about the Pontifex's loss?" he asked.

"Well, I've only had the video a short while. I thought he would download it or send it to me, but he made me dig it out of the archives myself. But now I have it—" Akemi pictured two birds wheeling through the air in a tight spiral.

Drench groaned. "Stop, please. If you cannot tell me without picturing it, you must not tell me." He wiggled his roots and waited to regain his center. He could tell Akemi was rather contemptuous of his spatial weakness and he tried to brush it off. "Someday I'll think of an equivalent and show you how it feels."

"Yeah, you work on that. Anyway, I also found the files that recorded each motion of their capture gloves, and let me tell you, that's some complicated junk. It's not just finding out what each motion or finger movement or wrist twist might do, it's figuring out the *degree* to which each motion translates to wing extension, angle, pitch... ouch!"

Drench had given her an admonitory tap, as he would a sapling, when she started to picture the birds again.

Akemi lashed back at him, suddenly furious. "It's not my fault if you can't handle it. If you don't want to know, then go away."

Drench paused to let the sun warm away the negative feeling.

"Why are you angry with me?" he asked.

"I'm not," Akemi said. "I'm angry about other things. And I don't really care about the hawking. It's more important that I access the communications network."

Drench waited.

"I have a plan to get away from Faal. And to settle some scores while I'm at it."

"What scores? You sound like a Merith when you speak in that way."

Akemi ignored Drench, but he could still read most of her thoughts. She'd been momentarily glad to have him back, but if "he was just going to ask questions with that condemning tone of voice," she wished he'd never come.

"I came here for you," Drench said, "because you asked me to stay with you. I don't demand your gratitude, but I thought you would at least be glad. I'm afraid you're not yourself—and I'm afraid I know why."

24

AKEMI DIDN'T RESPOND to Drench. There was so much else for her to do. She was almost... yes! She now had access to the communications network of the palace, which also gave limited access to the broader planetary grid.

It should not have been that hard, but her mind kept wandering to the moment over a month ago, when Nat had fought the Rik outside the Spo embassy. It had been such a horrible moment. Akemi had seen Nat get somersaulted off the observation platform, and Nat's glasses had fallen all the way to the bottom of the chasm. For a few horrible moments, Akemi had thought she was seeing Nat's death. It turned out that Nat had grabbed an exposed pipe, and she managed to climb to safety on her own.

And no thanks to Claire or her Rik friends—they had looked Nat in the eye and done nothing to help her!

Hadn't they?

Yes, she could remember seeing them run away, leaving Nat dangling from the pipe. How dare they?

Focus, Akemi told herself. Plenty of time to think of that later.

"Akemi," Drench interrupted. "There is something I must tell you. It is painful—"

"Not now." A list of names was now available to Akemi, a directory of all the guests currently at the palace. It was the work of seconds to search the few hundred names and find the three which could change everything for her.

Sam Locklear

Natsuki Fujimara

Shara Davis

She'd known it was a possibility that Sam and Nat were here, but she'd hardly dared hope it was true.

And Shara...

Akemi mentally ground her teeth. She had quite a history with Shara. But what were Sam and Nat thinking when they brought her here? A Rik assassin? Who exactly were Sam and Nat planning to kill? Plus, the death chamber was less than a mile from here, where Rik were being slaughtered every day.

Hm. But Shara's presence *did* open up several possibilities. This could work even better than Akemi had hoped.

Since Akemi had access now, it would be simple to send a message to Nat's tablet, but she knew everything she did was being monitored. The Pontifex had made it clear that she was free to explore, but he was totally keeping tabs on everything she did.

How could she say anything to Nat with the Pontifex reading it?

Unless—would Nat still have her glasses?

On Selta, Akemi had communicated with Sam, Nat, and Claire through their smart glasses. Using a proprietary signal, she'd been able to see and hear what they saw and send text to their lenses.

It took Akemi nearly an hour to whittle out a place for her signal in the vast communications network of Merith Prime, but it wasn't impossible. When she had the space, Akemi started with a ping to the glasses. Even if the glasses were here, and working, she would have to reestablish the connection. Also, it was nearly dinner time, and she didn't want to make Nat freak out if she was dining with a bunch of aliens.

Akemi waited, tense, to see if there would be a response. It seemed like hours, but it was only a few seconds until the glasses responded with the handshake protocol. Akemi could have cheered.

Nat, she sent. *Do you have your glasses on?*

Nat didn't need glasses, she had good eyesight, but Akemi thought it was entirely possible that Nat still wore the glasses for sentimental reasons. Nat pretended to be a tough, no-nonsense cadet, but she had a soft spot for her sister.

Akemi felt a momentary stab of guilt as she thought of Nat. Nat wouldn't appreciate Akemi's new escape plan. She'd be appalled actually, but then, it wasn't her business.

Akemi had every right to finish things her way. Her life had been destroyed by the Rik, and by Shara in particular. A swirl of memories threatened to sweep over Akemi again, but she fought it off. The Rik deserved everything they were going to get, and Akemi was going to make sure Shara didn't weasel out of it. She deserved death as much as the rest of them, as did anyone who helped the Rik.

"Akemi, is that you?" Nat's voice came weakly at first, and then louder as she 'pinched' the right lens to increase volume. "Can you hear me?"

Yes, I'm here.

Nat fumbled with the glasses, nearly dropping them in her excitement. "Are you alright? Talk to me. Basher messaged us that you were here."

Basher? How did he know I was here?

"He went to Faal's estate to get you. We thought Faal had left you there. Are you alright?"

I'm fine. Better than fine, as a matter of fact. I have incredible clarity.

"Good, good—Sam, I'm talking to Akemi," Nat said. She was breathless, and Akemi could hear tears in her voice. "She sounds okay."

Sam came into view, smiling at her. "Akemi, I figured it wouldn't be long before you found a way to contact us. Claire and Basher told us last night that Faal brought you here."

Akemi tensed up at this.

Claire and Basher? she asked. *What was* she *doing there? Was this your plan?*

"It was and it wasn't," Nat explained. "We planned to get Faal here, but we hoped he would leave you at home. Claire and Basher went to rescue you."

Akemi laughed mirthlessly. *How did that work out for them?*

"Er, they didn't get caught, thankfully," Nat said. "But they were really disappointed you weren't there, obviously."

Pity, Akemi said.

"That's..." Nat seemed at a loss. "Is that all you have to say? Claire risked going back to the zoo to get you. I thought you'd be grateful—"

Grateful? It's her fault I was at his estate in the first place! I guess I am grateful, even if it's too little, too late.

Akemi heard Nat gasp, and she saw Sam's frown as Nat repeated the gist of what she said.

"Akemi, what did Faal say to you?" Nat asked with careful intensity. "Not that I blame you for being bitter. I have no idea what you've been through, but you were the one who chose to go with Faal. You saved Claire."

I saved her? Why would I save a Rik-loving tramp like her? She bartered me to Faal for her life. She owes me.

"It wasn't like that... I was there."

Do you think I'm lying? Claire would have done anything to get away from him. She offered me up while we were in the elevator with Faal.

Nat repeated her words, and Sam rubbed his head, wincing when he hit the bruise. "Akemi must be confused. Something's happened to her..."

Darn right something happened to me, but I am not confused, Akemi sent. *I know exactly what happened. I can picture it perfectly.*

"Well." Nat made a pushing gesture, as if to put all that to the side. "We can figure that out later. Right now, I want to get you away from here. Where are you?"

I have some things to do first.

"Things to do first?" Nat echoed. "Are you joking? What's more important than getting you to safety?" Nat turned around as the door to her suite opened. Through her lenses, Akemi could see Shara entering the room. Akemi felt an unfamiliar tightening of hatred.

Shara was the one who'd started this whole nightmare for them. She was the one who'd tricked Akemi into trusting her, and then used Akemi as a hostage to get Nat. Then she'd put them in a shuttle and sent them to her Rik supervisors who had tortured Nat and then torn Akemi's brain out of her body.

Tell Shara hello for me.

Nat's hand was shaking as she adjusted her glasses. "Akemi says hello," she said.

Then Merith soldiers burst in their door.

After forming her own miniature communications network during the talk with her sister, Akemi had also sent a message to the palace administrator informing him that one of the humans visiting the Pontifex was not a human at all, but rather a Rik. She'd provided enough evidence of Shara's appearance, past, and credentials to make that official take notice.

The four soldiers surrounded Shara and put electric cuffs on her ankles.

Shara put her hands on her hips. "Excuse me. What's happening?"

Another large cuff went around her neck.

The first soldier spoke. "A secure source has informed us that you are a Rik masquerading as a human. The Pontifex does not tolerate deception."

"But—" Nat started to speak and then stopped.

"It is our understanding that you were not aware of this deception. Is that information correct?" the soldier asked.

Akemi had orchestrated this carefully. She didn't want Nat sent to the death chamber with Shara.

Tell him it's correct. Don't be an idiot.

"Why are you doing this?" Nat said. "She's your friend."

a) She is not my friend; she destroyed our lives, and now she's going to pay for it.

b) It'll be leverage for me with the Pontifex.

c) She talks too much.

The soldiers apparently took Sam and Nat's stunned silence as confirmation, and they proceeded to take Shara away. Sam and Nat watched the soldiers frog march Shara toward one of the low outbuildings.

"Where are you taking her?" Sam called.

One Merith looked back over his shoulder. "Temporary holding cell. She'll be taken to the death chamber tomorrow."

25

FAAL HAD SETTLED into his usual suite. It was the finest in the front wing of the main complex, with jeweled windows and a balcony that was nearly as large as the entire bedroom.

He received the Pontifex cautiously that evening, knowing that he played a dangerous game during this visit. They went out to the balcony while one of Faal's servants brought them a Tergre Slack, a drink they both enjoyed.

"You were right in your guess," the Pontifex said, looking up at the clear, starry sky. "The Akemi computer reported the false human today."

Faal gave a grim smile. "As I told you. It's an extremely capable adversary."

"As are you, my friend. Congratulations again on the hawking match. It's a game that will be replayed for years."

Faal inclined his head but did not speak.

"That reminds me. Is there a connection between the computer and the other humans? She asked me about them."

"Ah. Did she?" Faal remained noncommittal. He knew, of course, that Sam and Nat were involved in some complicated plot to get Akemi back, and he did not appreciate that they'd involved the Pontifex and the Diadina in their plan. It had inconvenienced him at an inopportune time, but he'd devised a rather ingenious way to make them pay for it.

"You don't answer," the Pontifex said. "Are they connected?"

"Yes. But may I say that this is a show you would enjoy more if I don't tell you the climax?"

The Pontifex laughed. "If you say so, I believe it. You are one of the only people in the world who never fails to impress me." He took a sip of his drink. "The Diadina is the other. She certainly took Akemi in violent dislike."

"She occasionally has excellent instincts."

"Generous! I must tell her you said so."

"Please do." After a respectful interval, Faal drew forth a parchment. "Have you considered my proposal for your Act of Service?"

The Pontifex nodded. Every eleven years it was traditional for the Pontifex to perform a service that would benefit all the Merith people—a somewhat flexible definition. The Act of Service was an opportunity to solidify his position, but finding something that actually benefited most of his species was no small job.

"I have considered your proposal." The Pontifex threw back the rest of his drink. "And I agree with you. The events today only confirmed it. A Rik penetrated my palace. Where else may they be? It provides the perfect context for this Act of Service."

The Pontifex took the documents from Faal and signed the declaration.

When he left an hour later, called away to mingle with other guests before the midnight fire-show, Faal remained on the balcony. The declaration contained the plans for a complete eradication of the Rik species—all of them—not just the ones who'd taken human bodies. It also contained a provision to exterminate any human found off Earth, who could be considered a Rik sympathizer. If the humans did not agree to this restriction, the Pontifex committed to complete war with no less than the invasion of Earth and subjugation of their species. It would be a glorious Act of Service from a political standpoint, as the Rik body-stealing technology could truly be considered a threat to all the species of the galaxy. The human planet was also known to be a rich plum, and most Merith would relish a new, almost certain-to-succeed war effort.

Now that these plans were marked with the seal of the Pontifex, Faal would be his deputy to carry out the eradication. With the Pontifex's backing, the main Merith leaders would be united with him.

The first flare of the fire-show rose into the air several minutes later. It was a concentrated chemical flare, and as it reached nearly to its zenith, it hit a pocket of methane trapped in the lower atmosphere, and the gas exploded with a flash of purple light and an audible pop. The fire-shows at the Pontifical palace were, of course, beyond compare.

They used to take advantage of random pockets of natural gases that formed over the tectonically active deserts. Now the pockets were seeded before the show, with slightly varying composition, to change the color, size, and shape of the explosions. Faal finished his drink and absently watched the next flare.

This would indeed be an life-changing year for him.

He'd been unsure whether tampering with Akemi's brain would work, but so far it was succeeding better than his cautious technician had promised him.

Faal had conceived the idea of reprogramming Akemi on the night that he'd received the summons from the Pontifex. He'd shut Akemi down in the heat of his anger at her continued impertinence, and it suddenly occurred to him—why should he not adjust that part of her? She said that he could not harm her, but she missed the point. It didn't matter if he could harm her, if he could *change* her.

He'd known his plan was tenuous at best, but he'd sown the

seed right then, threatening to turn her off for the duration of the trip to Merith Prime. He'd pretended to do it in a fit of pique, but he knew that it would be the perfect opportunity to try out his idea.

Part of the lie had been truth. She *could* have gone insane during the trip, but he was willing to risk it for the possibility that she might be sane... Frighteningly sane, and with a different set of priorities.

It wasn't possible to simply change her personality or thoughts. Or at least, if it *was* possible, his technology specialist had no idea how to do it. Faal had been on the verge of throttling him when he finally said what he could do.

He thought it might be possible to make a complete copy of the template of her brain, alter the copy, and re-uploaded it to the biocomputer.

The copy could be manipulated, memory banks altered, connections and keywords added, and whole sections deleted. The copy could then be inserted into the biocomputer while Akemi was "off" and when she was rebooted, the copy would be incorporated into her operating system.

While the copy would not necessarily *supersede* the original, it would drastically alter the composition of the whole. The technician speculated that changes emphasized with strong emotion would be more likely to overwrite her prior experiences.

Of course, this would create a dangerous and unpredictable split personality, which had made the technician very uncomfortable. Faal himself had taken a whole evening to ponder the possible ramifications of introducing a dangerously unbalanced entity to the Pontifex's palace. On the whole, he'd decided that the potential success outweighed the potential disasters.

After careful deliberation (the technician explained that changing memories would be extremely time consuming), they'd selected three memories to alter.

The technician selected the first. He'd explained that Akemi's emotions and memories involving her sister were by far the most powerful. It was the central relationship of her entire life, and they could use that to fuel the changes.

The Rik had done her and her sister tremendous personal harm, but somehow, she'd managed to largely subdue the worst memories. The most painful one was when she'd seen the Rik trying to re-contour her sister's brain. The specialist didn't even have to change that memory, he merely substituted out the word 'experiment' and put in the word 'torture.' Then he copied and pasted it into five more subsets of her memory. Every time she lost focus, she would remember her sister screaming as the Rik *tortured* her.

The second memory was related. She'd told the specialist how three Rik saved her sister after an assassin knocked Nat into a deep chasm. They had risked their lives to rescue her, and this seemed to have gone a long way in reconciling both Nat and Akemi to them.

Changing this memory was a bit more technical and required an actual visual change. If the changes took effect correctly, Akemi would remember the Rik walking away from Nat in her moment of need.

The last memory was a bit easier, as Faal had actually been present and knew exactly what had occurred. It was the memory of Akemi offering herself to Faal in return for Claire's freedom. Faal merely had the technician delete all the protesting and tears that Claire had actually displayed and replaced them with a simple statement: 'Take her, not me.'

Besides the three memories, they had added a bit of knowledge to her memory banks. Specifically, some damaging information about the Diadina. It was far easier to add information than to alter existing data.

One of Faal's servants came onto the balcony with another drink, interrupting his thoughts.

"There's a note for you, sir." The servant handed him a small slip of paper.

Shara has been taken to the death chamber, as you requested.

Faal crushed the note in his fist. He swirled the dark amber drink and sipped appreciatively. Already his work with Akemi was bearing fruit. He'd experienced a moment of real anxiety when he booted her up, knowing that he was introducing a wild card into his situation with the Pontifex. But if he won his gamble, he would win all. The impertinent computer could solve all of his problems.

Now she'd turned on one of her friends, and revealed a Rik in the Pontifex's court. This proved that the false memory work had succeeded, *and* it encouraged the Pontifex to accept Faal's proposal for their eradication.

The execution of the Rik would continue, and the humans would be coerced or beaten into submission as well. Faal could not ask for more.

There were Merith religious standards that governed the killing of sentient species... and if Faal violated the standards without the Pontifex's permission, there would be problems. The Pontifex could strip him of the faaldom of Merith II, and the other faals would be only too happy to unite against him and strip him of his personal holdings as well.

The Pontifex would not turn against him now, however. In this Year of Unity, the Pontifex's contribution to the security of his people would be the neutralization of the Rik threat—in whatever form Faal thought necessary.

26

AKEMI HAD SOLIDIFIED her own space in the network now, enough to really dig in and flex her muscles. Enough to accomplish the next task on her list, after dealing with Shara.

Most planets had a similar orbital network system for communicating off planet and with spaceships. Part of the network was to store ingoing and outgoing messages. On Selta, she'd heard Basher call it the planetary mailroom, because messages waited there for shipbound passengers until their ship checked in after a series of jumps. When she was ready, Akemi would leave a message in this planetary mailroom for Claire and Basher. They would see it when they checked for any messages from Sam and Nat.

Akemi was placing a few more careful alerts in the mailroom when the Diadina arrived in the treasury. She looked furtively over her shoulder as she shut the massive door behind her. She even took a goblet of white gold and set it on the handle of the door as a makeshift alarm.

"I have come to speak with you," the Diadina said. "I hope that while we are alone, we might be honest with one another."

That was what she said aloud, anyway, but Akemi could sense her unease and suspicion. The Diadina did not expect Akemi to be honest, and she did not have the remotest intention of being honest herself.

"Do you hear me, *bruck?*" the Diadina demanded.

"I hear you. What would you like to talk about?"

The Diadina came a little closer. "I will start at the beginning. Your friends came to me on Selta and told me Faal had acquired a questionable computer." She gestured to Akemi. "They gave me the chance to use that against him and I took it. It has not gone precisely as I hoped, but thus far I understood the plot."

She paused and Akemi could feel her weighing her words. She was being as truthful as possible in order to entice Akemi to do the same. "Now I want to know why your friends brought a Rik here, and why you turned on them."

"I did not turn on my friends—I only turned on the Rik they mistakenly trusted. She deserves the death chamber." She would also further Akemi's own plan by being there, but the Diadina didn't need to know that.

"I expected to find you opposed to Faal in every respect, and yet I find you in apparent agreement with his Rik extermination. I also sensed during your telepathy, though perhaps I am wrong in this, that you know things about me that only he knows. Forgive me, but you seem more his aide than his captive."

Akemi felt a shuddering within her, as if a door opened halfway through which she caught a glimpse of Shara and Nat's smiling faces... but the door slammed shut as she pictured, for the hundredth time, that horrible memory of Nat screaming and writhing on a tiny cot as the Rik *tortured* her.

"I loathe Faal," Akemi answered slowly, "but he has never injured me or the people I love as much as the Rik have." She thought of Claire—trapped in his zoo—but that was hazy as well...

"So you agree with him? You would have *all* the Rik die?"

"No. But I would have them punished." Once again, Akemi remembered (discovered?) one of the reasons Faal hated the Diadina. The information was there in her mind, but she couldn't remember where she'd learned it. She slowly verbalized it. "One of your ancestors was a Rik, weren't they? They stole a Merith body and you are a descendent. That's why Faal detests you."

The Diadina stiffened, but Akemi could tell she wasn't shocked by this revelation—she'd already suspected that Akemi knew.

"I don't deny it," the Diadina said. "It was my grandmother. During the upheaval around the time of a former Pontifex's death, the Rik decided to make a try for the Merith high families. My grandmother was not the only Rik infiltrator. On her deathbed, she confessed the truth to my mother and gave her the names of thirty other Rik/Merith spies." She breathed deeply. "Their plan failed, obviously. Most of the Rik became so thoroughly Merith, like my grandmother, that they never spoke to their kind again."

Despite her jumbled and vindictive emotions, Akemi couldn't help being fascinated by this bit of Merith history. For a moment, she felt nothing but a familiar sense of awed curiosity. "Wow. So that's why Faal hates you: you're part Rik."

"I am *not*," the Diadina spat. "I am a Meritha of Merith. My grandmother—whatever else she did—bore and raised eleven children to the honor of her husband and her planet. My mother was a Meritha of renown, as am I."

"Huh. I guess technically the offspring of a Rik-turned-Merith and a Merith would also be Merith. Claire certainly thought that if she married Sage their children would be human..." But the thought of Claire jolted Akemi. Claire had betrayed humanity for her Rik boyfriend. She'd even betrayed Akemi to Faal which was why she was in this mess to begin with...

"Are you planning to tell the Pontifex?" the Diadina asked. "That is the crux. I've prevented Faal from spreading these rumors about me for years. If he began to cast aspersions on my grandmother or my lineage, my husband would assume it was only his resentment speaking. But now Faal has devised a way for the information to come from a third party. Nothing you could do would please him more."

Akemi felt more than a bit conflicted. The Diadina was at last speaking the exact truth. Faal wanted this information to come to the Pontifex through her. Akemi did not want to please Faal, but she also didn't particularly care for the Diadina either.

"You realize Faal won't keep your secret forever?" Akemi asked. "He has begun a Rik eradication and if you think he won't try to extend that to you, you're a fool."

"We may all be fools, but—"

The goblet the Diadina placed on the doorknob fell off and landed with a loud, metallic *clang* as the door opened.

The Pontifex entered and his sleepy, turquoise eye opened wide for a moment at the sight of the Diadina standing beside Akemi's computer. He eyed the goblet, but did not mention it.

"Well, my dear, I'm glad you reconsidered." He came closer and touched her cheek. "It is a most interesting entity, is it not?"

She nodded. "It is. Most interesting. But I'll leave you, my love, as I'm sure you wish to question it alone."

The Pontifex watched her leave with a smile. "I'm ready," he said to Akemi when she was gone. "Tell me how I lost at hawking."

"First tell me about Shara," Akemi said. "I assume you gave her to Faal for execution?"

"The Rik girl has been sent to the death chamber. I don't know that Faal will order her execution yet. He might want to be present."

"Ah."

He narrowed his eyes. "You are a strange one. You've made no secret of your distaste for him, and yet you provide him more victims."

"A reversible weapon," Akemi said. "Isn't that the phrase you

Merith use? I'm willing to use Faal to achieve my own purposes. As you are."

"Indeed. But you keep harping on minor subjects—my main concern today is hawking. How did I lose?"

Akemi hedged. "I am making progress, but I need something else in order to fully understand. I need to do it myself."

The Pontifex whistled. "That's a bold request. How would you do so?"

"Teach me to play. You could easily connect one of the birds to a computer instead of those gloves. I would have the advantage of instantaneous reflexes, but the disadvantage of a theoretical understanding of flight and a novice's grasp of the game. I think you would find it interesting."

"I have never taught a beginner."

"In the human sport of karate, which I learned as a child, it is considered essential to instruct others. That is part of how 'master' is defined."

The Pontifex laughed suddenly. "Your continual boldness pleases me. Let us have a hawking lesson."

"And if I can beat you," Akemi said, "I would like a favor."

He put his hand on his throat theatrically. "If you can beat me, you may have three."

"Shall we play now?"

"So eager. I must attend to several matters and observe the Rik executions with my guests. Then we shall play."

27

SAGE WAITED NEXT TO JULIET.

"This is awful," she said as the guards shoved them into line in their cell. It wasn't her first day to await executions, but it seemed to bother her more every time.

"I know. Francois was protecting me all this time, but now that he's gone, the dread is worse than it was before," Sage admitted.

Juliet smiled sympathetically. She stood straight with her shoulders back, poised despite her dirty hair and torn dress. Sage was struck by how different she was from the immature rich girl he'd originally transferred to this body.

"You're actually taking this well," he said.

"I'm scared of the pain, but I'm not scared of dying. The worst is seeing the others."

"After all our study to be human," he said wryly, "I think you've gotten closer than any of us."

"I didn't do it myself," Juliet said, "I just found the right gate."

"Gate?"

"Yes. I mean, we were trying to steal Earth. We were trying to climb a wall and steal what we wanted from inside. But what if we just asked for it? You remember that translated book Francois got us? I tried to read it."

"That Crosspoint religious text?"

"Francois called it a children's book. I didn't really understand it, but he found me a human book, so I read that one, instead." She shrank back from a Merith glare, as they were ushered out of the dungeon toward the stairs. "Francois said that compared to what the Crosspoint have written about the Speaker, this book 'was but a chapter. And not the last chapter.' But worth reading."

"That sounds like him."

"But Sage, if you could have read it—they knew all about us."

Sage gave her a skeptical look. "I've read lots of human literature in my research. I didn't see any Rik prophecies in their religions."

"He was called the, 'Son of Man,'" Juliet argued. "Even though they knew he wasn't entirely human."

"That's not what they meant."

"He said he could take a heart of stone and give you a heart of flesh. Doesn't that sound like us?"

"You really think this human religion is offering to make aliens human?"

"Yes, I do think so. Another part says, 'you are no longer strangers and aliens, but you are fellow citizens...'"

"That's *definitely* not what they meant."

"I know originally it meant foreigners, but I think it *does* offer something that makes me human. I think it already has."

"What do you think it is?"

"I think it offers guilt."

Sage startled at the word. He had expected her to say love or faith or something like that, and he certainly hadn't told her of his growing obsession with guilt. And although he *was* interested, he couldn't help mocking her. "You read the whole book to make yourself feel bad?"

"In a sense—yes. Our culture is dead, Sage. The two things that define us are a sense of entitlement and one cutting-edge technology. We accept that we have no culture and no art—that's why we were going to steal it from the humans. But the real problem is that we have no guilt. No shame. No lines we know we shouldn't cross."

Sage walked just behind her up the stairs. "I've flirted with guilt, but I don't know that I want it like that."

"We don't get to choose our guilt." Juliet looked over her shoulder at him. "The guilt is already there; we're trapped in it. But we can't be free of it until we feel it. It's called remorse."

"I know the word," Sage said. "I've even tried to feel it."

"Remorse is what I got from the book," Juliet said. "'Those who weep will be comforted.'"

Sage looked away as they reached the arena floor. It was a misty morning, as the sun had not yet come up to burn the moisture away. The tiny droplets clung to his eyelashes like unshed tears, but the desert would be blazing in another hour.

"You can ask for it," Juliet said. "I don't know if it'll work, but it couldn't hurt to try. Francois says you can ask in your head the way the Crosspoint do."

The guards were putting together a new guillotine with an extra blade.

"I'm going to die in the next few days, if not today," Sage said. "I'm not sure I want to die with that kind of gift."

Juliet grimaced. "You've already seen what it's like to die without it."

Sage blinked, remembering the first execution he'd seen, with the woman screaming theatrically for a bored crowd. And the others since then. Anything would be better than dying like that.

They stood silently for a while while the rest of the captives were brought up. The nooses and guillotines shone in the morning sun. It was already a hot day.

"Who would I even ask?" Sage said finally. "This human god, the Son of Man?"

Juliet shrugged. "Francois said he was the same as their Speaker, but I don't know."

Sage took a rueful breath as the Merith began to select victims for the day. "Fine. Speaker of the Crosspoint, if remorse and peace are yours to give, I want—"

A crippling pain brought Sage to his knees before he'd finished. A feeling of absolute horror flooded his mind, and he thought of a Spo saying he'd once read, "To hate yourself is the last hell."

If this was remorse, he would rather face execution. Who had he invoked? What had he done?

Sage could hear guards yelling at him to get up, but he couldn't respond.

He felt naked and exposed, diseased and disgusted by his own soul. So many moments rushed by him, things he'd called success, necessity, and normalcy—which now became murder, torture, and cruelty.

He wanted to strangle Juliet for doing this to him. He wanted to strangle Francois for not warning him.

And for the first time, along with those thoughts, he felt culpable. He felt guilt. Savage, mind-searing guilt.

Sage vomited, gasped, and passed out in his own filth. It felt deserved.

Akemi swooped on the Pontifex in savage delight. This was the freest she'd felt in... forever. The gauntlet gloves would have been difficult and time consuming to learn, taking a lifetime to master, but she didn't have to do that. She *was* the hawk, and the tiny sensors in the animatronic bird were her eyes, ears, and nerves.

Drench had completely shut her out when she got inside the bird. They'd had another argument, and she was ashamed to admit it, but she'd taken quite a bit of satisfaction in nauseating him with the bird before he shut her out.

The Pontifex walked her through take-off and a few types of movement: side-slipping, diving, and draft riding.

"What about landing?" Akemi asked him. He'd had his people rig up her 'voice box' in a portable pouch so that he could carry it with him.

"Land?" The Pontifex laughed. "Only the best players land. Everyone else gets torn out of the sky."

He taught her a few common strategies—diving out of the light, oblique angles, gravity punches. "These are techniques you might learn in the first year of hawking. Mastering the use of them is more than technical skill or intuitive timing. It is knowing your opponent's strengths and weakness, knowing when they expect a dive, or whether to side-slip or flip."

The Pontifex's bird suddenly spun over, sank its claws into Akemi's belly and fell like a stone. They hit the ground with a puff of dust. Akemi felt dizzy.

"I would normally have torn out the nervelines," the Pontifex explained, "to render one or both of your wings useless."

They took off again, and Akemi matched him in a tight spiral with a feeling of sheer joy.

Akemi's mind felt clear for the first time since she'd awoken. She wasn't sure if it was because she was learning something new and clearing out a few cobwebs, or if it was the different venue. Either way, she was glad to set aside the tiresome memories.

She knew it would be next to impossible to beat the Pontifex at his own game... But then, she was mildly telepathic now. Could she read his mind enough to anticipate him?

"Very good spiral," he said. "We do that to establish a baseline synchronization—"

Akemi clutched his wing with her talons, but the Pontifex

dexterously snapped his wings in and twisted beneath her. The sudden tumble confused her, and she let go.

"Not bad," he said. "But I know how to counter every simple attack. Every complex one also."

"Yet you lost to Faal," Akemi said.

"Yet I lost."

She focused on getting a read on his mood. He still felt frustration and resignation at his loss, and a slight pleasure at eluding her. The pleasure was slight, because he didn't consider her a serious opponent.

Akemi felt when his mood shifted slightly, and she took a hard right and caught an updraft, narrowly avoiding his oblique attack.

"That was excellent!" he exclaimed. "Much improved."

Akemi circled above him and then dove. He avoided it as she expected but applauded her attempt. When he next began an attack, dropping at the right moment to land on her back, she felt his attack mood and dived also.

Still, he almost caught her, because she copied his straight dive, too predictably.

"Good effort," he said, "but it's better to side-slip away from a straight attack."

Akemi could tell that he was replaying his loss with Faal as he explained another type of attack. His bird was almost on top of hers when she quickly flipped and sank her talons into his bird's torso and tucked her wings. It was the same move he used earlier.

Their birds hit the ground before the Pontifex could speak.

Akemi remained silent. The Pontifex was shocked, but she couldn't tell if he was angry or not.

"Um. Does that count?" Akemi asked finally.

"That was more my loss than your win," he said ruefully. "I wasn't paying attention."

"I know. I could never do it again. It only worked because I knew you were picturing your game with Faal."

"Ah. And has my lesson helped you understand how I lost to him?"

"I think it might have, but I can only offer an intuitive answer. I still don't have the technical skill to analyze any further."

Akemi disentangled her bird and took off again, circling. She would probably never get to do this again, she might as well enjoy her last few minutes of freedom. "Hawking is all about expectation. Faal's injury seemed like a liability to you, but it wasn't. It was a chance for him to change your expectations."

"But I didn't underestimate him," the Pontifex protested. "I knew he was still a formidable player despite his injury."

"But do you know what his injury has done to him?" she asked.

Flying was exhilarating, but that brought its own temptations. From this height she could see over the wall that surrounded the palace. What if she just flew west, toward the ocean? Her connection wouldn't last of course, eventually the bird would fall out of the sky. But would her consciousness snap back to the computer? Or would she sink into the waves of sand and disappear? And why did that seem so appealing?

"What did his injury do?" the Pontifex asked, recalling her thoughts.

And that made Akemi think of Claire. A sudden echo of dislike reverberated through her. Claire, who helped the Rik escape, who stole Basher, who gave Akemi away...

For a moment, she remembered Claire's face, tears streaming down her cheeks, "Don't do this..." Claire had whispered.

But no. That couldn't be what happened. Akemi could hear Claire's voice saying, "Take her, not me." That line bounced around in her head, and Akemi hated her more each time.

"Akemi? Did you hear me? What are you saying about Faal?"

She snapped back to the present. "Sorry. The point is—Faal's injury marked a change in policy. For years he maintained a status quo, but his injury changed that. He has to go up or down now and find a new level. It's rippled into the rest of his life, and he's burning the status quo with the Rik, with the humans, with the Diadina... and even with you."

"Is he?"

"You have a deeper expectation of Faal than that of the game —you expect him *not* to challenge you, politically or personally. That expectation is what tripped you up. Because Faal isn't playing by his former rules anymore. His injury is a handicap—but it's also a symbol. Of his obsession."

The Pontifex didn't immediately answer, and Akemi wondered if he believed her.

"You've given me much food for thought," the Pontifex finally said. "And I believe I owe you three favors."

28

CLAIRE HAD to watch the videos of the executions. How could she not? She couldn't just abandon Sage to his fate. That would be killing him in her thoughts before he was even dead.

After the ship was done jumping, she brought her tablet to Basher. He was by the tiny table, fixing himself some coffee.

"How do I... Where are the videos?" She felt no need to be specific.

Basher silently took the tablet from her hand, typed in a few things, dragged something to the corner, and then typed one more thing.

"The icon in the corner is the Merith Prime news feed. It'll update automatically when they release the next video."

She nodded and felt him watch her as she left. She curled up on her bed, pulling her new blanket all around her before touching the small, ominous icon in the corner of her tablet. It was a Merith symbol of a skull, a bird skull.

A list of videos appeared, in reverse chronological order, so the most recent execution was at the top of the list. She wanted to know how long Sage had been captured, but she didn't think she could handle watching all the videos it would take to figure that out. So she settled for touching the most recent on the list, from yesterday.

It started abruptly, showing the amphitheater she'd seen on the first few videos. A smattering of Merith sat in the tiered benches. Her eyes skittered off guillotines and platforms to the ragged crowd of humans—Rik actually—that were corralled on one side. She tried to zoom in the video so she could see them more clearly, but it didn't zoom. There were more men than women in the group, and it was hard to tell for sure which one was Sage.

Then the guards started selecting prisoners, and the view switched to a closer camera. And there was Sage.

Claire caught her breath and paused the video. She knew Sage didn't die in this video; Basher would have told her, but that didn't help. He *would* die, if not today, then tomorrow or the next execution, and she wasn't prepared for it. There was no way *to* prepare herself. Claire started it again, and watched Sage as he stared forward, his jaw clenched in either anger or disgust.

When the video was over, she lay still for a long time.

Basher and his partner were in the piloting room when she joined them.

Basher looked at her cautiously.

"I'm glad you told me," Claire said. "I know it's not your fault that he's there... but, well, I needed to know."

Basher nodded. "I can at least tell you that Francois is alright. He was released nearly a week ago."

"Wait, they had *Francois?*"

"Yes, he was with Sage, I gather, and Faal pulled strings for his arrest. But like I said, he was released."

"Released a week ago," Claire repeated. "So, how long have they been there?"

"A while..."

"How long have you *known?*"

Basher paused. "Several weeks. You never asked—"

"I didn't *ask*? Are you kidding? I want to know if any of my friends are caught! I didn't think I needed to spell that out."

"You don't. But you seemed so sure that everything was fine—I didn't know if I should ruin that for you, when there's nothing you can do."

Claire took a deep breath and Basher started to speak again, but she held up her hand to stop him. She took another breath, and forced herself to relax her shoulders as she exhaled. She was furious with Basher, but it wasn't entirely his fault. She'd thought everything was fine because she received that letter from Sage. She'd known it was older by the time it arrived, but it made her feel as if Sage was still out there and safe. If she'd told Basher about the letter, he would have been forced to tell her about Sage. She respected him enough to believe that he wouldn't have lied to her.

But she hadn't told him about the letter, so he'd never been forced to tell her.

"You don't have the right to decide whether or not I suffer," Claire said finally. "It isn't your place to make that kind of decision for me." She rubbed her eyes. "I received a letter from Sage before we went to the Herayung—during the tribunal hearing; Sage said he was fine. He was going to visit Francois's home estate on Cross. That's why I never asked."

BASHER STARED AT HER. He'd never dreamed that Sage might have the audacity to write to Claire at the embassy.

The mere thought of Sage, if he indulged it too long, made Basher furious. The Rik had destroyed countless lives as he collected and chose suitable human bodies for his experiments. He was the worst of the worst, as far as Basher was concerned—an alien who'd planned, initiated, and carried through the crux of the plot against humanity.

When luck brought Sage into contact with Claire, (good luck for Sage that is, terrible luck for Claire) he'd used the opportunity to manipulate her into falling for him. And Claire, emerging from three years locked away in Faal's zoo, had been easy to manipulate. Basher didn't blame her for that, but he'd hoped now that Sage was out of her life she'd be able to see how he'd really used her.

"What?" Claire said. "Go ahead and say it."

Basher shook his head, but Claire wouldn't drop it. "No, I know you're just itching to defend yourself and tell me how Sage deserves this. You don't know him at all—"

"Neither do you." Basher's pent-up frustration suddenly found a voice. He knew it wasn't wise to say all this when Sage was going to be executed, but it only made him angrier that somehow Sage could avoid criticism because he was dying for his crimes. "How dare he write to you? Sage made sure you were loyal to him, and when an opportunity came, he cashed in on it immediately. He put you in incredible danger by bringing you almost directly to Faal at the embassy. He even convinced you to steal from me—from your own kind. And Sage got what he wanted: the ink to make the human tattoos. You got a bullet through your leg, and a broken arm. Yes, I know you'll say that was for Akemi, but if not for Sage's distraction at the embassy, Faal would never have had the chance to steal her in the first place. You would have been protected, and you wouldn't have had to ditch them and go alone. Sage doesn't deserve your loyalty."

Claire took a step closer. "He didn't manipulate me into stealing the ink. I *chose* to help my friends! Just because you hate the Rik, you think anything I did for them was coerced. I *wanted* to help him!"

"Of course you wanted to help him!" Basher said. "That's how *manipulation* works. I know they didn't force you to do anything, and that little Rik girl seemed genuinely fond of you, but Sage knew exactly what he was doing."

"Maybe I *knew exactly what I was doing* as well," Claire said, mimicking his words. "Maybe Sage actually cared about me. Why is that so hard for you to believe?"

Basher had refrained from saying any of this to Claire before, hoping she would see it on her own, or that possibly Nat would help her cope with things. And it wasn't even about him. Yes, Basher admitted to himself, Akemi had been right when she saw that he was falling for Claire. But Basher wanted Claire to see through Sage for her own sake. Whether or not she ever looked at Basher that way, she needed to learn when to doubt someone.

"That would be worse," Basher said. "Because if he cared about you, then what he did was even more selfish—and more dangerous."

"You just took me to Faal's estate. How is that different?"

"It's entirely different. I knew Faal wasn't there. And *you* wouldn't take no for an answer. And this is not about me—"

"I think it is!" Claire was beside herself. She'd found an outlet for her grief and confusion about Sage and she didn't care what she said to Basher. "You think you have a shot with me if he's out of the picture, so you keep trying to convince me that he's evil. And now he's going to be executed, and you're still trying to spin it!"

Basher stepped back, almost as if she'd slapped him. Claire wanted to cry, and she wanted to be angry, and she wanted to hurt him. "*We* are not going to happen, do you understand?" she said brutally. "I don't trust you, and I don't want to be with you."

Claire felt a hard, burning ball lodge in her chest.

Basher nodded, not quite meeting her eyes. "If that's how you feel, that's absolutely fine. It doesn't change what I've said." He spoke quietly and calmly now, and if he felt any pain at her harsh rejection, he wasn't showing it. "Sage was bad for you."

Claire ran out of the piloting room, back to her bunk in the hallway. She faced the wall, resenting that the only thing she had to hold onto was the blanket Basher had given her.

The ship was so tiny, she could still hear the tapping of the computer in the piloting room from her bed. A chair creaked, probably Basher sitting down.

His partner's gravelly voice was still easy to hear. "She's right."

"About what?" Basher snapped. Claire had never heard him speak that way to his partner.

"You took her into danger also. You blame the Rik for doing it, but when it was necessary, you did the same thing."

"It's different."

His partner was silent.

"It *is* different."

Silence.

"It's... I didn't do it for *me*. I took her for Akemi's sake."

"That changes the danger?"

"No. But it's... Okay, it's similar. Are you happy now?"

His partner sounded confused. "Why would that make me happy? As your friend, I am merely revealing your error to you."

"Thanks so much."

"Also, I was hesitant to interrupt your lively discussion, but there was a message waiting for us when I checked into the network of Merith mainspace. It is from the Pontifex's palace."

"From Sam? Did he get our message?"

"It is not from him. It seems to be from the palace network itself. It is directed to Claire, and I have not read it."

"Show me," Basher said. "If Faal is trying to send her a message..."

Claire waited to hear who it was from.

And waited some more.

"Claire," Basher finally called, a strange sound in his voice. "Could you please come back in here?"

The message was short.

Claire,

It's me, Akemi! Faal brought me to the palace and the Pontifex is such a duck. I'm going to have him eating out of my hand in no time. Literally. He agreed to grant me three favors if I could beat him at this dumb hawking game, and I did it! Can you guess what one of my favors will be? I can get Sage released from the death chamber!

Get to Merith Prime, he may need a quick getaway. I'll see you there!

Akemi

P.S. Shara says hi. :-)

29

WHEN SAGE WOKE UP, he was back in the dungeon, and there were fewer Rik. Juliet was near him, and she'd used the skirt of her red dress to clean his face.

He didn't feel the same gut-wrenching pain he'd felt earlier, but he slowly sat up and scooted back to lean against the wall. He felt like he'd just recovered from a severe illness—sore muscles, headache, and fatigue.

"Well." Juliet looked uncertain. "You weren't executed. I guess they want people who are awake."

"Probably." Sage leaned his head against the wall and closed his eyes. "Did you know that would happen? I felt like my appendix ruptured."

"Um, no. I didn't quite expect that." She paused. "But it worked, didn't it? Can you feel it?"

Sage tried to analyze himself critically. Had he really been changed as Juliet thought or had this fun-loving Speaker just punched him in the kidney?

"Think about what you felt this morning," Juliet offered.

Sage didn't have to try hard. The disgust he felt for himself flooded back, and he nodded grimly. "Yes, it worked. Cheers."

"But see, he accepted you. Now you can change. We die to

ourselves, and then he lives in us and we live in him. It's just like we do to them, but the new life is a hybrid of us *and* him. And in our new life, we're not guilty anymore. Because we died!"

Sage opened one eye to look at her. "You sound drunk, and I feel hungover."

"I know, it's kind of ridiculous, but I'm not making it up. It really says that." She brought Sage one of the water buckets and he took a long drink.

"I know," he said, "I remember."

The superstitious guy, the one who kept kissing the clover-shaped rock, was watching Juliet and Sage. "Personally, I don't care what you said to him," he told Juliet. "Seeing him double over and turn inside out like that was deeply satisfying. His sort need a little more of that." He glanced significantly from Sage to the Director.

The Director pursed her lips, but she seemed unable to let Clover Guy's insults go by, even when they only glancingly referred to her.

"His sort? What sort is that?" the Director barked.

Clover Guy rubbed his knuckles against the rock. "You know what I mean. You sort that got us into this mess."

"We all got ourselves into this mess," Juliet said. "You think it was just the Migrationists? We all wanted what we couldn't have, and we were all willing to steal to get it. But real life can't be stolen, it's a gift."

"The humans weren't about to give us anything," the Director said bitterly. "I did the best I could. It was a gamble, yes, but it would have gotten us everything we wanted."

The argument was interrupted when the guards came to the door. They shoved a new prisoner inside. She was short and blonde, and looked annoyed. She glanced around the room, frowning. "What a dismal place."

She would have settled in a free spot against the wall, but then she spotted him. "Sage! Is that you?"

She came closer and he studied her. She did look familiar, but he couldn't immediately place her...

"You trained me for a year after I got my body," she said. "Before passing me off to my next instructor. I was sent to Earth a few weeks before the trial."

"Shara," Sage remembered now. "How did that job work out for you?" he asked sarcastically.

"Well, I ditched it, obviously. The humans were pretty chill about letting me switch sides." Shara sat down near them and crossed her legs. Being significantly cleaner than anyone else in the room, she seemed to take unconscious care not to touch anything. "I hear you've been getting around. I spent the last few weeks at the Spo embassy on Selta, and they're all ticked that you stole their ink."

Juliet caught her breath. "Was Claire still there? Is she alright?"

"Oh, she's fine. Got her cast off and everything. Er—not to be awkward, but does she know you're here? Because she didn't mention anything to me."

"She probably doesn't," Sage said. "I sent her a letter that must have arrived around the time I was arrested."

"*That's* what it was," Shara said with satisfaction. "I knew she was reading something secret that night. She was rude to me. She's not a very friendly person."

"She's a *very* friendly person," Juliet shot back. "*You* were probably the rude one."

"Whatever."

"How did you end up here?" Sage asked.

For the first time, Shara looked troubled. "I don't know exactly. Apparently a friend... turned on me? But I can't quite believe it."

Juliet looked even angrier. "If you mean that Claire turned you in, I don't believe it."

"No, it wasn't her. A different friend."

The food came then, brick-like protein bars, and Shara sat with Sage and Juliet, despite Juliet's somewhat hostile attitude.

"I heard some people talking while they brought me here from the palace," Shara told them. "There's going to be a big execution tomorrow. The Pontifex and the Diadina are coming to this one. Faal will escort them."

Sage grimaced. "That's not good. I'm sure he hasn't forgotten how Juliet and Athlete and I beat him in Francois's restaurant. I hope he doesn't notice us."

"It's a good thing Claire's not here," Juliet said. "She's the one Faal was really angry with."

That night Sage was awoken again by the woman crying for her baby.

"Where is he? Where's my baby?"

Juliet held her again while she cried and this time she asked her, "What was the baby's name?"

"She never had a baby," Sage told her. "It's only a flesh memory."

The woman sobbed harder. "It's *not*. I had a baby before I got my human body. They told me he could be changed, too. That we could be together on Earth. But there was something wrong with him, he was one of those that can't change."

"A mono-rat?" Sage asked. "That's not uncommon in the younger generation."

"But I didn't know that! I'd never heard the term mono-rat and no one told me. By the time I realized," she sobbed again, "it was too late. He'll always be a Rik, and I'll always be a human. I can't even hold him—his skin was too sensitive to the salt of my sweat. I couldn't speak to him without a mask—I couldn't even speak his language anymore." She clutched Juliet. "Now I'll die, and he'll never even know why I left."

Sage twisted sideways, facing the wall. He felt a painful constriction in his gut, as the newly-present guilt mixed with pity and hate for the woman making him feel this way. The remorse was worse than he could ever have guessed.

AKEMI'S SLEEP was more disturbed than usual. Unfocused nightmares merged with brief moments of panicked wakefulness that may only have been more nightmares. She startled to a gentle touch, and then grumpily pushed Drench out of her mind. "Why are you waking me up? The sun isn't even up yet."

"Your dreams were concerning me. I think you were calling to me."

"Don't flatter yourself," Akemi said.

Drench wasn't amused. "There is something very wrong with you. I think the trip caused your brain to degrade. Parts of your presence are not lighting up the way they used to, and other parts are flaring. You're making strange decisions—"

"*I'm* making strange decisions? Your whole race are slaves to the Crosspoint."

Drench ignored her interruption. "You suddenly hate the Rik, and you suddenly hate this girl named Claire—you didn't feel that way before. Don't you remember?"

"Of course I hate the Rik. I told you what they did to me! You're the one who said it was like chopping off the roots and branches of a sapling."

"I recall what I said. But one of the things I found most fascinating about you was how you didn't hate those who'd injured you. Even Faal you treated with a casual contempt but not a settled hatred. We debated whether you were characteristic of humans or not... we thought not. We were impressed."

"Well, I'm sorry to disappoint you, but I'm not going to forgive the people who tortured my sister and chopped off my limbs."

"Are you not hurting your sister?"

"Nat will get over losing Shara. I'm her sister, and she loves me more than anyone."

"But what about the other girl? Will she forgive you for that?"

Akemi suddenly caught the thought behind Drench's words. There was more going on in this conversation than she'd thought.

"You wouldn't dare try to stop me," Akemi said. "I know your secret, remember?"

"I can hardly forget. It is causing me considerable anxiety given your present state."

Akemi laughed, but it didn't make her feel better. "Drench, I have serious plans today. If you don't mess with me, I won't mess with you."

She could feel his deep disapproval, but he didn't say anything in reply, and she took that as tacit agreement.

Akemi felt a ping as one of her message alerts was tripped. Ah, yes. She'd been expecting this. She'd set up an alert to notify her if Sam or Nat left any messages in the planetary mailroom.

Nat had just left a message for Claire and Basher. Apparently everyone was up early today.

Basher,

I don't know if Akemi has contacted you, but something is wrong with her. She turned Shara over to the Merith, and they took her to the death chamber. Akemi doesn't seem to remember things correctly, and I don't know why. Let me know immediately if she tries to contact you or Claire.

Nat

Akemi deleted the message. She was remembering things just fine. She remembered Nat screaming, and Claire laughing with the Rik over an open soda bottle, and Basher looking at Claire... Akemi tried to get control of her thoughts. She seemed to be sucked into her memories whenever she let herself go. It was distracting, but there was no way she was remembering all those things wrong—if anything, they were too insistently real.

But today she would lay many of them to rest.

Akemi rewrote the message.

Basher,

The Merith discovered Shara is a Rik and they've taken her to the death chamber here on Merith Prime. Our only hope is that Akemi has won a favor from the Pontifex. She can get Shara and Sage free. I know it's dangerous, but I think you'd better come.

Nat

Akemi composed her next message more simply, sending it to the Pontifex through the inter-palace network.

I would like to cash in one of my favors. I understand there is a special performance at the death chamber today, in honor of the Unity celebration. I would like to attend with you and the Diadina, along with the other humans. I promise to make the show even better.

She didn't have to wait long for a reply.

An interesting request, he sent. *I look forward to the occasion.*

30

SAGE SAID a foul word as the guards prodded them into line, and he wasn't the only one.

"We haven't even had breakfast yet!" someone yelled. "It's too early." No one seriously put up a fight, however, as they took the now familiar path up the stairs to the arena.

To Sage's left the sky was turning purple, but the sun wouldn't break over the horizon for a while yet. It was cold, as only a pre-dawn desert is cold on a day when you will probably die. The wind whistled through the amphitheater. The rows of benches were completely empty, and two new gallows had been built in the center of the death chamber. They were at least eighty feet tall, if Sage had to guess, and they were rigged for synchronized double-hangings.

Ahead of him, Juliet squeezed the hand of the woman she'd comforted last night. "Be brave."

All the Rik were being brought out to the arena, not just a few of the cells like usual. There had to be a thousand, no, two or maybe even three thousand. Sage had never gotten a firm idea of the numbers that Faal had captured; it was far more than he'd thought.

In the dimness, Sage hadn't seen Faal until he started to move.

That painful limp was Claire's legacy to her former owner. Sage shifted slightly to put someone between himself and Faal's gaze. If Faal recognized Juliet or him or Shara, their time was up.

"I've brought you here early," Faal began, "to make certain things clear." His resonant voice silenced the murmuring like a gong. "Today will be a special performance for the Pontifex himself, along with the other guests of the Unity celebration and thousands of off-world visitors. I will tolerate absolutely no 'incidents' during today's execution."

His beak glinted starlight. "You may ask yourself, 'What's the worst he could do? Kill us?' To which the answer is, of course, yes," Faal said. "All of you will die here, and you had best marshal whatever part of your foul minds you use to put one foot in front of the other to believe that. However, if you create any untoward situations—you will die sooner. Unnoticed, meaningless." Faal suddenly pointed at a woman. "Let me demonstrate. I need to test this new apparatus anyway."

A rustle went through the crowd of Rik. "But there's no one here!" one of them shouted.

"What's the point?" another shouted as the woman was taken.

Juliet gasped when she realized Faal had picked the woman she'd held earlier, the one who kept crying for her lost baby.

Faal pointed at the one who shouted, and the guards immediately pulled him forward. It was Clover Guy, the superstitious botanist.

Sage swallowed his rising bile and raised his eyes to count the last visible stars. Juliet was breathing raggedly, tears running down her face. Sage felt again the rush of pity and hatred for the condemned for making him feel so helplessly horrible.

"We all tried to steal new lives for ourselves," Juliet whispered brokenly, "and now she's lost even the old one."

"Would you stop?" Sage murmured.

"I can't help it. We did this to her."

"You didn't do anything. *I* did it—is that what you're angling for? Yes, I admit it. I'm disgusted by what I've done to these people. I feel ill." With his newfound sense of guilt, he could barely stand upright. He had no idea a conscience could make one's whole body *hurt*.

Juliet stepped close enough to touch his hand. "I didn't get to finish," she said. "You can be free of the guilt."

"Shut up. This is not the time."

The two prisoners climbed separate ladders to two high platforms. They moved their hands and feet with excruciating slowness.

"You were already guilty, you just found out about it yesterday," she said. "Now you can be forgiven."

"None of these people are going to forgive me."

Juliet gripped his hand. "I do."

The two were fitted with nooses. They, at least, would die quickly, dropped from such a height.

"But you don't need my forgiveness or theirs," Juliet said. "You have to be forgiven by the one who made us."

"*I* made us," Sage said. "Well, not Clover Guy, that was probably Anderson's work."

"I mean—"

"I know what you mean; I read the book. But I don't think it works like that. If I deserve to die, nobody else's death changes that."

"I know. But he gives his death to you—then you die and he lives. It says, 'I have been crucified—'"

"For pity's sake, don't mention crucifixion here!"

His last words were drowned out by a gasp as the trapdoors opened simultaneously. The rope on the left pulled taut, but Sage didn't see the women's moment of death, because the other rope snapped in two and Clover Guy hurtled to the ground.

The sound he made when he hit the ground punched through Sage like a spear.

"That's why we test these things," Faal said, almost conversationally. He spoke calmly to nearby guards who went to move the body away. Another guard picked up a length of chain, hung it on his shoulder, and began to climb up.

Juliet bit her lip. "It could be us next—"

"Not if you would shut up," Sage hissed.

"I want you to know what I read. It says, 'the same one who descended also ascended higher than all the heavens, so that he might fill the entire universe with himself.'"

"Be quiet." Sage saw that the guard had almost finished attaching the chain to the post. Clover Guy's body had been carried out of the way, and Faal looked at the crowd of Rik again. His gaze lingered on Shara, who was several rows in front of them. Something was making him smile.

Faal finally moved on from Shara... and fixated on Juliet. Then himself.

"No," Sage breathed.

Faal's gaze flickered between Sage and Juliet, and the muscles around his beak tightened in pleasure. "I had not realized I already possessed several Rik celebrities. You'll be interested to know that I did some research after our last encounter. I had no idea who I was dealing with."

They were going to die. Faal limped toward them and the Rik parted like water.

"You are arguably the architect of the Rik to human transition," Faal said to Sage. "I have high hopes that your death will be most apropos later today. However, you," he turned to Juliet, who was still standing close to Sage. "I was most impressed that you managed to disarm one of my guards so handily. You can die now. I don't want anyone with your skills around during today's performance."

Sage reflexively clutched Juliet's hand.

"However, I respect competence." Faal made a show of looking around the group. "I learned in the course of my research that you are the daughter of the Director, whom I believe I already... ah, yes."

Faal pointed to the Director, who looked absolutely furious.

"Perhaps a Spo-style, family execution?" Faal offered. "I think I owe you that much consideration, my dear Juliet."

One guard came for Juliet, but Sage wouldn't let go of her hand. "No, you can't, not her—I *cannot*—"

"Sage." Juliet's face was pale, but calm. There were tear tracks, but they were drying into faint trails in the early morning light. "It's okay."

"It *isn't*—you're the only one here who *doesn't* deserve to die."

There was a murmur of assent from those around them—those who had been in the cell with her.

Faal laughed, seemingly content to let them play it out.

"I'm not afraid to die." Her chin quivered as she tried to smile. "Or not much. I'll live even if I die."

Sage didn't know what to say to her. This moment would haunt him for the rest of his life. He couldn't save her, and what was there to say in such a moment that would make any conceivable difference?

Faal laughed. "The little Rik is convinced her death has *meaning*. Survival is sanity, little one. Your death means nothing."

"Survival isn't sanity," Juliet said. She raised her voice, "Survival *isn't* sanity! The whole galaxy is wrong about that. We're all slaves to the fear of death, but sacrifice is better than survival."

Faal flicked a hand for the guards to pull her away. Juliet's fingers loosened, and the guards shoved her toward the ladder. Faal's lingering gaze of satisfaction disgusted him, Sage could not stop his tears.

Sage finally understood what motivated tragic lost causes and futile last stands. He lunged for Faal, but the guards were ready. They grabbed Sage's arms with their taloned hands. He was held taut between two of them.

Juliet squared her shoulders and took a deep, shuddering breath. The sky was lighter but the sun was still not over the horizon. She climbed rung after rung up the ladder. She looked back at Sage only once. Her lips trembled but she kept climbing. In the dead silence, Sage heard her start humming and then singing a song she'd learned from Claire.

When Sage couldn't bear to look at Juliet anymore, he was not surprised to look around and see more than a few distraught faces. In the short time she'd been in their dungeon, Juliet had formed connections. This was the most human the crowd had ever looked, and her voice seemed to pierce each of them as it filled the air.

When she was at the top, Sage couldn't see the details of her face clearly anymore. She had to wait while the Director, her mother, was shoved up to the twin platform. Juliet's stance was calm.

When the loop was put around Juliet's neck, Sage felt blood rushing to his head. Where was the last-minute rescue? Where was—?

The trapdoor opened and Juliet and her mother fell.

A horrible sound tore out of Sage's throat. The moment seemed to last forever, while his heart hovered between one beat and the next. Then Juliet dangled from a broken neck. Her black hair fell over her face. Sage's knees sagged, and he was only held up by the grip of the guards.

"What are you trying to do?" Sage surged towards Faal again, although his arms were nearly dislocated as the guards wrenched him back. "We already lost our chance with Earth. Did you think we would try for Merith next? Why do you care? Why kill *her*?"

Faal smiled a little. "I think the question is, why do you care?" He gestured at Juliet's body swinging above them. "Are you finally gaining a little humanity, Rik? Claire had more effect on you than I realized."

Sage didn't even want to ponder why that made Faal smile. "None of us can do anything to you," Sage continued. "We already switched bodies, and you know it can only happen once. We're actually the *least* dangerous Rik in the galaxy. Juliet least of all."

"Oh, I know," Faal said. "But exterminations can only happen in stages. The visible and obnoxious must come first, to whet the appetite. The bulk of the meal can occur only after the craving has taken hold."

"You're going to destroy *all* the Rik."

"As you've said, you and your compatriots are no longer a risk; but a planet full of unchanged Rik, just waiting for a chance? Only a fool would ignore such a threat."

"But—many young Rik cannot even change," another man spoke up. "We call them—"

"Mono-rats? Yes, I know. But really, what would be the point of sparing them? Your culture is bankrupt, your adult generation soon to be non-existent. Such pity would, in fact, be cruelty."

CLAIRE STOOD in the piloting room behind Basher and his partner, reading over their shoulders. Basher had been scrupulously polite with her since their argument.

"You see?" Claire said to Basher, who was re-reading Nat's message yet again."Nat says we should come to Merith Prime. I don't think there's any question. If Akemi can get Shara and Sage free, they may need a quicker exit than Sam and Nat can provide. And if Akemi is getting all this done—perhaps she can maneuver her own escape! Who knows? We need to be there in case they need us."

"But—I'm surprised Nat doesn't explain *why* she wants us. This is a rather cryptic message considering the risk she's asking us to take."

"But—"

Basher raised his hands. "I'm not saying we won't go—I can hardly say no since Akemi herself requested it. I just think this is strange, and we're going to be extremely careful."

His partner broke in, "Does that mean you want me to make the final jump to Merith Prime?"

"Yes, go ahead." Since they were still in Merith mainspace, they'd been able to maneuver to Merith Prime fairly rapidly.

Basher and Claire held onto a railing, and she avoided making eye contact with him. She was ecstatic to get Akemi's message that Sage—and now Shara—might be saved, but it made things more awkward than ever with Basher.

When the brief jump was over, Basher and Claire went to pack up what they might need. Basher reached up to get his satchel from the top bunk where he'd been sleeping, and Claire knelt on the floor to get hers from the tiny cabinet below the bottom bunk.

"You have the extra glasses?" Claire asked. Since they'd been planning to get Akemi from Faal's estate, they'd brought both pairs of the smart glasses that Akemi had used to communicate with them. Claire also had her own pair, which made three altogether that Akemi could potentially use.

"I've got them." He put three fresh water bottles in his bag. "You realize Faal is going to be there? Legally you should be safe, but we can't be sure..."

"I know, but I trust Akemi. I think she must have a plan."

Basher nodded tightly and pulled out a black case. "I'm sure she does, but I'm bringing more than a tranquilizer gun to the death chamber."

"Not gonna argue," Claire said.

Basher swung his bag over one shoulder. "Let's go get in the shuttle then."

32

THE DIADINA LOOKED in her hand mirror before she left her room. She barely resisted the urge to throw it against the wall. Despite all her efforts, her eye still looked bloodshot, and the skin around it was positively haggard. She did not look her best; that was certain. This morning she would be attending the executions at the nearby death chamber with the Pontifex. They were to be Faal's special guests, and she hated presenting such a stressed appearance to her enemy.

But how was she to be calm and rest when the threat of that deviant computer called Akemi rested over her like a hanging blade? Faal had outplayed her in this round, and she did not know her next move. She'd never considered that Faal would tell her secret to the computer, but now she wondered how she'd overlooked the possibility.

She had hoped to play on the computer's hatred of Faal, but after their short conversation, the Diadina did not feel at all confident of Akemi's motivations. Generally the Diadina was excellent at ferreting out loyalties and alliances—but this Akemi was strange and inconsistent. The Diadina could not determine what the computer wanted, which made her deeply uneasy. At any moment, the computer could decide to spew out the Diadina's secret ancestry in a damaging way.

The only good thing about this morning's activities would be leaving the computer's instability and disruption behind for a time.

The Diadina, followed at a discreet distance by her maid, attempted to walk calmly to the front courtyard, but she feared her sleepless night showed in the ungraceful heaviness of her steps. When she reached the courtyard, where the Pontifex had recently planted that huge Melifleuran tree, the caravan was being set up. Twelve litters would carry the Pontifex and herself and a few of their more illustrious guests to the death chamber. The arena was situated less than a mile from the palace, if you could fly directly there, but the elevation dropped significantly, and the road leading to the entrance circled nearly two miles around the wall of the palace.

Faal, thankfully, had gone on ahead to the death chamber the night before in his private shuttle, for which the Diadina was devoutly thankful. She did not think she could bear being enclosed in a small litter with him and the Pontifex for an hour. She just wasn't up to a battle of that intensity this early in the morning.

She made her way to the front-most litter. It was a small platform of light but strong wood powdered with sparkling iron pyrite and provided with cushions stuffed with the feathers of dead Merith. It was all of the best, if you liked that sort of thing. The Diadina usually did, but she froze at the sight of a round black container bristling with wires and plugs. It sat in the center of the litter, and it was connected to a small box with a tiny, but visible lens. It also contained a microphone and speaker.

She eyed the thing as if it were a Spo trouncer that might attack at any moment. No one seemed to be watching the thing, and the Diadina looked around in confusion. Why was the computer *here*? As difficult as this day was going to be, she had not expected to have to ride with the *thing* all the way to the death chamber. It was almost worse than Faal.

"Not worse than Faal," came a lilting voice from the box, and the Diadina bit her tongue to keep from visibly reacting. "I hate Faal as much as you do—we have at least that in common."

"Reading my mind, are you?" the Diadina asked with false lightness. She glanced around to see if anyone else was watching. Was the computer trying to tell her that she'd decided to keep the Diadina's secret?

"I'm not reading your mind; I'm reading your face. I have many other things to focus on this morning."

The Diadina glared at the computer. It wasn't enough for the thing to potentially ruin her life; it had to belittle her as well.

She turned away from the litter and went to stand in the shade of the tree. Already the cool of the morning was burning off, and the sun was barely over the wall. This was a beautiful tree, she had to admit, and she leaned against its trunk. For a moment, she felt a loosening of her tension and she sighed faintly. If only she could stay here instead of going to the arena at all.

DRENCH OBSERVED the Merith gathering under his spreading branches. He also sensed Akemi's change in position. "Where are you?"

She didn't answer right away, and Drench felt more and more concerned. Although her memories of their previous interactions seemed to be intact, talking to her was like conversing with an entirely different person. He'd explained to her how she'd changed, but she didn't believe him.

Drench listened to the Merith around him and answered his own question. They were going to the death chamber. He'd heard that it was nearby, but he had tried not to think about it. There were no Melifleurs there, so it was essentially off his radar. He wondered if he would be able to talk to Akemi there or not.

Her behavior left him in a real dilemma. He had no right to interfere in her affairs—he was not her sire or brother or forest lord. The Melifleurs were committed to non-interference; they only watched and listened. The Crosspoint were on-board with this policy, of course, as it suited their needs, but Drench was not the only Melifleur who at times stretched the meaning of 'non-interference.' Or ignored it completely.

If Drench decided to stop Akemi, he probably could. He could plunge her back into the trance state she'd traveled in, though without the other Melifleurs to help him, he wasn't sure it would work quickly enough. If she fought back, which she definitely would, Drench might struggle to hit the delicate balance of calm unconsciousness.

It would be far easier to kill her. Drench considered the thought, even though he shrank from the necessity. Putting her into a trance was a delicate operation, but if he was merely trying to quench the flame of her thought once and for all— that would be simple. Akemi didn't think he was particularly active or powerful, so she wouldn't think he was capable of it.

And if she was about to kill someone he knew she cared about —her sister or her good friends—wouldn't she want him to stop her? The real Akemi would. The one he'd gotten to know at Faal's estate.

With her treatment of the Rik, however, he was at a loss. He knew about the Rik imposture, their attempt to discredit humanity with a disguised attack and a rigged trial. It had been much discussed by the Melifleurs at Faal's estate, and they agreed that a Rik pretending to be a tree, while it would be amusing to observe their attempts to blend in, would have to be chopped down. He had no right to stop her from punishing those who had so deeply injured her.

But until she'd come here, she didn't seem to *want* revenge. Akemi's lack of rancor for the Rik had also been discussed, usually while she was sleeping. Had she only temporarily subdued her anger, and this new, vengeful person was the real Akemi? How far could he trust his instincts about an alien animal?

The Melifleurs liked the old Akemi. She'd been a novelty to them, and a fascinating source of information on the new barbaric races.

He'd once used the word *barbaric* with her accidentally, but never had he thought it appropriate until now—when her presence felt truly barbaric.

"I'm sorry you disapprove," Akemi said. She'd been paying more attention than he realized. "But it's none of your business. You're welcome to pass the story along at some point when you check in with your Crosspoint keepers, but today I don't have time for your angst."

Drench deeply regretted telling her about the Crosspoint arrangement. While he may not have the right to kill her for taking vengeance on her enemies, if she was going to reveal the Melifleur-Crosspoint alliance, he would have to act. That was not her secret to tell.

33

NAT WAS cautious as she and Sam came to the courtyard. Lots of Merith in red tunics stood around waiting (the litter bearers, Nat supposed), and many guests milled around forming small groups. The Tergre and Vel guests tended to clump together, and the two token Spo looked rather at a loss.

Don't worry! I've got everything under control. You'll be perfectly safe. Akemi sent the message to Nat's glasses.

"But I have no idea what you're planning," Nat said carefully. "Why would you get us an invitation to the death chamber?"

If my plan works, we'll be on our way home by tonight. Together. Doesn't that sound good?

"Yes, except for the part where you get Shara killed." Nat followed Sam further into the courtyard, which was crowded with shiny platforms furnished with silky pillows.

Shara's hardly my friend. And you can barely stand her! Don't pretend it's not true. She annoys you to death.

"Yes, but I've always put up with her for *you.* Because you connected with her—"

Sam lightly squeezed her elbow. "Starting to draw attention," he said. Several Merith were watching them, and Nat raised her chin, looking squarely back at them.

"Ah, my human friends," said the Pontifex, coming up behind them.

Nat spun around a little too fast, but Sam reacted calmly, inclining his head correctly. "We appreciate your invitation. But I do not know if there is space for us on any of these litters."

"You'll ride with me," the Pontifex said. "It's all arranged."

Yes, it's all arranged. You'll be safe with him. And this'll give you a chance to get on his good side, Akemi sent.

"Thank you," Nat said to the Pontifex. "I hope we won't inconvenience you or the Diadina."

The Diadina gave her a dirty look, which Nat could only assume meant that she did not appreciate how their scheme was working out for her. Nat didn't blame her. Nothing was happening as they'd intended when they spoke to her at the Herayung.

The Pontifex led them to his litter, and when Nat saw the computer that housed Akemi her pulse began to race. She hadn't seen it since Selta, and she hadn't been sure if Akemi would really be coming in person, or just 'coming' through use of a signal boost or something. If Akemi was *physically* at the arena, their chances of escaping with her went dramatically up.

"Hello," Akemi's voice came from the box, "It's a pleasure to meet two fellow humans."

Pretend you don't know me, Akemi sent.

Since Nat had already given a genuine jerk of surprise at Akemi's 'voice', this was not difficult.

"Another human?" Sam asked.

The Pontifex shrugged. "I'm not aware of the whole story, but I believe so. A Rik experiment gone awry. She is called Akemi."

"It is always nice to meet a fellow human, no matter the occasion," Sam said.

Nat choked out something suitable and cursed her suddenly awkward tongue. She was a language expert, darn it, and good under pressure. She should be able to acquit herself better than this despite Akemi's unpredictable behavior.

They arranged themselves on the litter, shaded by a gauzy maroon cloth that stretched over them. Six Merith held onto the long poles and hefted them into the air.

It felt dangerously tippy to Nat, who automatically reached forward to clutch Akemi's computer in case it should roll to the edge.

The Pontifex eyed her hand, but he looked unsurprised. His lack of reaction was unnerving. Clearly he knew more than she thought about the situation, and Nat desperately wished she could talk to Akemi without them listening.

Nat knew Sam well enough to tell that he was having the same realization, as his gaze went from Akemi's computer to the Pontifex and Diadina.

The Pontifex seemed content to let the silence linger, but the Diadina was not at ease.

"It's going to be a scorching day," she said, adjusting a bracelet. "I wish Faal had chosen another time for his display. A nighttime execution would be a novel change."

"I shall suggest it," the Pontifex said. "But I'm afraid we are obligated to him today. Have you ever visited a death chamber?" he politely asked Sam.

"Yes, sir, once. During our Spo cadet training, we visited one on Comboda."

"I've never been," said Akemi from the voice box. "I was selected for the Spo program, but I didn't get to go."

Nat took a shaky breath and felt the Pontifex's sharp eye on her. She just didn't know how to deal with Akemi this way. Akemi sounded angry that she didn't get to join the Spo cadets, when actually Nat had taken her place to try and save her life. Perhaps Akemi had some unknown purpose for this act, but Nat could not see through it.

She came to an abrupt tactical decision. "I should probably inform you that I already know Akemi. In fact, she's my sister."

What? Why did you say that?

"The Pontifex already knew," Nat said. "Or guessed. Am I right?"

"I knew you were connected," the Pontifex admitted. They were passing through the front gate of the palace now, back into the desert.

Nat tapped her glasses. "I can communicate with her through these."

"That I did not know," he admitted. "A neat plan. Now when you say *sister*—does that mean the same thing it does for us? Two daughters of a mother?"

"Yes, in most cases, it means two daughters of the same mother and father. We were very close."

This was not part of my plan, Akemi sent.

"We grew up together until I was conscripted into the Spo cadet program. Then, around the time of the human trial, the Rik were trying to infiltrate the cadets, and they kidnapped both of us."

The Diadina stirred uncomfortably.

"I can certainly understand her hatred of the Rik, then," said the Pontifex.

"Yes, but you see, that is something entirely new for her. I think that Faal has influenced her to feel that way."

You're not helping at all!

Nat knew she was taking a risk, but it was a calculated risk. She was still absolutely determined to rescue Akemi, but that didn't mean she trusted her. After Akemi was safely home with them, Nat could figure out exactly how Faal had reprogrammed her. For now, Akemi was at best a damaged ally, at worst—a hostile participant.

In this scenario, the best way Nat could safely undermine

Akemi was to start aggressively telling the truth. This had the added benefit of appealing to the Pontifex, who everyone knew appreciated boldness and strength and was reportedly excellent at sensing deception. Telling him the truth against Akemi's wishes made the Pontifex a temporary ally, emotionally.

"I would not be at all surprised if Faal has indeed influenced Akemi," the Pontifex agreed. "As long as you are being so forthcoming, may I inquire the purpose of *your* visit to my court?"

The Diadina looked positively pinched at this question, but she remained silent.

"We didn't know Akemi would be here," Nat said, "if you were wondering. That is the truth. Our main reason was merely to ascertain that Faal was truly here."

"Ah. Was that all?"

"Well, we'd also like to end the potential Merith war with Earth, as long as we're here," Sam added.

"Only natural!" The Pontifex laughed and turned to the Diadina. "Do you not find such candor refreshing, my dear? I'm not sure I would wish to live with it all the time, and it would be fatal in politics, but it is refreshing."

They were still bouncing along the track that led around the outside of the palace wall.

"What of the Rik?" the Pontifex asked.

"We'd like to end the extermination," Sam said.

"Ah, now that is interesting. After they tried to steal your planet? I should think you would be the first to thank us for our interference."

"Nonetheless, we're not. And as they're *our* enemy, we feel we have a stronger right to decide their fate than you do."

"And do you speak for the rest of humanity in that?"

Sam sighed. "Probably not. I've tried to do that before, and it hasn't worked out terribly well. But I'm the one here, and that's what I think."

"If I were inclined to halt the human war," the Pontifex said, "which I am not at all sure that I do, would you be willing to leave the Rik to us?"

"Yes!" Akemi spoke up. "Don't be an idiot, Sam. That would be an incredible offer and the removal of a real threat. It makes sense."

"I'm afraid it's that or nothing," the Pontifex agreed. "The human war—it is not very dear to me. The Rik are another matter. I've pledged myself to render them harmless—it will be my Act of Service. Every eleven years, you see, there is a Unity celebration, but it is not just any grand gala. It is a year in which the Pontifex proves his worth by doing good to the whole of the Merith race."

"That sounds challenging," Sam allowed.

"Yes, finding a task that can reasonably be accomplished in a year and that most Merith consider a benefit is no simple chore. I've performed five Acts of Service thus far, and the sixth one will be the eradication of the Rik. That much is settled." He turned to look over his shoulder. "Ah, and here we are in sight of the arena. Is it not magnificent?"

34

BASHER FELT DEEPLY uncomfortable as he landed their shuttle on Merith Prime. The airfield was crowded with craft broadcasting high-level security IDs. Thirty-nine of the fifty high families of Merith society were already here. There were also Vel, Tergre, Spo, and even *Melifleuran* royal IDs in the incoming queue, and while Basher found it helpful that so many people seemed to be headed in the same direction as them, he also found it uncomfortable to be lumped in with such illustrious guests. The upper crust of the galaxy, like elite societies everywhere, did not appreciate counterfeits or social mushrooms.

Basher looked at Claire one more time, wondering yet again if there was any possible way he could talk her into staying on the ship. Akemi and Nat's messages made it almost impossible for him to refuse, but Claire could stay on the shuttle...

"Absolutely not. I am not staying on the shuttle," Claire said.

"I wasn't going to say anything—"

"Oh please, you keep looking at me like you want to tie me to this chair until you get back. It's obvious what you're thinking, but I'm not going to wait here for hours and hours going crazy. If Akemi and Nat think this could work, I'm coming."

Basher feared Claire was feeling overconfident after their trip to the zoo. She'd seen the zoo again, and though she'd been terrified, she'd made it out. She'd faced some serious fears from her past, and the emotional high was still going strong. Now she felt ready to face another fear from her past, Faal himself. Normally Basher would be in favor of anything she felt capable of handling —but Faal was a real threat to her. Therapy was all well and good, but if someone had a deathly fear of crocodiles, tapping the biggest, wildest one on the nose was not a good way to overcome it.

Obviously she was also excited at the thought of rescuing Sage. That didn't require any analysis. Basher slung his satchel over his shoulder. "We're ready to go."

They went down three steps to the ground, and Basher took several deep breaths to acclimate to the air of a new planet. It was morning here, and the sun was on their left, casting long, twisted shadows from the many strange ships on the huge field. The spindly Vel shuttles looked particularly picturesque in the side light, like miniature pagodas in yellow gold.

Opposite the mid-morning sun, on Basher's right, was a barren mountain range that showed signs of relatively recent volcanic activity. The sky was a cloudless hue that, although blue, was completely unearthly. The sunlight seemed to cast a path in the air, an iridescent shimmer that made the sky look more like an ocean than an atmosphere.

"It's beautiful," Claire said.

"Butane gas trapped in the ionosphere," Basher said. "We got a warning about it while landing." Not that he wouldn't enjoy sharing a sunrise with Claire, but he wasn't going to wax poetic about gas while they went to rescue Sage.

On the far edge of the airfield, at least half a mile away, rested the distinctive stone arena of the death chamber. It was situated in a natural valley, and the pillars surmounting the rim made him think of a Roman coliseum.

"*Fleck'krut. Fleck'krut.*" A Vel female who had exited a ship near them waited for a response.

Claire laughed nervously. "Do you speak Vel?"

"Nope. Do you?" Basher asked.

"Not yet. We'd better walk."

They threaded their way toward one of the pedestrian walkways and joined the crowd flowing toward the arena. They were getting many strange looks. Basher wasn't sure whether people thought he and Claire might *be* Rik, or they just thought it strange that humans had been invited to this party.

Basher glared at one of the more aggressive aliens, and to his surprise, it quickly looked away and skirted cautiously around them. Huh. Unlike the aliens who lived on Selta, none of these aliens had probably ever seen a human or a Rik up close. The humans had a reputation for violence already, and the Rik were unpredictable at best.

"Wow. *We're* the scary aliens here." Claire eyed the jewel-encrusted gown of a nearby Meritha. "I also feel under-dressed." They'd brought serviceable clothes on their way to Faal's estate, but nothing fancy. Claire pulled her hair into a messy bun.

"I'm glad they're nervous around us," Basher said. "I'll take any advantage we have."

You'll take what? The words appeared on his glasses and Basher almost tripped on his own feet. "Akemi? Is that you?"

Who else? I just got in range of the death chamber and searched for your glasses. I figured you'd have them if you were planning to rescue me. :-)

"What's the plan then? Where are you? What should we do?"

Claire nodded along. "Ask her if Sam and Nat need to get out, too. Ask her about Sage."

I have a few things to wrap up first. Then we'll leave. Go on into the arena and sit somewhere in the middle section. I'm glad you came.

"Akemi, I need more than that. Where is your computer? How does Faal fit into all this?" Basher demanded.

Sorry, can't talk. Sam and Nat are making a mess.

"Akemi!"

Trust me.

She didn't say anything else, and Basher felt more frustrated than ever as he repeated her brief words to Claire. "I have half a mind to wait in the shuttle. It'll serve her right for being this annoying."

Claire shook her head.

"I know, I know, I don't mean it." Basher had gotten to know Akemi well in the weeks she'd kept him company at the embassy. He cared too much about her to risk ruining her plan now. When he'd first gotten to know her, he'd found it hard to remember that she was only a teenage girl, but now it came back to him loud and clear.

"I guess we just go find some seats," Basher said. "In the middle."

This wasn't a ticketed affair, like the Herayung, but Basher was still surprised that he and Claire could walk right in. They flowed with the crowd into an avenue of majestic columns which led to the towering wall of the amphitheater. A broad tunnel led into the arena and to a large stairway. The steps were slightly deeper and wider than was comfortable for a human, and Basher found it annoying to alternate between two short steps and one long one.

The stairway led out onto a platform about halfway up the stands of the amphitheater. A Merith was stationed on the platform, in a red uniform, and he seemed to be directing people to different areas. Basher waited uneasily for their turn.

"Whom are you a guest of?" the Merith asked.

"Ah, we are not guests," Basher said. "We're just—visiting?"

"Very good. Please choose seats in the upper tier."

The Merith turned to the next group, and Claire took a deep breath. "That was easy. I guess this is a public event."

They made their way up another stair to the highest seating levels, near the middle-top. Basher was boggling at the size of the place. He estimated that the spectators already numbered at least ten thousand aliens. And the nosebleed section where he and Claire found space wasn't even crowded yet.

Claire hugged herself, putting her hands under her armpits as she stared at the two giant gallows in the middle of the arena. Chains dangled from the crossbeams instead of rope, but other than that, it could have been straight from a textbook on medieval Europe. Worse than the large gallows, on either side of the stage two bodies twisted slowly in metal cages. Though the cages dangled at least twenty feet above the platform, Claire and Basher were seated so high that the cages were below them.

Claire avoided looking at them. "Please tell me whether they're dead or not."

"Oh. They're dead," Basher told her. "You can tell because— well, they're dead." But as he looked more closely at the bodies, particularly the one that faced them, he felt a cold burn of recognition. He couldn't be positive at this distance, but the corpse looked a lot like Juliet, one of the Rik girls Claire had gotten to know at Francois's restaurant. Basher spent hours watching those Rik through Claire's glasses, and he knew their faces well.

Claire exhaled slowly. "Okay. It's terrible, but that's better than—"

"Don't look!" Basher said sharply. "Just don't look at them."

"I wasn't going to."

Basher wished they were further to the right or left, where they wouldn't be able to see the dead girl's face, and he wondered briefly if Akemi had known about this. Surely not?

There must be some other reason she wanted them seated dead center. Probably so she could give Sam and Nat a location...

but it was unfortunate. Claire was bound to look at those bodies eventually, if only by accident, and see her friend. And he'd learned his lesson about trying to protect her.

"I think you know one of them," Basher told her quietly. "I think one of the twins is down there."

Claire's eyes flew open, and he heard her gasp of recognition.

It's called gibbeting, this display of dead bodies. Distasteful, isn't it? Akemi sent.

Basher put his arm around Claire, who buried her face against his chest. "It's Juliet," she moaned.

Tell Claire to be quiet. Here comes the Pontifex. It's about to start.

"THAT WAS CRUEL," Drench said to Akemi. "Extremely cruel. Why are you hurting your friends?"

"I'm not hurting anyone. Claire chose to give her loyalty to a bunch of aliens. If the sight of a dead Rik hurts her, that's her problem."

"Just tell me this—and I am amazed that I must ask—are you going to get Claire killed?"

"No, why would I do that? Faal is executing Rik, and she isn't a Rik. Plus, I have a better plan for her."

Drench read her thoughts and was confused. "You're going to trade her to Faal for your freedom? That's what *you* did for *her*."

"No! She traded me to Faal for her freedom, so that she could have Basher and I got... No, she traded—I offered—" Akemi's thoughts trailed off in confusion.

"You don't know what happened, do you?" Drench asked. "There's something wrong with your memory."

"No. I *do* know what happened. I remember what it feels like to be left behind, to be betrayed..."

"You're confused. Admit it. Your memory is failing."

"Just stop. I remember what it felt like and that's enough."

35

NAT SHUDDERED at the sight of the dead bodies hanging on the sides of the arena. She and Sam were entering just behind the Pontifex, along with the rest of the aliens from the palace. He'd led them through a rear tunnel that was only for dignitaries.

Now they followed him onto the rough sand of the arena floor, skirting the stage and walking directly below one of the hanging bodies. The crowd was centered mainly in front of them, and there was loud applause at the sight of the Pontifex.

One of the Pontifex's minions was bringing up the rear of their procession carrying the biobank and the voicebox of Akemi's computer. Nat would have preferred to carry it herself, but there was a difference between aggressive honesty and foolish provocation, so she didn't ask.

The sun was getting hot, and Nat shaded her eyes as she tried to look at the spectators. Thousands of eyes, singular and plural, stared back at them. Nat muttered to Akemi, "I hope you know what you're doing."

Basher and Claire are here. Akemi sent unexpectedly. *They're directly in front of you, near the top.*

"What? Why are they here?" Nat noticed the Diadina

glancing back at her and tried to pitch her voice even lower. "Basher should know better than to bring Claire here."

There's a very good reason. Just stop messing with my plan. If you and Sam will trust me, we can get things done.

At the front of the stage, the Pontifex stopped and faced the enormous crowd in the stands. Nat and Sam and the others were directed to fan out around him, also facing the crowd. A special platform with four empty benches and one throne-like chair was on the edge of the arena. Nat assumed that was where they would sit in a moment. Unlike the structure of a Roman coliseum, the Pontifex's special platform was unusually close to the floor of the arena. Faal had been resting in the throne-like chair, and he rose slowly to greet them.

He bowed profoundly to the Pontifex, who formally extended his left hand to raise him back up. Extended cheers rose for both Faal and the Pontifex.

The Pontifex bowed toward the crowd. His voice was somehow being enhanced, and it reverberated around the stadium. "We are come to the sixty-sixth year of my reign, and the sixth Unity celebration. It is my honor and privilege to announce my Act of Service for this Year of Unity."

He waited until there was relative silence.

"My Act of Service will be to rid the Merith of a pernicious and unpredictable threat. I undertake the eradication of the Rik species. I pledge to neutralize them by whatever means necessary. Their illicit technology and malignant culture have been allowed to prosper for far too long. If the Galactic Council is too squeamish to take the steps necessary to protect the sentient races of the galaxy from this threat... I am not."

A resounding cheer broke out in the stands—the clapping of Tergre, the clacking of Vel, and the loud cawing of Merith. Nat glanced at Sam and his mouth looked grim.

"I will do whatever it takes," the Pontifex continued. "If the humans will not bow to our necessities in this, I will even take steps to secure their planet for the safety of all Merith and the good of the greater galaxy. In honor of this pledge, the culmination of the Unity celebration is being held here today, hosted by the most excellent Faal of Merith II, my deputy in this undertaking."

Nat felt faint. This was even worse than she'd expected. The Pontifex's pledge more or less guaranteed that Earth would be invaded before this 'Year of Unity' was over.

"As the waves weather the rock, let the deaths erode the mountain," concluded the Pontifex.

He took the throne-like chair, and Nat and the others were directed to the lesser benches around it. Nat ended up right behind the Diadina and the Pontifex. Akemi's computer was situated on a cushion on the other side of the Pontifex.

"This is really messed up," Nat whispered to Sam.

Faal came to sit directly next to the Diadina, putting three of the most powerful and antagonistic Merith in the galaxy within spitting distance. Nat realized she was chewing her thumb nail and clenched her hands in her lap.

Faal leaned over to speak to the Diadina, and Nat saw with a start that the Diadina was perspiring heavily, although her inner eyelid looked as dry as sandpaper.

"Don't you approve of your husband's Unity task?" Faal asked malevolently. "No more Rik threat. Anywhere."

The Diadina gave him a look that probably was intended to be sophisticated disdain but fell short. He'd definitely rattled her, and the Diadina couldn't hide it.

"Have you decided to change your strategy after all these years?" she asked.

"It's an evolving game, my dear Diadina."

She stared at him and then looked down at her hands, which Nat saw were shaking slightly. "As you say."

Faal turned away, ending the conversation.

Only because she was so close, Nat heard the Diadina whisper, "So be it."

Nat didn't know exactly what drama was playing out there, but she was sure there were entirely too many plans snaking their way through this arena.

"Akemi," she hissed. "*What* is the plan? Why did you bring us here to watch these poor Rik die? And did you understand what the Pontifex just said? We're next."

Please, give me some credit. I brought you here to make an alliance with the Merith, a trade with Faal, and a safe escape with Basher. Trust me.

The Rik filed in from another door set low on the far side of the arena. They blinked in the harsh sunlight and slowly lined up in a multitude of rows before the Pontifex. Nat immediately spotted Shara.

Faal stood up and gave the spectators a brief synopsis of the day's attractions—but Nat was watching Shara with a growing sense of helplessness. Shara's eyes had locked on the computer. She glanced at Nat and then back at the computer, and gave a brief thumbs up. She was clearly signaling with her eyes, "Akemi's here! We have a plan."

Akemi clearly *did* have a plan, but Nat was very afraid her plan included Shara's death. Shara was as narcissistic as a Rik could be, and she frequently annoyed the heck out of Nat, but she was their friend. She was sincerely attached to Akemi.

"There's Sage." Sam pointed out the man next to Shara, and Nat grimaced again. It was the Rik guy Claire had had some kind of relationship with before she'd come back to the embassy. Nat had only met him briefly, when he and the other Rik had saved her life.

Seeing Sage and Shara together, Nat suddenly put several things together. She was afraid she knew why Akemi had gotten Basher and Claire to come here.

Nat clenched Sam's hand. "We have to warn Claire."

Akemi had accused Claire of trading her to Faal, and while Nat knew that wasn't what had happened, Akemi was clearly furious about it. She'd surely known that Sage was here, and used that to lure Claire. And given how unhinged Akemi seemed to be, Nat was guessing that a touching reunion was not in her plan.

In fact, Akemi had just said the second part of her plan was 'a trade,' and that explained everything.

"We need to get Claire out of here."

"Why?"

"Akemi is going to give her back to Faal."

Akemi's voice suddenly spoke from the voicebox, and Nat wasn't the only one who jumped. The Diadina almost jabbed herself in the eye with a tall flute of wine she was bringing to her lips, and Faal shifted uneasily in his seat.

"Perhaps the first two deaths of the day," Akemi said in a ringing voice, "could go to my two particular friends? It would be an honor of some distinction."

CLAIRE WAS unable to keep the tears from leaking down her cheeks while Juliet's body rotated for the crowd to watch, but she'd forced herself to calm down enough to witness Sam and Nat's arrival with the Pontifex. Basher also pointed out the Merith holding Akemi's computer.

From their high vantage point, they could still see the Pontifex when he sat down. Basher squinted down at them, the light in his eyes. "I think Sam and Nat are close behind the Pontifex, and Akemi is right there too, but Faal is nearby. I don't see how Akemi is going to work this out. Sam and Nat can't just walk away with her."

The Rik filed in, and Basher immediately spotted Sage and Shara.

"Okay, this is it," Claire said, wiping her cheeks. "If Akemi has a favor to use to get them free, she'll use it now..."

The Rik stood there and nothing happened, but it looked like there was some discussion happening around the Pontifex. The crowd rumbled expectantly.

"I hope this means Akemi is calling in her favor," Basher said. "Because I'm—I'm increasingly worried her plan isn't what we thought."

36

AKEMI REPEATED HER REQUEST. "I would be honored if the two Rik known as Sage and Shara might be executed *first*."

Faal smiled and looked at the Pontifex. "I have no objection to granting this request. Do you?"

"You are the host," the Pontifex said. "Do as seems best to you."

Faal waved his hand. "Call forward those Rik."

Shara's eyes got wide as she heard her name called. She and Sage moved forward until they were no more than ten feet away from the Pontifex.

"No," Nat burst out. "Akemi doesn't want that! There's something wrong with her and—"

"I can speak for myself, thanks to this nifty voicebox," Akemi said, "so please believe me when I say: I know exactly what I want."

"No, you don't!" Nat said. "Don't you remember how you urged me to let Shara come with us? Don't you remember that Sage and the others saved my life—just weeks ago? For that alone, you owe them better than this."

"He didn't save you. I saw it. He—you fell—Claire—" the

voicebox made an odd noise like bad feedback on a microphone. "He doesn't deserve anything."

Nat glared at Faal. "I don't know what you did to her, but if she's broken, it's your doing."

He spread his hands. "I do not deny that I break things that are breakable, but I'm not the one who put her in that box. If she wishes to take revenge on those who plotted her death, even I would not deny her that."

Shara could hear the conversation now, and she looked heartbroken. "Akemi, you know I never wanted you to die. You're my best friend."

"Best friend? You turned me over to the Rik. You didn't hear Nat screaming for hours. You didn't feel the cold vacuum when they tore out my brain and discarded my body."

"I know, but..."

"But what? What can you possibly say to defend yourself?"

Shara spread her hands. "Nothing. But I thought you forgave me."

CLAIRE ABRUPTLY STOOD up and started down the stairs. "I can't stand this. We have to get closer to hear what they're saying.'

Basher jumped several stairs to catch up with her. "We're not getting anywhere near Faal."

"Not too near—but something is happening. Look! There's Shara and Sage at the front. Akemi must be working this out. Let's get close enough to be ready when it happens."

Basher followed her down the stairs. The other aliens, growing bored with the long and unexpected wait, watched them with interest.

"I don't think Akemi's plan is working," Basher said. "Shara looks upset, and—I think you need to prepare yourself for the worst."

Claire glanced back at him with a strange expression. "I don't even know what that would be."

She jogged down the steps and when they reached a broader walkway, she took a nearby aisle that led down to the Pontifex's platform. When they were only twenty rows from him, Claire still hadn't stopped, so Basher was forced to grab her arm.

"No further," he said firmly.

There was absolutely no room in these packed rows for them to sit down, and he felt exposed with them standing on the stairs. They would be clearly visible if Faal turned around to face the crowd again. Basher pulled her down to sit on the step next to him. They were still rather too obvious, sitting in the aisle, but at least they were at the same height as everyone else.

"I don't know if we can hear them from here," Claire said, but then Faal started speaking, and they could hear him just fine. Too well, in fact.

"The crowd is restless, and I must begin," Faal said. "The Pontifex should have the final say on the first executions."

The Pontifex turned in his chair to look back at Nat. "I understand your concern, but I still agree with Faal. Akemi asks a reasonable favor, and I owe her three."

Claire took a deep, excited breath. "She did it. He's giving her a favor!"

The Pontifex waved his hand. "Begin with those two."

"Wait, begin with those two? What does he mean?" Claire sputtered.

Four guards surrounded Shara and Sage, shoving them toward the ladders that led to the tall platforms and the gallows.

Claire stood up. "No!"

AKEMI HAD KNOWN Claire wouldn't be able to stay away.

In a way, what was about to happen next wasn't even Akemi's

fault. If Claire had the strength to stay away from the Rik, she would have been safe.

"Claire," Akemi called, using her voicebox at its highest level. "Can you hear me?"

She knew from Claire's jerk and Basher's gasp that they could.

Sage spun around and searched the front rows with his eyes. The guards grabbed his arms and turned him around again, but he craned his head back, still looking for Claire.

"Claire, didn't I warn you about falling for a Rik?" Akemi said. "If you have anything to say, this is your chance."

Claire stumbled down the steps, despite Basher trying to hold her back.

Akemi laughed. "Ah, there you are. Sorry, Basher, this will only take a few more minutes."

Faal looked at Claire with satisfaction. Akemi didn't like the look, but she couldn't care about that, because... Akemi's thought trailed off. She had to remember her plan and stick to it.

"Faal," Akemi said, "at the conclusion of this execution, I would like to propose another trade. You may have Claire back, and I will go with my friends. I think you are honest enough to admit that our relationship was useless to us both."

37

THE DIADINA QUIVERED WITH DREAD. The computer was completely out of control, and Faal looked as smug as a Velusian dung beetle. This was clearly working out exactly as he'd wanted, and that meant something terrible was in store for her as well.

So far the computer had been focusing on her own friends, but the Diadina knew that her turn must be coming.

Even watching the computer destroy these other humans was unexpectedly painful. The Diadina had liked Claire during their time on Final Say, even though the Diadina couldn't trust her enough to be considered a true confidant. They both had lived on the edge of Faal's knife long enough to have a certain commiseration for one another.

She saw Claire stumble down the stairs open-mouthed and with a face furrowed with horror. She was shuffled off to the side and secured between several guards. Her eyes were fixed on the voicebox.

Many years ago, Faal had told the Diadina that he had nothing but respect for the unbreakable, but he could never be sure that something deserved his respect without testing it. Very few things remained unbroken in his hands.

The Diadina could see that he'd broken the computer, and at

least two of these humans were on the point of shattering. Faal must be thrilled.

And that brought her back to her own danger. She had to decide what to do, because doing nothing right now might be the worst mistake of her life. She could wait for Faal or his broken computer to get around to revealing her secrets, or she could somehow pre-empt it and make her own disturbance.

The guards had the first two Rik at the ladders. The male Rik looked back at Claire and his face twitched, as if he was trying to smile but not able to do it.

The Diadina's body was clenched so tightly she had difficulty taking a deep breath. She knew what she had to do to save herself, but she was afraid. She could wait until this unpleasantness was over, but that would be the path of weakness and cruelty. She had to do it now.

The computer spoke again, and its voice was like a jolt of ice water down her spine. "The Pontifex may be interested to know that the blonde Rik known as Shara was responsible for turning the human trial. She betrayed her species and revealed several key pieces of their plot. Of course, Faal knows that already. He is very good at keeping secrets. For instance, it was *he* who hired the Rik to sabotage the Spo space station. Would anyone like another war with the Spo–?"

"Apparently you're rather good at keeping secrets as well," Sam said harshly. "Akemi, examine your memory. Something has clearly been done to you."

"The Pontifex has made his decision," Faal said. "You disrespect him with your continued argument."

Sam looked at Faal intently. "*What* is your stake in this? I understand why you want to punish Claire, and I get why you might have messed with Akemi—but why do you care about the Rik at all? Why those bombs in the space station, if that is true? *Why* is this your passion?"

Faal laughed at Sam, an almost maniacal look in his usually rigid face. "Don't you realize you caused this much more than I? The Rik *lost* the trial. If you had left well-enough alone, they would be irrelevant by now. I tried to tell you at your trial, but you were too full of your own self-righteous compassion to hear me. And now look what you've done." He gestured at the gallows, the row of guillotines. "If you'd let them lose the trial, I would have done nothing—the Merith would have been safe. But you had to give them a second chance. That's why they're here."

"But they're not trying to take over another species now," Sam said, speaking loudly so others could hear. "Why can't you just wait? In another few generations, they'll have their own culture, and the 'Rik' will be effectively gone."

"That is the problem with you humans, you optimistically leave problems for future generations. I will not do that. I am already part of the generation that was left with the problem. And I will solve it."

"By killing anyone remotely connected to the Rik?"

"If my own father stood before me accused of a Rik connection, I would kill him with my own hands." He focused on Sam again. "So don't think to move me by pity. Pity is the worst kind of cruelty."

The Diadina took another painful deep breath. It was now or possibly never. She wanted to put her hand on the Pontifex—to touch him in some way while she told him the truth—as if that would convince him more fully of her identity than their years of marriage had. She resisted however, because she knew he would see a touch as neediness, and that would lend the wrong color to her words.

"Could Sam be right?" the Diadina said. "Isn't it possible that the Rik could become their own people? That those who're already human," she gestured to Sage and Shara slowly climbing the ladders, "That they might assimilate harmlessly into society and disappear?"

The Pontifex frowned, looking at her in a perplexed way. "I thought the extermination of the Rik was one of the few things you agreed upon, my dear. Faal has done more study on the Rik phenomenon than I have, and he considers them even more of a threat than the Spo. We've talked about this. He even has that theory on how they tried to infiltrate the Merith in past generations."

"Faal is obsessed with that idea," the Diadina said bitterly.

The Pontifex raised his hands. "I know you both loathe each other, but this is not the time to air it again."

She hadn't been married to the Pontifex for eleven years for nothing. He might still have her executed, but he would not hate her. "But you do not know *why* we loathe each other." Her shoulder feathers twitched in fear. "Faal's detestable theory is true."

The Pontifex studied her, trying to figure out her angle in suddenly agreeing with her long-time enemy.

"He knows it is true," she continued, "because it happened in his family. His grandfather was a Rik who took on Merith form." She paused. "You look skeptical, but you can see how it could be so. When his grandparents were young, the Merith were in uproar. It was two years before you became the Pontifex and began your Years of Unity, and the Rik thought there was an opportunity. His family, though not high, was wealthy and influential. I suppose the Rik thought it a safe place to start."

The Pontifex put his hand on her arm. "This is ridiculous, my dear. I know he has antagonized you, but this tale is pure foolishness. If the Rik were going to try for Merith, they would have infiltrated the high families, the ones who might have gotten a Rik in my place."

"Like *my* family?" The Diadina took another deep breath. "My family, the Skrenni, was at the pinnacle of the aristocracy at that time. That's why you invited me to the last Unity celebration. The reason I know all of this—is because it happened in my family as well."

The Pontifex froze. "What are you saying?"

The Diadina strove to remain outwardly calm. "It was my grandmother. If you consider, you will realize how this fits with what you know of both of us. From his grandfather, Faal learned who else was an imposter at that time. He has held this knowledge of tainted blood over my head since our first meeting, and I him. His vendetta against the Rik is entirely personal."

The Pontifex grasped the edge of his rocky throne, and his talons scraped the sides. "I do not believe you."

"You do, or you would not be so angry." She hurried on before he could answer. "And I do not tell you to weaken your position, or even to denigrate Faal, but to prove how weak the Rik truly are. Do you know any woman more Meritha than I? Or any Merith more fierce and cunning than Faal? We are Merith of Meritha, both of us. The Rik are nothing. A drop in an ocean that does not retain its shape." Her throat felt more open now that the worst was over. "Faal would no doubt have me die as well during the course of his eradication. He murdered his father and grandfather, when he discovered the story. He won't rest until every drop of Rik is gone. Please end this and spare my life."

She rose to her feet in agitation and might have said more, but the Pontifex slashed his hand at her. "Be still. I must think." He rose from his throne and paced the length of the platform.

One of the guards held up his fist for the executioners to wait until the Pontifex was seated again. The two Rik were on their respective gallows' platforms, the chains looped around their throats.

That had not gone as badly as it might, but what was the Pontifex thinking now? Did he suspect her of insinuating herself into his life to get to this position? Surely not. He knew better than anyone that he'd chosen her of his own accord.

Her limbs were shaking, and she sat down heavily.

Faal leaned close to speak in her ear, a controlled tone that sent vibrations through both her stomachs. "You should not have done that."

FROM THE HIGH PLATFORM, with the metallic weight of the noose hanging around his shoulders like the heaviest necklace in existence, Sage watched the Pontifex stride angrily up and down the platform.

Sage discovered he had enough selflessness to wish Claire wasn't here to see him die. With his new clarity of thought, he knew that he didn't deserve the loyalty she'd given him. He'd known how vulnerable Claire was when he met her, and he'd taken advantage of that to gain her affection. He'd been genuinely fond of her, but he'd still manipulated and used her.

Curse Juliet and her soul-killing guilt, Sage thought savagely. And now she was gone, leaving him to die alone in his own horror. He had half a mind to go ahead and jump off this blasted platform just to get it over with. Just to finish this intolerable pain. But—and Sage hated himself even more at the realization—he didn't have the courage to do it.

Sage kept watching Claire, who seemed riveted by the argument going on below, but he couldn't hear what was being said. Her eyes did finally flicker to him and over to Shara, and he glanced at Shara as well, wondering how she was handling the wait at death's door.

While he was having a moral crisis, she was otherwise occupied. The guard next to her was riveted on the altercation down below, and Shara had worked one hand under the chain around her neck. With tiny incremental movements, she loosened it so that it would slip over her head and off.

38

THE PONTIFEX PACED BACK toward the Diadina, examining her with fresh eyes. She sat with a straight back and composed features, despite sitting next to her mortal enemy. The events of the past eleven years slotted into the new template that his wife had revealed, creating new patterns.

She was descended of a Rik, and Faal had known the entire time. Astounding.

She ought to have told her husband, of course, but when? She would have been mad to tell him *before* she was the Diadina. He might have had her executed on the spot as a Rik sympathizer.

And after he'd selected her to be his Diadina, essentially unknown to him, she would have been a fool to come to him with this secret.

The Pontifex paced away again. And she'd known the same destructive truth about Faal, and she'd not used that weapon either! She was an endless source of surprise and fluidity, and the Pontifex was amazed at the strength of his feeling for her—now that it was put to the test.

If he was honest with himself, he was more impressed than ever at the masterful way she'd dealt with an untenable situation. He'd felt many things for her over the years—respect, curiosity, amusement, and affection. He'd been proud of her unprecedented popularity. He'd enjoyed her company for eleven years.

The Pontifex spun to pace back towards them.

Faal was speaking in a low voice to the Diadina, something that made her eye flicker with fear, and the Pontifex felt a surge of hate. Over the years, the Pontifex had regarded Faal with wariness but also appreciation for his wit, ruthlessness, and intelligence. He'd not always *liked* Faal, but he'd indulged him.

But in this, having tricked the Pontifex into making a pledge that would lead to his wife's death, Faal had gone too far.

The Pontifex stopped pacing. "Tell me Faal, would you have been the last to go up on that gallows, when the Rik planet was wiped clean and the last remote connections were obliterated? Would you have explained yourself then?"

DRENCH FOLLOWED the confrontation through Akemi's thoughts, but they were becoming so chaotic he struggled to gather the truth from her.

The Diadina—she ruined everything! I can see it in the Pontifex's ugly blue eye; he's changing his mind.

"She's turning the Pontifex against Faal," Drench protested. "And you hate Faal. Did you forget about that?"

He could sense Akemi getting lost in her own mind. The layers of her thought were spreading, like vapor rising off a lake.

I do hate Faal—but I hate the Rik so much more. They deserve —I feel like they deserve—

"Pause for a moment," Drench commanded her. "You're a sentient being and you can do better than this. *Think.*"

I can't think! I just know I had a plan, and now it's gone.

THE PONTIFEX WAITED until Faal answered his question.

"Yes," Faal said finally. "I would have been the last to give my life to rid the galaxy of this species and their offspring."

There was silence.

"Oh, for heaven's sake," Sam burst out. "Can we at least agree that he's lying *now*?"

Faal slashed a hand to silence him, but Sam didn't stop. "Faal has convinced himself that he's the purifier of the race, but to sacrifice himself would take a kind of humility he's totally incapable of. That's how this type works." Sam waved at the swirling cameras of newscasters, a flock of tiny drones. "He would *never* finish purging the galaxy of Rik, or so he would claim, and therefore he would never give up his power."

Faal's expression wavered, and the Pontifex knew instinctively that Sam was correct in his assessment.

The Pontifex glanced at the Diadina. "I have already committed to this action. I signed the Declaration of Service and swore to neutralize the Rik threat. I will not undo my oath. But I can change the order."

The Pontifex turned to Faal. "Instead of the last, you will be the first."

The spectators near enough to hear what was going on had been dead silent, hanging on every word, but when the Pontifex threatened Faal there was an audible gasp. There was even a ripple in the drones.

The Pontifex turned on his amplified voice. "Bring those two down from the gallows. There has been a change of plans."

"No. *No.*" Faal snatched up the round biobank computer that housed Akemi's brain. He shook it viciously. "*You* did this."

He backed away from the Pontifex. "You abomination of a machine. Who do you think *planted* that information in your mind? Yet you warned the *Diadina*? I'll destroy you for real this time."

He raised the biobank to slam it into the rock. "You have nothing left to offer."

"No, wait!" Akemi said. "I have one more secret to trade."

Don't do this, Drench commanded her. *I can't allow you to reveal the Melifleuran secret.*

"I already knew you killed your father," Akemi told Faal. "I already knew all about you because—"

I will stop you, Drench warned.

"Just try!" Akemi screamed. *Please, try,* she begged.

Shara saw the lights on the biobank go dark just before Faal slammed it onto the rock hard enough to crush the exterior and send pieces of metal flying in different directions. The grey brain tissue inside was dislodged, fallen on the sand of the arena.

Faal stomped on it.

Nat and Claire screamed, but a worse cry came from Shara's own throat, as she watched from the platform above them. She vaguely heard her scream echoed by a roar from the crowd.

Shara slipped the chain from her neck in one smooth motion. With a feral yell, she jumped off the back side of the platform.

She held the chain in both hands but it was also wrapped around her left arm. When she reached the end of her freewill, with a bone-shaking snap, the looped chain prevented her flying free. She felt an agonizing pain in her left shoulder—it was probably dislocated—but it worked.

The chain caught the lip of the platform and swung her forward toward the crowd. She let go at the right moment and slammed into Faal from behind. They both crashed to the ground, and Shara rolled on top of Faal.

Her left arm was useless, but she planted her knee on Faal's throat. "How dare you kill my friend!"

The pupil of his large Merith eye contracted in hatred. "I will kill every last one—"

"It was a rhetorical question." Shara jumped and brought her full weight down on her knee, on Faal's throat. She felt cartilage snap.

Shara was an assassin, first and always, and it only took her moments to finish the job. She felt dizzy and light-headed, but she saw the light fade from Faal's eye as he died, blood trickling out of his beak.

As if from far away she heard Sam say, "I never really believed she was an assassin until now."

The camera drones were in a frenzy, but the Pontifex and the Diadina—everyone really—gaped in shock.

Several guards, though stricken nearly dumb by Faal's death, recovered themselves enough to tackle her—a rogue Rik who'd just murdered a Merith.

Shara's head hit the ground with such force from their tackle that she blacked out.

39

BASHER COULD HEAR nothing over the sudden uproar of the crowd as Shara was taken down. The audience was turning into a dangerous mob as many tried to surge down and see what had occurred. Still more were trying to flee and some fights were breaking out among different species. When Basher tripped, the only reason he didn't topple down the unforgiving stone stairs was the crush of aliens holding him up.

Basher shoved and shouldered his way to Claire, who was no longer surrounded by guards, but slumped on the lowest bench. He couldn't tell whether she was staring at the remains of Akemi's brain smeared on the sand, or the ghastly sight of Faal's tongue protruding from his beaked mouth.

"We need to go," Basher said, pulling her roughly up. He was horrified by what had happened to Akemi, but the mob was already spilling down onto the platform and the floor of the arena. The Rik prisoners were pushing back, trying to escape into the crowd during the chaos. Some guards surrounded the Diadina and the Pontifex, but others had jumped the short distance to the sand to round up the Rik. Some just seemed stunned.

The Pontifex gave a piercing whistle, which although it didn't silence the crowd at all, made the guards look at him. He whipped his hand in a circle—indicating Sam and Nat, Basher and Claire, and many of the aliens who'd come in the litters with them. "Bring them," he said. "Get those two Rik as well. Rear exit."

Basher didn't need to be told twice. There was no way they would be able to get back to the airfield in this riot. Their only chance was to go with the others. The aisles and stairs were thronged, impassable. The Pontifex went to the front of his platform and leapt lightly off, into a small space the guards were holding on the sand of the arena.

The Pontifex's platform was only about five feet above the sand, and Basher jumped down to the sand, helping to steady Claire as she followed. Other aliens followed as they could, but the Pontifex was already headed straight under the gallows to the rear of the arena. The Rik prisoners were fighting for their lives now, as the Merith mob screamed and tore. Basher ran after the Pontifex, pulling Claire with him. A Merith broke away from the fighting and ran after them.

"Murderers!" he screamed.

Basher pushed Claire to run ahead of him between two rows of guillotines with shining diagonal blades. "Go, now!"

Basher drove his shoulder into the torso of the screaming Merith to arrest his momentum, and Basher only narrowly slipped away from his talons. The Merith got in a blow to his side, but a one-two punch to the Merith's head dropped him to the ground. More were coming.

Basher sprinted after Claire, glancing over his shoulder and nearly falling off the edge of the guillotine platform. She helped him get his balance and they ran on. The Pontifex disappeared into a narrow tunnel that was being protected by guards.

They ran up to it breathlessly, but the guards didn't move.

"Let us through!" Basher said.

The guards raised their guns. "Back away, Rik!"

There was screaming from behind as the Rik began to escape into the stadium. Others were headed toward them.

"We're not Rik." But Basher was unknown to them, of course they wouldn't believe him.

But then Sam and Nat, who must've been delayed in the mob, reached the tunnel. They were disheveled and Sam had a nasty bruise on his face. Nat had tears streaming down her face.

"Let us all through," Sam ordered the guards. "You know I arrived with the Pontifex, and these humans are with me."

The guards hesitated but then moved aside. They piled into the relative darkness. Another guard was marching Sage head of them down the tunnel, and a fourth carried an unconscious Shara in a fireman's hold.

A keening Merith tried to come into the tunnel as well, but the rear guards were back in place, protecting the tunnel.

They all followed the retreating guards down the dark corridors until Basher could see daylight ahead.

When they came out of the tunnel into the bright sun, Basher looked at the fancy litters of the caravan in disbelief. This was the fastest getaway they had? What was to stop the mob from following and tearing them apart? He and Claire would be better off running away than sitting on these stupid litters.

He was opening his mouth to say so when a shuttle appeared in the sky. It settled in the sand thirty yards away, and the Pontifex jerked his head toward it. It was a large shuttle, and all the aliens and humans with the Pontifex fit into it, though there was standing room only by the time Basher and Claire got on.

Only minutes later, the guards who'd been holding the tunnel came running out and sprinted up the ramp. Despite his impatience to get away, Basher thought better of the Pontifex for not leaving his bodyguards behind.

The doors closed. The sudden silence fell like a hammer.

Nat leaned gainst Sam's chest, tear-less now, but with a blank, unseeing look in her eyes. Sam stroked her hair and whispered something to her, tears in his own eyes.

Claire was sandwiched against the wall, and she and Basher looked out the shuttle window, studying the mob scene as they flew high and circled above the arena.

The rest of the cabin was crowded with silent Merith whose stares felt like lasers on Basher's skin.

SAGE LOOKED out one of the shuttle windows as well. The guard who'd brought him along kept a heavy hand on his neck, and Sage didn't blame him. He was just grateful that the guard hadn't left him to die at the hands of the mob.

Sage's neck and face were painful and scraped where the guard had jerked the chain off his head. In a brief moment of unity, they'd both skimmed down the ladder as fast as they could. Sage had fallen the last few feet and twisted his ankle—perhaps sprained or broken it—but the guard had half-pushed, half-carried him to the escape tunnel.

Sage had already realized that his only hope of survival was to go with the guard, and he did his best not to slow him down. He'd had no illusions though. This wasn't over. He'd heard the Pontifex declare that his Act of Service would be to destroy the Rik, and that wasn't the kind of thing he would or could take back.

Sage leaned against the wall and shifted his weight away from his painful foot, closing his eyes and taking a shallow breath. In all likelihood, he would end up right back in the death chamber by the end of the day. And if he had to deal with any more moments like Juliet's death this morning, or Claire's face as she watched him climb the ladder, he would be begging them to go ahead and finish him off.

Sage's thoughts were interrupted by a commotion toward the front of the shuttle. He and the others were all packed so tightly that he couldn't properly see what was going on, but it sounded like a bit of a scuffle. Sage strained up onto his toes to see what was happening.

Two Merith guards stood on either side of Shara, who had clearly just regained consciousness. One guard was trying to catch hold of her wrists, but her elbow flew to a weak spot on his arm. Her instinct was to fight, and she was good at it. Another Merith trod on Sage's foot as he tried to get out of her radius.

Sam shoved past him and went to Shara. The other aliens made as much room as possible, not wanting to be near the deranged Rik.

"Shara!" Sam tried to get her attention, but she still looked disoriented. He shook her shoulder and caught a punch as Shara turned to him. She sagged, her hand gripping his arm. "He killed Akemi," she said. "I—I didn't stop him. I'm *so* sorry."

"I know." Sam looked around. He probably didn't want to get into Faal's death surrounded by other high-ranking Merith. "But you've got to calm down for now. Nat and I will do what we can for you."

"I told you all along I could kill him," Shara moaned. "Why didn't you let me?"

Several Merith started muttering at this and others hissed. "They came here to murder one of our own. Assassins and Rik sympathizers."

"We didn't come here to kill anyone," Sam said distinctly.

"Oh, please," Shara said, swiping angrily at her eyes. "We totally came here to—"

Sam glared fiercely at Shara who finally seemed to catch on.

"—we totally came here to—meet the Pontifex. And see— *stuff*."

Sam curled his lip at Shara's lame attempt to change her statement, but he also nodded. "That's right."

Sam brought Shara to stand with Basher, Claire, and Nat.

Nat put her hand on Claire's arm. "I owe you an apology. Akemi was broken—I don't know. I'm sorry she brought you here; I'm so sorry about Juliet."

Claire wiped tears off her cheeks. "I'm not going to think of that as Akemi. None of this was *her*. She's the one who kept me company, who saved me from Faal. I don't know what he did to her these last few weeks, but I'm only going to think of today as Faal's failed scheme—not Akemi's."

"You're right," Nat said. "It was his doing—but I still wish I knew *what* he did. Because she was still there; she was still *Akemi* under all that. But Juliet—"

Claire embraced Nat, who clung to her in return.

Eventually Nat pulled away. "We're almost to the palace—should we talk about what's going to happen next?"

Sam took a deep breath. "We should. The Pontifex has some decisions to make. On the way to the arena today, before all this, he sounded open to the idea of leaving Earth alone—as long as we let him have jurisdiction of the Rik and their planet. But now with the Diadina's revelation—I don't know. Perhaps he'll be willing to compromise?"

Sage scoffed. "He already committed to destroying the Rik for his Act of Service. He can't compromise on that."

The Merith shifted, making him more visible to Sam and the others, and they all seemed to process his presence at once. Claire's eyes flickered uncertainly over him.

Nat seemed to take his interference in stride. "What is the exact terminology though?"

Sam shrugged. "You're the language expert. I thought that's what he said."

"I know the phrase extermination was thrown around by Faal,

but I think during his announcement the Pontifex actually said, 'Neutralize them by whatever means necessary...'" Nat said. "Or render them harmless."

"It comes to the same thing," Sam said. "They consider the Rik a threat by their mere existence. I don't know how he would 'neutralize' or 'render them harmless,' except by killing them."

Sage agreed with his interpretation, though the words did start a slow churn of thought in the back of his mind. Harmless... was there any way besides death that the Pontifex would consider the Rik harmless?

Claire avoided looking at Sage, but he wasn't sure why. Was she just feeling self-conscious? Was she embarrassed to show affection to him in front of her human friends?

Or was she ashamed to show him that she didn't care about him anymore? That couldn't be entirely true, he'd seen her face as he climbed the ladder to the gallows. He knew she still cared. But did she care more for Basher now, as he clearly did for her?

Claire finally looked at him as they were landing in the courtyard of the palace. "I'm glad you're okay."

"I'd rather it was Juliet."

"Yeah."

"Did you, er, ever get my letter?" Sage asked.

"I did, yes. I'm glad the Merith released Francois after you were caught."

"I was, too. I heard the Spo gathered a coalition to demand his freedom. Was that you?" he asked Basher.

"Ah—yes."

"You didn't tell me that," Claire said.

"I wasn't sure it would work."

"It was for the best," Sage said. "Francois wanted to save us, but he would have been broken if he couldn't—"Sage trailed off, not wanting to say it.

"Couldn't save Juliet?" Claire whispered.

"Yes."

"Were you there?" Claire asked. "Was Juliet—? No, I take it back, I shouldn't ask. I just hope she didn't suffer long."

Sage shook his head. "She was scared, but she died more bravely than any Rik I've ever seen. More bravely than *any person* I've ever seen. No one who saw it will ever forget."

40

THE PONTIFEX ORDERED his pilot to land in the central courtyard of the palace, a thing that had not happened in nearly two centuries. Aircraft were only allowed on Pontifical grounds in emergencies.

During the flight, the Pontifex had busied himself deploying troops to quell the violence in the arena. Another of his aides was monitoring the news channels, compiling an update of what was being said. He looked grim.

The shocked silence in the shuttle had given way to rampant speculation, exclamation, and accusation. When the doors opened, his guests spilled down the ramp into the courtyard. The Pontifex ordered his guards to escort both the Rik—Sage and Shara—to a holding cell immediately.

The Diadina was still seated in the copilot's chair, facing away from him, visibly pulling together her shattered poise. She straightened her neck and shoulders, took a deep, steadying breath, and smoothed her shoulder feathers. When she rose, her legs neither shook nor wobbled. He saw the moment when she turned and realized he was observing her.

It was obvious to him that she was afraid, but she did not show fear. She inclined her head slightly. "Thank you for securing my safety so promptly."

"Of course, my dear."

Her shoulders loosened slightly at the endearment. "Do you wish me to retire? Until—later?"

"No. While I'm certain you are exhausted, there are several things that must be discussed. Please await me in the small war room." He looked out over the crowd. "No—make it the large war room. Please have refreshments brought in half an hour."

She bowed and withdrew.

The Pontifex stood at the top of the shuttle ramp and raised his hands. The humans had grouped themselves uncertainly under the new tree in the center of the courtyard, looking more than a little defensive. Silence quickly descended.

"I apologize most abjectly for the danger in which you were all placed. As my guests, your safety and well-being are my privilege and priority. Should you wish to depart, I will arrange transport as soon as the airfield is secure. I hope, however, that you will remain and recover here. If you need medical attention, please proceed to the infirmary. It is just to the north of the hawking fields. Please make any other needs known to my staff, who will assist you in every way."

He lowered his hands, and the crowd began to buzz again. He saw several Vel help a limping comrade toward the medical quarters.

The Pontifex said, less loudly, but still in a perfectly audible voice, "My faals will assemble please in the large war room. Immediately." He looked around for the human group. "Sam, you and your associates will join us."

The large war room was one of the Pontifex's favorite rooms. It had a vaulted glass ceiling that he had commissioned himself, while the marble floor had been hand-pieced nearly two millennia ago. It was a glorious depiction of the most complicated sand table pattern—the diving death. And though he did not possess a death-glass table like the Spo emperor—it was one of the only things he envied the Spo emperor for—the Pontifex did have a very fine table of petrified wood from the ancient forests of Merith Prime.

The Diadina waited at the table, having satisfied both pride and discretion by placing herself behind the chair that would be at his right hand, but not sitting down. By this she indicated that it was her place by right, but only at his word would she take it.

He smiled slightly and gestured for her to sit. He had not yet had time to consider the ramifications of Faal's sudden demise, but he was strongly inclined to feel that if things had been reversed, and the Diadina had died in the arena and Faal now sat before him—he would be much less pleased.

Though perhaps the situation would've been less complicated.

The four lesser faals took their places quietly with some shifting of eyes. Faal's death left a hole both physically and politically in all previous hierarchies.

Sam and Natsuki sat next, followed by the other two humans.

The Pontifex sat last, as it was his right to have the last word in this discussion. "Before we address the events of the day, we ought to make ourselves known to each other." He introduced his four faals, stating their name and planet.

"Sam, please introduce us to your companions and their status in your government."

Sam inclined his head. "I'll ask Nat to do the introductions. She is the most fluent in Merith."

"I am Natsuki Fujimara, and this is Sam Locklear. We are not currently representatives of the Earthly government, but we were trained in the Spo cadet program, and can take responsibility to negotiate—for some things. Any agreement would need to be ratified by our government to take effect. This is Basher Kapur and Claire Kindler. Basher has been stationed on Selta for the last three years, tracking and arresting Rik criminals. He is as familiar with the Rik problem as any human. Claire—was a guest of Faal at his estate on Merith II for some years, and is a personal friend of ours."

His guards then appeared with the male Rik, Sage, and the Pontifex gestured curtly at him. "Is he known to you? I can have him put in incarceration with the Rik assassin, but as he is here and the fate of his race is at stake, I thought perhaps he would be of use."

"He is known to us," Nat said. "He was a—scientist."

"I was a senior scientist and manager of the Earthly migration project. I am also 'not currently a representative' of my species," he quoted Nat, "but I have as much right as anyone left alive to take that role."

"Then sit," the Pontifex said.

Several servants arrived with refreshment, and the Pontifex waited while everyone received a tall tumbler of warm water and another drink of their choice. The humans sipped the warm water with expressions of distaste, and the Pontifex wondered if their species hadn't yet evolved back to the simplicity of enjoying pure mineral water. It usually took about eight millennia after the invention of spirits for a species to—he recalled his wandering thoughts. There would be plenty of time for anthropology later.

"First, the holdings of Faal of Merith II," he began. "I will appoint a temporary administrator of Merith II for now, but eventually, in the interests of the planetary population, I must appoint a permanent Faal. Would any of you like to make a case for your qualification?"

There was silence.

"Come, come. No false modesty, let's hear it."

The Pontifex knew almost exactly what his faals were thinking, but it amused him to put them on the spot. These four had maintained a loose alliance *against* the late Faal, and the first to break the alliance would henceforth be on the outside. The management of Merith II would counterbalance that loss, but it was still a risk. Even worse, if they broke the alliance by making a claim to Merith II but the Pontifex did *not* appoint it to them—they would have lost on both sides.

He might take pity and select one—but he valued the boldness of risk takers, and he was curious to see if any of them would take the gamble.

To his surprise, the first voice he heard was from the dark-skinned human girl, Claire.

"I know I have no say in this, but I would nominate that one." She pointed to the youngest faal. "He—has often visited Merith II and is no doubt as familiar with the planet as any of them. And he impressed me on his visits to Faal's estate." She shrugged. "For whatever that is worth."

The young faal was too bewildered to hide his reaction. "Forgive me, human, but have we met? I have no recollection of it."

"I was in a cage beneath Faal's estate. Near the spiders."

"A cage?" His eye widened in recognition. "Ah—I remember—I regret—"

"Don't hurt yourself," she recommended. "The past is the past. But I know he offered to make you his protégé a few years ago. Somehow you avoided it without making him your enemy." She laughed nervously. "If that wasn't a good decision, I don't know what was."

CLAIRE REGRETTED SPEAKING UP, now that everyone in the room was staring at her. It had been a whim, probably brought on by emotional exhaustion and the surreal feeling of sitting between Basher and Sage in a Merith war room.

She did remember the young faal from his visits to the zoo. In fact, she recognized all of them, once she realized who they were. Faal usually took his guests on tours of the zoo to show off his newest acquisition or to allow them to visit their old favorites. That particular faal was the only one who'd looked as disgusted as he should have at many of the zoo's arrangements. She'd overheard conversations between him and Faal, also, and the zookeeper had once let slip that Faal preferred this one.

She wasn't surprised that he didn't remember her, because he'd always tried to look at the 'animals' in the zoo as little as possible. Claire shifted uncomfortably under the scrutiny of the Pontifex, and Basher gave her hand a quick, comforting squeeze under the table.

Finally the Pontifex inclined his head, apparently realizing she wasn't going to say anything else. "I will take that into consideration." He turned to the young faal. "Perhaps I'll give you a trial as the temporary administrator on Merith II, and we'll see how things progress."

"Of course. Thank you, my lord Pontifex."

"Onto the next issue then: the Rik. Claire, since you were willing to risk speaking up, you may have the honor of speaking first on this issue." He paused to organize his thoughts. "Here is the situation: I have committed to neutralizing the Rik threat. And yet the Diadina assures me they are not the threat Faal made them out to be, nor do I wish to execute her. Conversely, Sam tells me that they *are* a threat, but that the humans should have jurisdiction of them. And to complicate things further, Faal was the logistical manager of the eradication, and without him I will have trouble completing the task." He paused again. "Your thoughts?"

Her *thoughts?* What was she even doing here, talking to the Pontifex—the most powerful Merith in the galaxy—about the fate of the Rik?

"Er—well, I—I think," Claire floundered for coherency. She knew Basher considered the Rik who had taken human bodies to be killers. He was right. He thought they were a major risk. And though he'd admitted that Faal's executions were terrible, he hadn't exactly provided an alternative solution either.

Sage... Well, Sage was a Rik, and she'd fallen in love with him. She knew what that said about her, but what did it say about him? No matter what Basher thought, he wasn't all bad. And he wasn't a threat to the Merith, because he had already switched bodies and they could only switch once.

"The Rik threat is their ability to steal bodies," Claire spoke slowly. "Without the technology that makes it possible, they wouldn't be a threat to anyone. So perhaps there is another solution. Perhaps you could still fulfill your pledge by destroying their technology?"

The Pontifex looked a bit disappointed, and Claire bit her lip.

The Pontifex turned to Sage. "Tell me the truth—could the technology be destroyed?"

Sage shook his head. "I can't even pretend that it's a possibility. The machines could be destroyed, though there are many of them all over the planet, but the knowledge is something else. Too many people know how it's done." Sage sighed. "We were planning to take over the Earth—we had to accumulate a critical mass of qualified personnel and machinery to migrate efficiently."

Claire grimaced. She didn't often think about Sage's role on his own planet—or how close the Earth had come to being completely overrun.

"I knew as much," the Pontifex said. "Be glad you didn't lie about it."

Claire shook her head. "Okay. I guess the technology can't be totally destroyed, but surely there's some other way. If they're carefully watched, perhaps, until they have their own culture-- wouldn't the drive to migrate die out?"

Sam nodded. "That was our plan from the beginning."

The Pontifex shook his head. "Your species, forgive me, is young and naïve." He gestured to the nasty, warm water she was sipping, but Claire had no idea how that related to his point. "The Spo don't trust you to contain the Rik, and neither do I. Nor do I think even my own forces could contain the Rik for up to three or four generations. That would not fulfill my pledge at all."

SAGE SLAPPED the table and Claire jumped.

"What if—what if instead of destroying the machines, we *use* them?" he said.

Everyone frowned at him, but Sage only laughed. An incredible idea had come to him. Some strange, subconscious pondering of Juliet's words about substitution had abruptly come to fruition.

"You know that the Rik can only change bodies once?" Sage said. "Only *once*. I can never be Rik again, because I've switched bodies. Nor could I take another human body or a Merith or Vel, etc. We are safe after we switch. But it doesn't have to be *across* species. There have been experiments with moving a Rik from one Rik body to another."

There were several sounds of disgust from the Merith and from Basher also. Sage pressed on. "We tried it with criminals, for longevity purposes. But that's not the point. We built up the technology and manpower to transfer every Rik into a human body in the next decade—but what if instead we used it to—to switch every Rik into another Rik's body? We could—swap. The technology could be used that way. It's never been a priority, because we didn't want to go back to our old bodies and had no desire to preserve the host. But it wouldn't be a complicated change."

Basher leaned forward. "So—you think *every* Rik would be willing to switch with another Rik? And if they did, they'd be incapable of switching bodies again?"

"Completely incapable," Sage said. "And in another few generations, the ability will be gone. That was our rush with Earth, you know. Our sociologists project that in another forty years half the population won't be able to switch at all. Already the incidence of genetic mutation limiting transition has gone up."

"But would they be willing to switch bodies with each other?" Basher asked. "That's still a big deal, isn't it?"

"Well, they won't love it," Sage admitted. "But it beats genocide."

Sam nodded slowly. "It would be an interesting test for your species. They would *have* to cooperate in order to survive—they could no longer be slaves to self-interest."

"And if they refuse," the Pontifex said. "I would kill them; that is a motivating factor."

Basher shrugged. "That sounds fair."

Claire opened her mouth to object to that, but Sage touched her hand. "It *is* fair, he's right."

Sam was seeing the brilliance of it, but he had reservations. "The culture will still need help—the Rik have spent too long planning to migrate. They've never owned their own cultural development."

One of the faals laughed derisively. "The Rik are incapable of culture. Everyone knows that; it's why they must steal."

Nat rubbed her eyes. "That is a problem."

Claire snorted. "What are you talking about? The Rik could *totally* have a culture if they wanted to. I've seen them sing, paint, pray, cook, tell stories... Shara can't get enough of color theory, and Diva was a musician if I've ever heard one. They're just lazy."

Sam and Nat looked rather dumbstruck.

Nat said tentatively. "But the Rik you knew were already human. Maybe the artistic talent and curiosity came from their hosts."

"Didn't we all agree that they kill the person when they take their body? Perhaps their physique was stolen, but their personalities were not."

"I guess that could be true," the youngest faal said, "but everyone always says how the Rik can't make their own culture..."

Claire shrugged. "Maybe that used to be true, but it's not what I've seen. I bet if they stopped telling their kids that from the time they're born, they'd be fine."

Sam laughed. "And it's not like there aren't programs in place for retraining the children of another species." He turned to Nat. "Maybe we could talk the Spo into running some Rik cadet programs. Or better yet, the Crosspoint. After the Rik have all switched bodies of course. Then no one could suspect their motives."

"Slow down," the Pontifex said. "I admit this is a suggestion that may have merit. It has certainly never crossed my mind—which is unusual. It requires reflection. The Diadina looks weary as well. We will resume in two hours."

41

BASHER ROSE as the Pontifex and the Diadina left the room. There seemed to be more air without them, and Basher rubbed his face vigorously. He hadn't formed any expectation of the Pontifex, but if he'd thought about it, he probably would have expected to dislike him as much as he'd disliked Faal.

The Pontifex, however, didn't repulse Basher the way Faal had. He had power and arrogance, but it was tempered by a healthy dose of practicality, and maybe even a sense of humor. He was also courteous to everyone, which Basher thought indicated greater dignity and class than Faal had ever had. When Claire had spoken up about the appointment of a faal for Merith II, Basher had expected him to give her a scathing set down. Instead, he'd seemed impressed by her boldness.

Sam was still excited. He turned to Sage. "Exactly what resources would you need in order to do this switch? I know you said the infrastructure is in place, but if the qualified personnel have left the planet—or been executed—what kind of numbers are we talking?"

Sage began to explain, and Sam and Nat leaned in to confer with him.

Basher caught Claire's eye. "Just like old times."

She smiled and Sage glanced at her, but Sam asked him another question, so he was forced to turn back to them.

Basher jerked his head at the door. "You want to go find some food?"

"I don't know if I can eat, but—I probably should."

"No kidding." Basher got to his feet. "We haven't eaten since— I don't know when. Feels like a long time ago."

Claire glanced at the others guiltily, and Nat said, "Go ahead, we'll come later." Sage was making a list of his associates on a pad of paper, and he didn't look up from it.

Basher walked with Claire through the quiet central courtyard. There was a large tree there, and the earth was still churned up around it. Its large root system must have required serious dirt-moving if it'd been recently planted.

"I feel like I've gone deaf," Claire said. "It's so quiet here, after the mob. I feel like I've been in a blaring concert and now my ears are ringing."

"Yeah. I feel like I've been sprinting on a treadmill that slammed to a stop, and I can't get my balance." He took a right onto a shrub-lined pathway on the north end of the courtyard. "Sage's idea is brilliant. I'm glad there's another solution for the Rik. The possibility of a solution, at least."

"It's so simple. I can't believe nobody thought of it before."

"That's the thing about great solutions; they usually seem ridiculously simple in retrospect."

"I guess so."

"This could be the solution to the human problem too. If the Pontifex is willing to negotiate about the Rik, perhaps he'll end the war before it's really started." They followed a gentle curve in the pathway.

"Hopefully." Claire's face suddenly lit up. "Oh! I wish we could see the faces of the tribunal when Sam gets to tell them *he* ended the war."

"Wow. That's going to be amazing. Though I give the politicians enough credit to think they'll be truly glad to hear the news, even if it's Sam's doing."

They came to a fork in the tree-lined walkway and they both stopped. Basher suddenly realized he had no idea how to get to Sam and Nat's suite from here. Or where to get food. They'd gone directly from the courtyard to the war room earlier and Sam had only quickly pointed out where the human suite was situated.

"I don't suppose you know where we are?" Basher asked.

"I was following *you*."

"I wasn't thinking. I guess we should go back to the central courtyard. I thought Sam said the guest rooms were across from the treasure room on the south."

"The west, I think."

They turned around and headed back the way they came.

"I'm so sorry about Akemi," Basher said. "And Juliet, also. She seemed really sweet."

"She was. I'm glad she wasn't terrified," Claire's voice wobbled, and Basher fought the urge to put his arm around her. "Sage said she was brave."

"Speaking of Sage—he seems a bit different than before."

"Maybe." Claire's voice was carefully neutral.

"We've only been back a matter of hours, and it's already clear that he's not the same. I..." Basher took a deep breath. "To be completely honest, I will always hate the idea of you and him together, but I can't say that it would be entirely wrong. You don't need my permission, but whatever you decide to do, I won't think less of you."

"I appreciate that."

He laughed ruefully. "Good, because it's not easy to say."

"And I agree that it wouldn't be wrong—but I'm not going to try it. I'm not in love with him anymore."

Basher was relieved, but he wasn't going to ask for more. She'd made her position on *him* clear enough. They took a left, retracing their steps, and the shadows of the trees fell on them with every other step.

"Aren't you going to ask me why?" Claire finally said.

"I'm pretty sure I don't have the right to ask."

They were back under the large tree, and Claire stopped walking to put her hand on its silvery bark. "I apologize for yelling at you on the ship. I shouldn't have said I didn't trust you. It's not true. I trust you more than anyone I've ever met."

Basher waited, sensing she wasn't done.

"When Sage was about to die, I was horrified, but I wasn't heartbroken. He's a friend, but you were right—my relationship with him was based on my loneliness, not what we had in common." She smiled a little. "I forgot to even be scared of Faal in the arena, because I knew you would do anything to protect me. I don't know if I—love you, but I don't want to lose you after all this. If you're still interested in—us, I'd be willing to give it a try."

She moved to tuck her hands in her pockets, as she always did when she was embarrassed at sharing too much of her past. Basher caught one of her hands. He knew what trust meant to her. In a way, it was a bigger hurdle than love. You can fall for someone dangerous, but you can't trust them.

"You're the most brave and generous person I've ever met," Basher said. "You went through the unthinkable and came out strong enough to still care about others. I shouldn't have criticized you for that. I would be *honored* if you wanted to give me a chance."

He could tell her also that he didn't need a chance, he was already in love with her. He could tell her that she could take years to make up her mind. He could tell her that he already knew he wanted to spend the rest of his life with her.

Or he could tell her all that later. He squeezed her hand. "And I think the first part should involve getting you back to Earth. You should go to Florida and find your family. I should go see my mother in New York. Maybe we could come visit; I'm sure she could use a vacation."

"That—sounds amazing. My dad could take us snorkeling, maybe. If that's still a thing. He used to love it."

"You have a lot to catch up on." Basher leaned one shoulder against the tree. "And now you have a chance to do it."

"I'd—really appreciate not going home alone. I kind of never want to travel through space on my own again."

"Then I'll be right there as long as you want me."

Claire squeezed his hand again and Basher felt a rush of joy. The tree warmed his shoulder, and the leaves danced over their heads. He really wished Akemi was still here. He knew she would have been happy for them, too.

"I think I'm hungry now," Claire said. "Let's *actually* find some food."

Basher pushed away from the tree and followed her down a different path.

42

BEFORE THE ARENA, Drench had already decided how to act if Akemi threatened to reveal his secret. It was a horrible thing to snuff out a living being, but he had known it would be necessary. In the forests of Melifleur, such things were understood and used when necessary.

Perhaps it would have been harder to follow through on his decision if he hadn't felt her deep horror and disgust at what had been done to her. She'd been incapable of arresting her free-fall descent into confusion and cruelty, but she'd *wanted* to stop. Her desire had been crystal clear for one brief moment. Though still confused and angry, she'd begged him to stop her.

And although Drench could have let Faal physically destroy her at that point—as he had done anyway—Drench despised the idea of letting Akemi be killed by her enemy. If anyone was going to snuff out her light, it should be a friend.

Drench had wrapped the bulk of his presence around her to smother her—a blanket of wet leaves over a flickering flame. This was only the second time in his life that he'd intentionally killed another sentient being, and he hoped it was the last.

To his intense pain and surprise, however, he'd found that Akemi could not succumb to death, even when she willed it. In those seconds when Faal raised her shell to destroy her, she instinctively fought Drench with the sudden force of a wildfire.

For the first time, as Drench locked into conflict with her fierce survival drive, he understood how she might have survived the Rik procedure that killed her body. The mere psychic horror of the act would have undone any Melifleur, but Akemi was not a Melifleur.

As Faal began to lower his arm, Drench was still locked in a burning struggle with her. He had a choice. He could withdraw from the struggle and leave Akemi to be smashed. That would be the prudent thing to do, because in the clarity of his pain, he realized she was capable of killing them both.

But Drench could still not bear to leave her to Faal. So instead he drew his consciousness back to himself—back to his firm tree self in the courtyard of the palace—and brought Akemi's fire with him.

She was beyond words, beyond understanding, and she fought even harder as he pulled her consciousness away from the biobank computer.

He felt the moment that Faal destroyed what was left of her physical body because it released her like the cutting of a rubber band. She suddenly had no anchor. They both snapped back into his space with a branch-cracking whiplash.

Indeed, several of his branches fell heavily to the ground, and all his outermost leaves withered.

And Akemi...was she gone?

Drench found her, a tiny thread of consciousness entangled with his own. Now that she had no corporeal connection to the world, he could effectively do what he had tried to do before. He could smother her.

Drench sighed. He was only kidding himself. He could never kill her now. She wasn't a threat to him or to any other Melifleur, and she would probably dissipate rapidly on her own, unanchored as she was.

He'd barely had time to hope that it would happen before she woke up and understood what was happening when she stirred.

He felt her instinctively reach for her senses. Five, eight, ten tendrils of thought slowly extended, searching for sight, sound, touch, taste, balance, and more. They recoiled at once.

I'm dead. It finally happened.

"No," Drench told her. "You are not dead yet."

Yet?

"The computer was destroyed," he said gently. "I think it will only be a matter of minutes."

Ah. Thank you, Drench. Thank you for saving me from myself. This is peaceful.

Akemi's mind wandered as she said goodbye to her life. She pictured different humans she'd known in her previous life, lingering long on her sister and her friends, saying silent farewells. Drench approved. It was a good way to finish.

The minutes passed slowly, but Akemi did not seem to be dimming. If anything, her mind was gaining clarity.

Akemi finally spoke again. *Well. This is awkward. Here we are waiting for me to die, but it doesn't seem to be happening.*

"Indeed." Drench was in something of a fix. He had expected their struggle to end in death, at least for her, if not for them both. He hadn't considered that they might *both live.*

Pessimist.

"Did *you* expect to survive the destruction of your brain?" Drench asked tartly.

I guess not.

Drench softened a little. "Do you remember what happened?"

Her mind flitted back over the last few hours, but it was patchy and confused. What she did remember was enough to make her soul cringe. *I suppose whatever he did to me—whatever software or programming Faal used to confuse me—must have been destroyed with the computer.*

Drench confirmed this.

I'm so sorry I betrayed you. I can't believe what I did to my friends.

"It was Faal's doing," Drench said. He wanted to say that it wasn't her fault at all, but he couldn't give her complete reassurance.

You can't hide your thoughts from me anymore, Akemi reminded him. *And I think you're right. Faal did something to my memory, but I was still the one in control. I don't know what that means about me.*

"It means you are the same as all lesser beings, such as myself," Drench said. "Capable of great evil and great good."

The shuttle landed nearby, and Drench shook slightly with the impact. The earth around his roots had not yet packed in firmly.

He and Akemi studied the crowd as they swarmed out of the shuttle. He gave her space, as had occasionally happened before, to share his sensory input.

There's Sam and Nat! And Claire and Basher—I'm so glad they're alright. Sage is with them, too. And there's Shara! She's alive.

"I thought your hatred of the Rik might persist," Drench noted. "I wasn't sure whether that was another of Faal's constructions or your true feelings."

I don't love all of them, but Shara is my friend. So is Claire.

As if she'd heard her name, Claire drifted toward Drench and the others followed her. They stood in his shade, but Drench was rather embarrassed at the state in which they were meeting him, with his branches scattered about and leaves in disarray.

Akemi laughed, and it was a wonderful sound. He hadn't heard her laugh like that since they arrived.

"*You* can laugh," he said dryly. "You're not a complete mess. They can't even see you."

Akemi sobered. *They think I'm dead. I completely forgot.*

The humans began to listen as the Pontifex made an announcement.

They don't seem particularly upset that I'm gone, Akemi said, sounding a bit grumpy. *I mean, they don't even look like they were crying.*

"In their defense, this is, hmm, the third time they've thought you were dead?"

You make a fair point.

"In the meantime," Drench said, "I am not sure how you can communicate with them. I could do so—when my Crosspoint contact comes. But that may not be any time soon. Also, if Faal finds out you're still alive, that could be problematic."

Yes. But I didn't see Faal get off the shuttle. Do you think the Pontifex got mad at him?

"I can only assume so, but I was busy with you. I don't know what happened after..." Drench trailed off uncomfortably.

After he smashed my brain to pulp. It's okay, you can say it.

"You have an animal's sense of humor," he said sternly, though he was remembering how much he enjoyed her company.

Aw, thanks. I like you too. Which is a good thing, because I think we're stuck with each other.

"Forests and firebrands; you may be right."

Can you curse? I didn't even know that.

"I like you well enough, but if I have you in my soul much longer, I will volunteer to furnish the Pontifex with a new table."

Drama, drama. You sound like a palm tree.

"Excuse me—"

Who's got all their branches in a twist?

Drench centered himself. "I was *going* to say, before I was so rudely interrupted, that we may be able to transfer you again.

Your consciousness or soul, whatever it is that's left of you, is clearly very elastic."

Akemi pictured a slingshot.

"I will lose more leaves if you do that again. Be good, Akemi, and let me think."

The courtyard cleared, and Akemi was getting a little bored by the time someone finally came back. Claire and Basher were back. Drench didn't recognize them himself—he could not tell humans apart easily because they all had the same number and arrangement of branches—but Akemi recognized them through his faculties.

She shamelessly eavesdropped and completely interrupted his train of thought. *This is it! They're finally getting together.*

She listened intently through Drench's excellent sense of hearing.

Yay! I totally knew Basher was in love with her.

Drench was confused. "I thought—though I may have been mistaken—that you cared about this one as well."

It's complicated for humans, particularly for girls. I do like Basher, but I always knew I couldn't have him. And if you can't have something, the next best thing is to give it to your best friend.

43

NAT CHEWED on a piece of rubbery potato that was part of the lunch the Pontifex had provided. Her eyes felt gritty with desert sand, and she seemed to have no tears left to rinse them out.

She hadn't yet dealt with Akemi's death. True grief would come later, but she was surprised to realize that she wasn't as devastated as she'd expected. Akemi could never have lasted indefinitely in that biobank... particularly not with the horrible changes Faal had wrought.

Nat pressed her eyes again, forcing her attention back to the matters at hand. Things were going well in this second impromptu negotiation, but not everything was perfect. The Pontifex was intrigued by Sage's alternative solution—but there were major logistical problems. For instance, how long would it take to poll the Rik and find out whether they would even choose to do this switch? How long would it take to adapt the machinery? How long would it take to do the actual work?

The Pontifex had a year to fulfill his Act of Service, and if any of this could be done in a year, it would be amazing.

And they hadn't even touched on the Merith war with humanity yet.

On the bright side, Nat had spotted Claire holding Basher's

hand after they came back to the war room, and that made her smile.

The Pontifex made another note on his clunky tablet and then leaned back in his chair. "I cannot commit the Merith to handling cadet programs for the Rik children. There is bad blood there, and it would weaken public perception of my Act of Service."

Nat didn't exactly like the Pontifex, but she appreciated his honesty. His main goal was to be a popular and long-lived Pontifex, and the means to that end was positive public opinion. It wasn't particularly noble, but it gave clear edges to the negotiation.

"Everyone agrees that the Spo and the Crosspoint have the best cadet programs," Nat said. "Of course, the Spo may not be inclined to help you, considering how often you seem to find yourselves at war with one another. The Crosspoint are also closely allied with the Spo."

The Pontifex waited.

Sam took over. "If you are willing to make a long-term treaty with the Spo and Crosspoint, contingent on their willingness to handle the Rik cadet programs, you could spin it really well. I can almost see the slogan, 'Making our enemies into our servants,' or something like that."

"That's not a bad notion," the Pontifex admitted. "You negotiate excellently well for other species. But what about your own?"

"Obviously we'd like a treaty as well," Sam said. "An assurance of planetary sovereignty is a must, but perhaps we could offer a temporary trade deal...or a small percentage on Earthly cultural exports."

The Pontifex carefully scratched the skin below his eye. "But Earth is such a fascinating place—I'm not at all sure that I wouldn't want to invade for my own purposes."

Nat had observed how the Pontifex liked to bait and challenge those around him, but she wasn't sure whether this fell into that category or not.

Sam shrugged. "Our military is quickly gaining proficiency with our new space fleet. I'm not pretending we could defeat you, but we could make it expensive. And you'll have many draws on your resources this year."

The Pontifex opened his beak to reply, but Nat never knew what he might have said.

Everyone stared at their various tablets as a message popped up. *May I interject into this conversation? I believe I have a final favor to ask of the Pontifex. :-)*

Claire squealed and clutched Basher's leg. Nat gasped. The Pontifex froze.

This is Akemi, in case you were wondering, and I am back to my normal self. Sort of. I elbowed some space in the palace network, and so...here I am.

Sam pinched the bridge of his nose. "You know what, Akemi? *You know what?* I'm not even surprised! It just stings to think of all the trouble we've wasted on someone who is clearly immortal."

You don't sound too excited to hear from me.

Sam laughed. "I'm always happy to hear from you."

Nat's hand shook as she touched the letters on her tablet. "How—*where* are you?"

That's a long story.

"Try us," Sam said.

Not in this company, my dear almost-brother-in-law. But I've got a whole new set of jokes. A Merith, a Crosspoint, and a Melifeur walk into a bar—

"Akemi," Sam said. "Are you drunk?"

I guess this isn't the time for jokes. I think I am a little giddy to be myself again, but in all seriousness, I am truly, deeply sorry for everything I have done since Faal corrupted my memory. Anything I can do to help, I will.

"That's good to hear. In fact, that's great," Sam said. "I think you'll be able to smooth out several of our last wrinkles here..."

44

AKEMI ONCE AGAIN CIRCLED A PLANET, but this time it was not Earth and she was not a space station. And this time, instead of a handful of curious people waving at her, there were thousands of aliens staring at the sky. Hundreds of thousands.

She had circled the Rik planet many times already over the last two days, altering her trajectory to cover all the settled continents with her cameras. She'd needed to see each continent during the night, and now she was on her final pass. She'd been counting the votes as she went. Emotionally, she had now cycled from being exhaustion to elation.

"I'm done, I'm done, I'm *done*," Akemi called out. Sam jerked upright. Indentation marks lined his sleepy face from where his head had rested on the control board. Basher was fast asleep, propped against the wall in the corner with Claire curled up against his side, her head pillowed on his shoulder. She was still fast asleep, also. They all had cabins they could be in, but they'd been waiting to hear the results of her final pass around the planet.

The Rik had been told of Sage's plan—arguably crazy though it was. If they agreed to undergo the switch and relinquish all rights to the technology thereafter, they were supposed to come outside to be confirmed and counted.

Nat had slumped sideways against the bulkhead and now straightened, rubbing her neck. "What time is it?"

"It's counting time!"

Sam waved a lazy hand at her voice simulator. "What are you on and where can I get some?"

"It's just the tree talking. Wake up!"

She and Drench had accomplished an impressive feat, hacking into the Pontifex's communication system. A Crosspoint expert had helped her figure out how to use the external processor now attached to Drench's trunk. Unfortunately, that had been the last of the miracles. Neither Akemi nor Drench nor anyone else could figure out how to separate the two of them. So Drench was, in fact, stuck with her.

His bulk filled a large part of the storage facilities on this ship, but currently he was dormant since he hated space travel. His presence was a warm, pulsing, green radiance that suffused her consciousness.

So Drench was in a trance for the moment, but Akemi thought he was growing resigned to her presence. After this mission, which she'd begged him to let her do, they were going to be taken back to Melifleur.

The Crosspointers were fascinated by Drench's situation, and they were eager to see what could be done on his home planet.

Drench was eager to be home, too, and though he didn't often express it, he was enthusiastic to show Akemi his planet.

The others were stirring groggily now, and Akemi waited for them to view the stats for the many orbits she'd made. "I'd call that a resounding success," she said.

They nodded dumbly. There were some holdouts, but the Rik had voted resoundingly for the plan. They had literally come out in droves to be counted. Over ninety percent had agreed to fundamentally alter their society by agreeing to the plan.

Sam rifled through the printouts. "Sage still has his work cut out for him, but this should expedite things a lot."

"Should I call the Pontifex?" Akemi asked. "And Greg?"

"Go for it. Only promise me you'll wake them both the same way you woke us," Sam said. "Now I'm going to bed."

SAGE STARED down at the planet below him. His planet. His responsibility.

He had never considered it profoundly. Always the plan was to migrate; always his focus had been on Earth. Now he studied the contours of the continents and wondered if he could grow to love it the way he'd loved the idea of Earth.

It would be difficult. For so long he'd had nothing but contempt for his own species. Could they truly become a worthwhile people without stealing the essence from others? He didn't know. Six months ago, he would have said no. But now he had known Claire, who had begun to change him. Now he had known Juliet, who had changed him even more.

He still had not found the quiet peace or the forgiveness of past wrongs that Juliet claimed was possible, but he thought perhaps that was as it should be. Maybe that wasn't for him. And he didn't know if his new perception of responsibility was due to Juliet or to some supernatural influence, but it could mean the difference between life and death for the Rik.

He was continually astounded that they even had that choice. If not for the Diadina, the Pontifex would never have been willing to spend this much money to allow the Rik to live. And Sage was perfectly aware of how undeserving—and ungrateful—many of his people would be for their unexpected salvation. If this was divine influence, it made no sense at all.

But Sage had come to believe that if they were ever to have a culture, it would have to be grounded in a new understanding of remorse and empathy. He had even seen some signs that other Rik were bothered enough by their empty existence to embrace a different truth.

He'd spoken to Sam and Nat about this, and they'd agreed. Akemi had even speculated that perhaps the redemption of the Rik had been the point of the last few years—for the humans, for the Diadina, even for the Spo. A plan that brought the Rik into close contact with humans and Crosspoint and also made them desperate enough to change....

He didn't believe that—but he did agree that the Rik needed *something*.

Everyone who had seen Juliet die that day—those who had survived the mob, and those who had seen it on video later—had voted for the plan. Some had even taken to getting a 'J' tattooed on their hand. He didn't know what exactly it signified for them, but it had to do with courage in the face of death—something entirely new for the Rik.

Sage sighed, looking down on his planet. Great change was coming, and he had a completely overwhelming job to accomplish over the next years. But at the end, perhaps the changes would leave something worthwhile in their wake.

He could only hope it might be so. For Juliet's sake.

EPILOGUE: LOS ANGELES, 6 MONTHS LATER

SAM AND NAT'S wedding celebration lasted five days. The ceremony was televised around the world and on all the Galactic Prime feeds. Nat wore a dress that was a cross between a traditional Japanese wedding gown and a western one, designed by Shara and Akemi.

Nat mostly ignored the galactic polls on her wedding dress, although Shara told her cheerfully that it was a major hit with both Tergre and Crosspoint.

They married in Los Angeles at the Crystal Cathedral, which had been the headquarters for the Spo press for several years. It was now used sporadically by the Human Coalition Government.

There were no posters on the walls.

Basher and Claire were on the first row, next to Nat's parents. On the groom's side were Sam's sister Claudia and her husband, Chris, as well as his mentor Greg, and many of his cadet friends.

Basher's mother and Claire's parents were also in attendance, looking rather shell-shocked at the presence of not only Spo, but Merith, Vel, Tergre, and even Crosspoint guests. Nat had extended an invitation to the Pontifex and the Diadina, but she had been frankly relieved when they sent polite regrets. Earth owed their current safe status to them, but Nat still didn't exactly like them.

Watching all the human guests at the wedding, Claire thought they were handling the alien presence with great aplomb. There were a lot of wide eyes, but most mouths were kept firmly closed.

At the first of many receptions following the ceremony, Sam and Nat were immediately surrounded by a group of old friends that Claire had met briefly—she caught the names Armen and Melanie among others.

Francois was there as well, and he seemed to have found his seventh heaven. He kept coming up to Claire to tell her another secret he'd learned in the kitchen.

In his excitement, he stacked and re-stacked a pyramid of champagne glasses before the amazed eyes of Claire's mother and about thirty other guests. He also caused the whole wedding cake to levitate about four inches off the table before Claire could urge him back to the kitchen.

Her parents only stuttered a little after seeing her intimacy with a telekinetic alien. She and Basher planned to visit Francois's family estate on Cross eventually—he'd invited them too many times to count—but her parents needed time before she left again. In fact, Claire was thinking of asking them to come, too. Now that the Earth had a more secure status—thanks to Akemi's favor and the Merith treaty—it was safe to travel through the galaxy.

Claire's father was currently eyeing the nearest Vel warily, rather like it was a 'gator that had slipped into the party. Claire knew he would jump at the chance to travel the galaxy. As a biologist, he was fascinated by the aliens. Her mother was a little less fascinated, but she was nobly holding up her end of a fashion conversation with Shara, which meant she had no small amount of patience.

"I forgot how capable my parents are," Claire said to Basher. "They're taking this all in stride."

"I'm not surprised. You had to get it somewhere."

The sound of an overblown trumpet interrupted them. It heralded the flashy entrance of a Merith retinue. They led in eight strange animals on a rope, which caused an even bigger stir. The animals were spindly and tall with brilliant plumage like birds of paradise, except they had more intelligent faces.

"The Pontifex sends his regard to the *royal couple*," the Merith began in a loud voice, emphasizing the last words. "He wishes to present you with this small addition to your menagerie..." He made a longish speech during which Claire snuck another croissant. Basher discreetly showed her a newscast on his tablet. "Sam Locklear—ruler of Earth and humanity!—receives a precious gift from his grace, the Pontifex of Merith Prime..."

When the Merith finished his speech, everyone looked at Sam and Nat. Sam looked caught between laughter and dismay.

Nat kissed his cheek. "Ruler of Earth and humanity, don't you have anything to say?"

"You know, someday I'm going to stop denying it and just make myself emperor." He cleared his throat. "But not today. I thank the Pontifex for his very generous gift to Nat and I, even though we are only *two private, non-royal citizens.*"

"He's messing with us, isn't he?" Nat said.

"Of course he is," Sam agreed. "The Pontifex knows perfectly well that neither of us are 'royal.'"

"What should we do these animals then?" She paused. "Oh, no. Do you think they're sentient?"

Sam threw back some champagne. "I guess we'll have to find out. We are starting to have a collection of alien animals, what with Nebbie and Kit. I say we find an island in the South Pacific—they'll love it. We'll send some exobiologists to figure out if they're sentient."

"I think you're enjoying this too much," Nat said sternly. But she went ahead and thanked the Merith as well, accepting the gift. The bird things were taken back outside.

The large hall was rather silent after they left. Sam rolled his eyes. "Aliens, right?"

There was a collective laugh and the murmur of socializing returned.

"I'm thinking Nat and I need a really long honeymoon," Sam said to Basher. "I want to let all this *royal couple* stuff die down. Like maybe a year or two."

Basher raised his brows. "But how will Earth function without you?"

"It'll probably implode while we're gone," Sam agreed, "but I'm willing to risk it. Point is, do you want to come? Nat's parents are coming, and my sister and her husband. Francois insists he has room for them and many more."

Basher looked at Claire. "I'm up for it if you are. Your dad would be thrilled; we just have to keep him from throttling any Vel."

Claire smiled. "I think we should go. I mean, how many opportunities do you get to tour the galaxy?"

"A lot, actually," Sam said. "But rarely in such good company."

The End.

AUTHOR'S NOTE

Thank you for reading *Imposters*! It was extremely satisfying to write the final installment of the Alien Cadets. I've grown attached to Sam and Nat, Basher and Claire, Sage, Juliet, and the others. This is the first series I've written, and I went a little crazy trying to wrap up all the loose ends I'd created. Much thanks to my husband and my sisters for reading the various versions and helping me put it all together.

Like my other novels, I based this story loosely on an Old Testament book, in this case, Esther.

I'd had the idea to use the Esther story since the middle of the second book, but I was thinking of Akemi as Esther. It wasn't until the middle of this book that it suddenly hit me that she wasn't Esther at all, it was the Diadina.

I have a whole lot more ideas about what happens after this story... Sage becomes a type of prophet, an Abraham-figure. A legacy and mythos grows around Juliet's story. The Rik people have a sort of rebirth... It's hard to leave all the research I did on the Japanese Meiji restoration on the table!—but it's time for me to move on. As the first series I completed, it's time to apply all the learning to new books.

If you enjoyed these, I hope you'll find more of my works!

Check out my website at corneliaclark.com, and come sign up for my mailing list to find out when new books are released. I also use that list to look for ARC readers—those who will read a free early version of a new book to leave a review.

Thanks again for reading, *bruck*! Stay strong out there.

Cornelia Clark

ABOUT THE AUTHOR

Cornelia Clark is the science fiction and fantasy penname of author Corrie Garrett. In all her stories, from historical romance to speculative fiction, her characters always face impossible odds, build deep friendships, and find lasting love. She lives in the beautiful hills of West Virginia with her husband and four kids. Some of her favorite hobbies are reading, hiking, and poking her fluffy cat with her toes. Cautiously, of course.